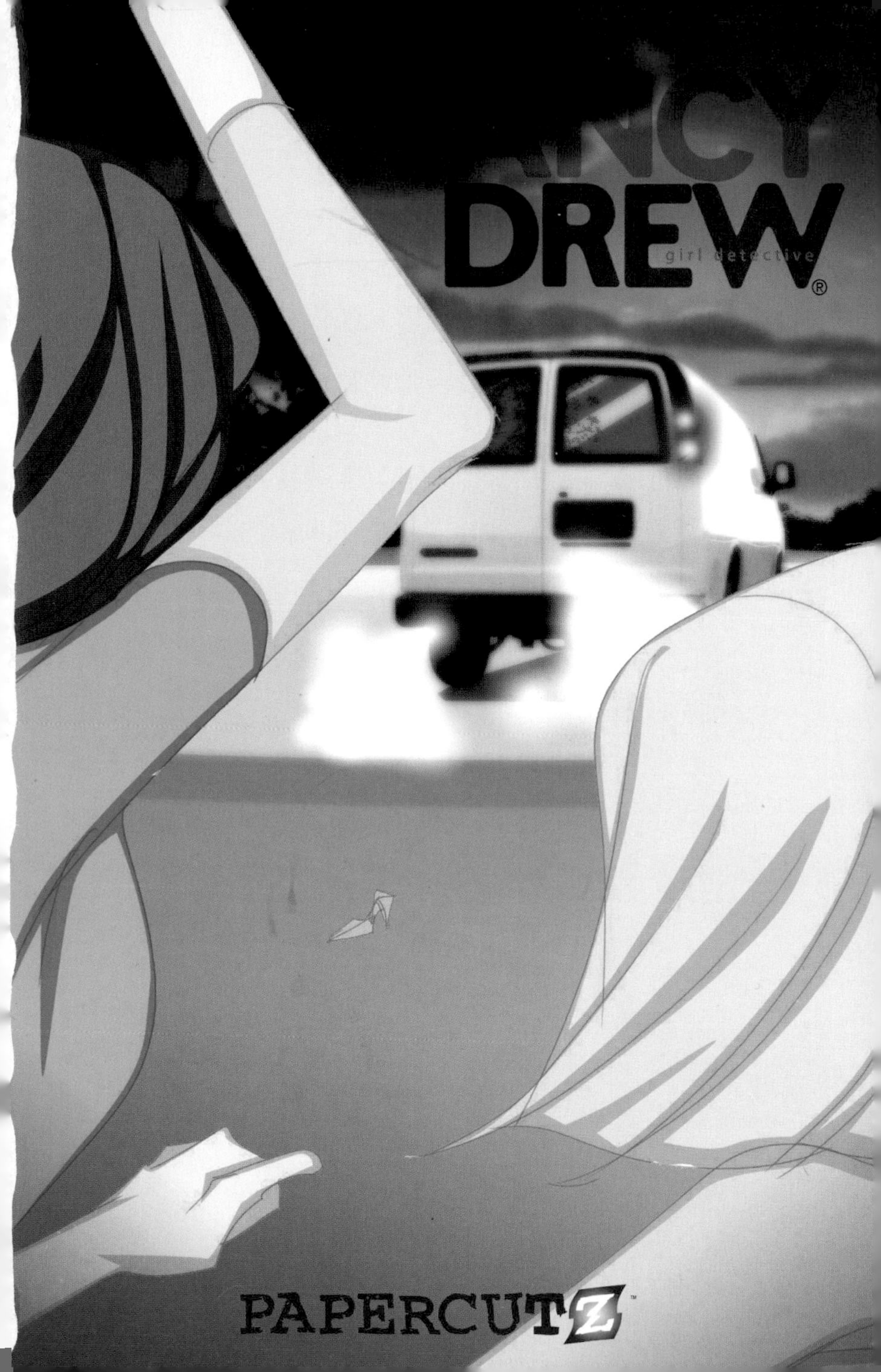
DREW
girl detective
PAPERCUTZ

NANCY DREW GRAPHIC NOVELS AVAILABLE FROM PAPERCUTZ

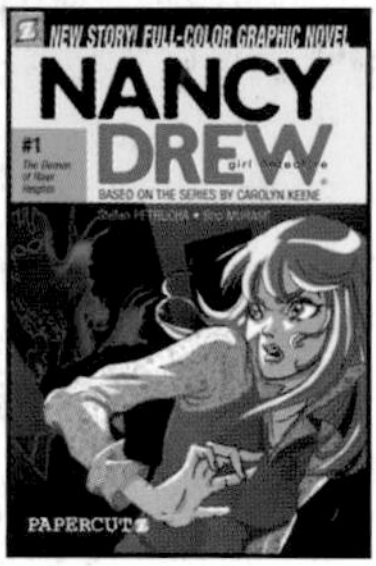
NEW STORY! FULL-COLOR GRAPHIC NOVEL
NANCY DREW
#1
BASED ON THE SERIES BY CAROLYN KEENE
PAPERCUTZ

Graphic Novel #1
"The Demon of River Heights"

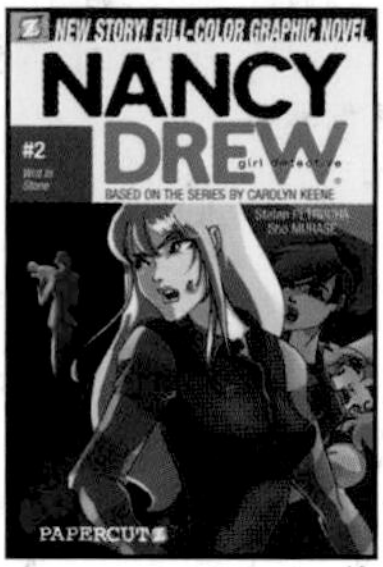
NEW STORY! FULL-COLOR GRAPHIC NOVEL
NANCY DREW
#2
BASED ON THE SERIES BY CAROLYN KEENE
PAPERCUTZ

Graphic Novel #2
"Writ In Stone"

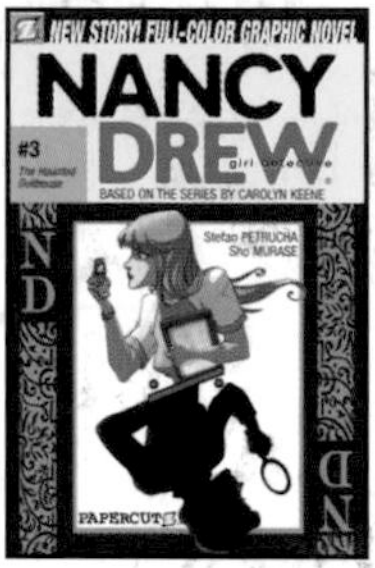
NEW STORY! FULL-COLOR GRAPHIC NOVEL
NANCY DREW
#3
BASED ON THE SERIES BY CAROLYN KEENE
Stefan PETRUCHA
Sho MURASE
PAPERCUTZ

Graphic Novel #3
"The Haunted Dollhouse"

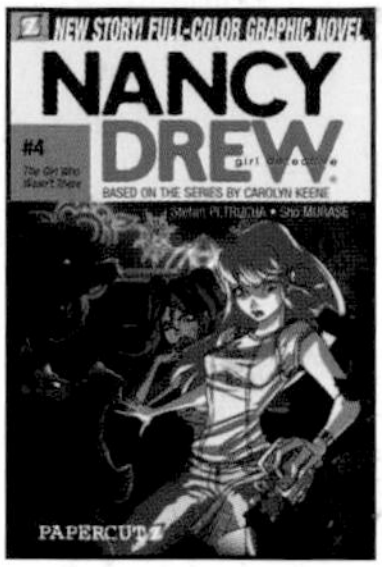
NEW STORY! FULL-COLOR GRAPHIC NOVEL
NANCY DREW
#4
BASED ON THE SERIES BY CAROLYN KEENE
PAPERCUTZ

Graphic Novel #4
"The Girl Who Wasn't There"

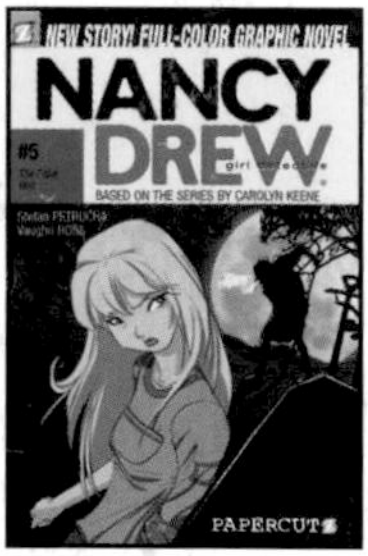
NEW STORY! FULL-COLOR GRAPHIC NOVEL
NANCY DREW
#5
BASED ON THE SERIES BY CAROLYN KEENE
PAPERCUTZ

Graphic Novel #5
"The Fake Heir"

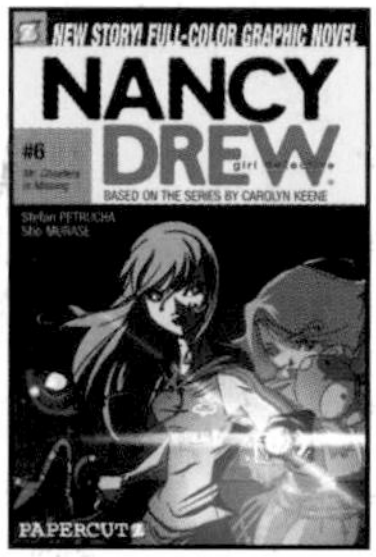
NEW STORY! FULL-COLOR GRAPHIC NOVEL
NANCY DREW
#6
BASED ON THE SERIES BY CAROLYN KEENE
PAPERCUTZ

Graphic Novel #6
"Mr. Cheeters Is Missing"

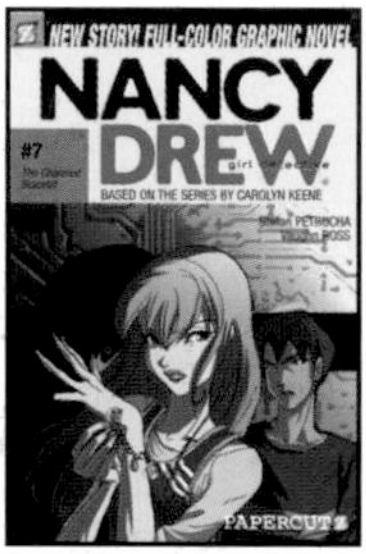
NEW STORY! FULL-COLOR GRAPHIC NOVEL
NANCY DREW
#7
BASED ON THE SERIES BY CAROLYN KEENE
PAPERCUTZ

Graphic Novel #7
"The Charmed Bracelet"

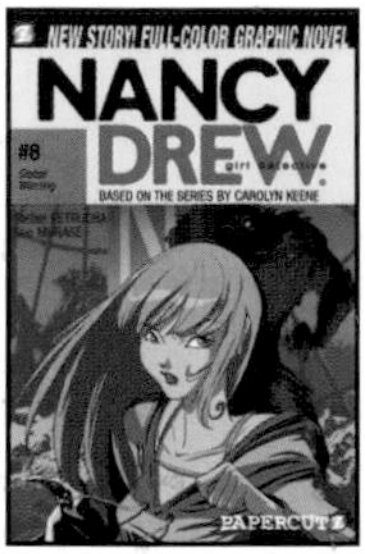
NEW STORY! FULL-COLOR GRAPHIC NOVEL
NANCY DREW
#8
BASED ON THE SERIES BY CAROLYN KEENE
PAPERCUTZ

Graphic Novel #8
"Global Warning"

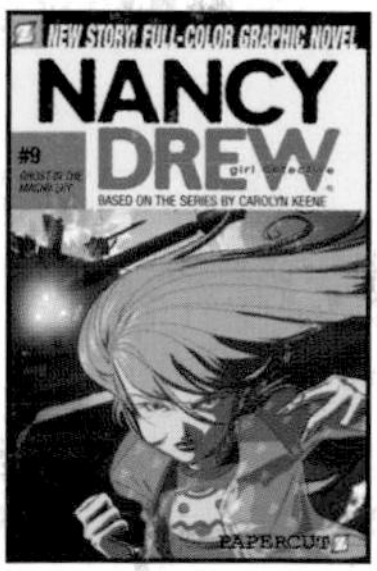
NEW STORY! FULL-COLOR GRAPHIC NOVEL
NANCY DREW
#9
BASED ON THE SERIES BY CAROLYN KEENE
PAPERCUTZ

Graphic Novel #9
"Ghost In The Machinery"

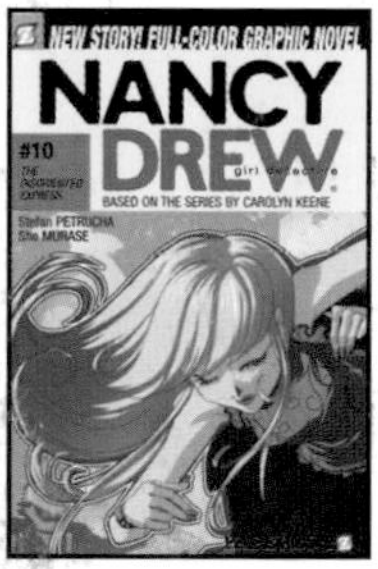
NEW STORY! FULL-COLOR GRAPHIC NOVEL
NANCY DREW
#10
BASED ON THE SERIES BY CAROLYN KEENE

Graphic Novel #10
"The Disoriented Express"

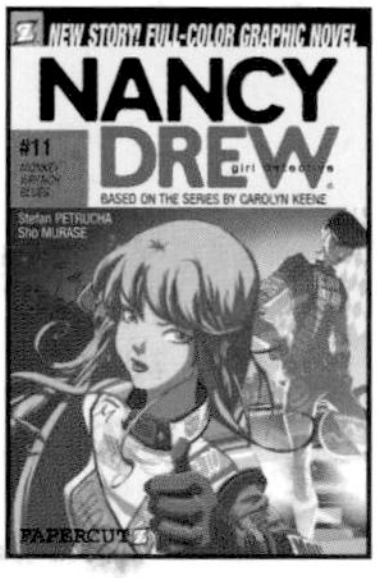
NEW STORY! FULL-COLOR GRAPHIC NOVEL
NANCY DREW
#11
BASED ON THE SERIES BY CAROLYN KEENE
PAPERCUTZ

Graphic Novel #11
"Monkey Wrench Blues"

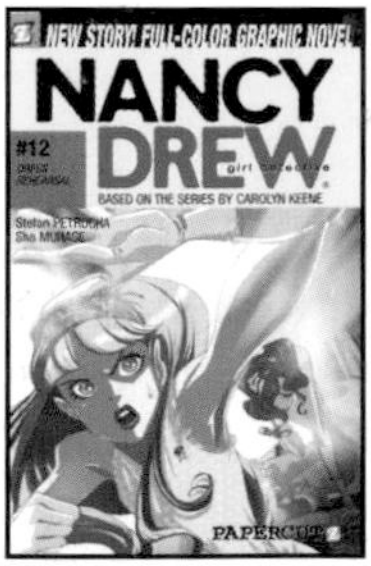
NEW STORY! FULL-COLOR GRAPHIC NOVEL
NANCY DREW
#12
BASED ON THE SERIES BY CAROLYN KEENE
PAPERCUTZ

Graphic Novel #12
"Dress Reversal"

$7.95 each in paperback, $12.95 each in hardcover. Please add $3.00 for postage and handling for the first book, add $1.00 for each additional book.
Please make check payable to NBM Publishing. Send to:
Papercutz, 40 Exchange Place, Suite 1308 New York, NY 10005 • www.papercutz.com

NANCY DREW

girl detective ®

#12

Dress Reversal

STEFAN PETRUCHA & SARAH KINNEY • Writers
SHO MURASE • Artist
with 3D CG elements and color by CARLOS JOSE GUZMAN
Based on the series by
CAROLYN KEENE

PAPERCUTZ™
New York

Dress Reversal
STEFAN PETRUCHA & SARAH KINNEY – Writers
SHO MURASE – Artist
with 3D CG elements and color by CARLOS JOSE GUZMAN
BRYAN SENKA – Letterer
JOHN McCARTHY – Production
JIM SALICRUP
Editor-in-Chief

ISBN 10: 1-59707-086-6 paperback edition
ISBN 13: 978-1-59707-086-7 paperback edition
ISBN 10: 1-59707-087-4 hardcover edition
ISBN 13: 978-1-59707-087-4 hardcover edition

Printed in China.
Distributed by Macmillan.

10   9   8   7   6   5   4   3   2   1

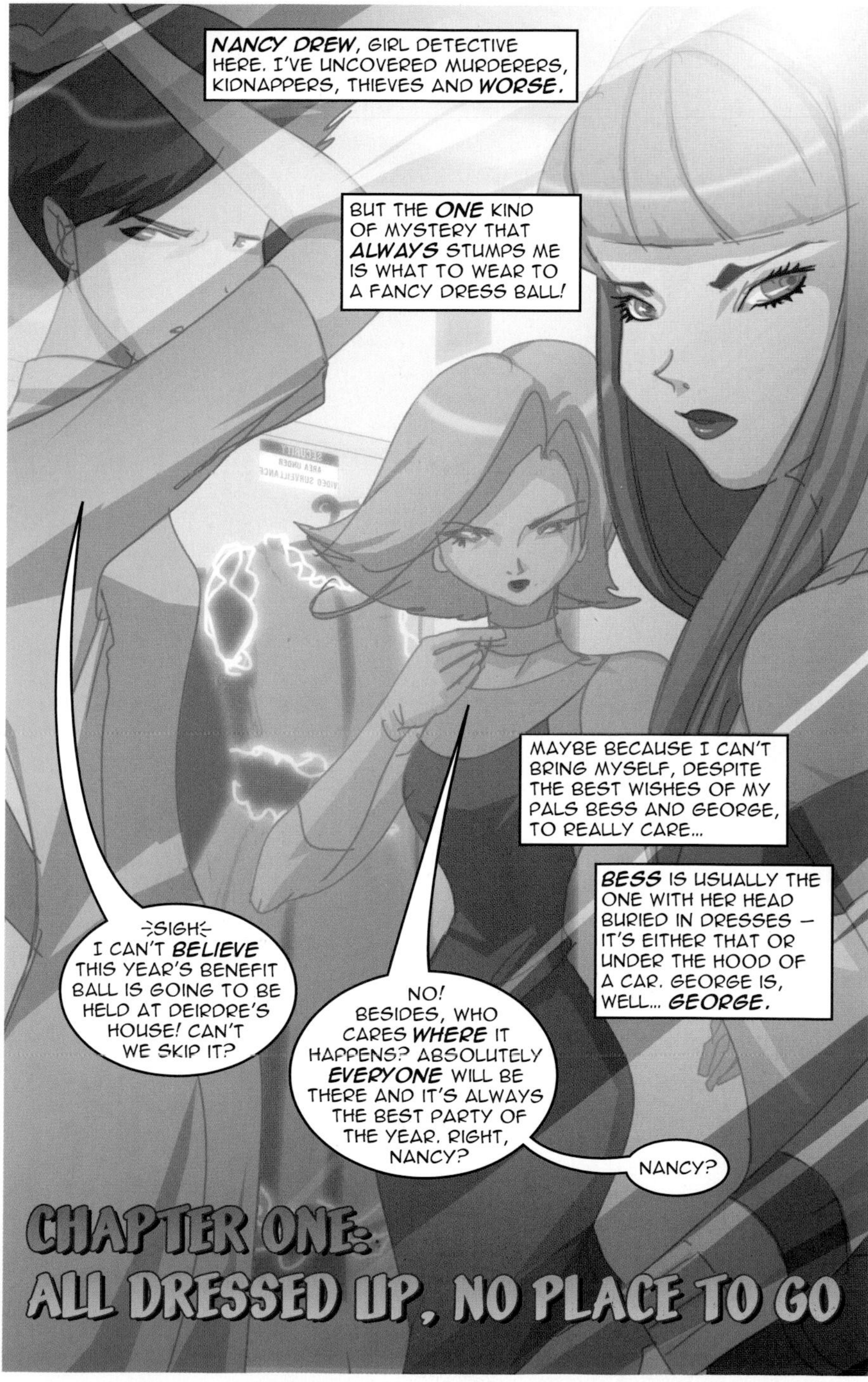
NANCY DREW, GIRL DETECTIVE HERE. I'VE UNCOVERED MURDERERS, KIDNAPPERS, THIEVES AND WORSE.
BUT THE ONE KIND OF MYSTERY THAT ALWAYS STUMPS ME IS WHAT TO WEAR TO A FANCY DRESS BALL!
MAYBE BECAUSE I CAN'T BRING MYSELF, DESPITE THE BEST WISHES OF MY PALS BESS AND GEORGE, TO REALLY CARE...
BESS IS USUALLY THE ONE WITH HER HEAD BURIED IN DRESSES — IT'S EITHER THAT OR UNDER THE HOOD OF A CAR. GEORGE IS, WELL... GEORGE.
SIGH I CAN'T BELIEVE THIS YEAR'S BENEFIT BALL IS GOING TO BE HELD AT DEIRDRE'S HOUSE! CAN'T WE SKIP IT?
NO! BESIDES, WHO CARES WHERE IT HAPPENS? ABSOLUTELY EVERYONE WILL BE THERE AND IT'S ALWAYS THE BEST PARTY OF THE YEAR. RIGHT, NANCY?
NANCY?
CHAPTER ONE:
ALL DRESSED UP, NO PLACE TO GO

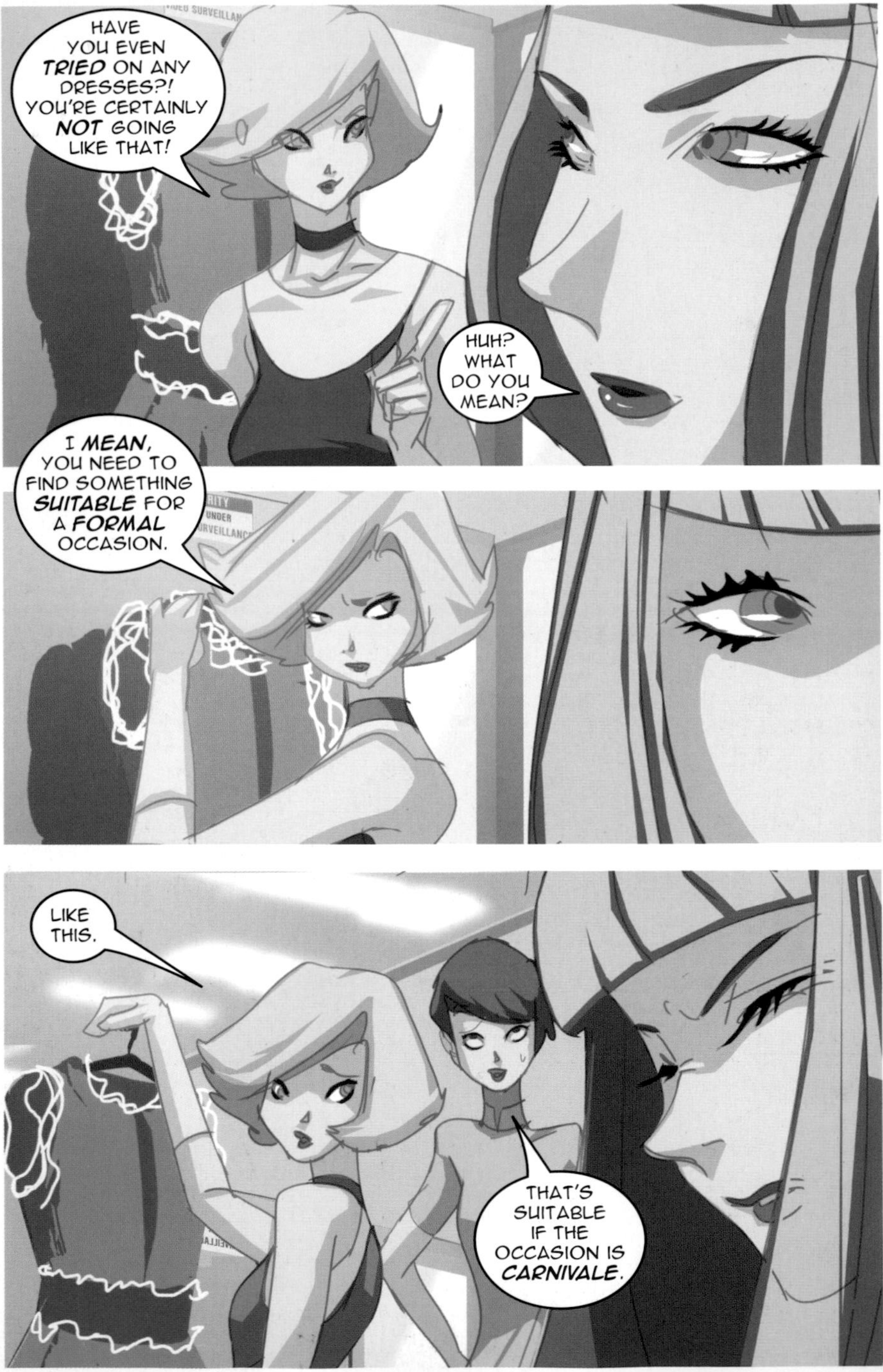
HAVE YOU EVEN TRIED ON ANY DRESSES?! YOU'RE CERTAINLY NOT GOING LIKE THAT!
HUH? WHAT DO YOU MEAN?
I MEAN, YOU NEED TO FIND SOMETHING SUITABLE FOR A FORMAL OCCASION.
LIKE THIS.
THAT'S SUITABLE IF THE OCCASION IS CARNIVALE.

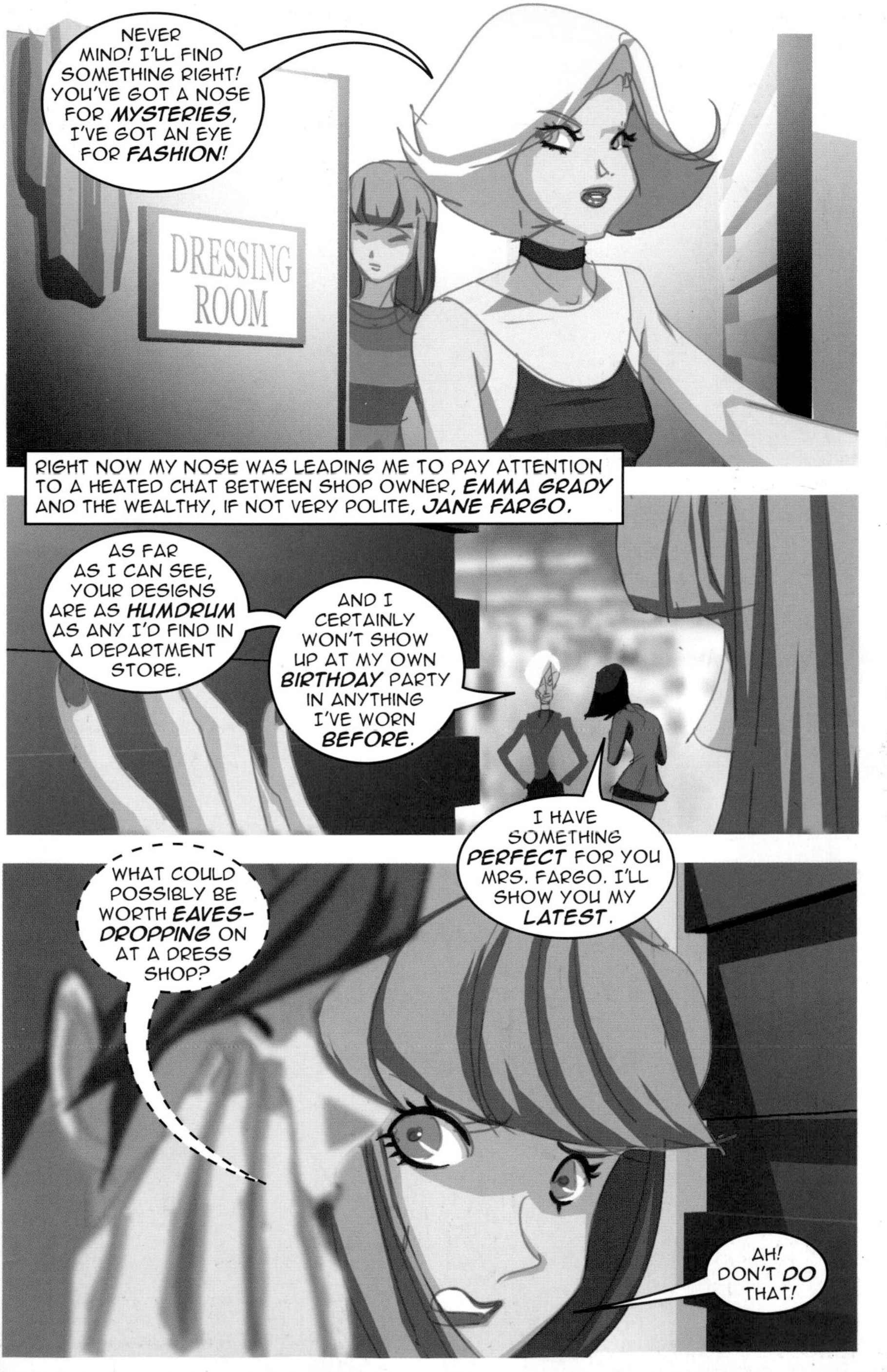
NEVER MIND! I'LL FIND SOMETHING RIGHT! YOU'VE GOT A NOSE FOR MYSTERIES, I'VE GOT AN EYE FOR FASHION!
DRESSING ROOM
RIGHT NOW MY NOSE WAS LEADING ME TO PAY ATTENTION TO A HEATED CHAT BETWEEN SHOP OWNER, EMMA GRADY AND THE WEALTHY, IF NOT VERY POLITE, JANE FARGO.
AS FAR AS I CAN SEE, YOUR DESIGNS ARE AS HUMDRUM AS ANY I'D FIND IN A DEPARTMENT STORE.
AND I CERTAINLY WON'T SHOW UP AT MY OWN BIRTHDAY PARTY IN ANYTHING I'VE WORN BEFORE.
I HAVE SOMETHING PERFECT FOR YOU MRS. FARGO. I'LL SHOW YOU MY LATEST.
WHAT COULD POSSIBLY BE WORTH EAVES-DROPPING ON AT A DRESS SHOP?
AH! DON'T DO THAT!

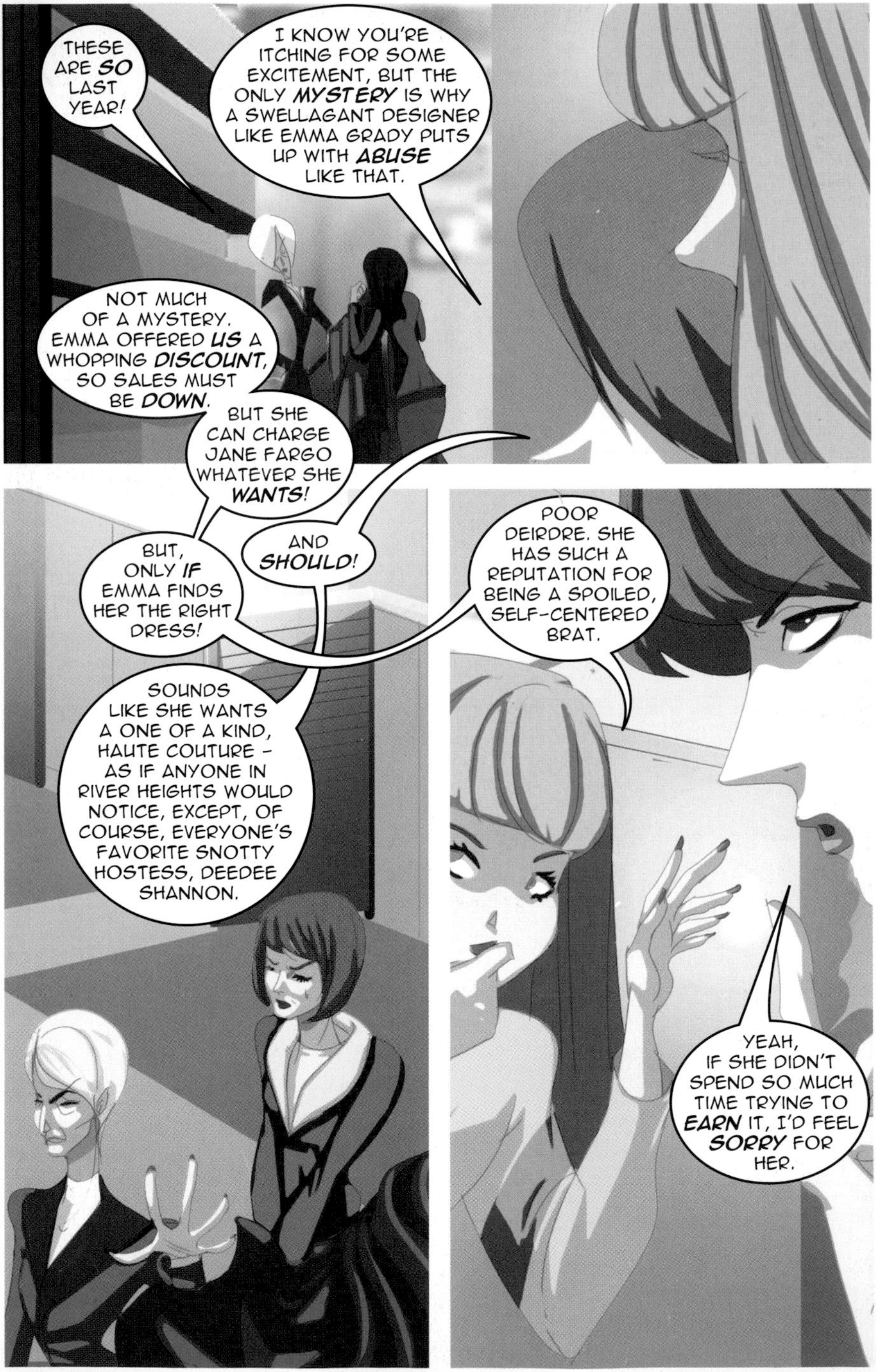
THESE ARE SO LAST YEAR!
I KNOW YOU'RE ITCHING FOR SOME EXCITEMENT, BUT THE ONLY MYSTERY IS WHY A SWELLAGANT DESIGNER LIKE EMMA GRADY PUTS UP WITH ABUSE LIKE THAT.
NOT MUCH OF A MYSTERY. EMMA OFFERED US A WHOPPING DISCOUNT, SO SALES MUST BE DOWN.
BUT SHE CAN CHARGE JANE FARGO WHATEVER SHE WANTS!
BUT, ONLY IF EMMA FINDS HER THE RIGHT DRESS!
AND SHOULD!
SOUNDS LIKE SHE WANTS A ONE OF A KIND, HAUTE COUTURE - AS IF ANYONE IN RIVER HEIGHTS WOULD NOTICE, EXCEPT, OF COURSE, EVERYONE'S FAVORITE SNOTTY HOSTESS, DEEDEE SHANNON.
POOR DEIRDRE. SHE HAS SUCH A REPUTATION FOR BEING A SPOILED, SELF-CENTERED BRAT.
YEAH, IF SHE DIDN'T SPEND SO MUCH TIME TRYING TO EARN IT, I'D FEEL SORRY FOR HER.

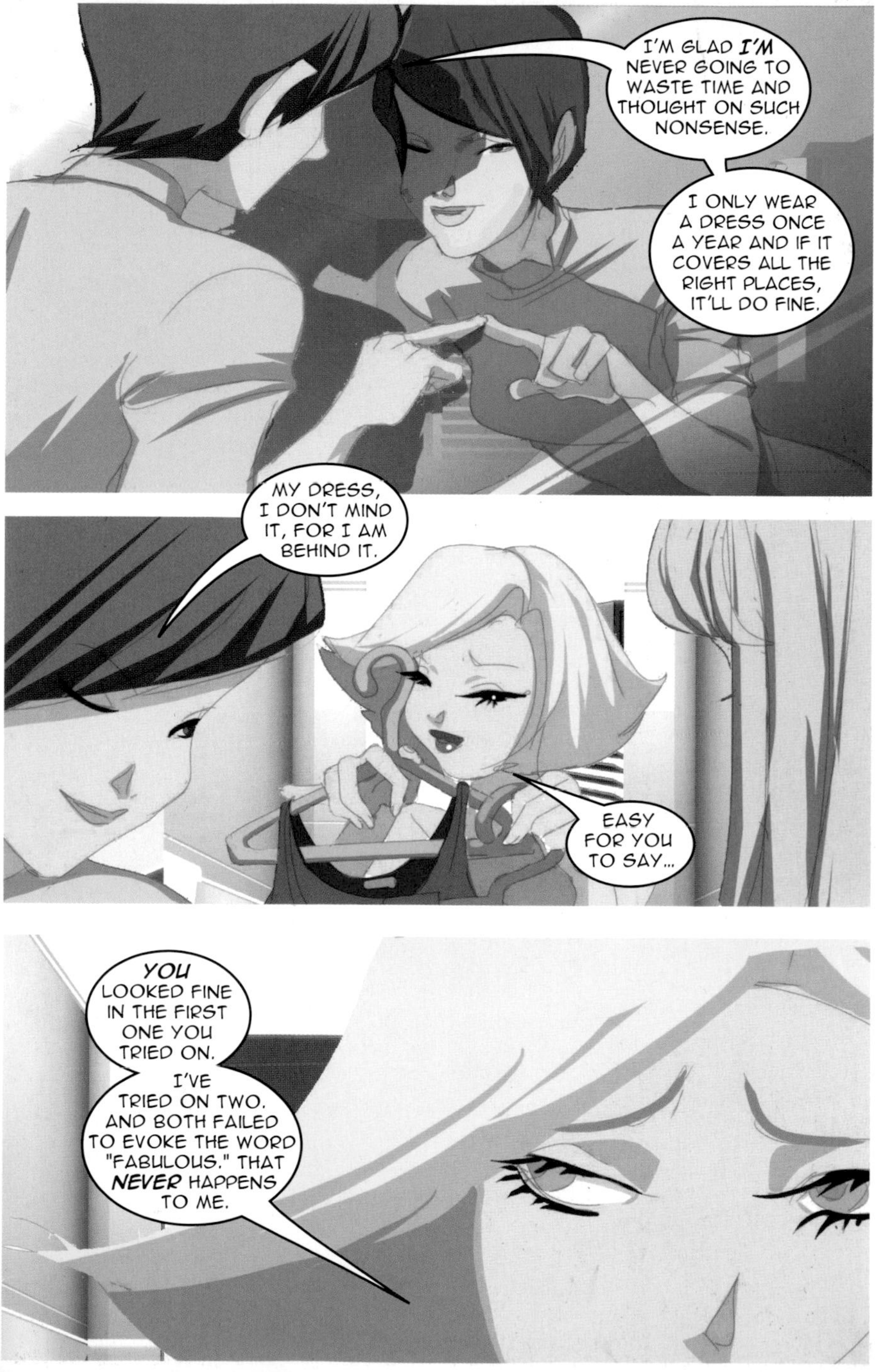
I'M GLAD *I'M* NEVER GOING TO WASTE TIME AND THOUGHT ON SUCH NONSENSE.
I ONLY WEAR A DRESS ONCE A YEAR AND IF IT COVERS ALL THE RIGHT PLACES, IT'LL DO FINE.
MY DRESS, I DON'T MIND IT, FOR I AM BEHIND IT.
EASY FOR YOU TO SAY...
YOU LOOKED FINE IN THE FIRST ONE YOU TRIED ON.
I'VE TRIED ON TWO. AND BOTH FAILED TO EVOKE THE WORD "FABULOUS." THAT *NEVER* HAPPENS TO ME.

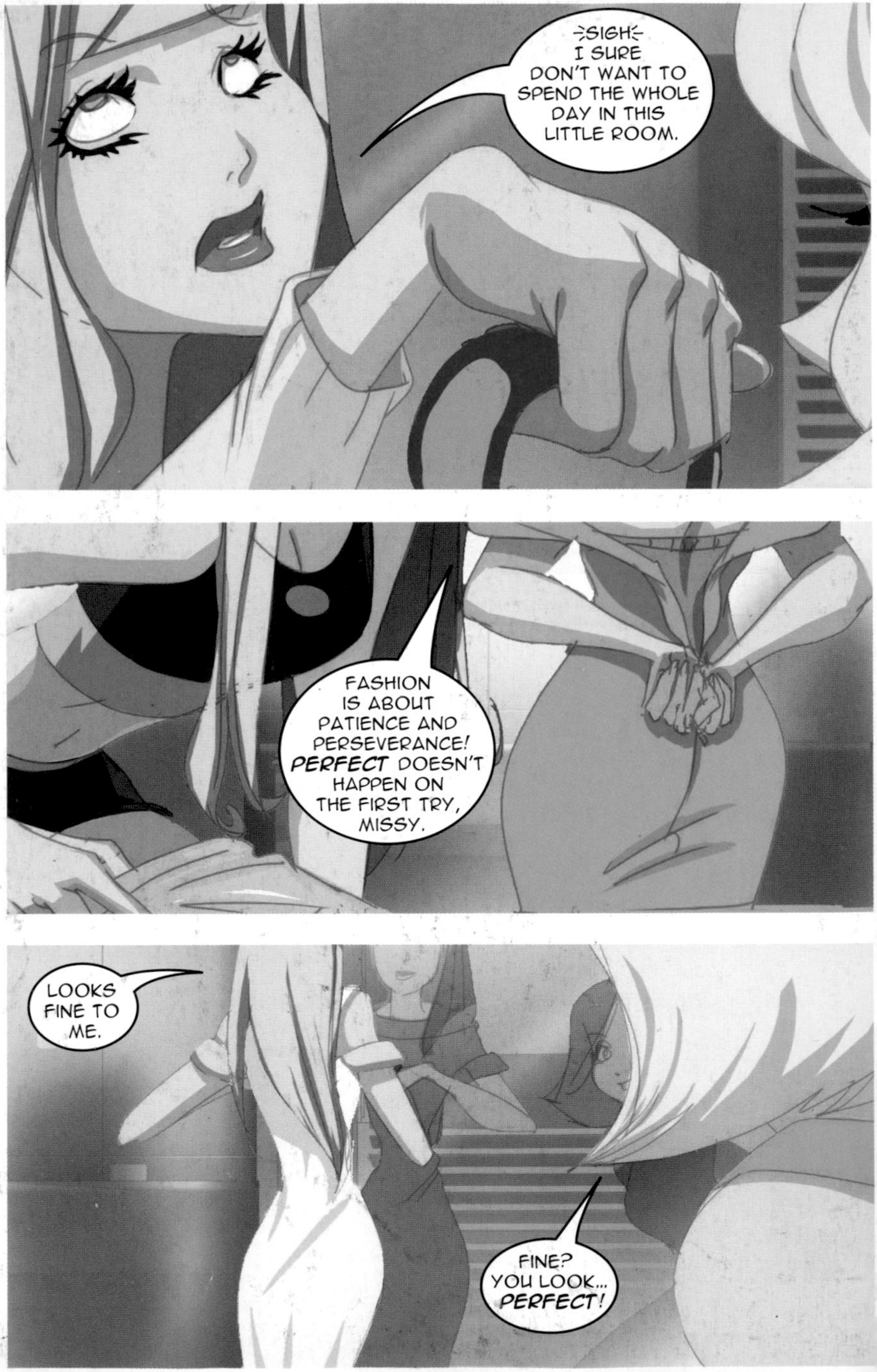

SIGH
I SURE DON'T WANT TO SPEND THE WHOLE DAY IN THIS LITTLE ROOM.
FASHION IS ABOUT PATIENCE AND PERSEVERANCE! PERFECT DOESN'T HAPPEN ON THE FIRST TRY, MISSY.
LOOKS FINE TO ME.
FINE? YOU LOOK... PERFECT!

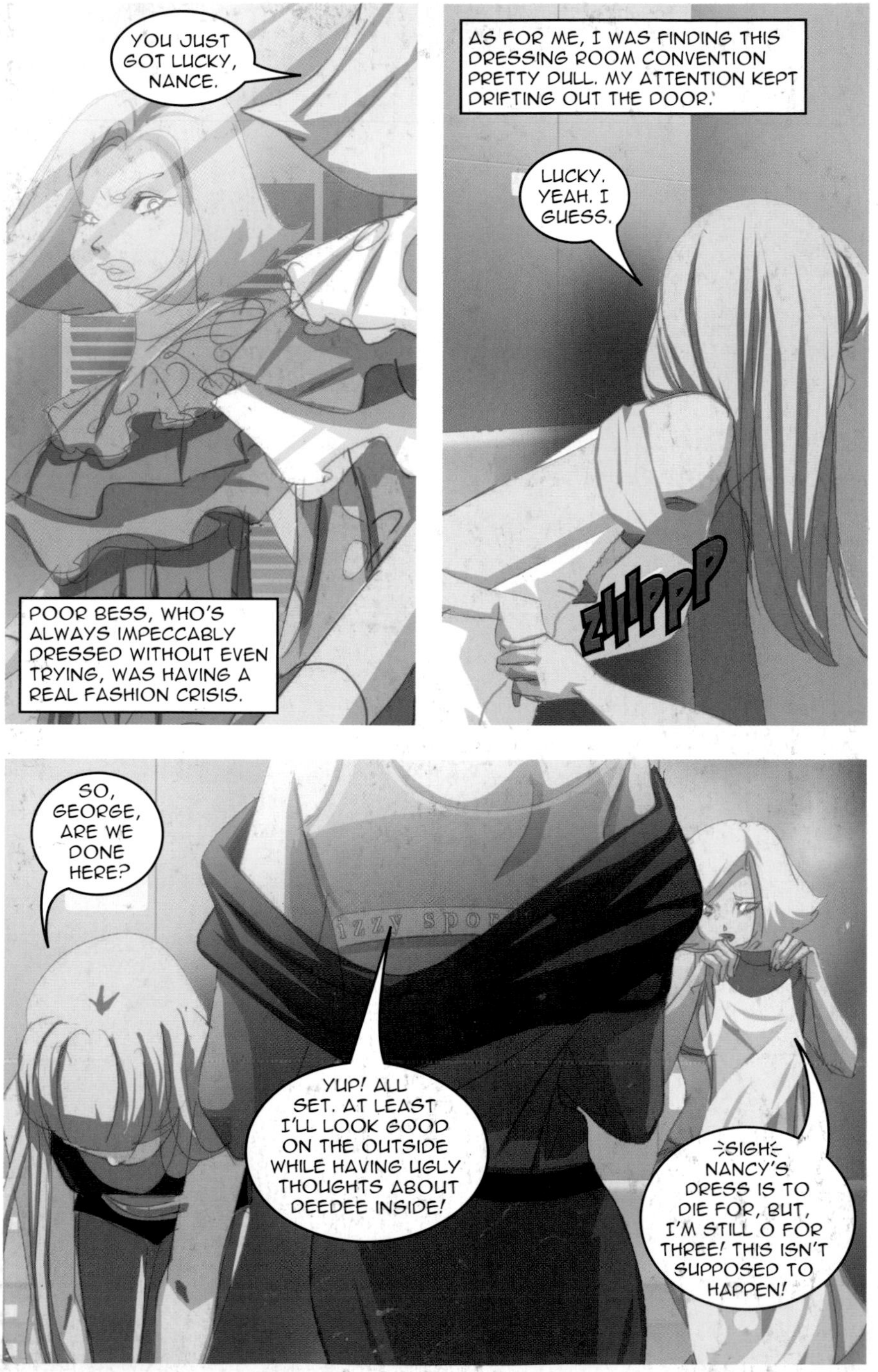
YOU JUST GOT LUCKY, NANCE.
POOR BESS, WHO'S ALWAYS IMPECCABLY DRESSED WITHOUT EVEN TRYING, WAS HAVING A REAL FASHION CRISIS.
AS FOR ME, I WAS FINDING THIS DRESSING ROOM CONVENTION PRETTY DULL. MY ATTENTION KEPT DRIFTING OUT THE DOOR.
LUCKY. YEAH. I GUESS.
ZIIIPPP
SO, GEORGE, ARE WE DONE HERE?
YUP! ALL SET. AT LEAST I'LL LOOK GOOD ON THE OUTSIDE WHILE HAVING UGLY THOUGHTS ABOUT DEEDEE INSIDE!
SIGH NANCY'S DRESS IS TO DIE FOR, BUT, I'M STILL 0 FOR THREE! THIS ISN'T SUPPOSED TO HAPPEN!

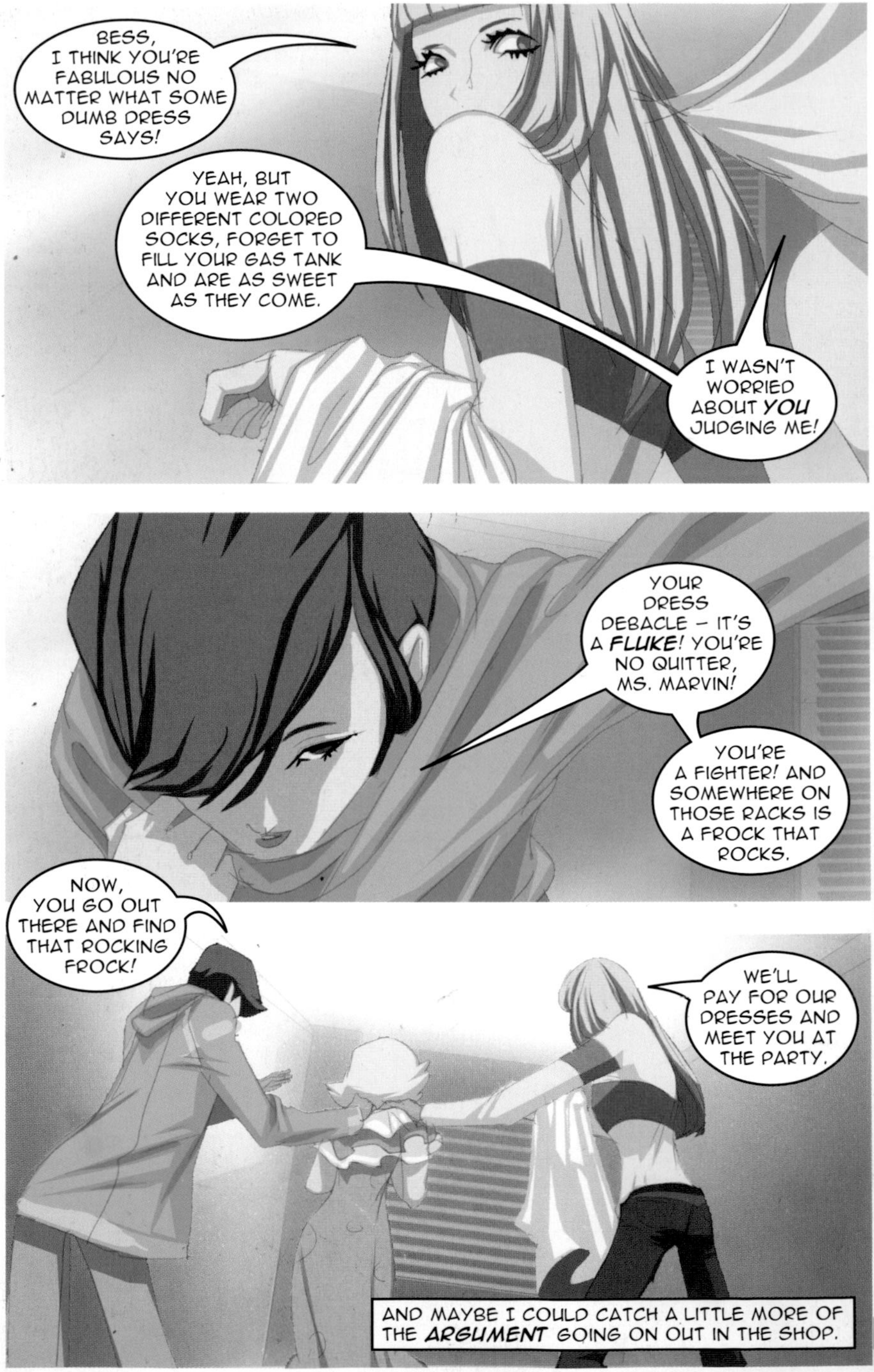
BESS, I THINK YOU'RE FABULOUS NO MATTER WHAT SOME DUMB DRESS SAYS!
YEAH, BUT YOU WEAR TWO DIFFERENT COLORED SOCKS, FORGET TO FILL YOUR GAS TANK AND ARE AS SWEET AS THEY COME.
I WASN'T WORRIED ABOUT *YOU* JUDGING ME!
YOUR DRESS DEBACLE – IT'S A *FLUKE*! YOU'RE NO QUITTER, MS. MARVIN!
YOU'RE A FIGHTER! AND SOMEWHERE ON THOSE RACKS IS A FROCK THAT ROCKS.
NOW, YOU GO OUT THERE AND FIND THAT ROCKING FROCK!
WE'LL PAY FOR OUR DRESSES AND MEET YOU AT THE PARTY.
AND MAYBE I COULD CATCH A LITTLE MORE OF THE *ARGUMENT* GOING ON OUT IN THE SHOP.

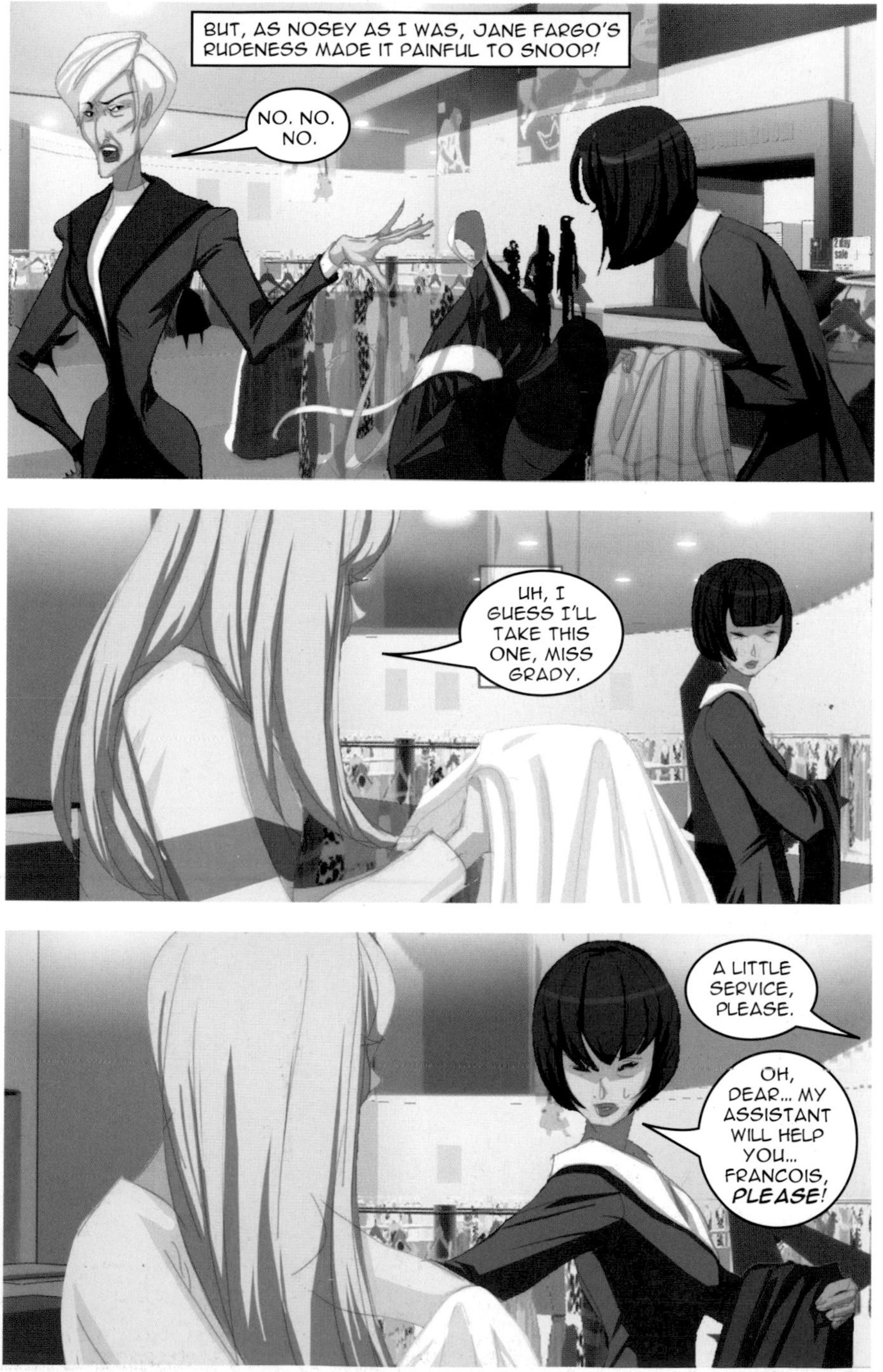
BUT, AS NOSEY AS I WAS, JANE FARGO'S RUDENESS MADE IT PAINFUL TO SNOOP!
NO. NO. NO.
UH, I GUESS I'LL TAKE THIS ONE, MISS GRADY.
A LITTLE SERVICE, PLEASE.
OH, DEAR... MY ASSISTANT WILL HELP YOU... FRANCOIS, PLEASE!

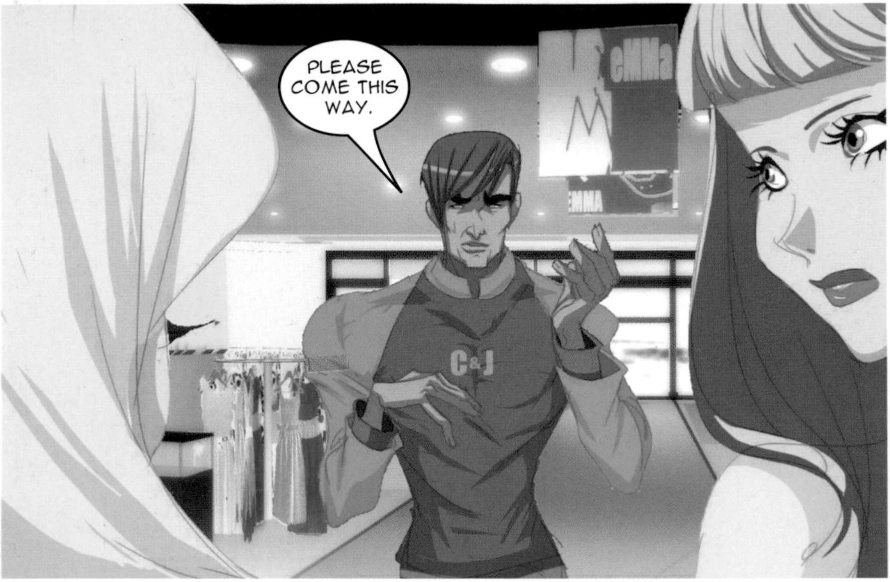
PLEASE COME THIS WAY.

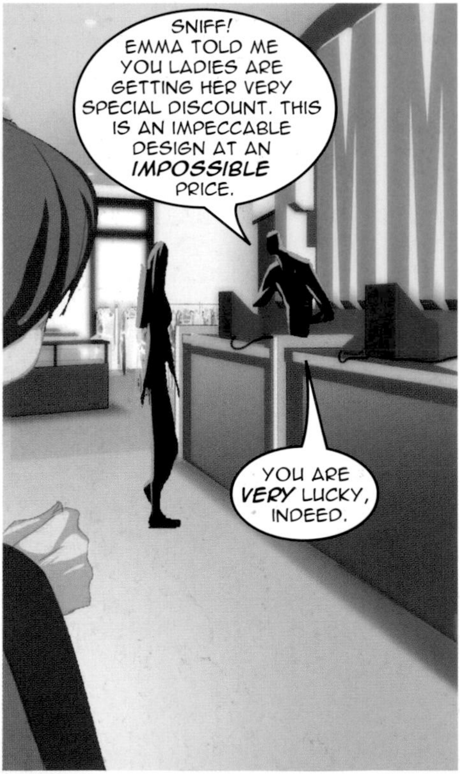
SNIFF! EMMA TOLD ME YOU LADIES ARE GETTING HER VERY SPECIAL DISCOUNT. THIS IS AN IMPECCABLE DESIGN AT AN ***IMPOSSIBLE*** PRICE.
YOU ARE ***VERY*** LUCKY, INDEED.

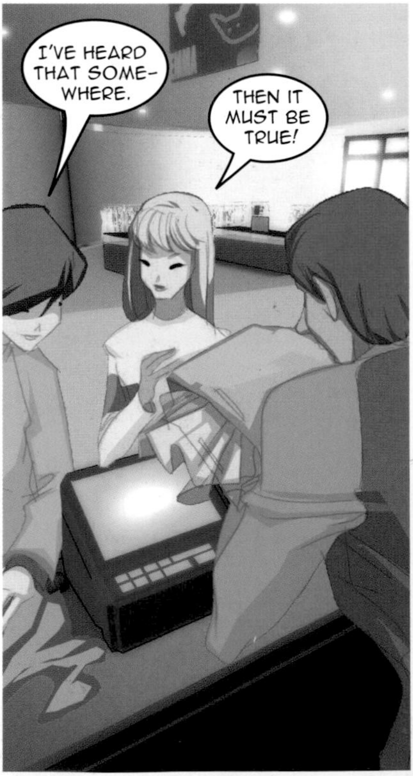
I'VE HEARD THAT SOME-WHERE.
THEN IT MUST BE TRUE!

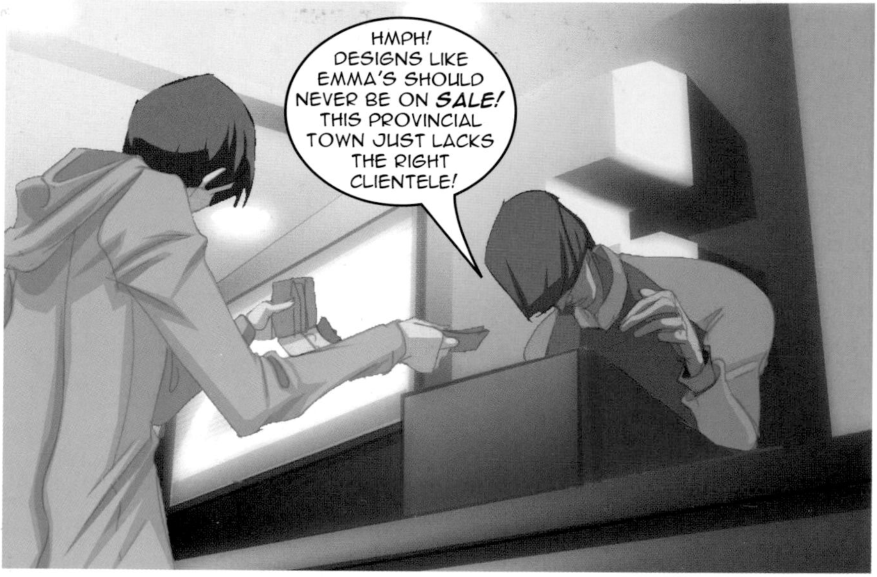
HMPH! DESIGNS LIKE EMMA'S SHOULD NEVER BE ON *SALE!* THIS PROVINCIAL TOWN JUST LACKS THE RIGHT CLIENTELE!

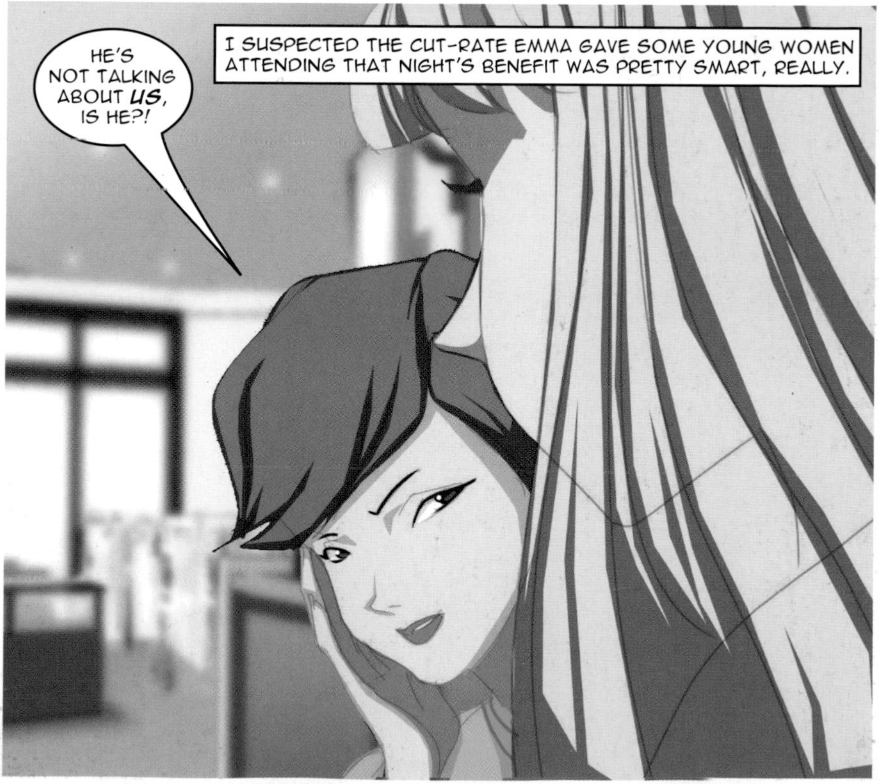
I SUSPECTED THE CUT-RATE EMMA GAVE SOME YOUNG WOMEN ATTENDING THAT NIGHT'S BENEFIT WAS PRETTY SMART, REALLY.
HE'S NOT TALKING ABOUT *US*, IS HE?!

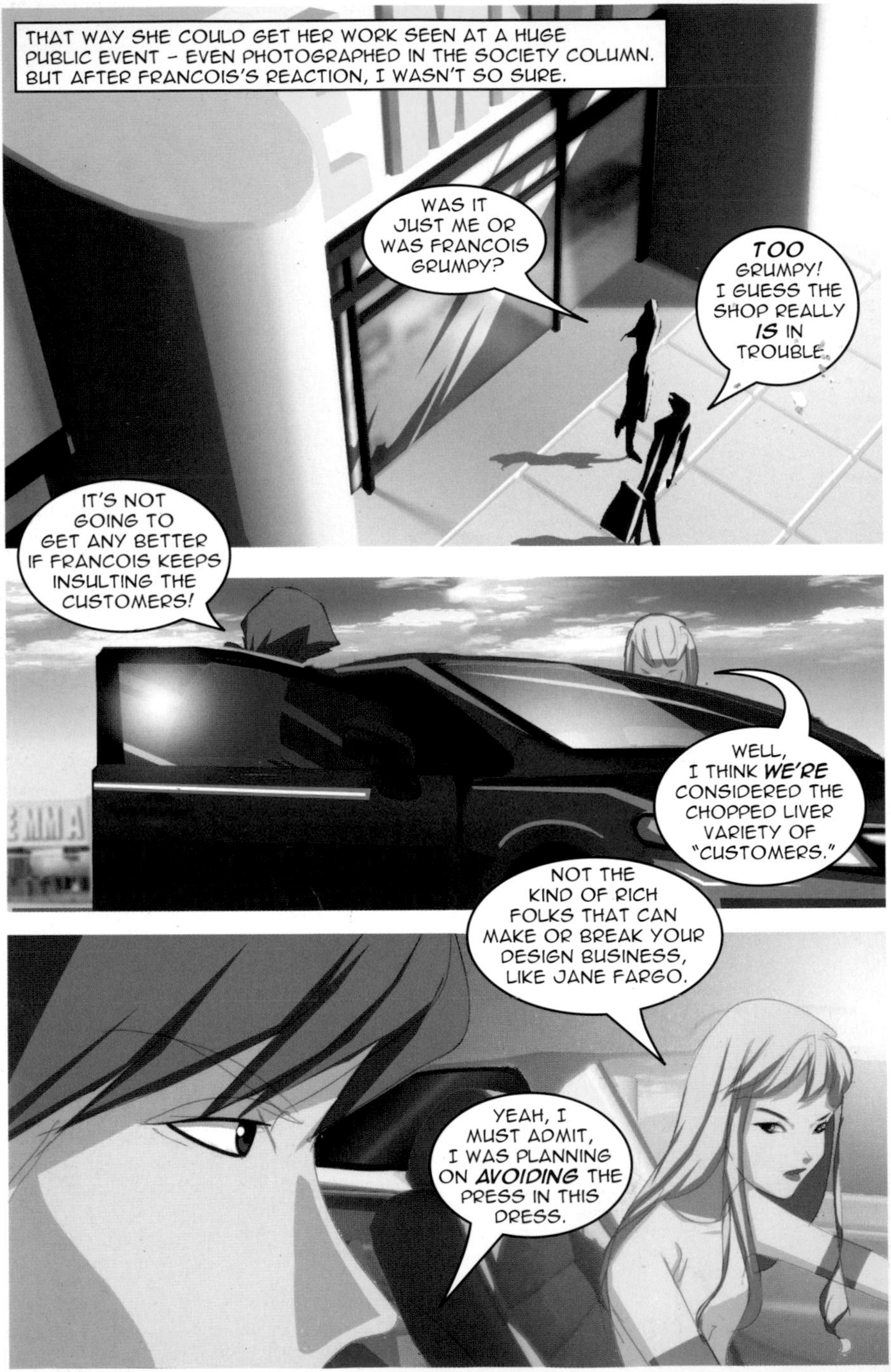
THAT WAY SHE COULD GET HER WORK SEEN AT A HUGE PUBLIC EVENT – EVEN PHOTOGRAPHED IN THE SOCIETY COLUMN. BUT AFTER FRANCOIS'S REACTION, I WASN'T SO SURE.
WAS IT JUST ME OR WAS FRANCOIS GRUMPY?
TOO GRUMPY! I GUESS THE SHOP REALLY IS IN TROUBLE.
IT'S NOT GOING TO GET ANY BETTER IF FRANCOIS KEEPS INSULTING THE CUSTOMERS!
WELL, I THINK WE'RE CONSIDERED THE CHOPPED LIVER VARIETY OF "CUSTOMERS."
NOT THE KIND OF RICH FOLKS THAT CAN MAKE OR BREAK YOUR DESIGN BUSINESS, LIKE JANE FARGO.
YEAH, I MUST ADMIT, I WAS PLANNING ON AVOIDING THE PRESS IN THIS DRESS.

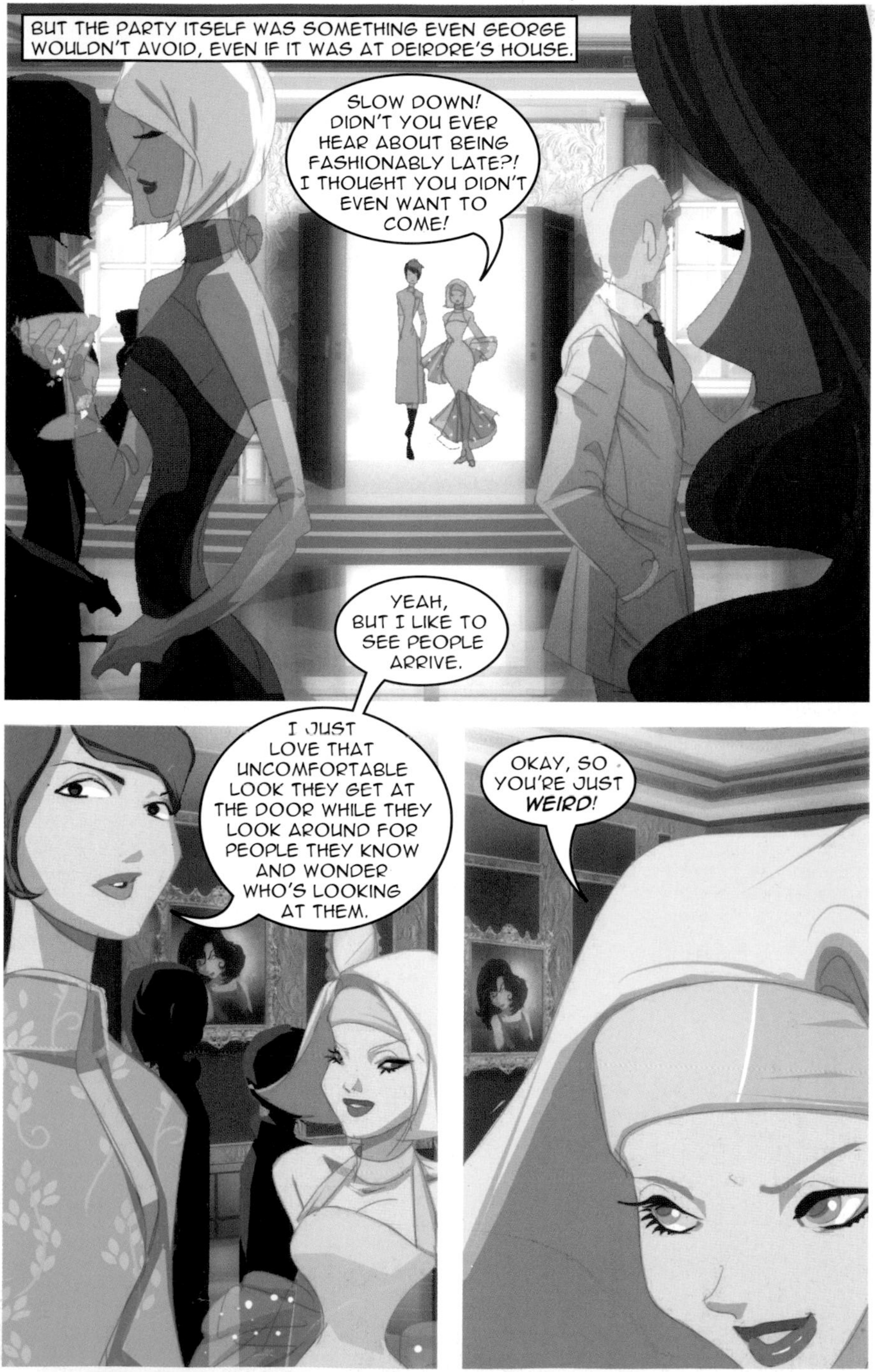
BUT THE PARTY ITSELF WAS SOMETHING EVEN GEORGE WOULDN'T AVOID, EVEN IF IT WAS AT DEIRDRE'S HOUSE.
SLOW DOWN! DIDN'T YOU EVER HEAR ABOUT BEING FASHIONABLY LATE?! I THOUGHT YOU DIDN'T EVEN WANT TO COME!
YEAH, BUT I LIKE TO SEE PEOPLE ARRIVE.
I JUST LOVE THAT UNCOMFORTABLE LOOK THEY GET AT THE DOOR WHILE THEY LOOK AROUND FOR PEOPLE THEY KNOW AND WONDER WHO'S LOOKING AT THEM.
OKAY, SO YOU'RE JUST WEIRD!

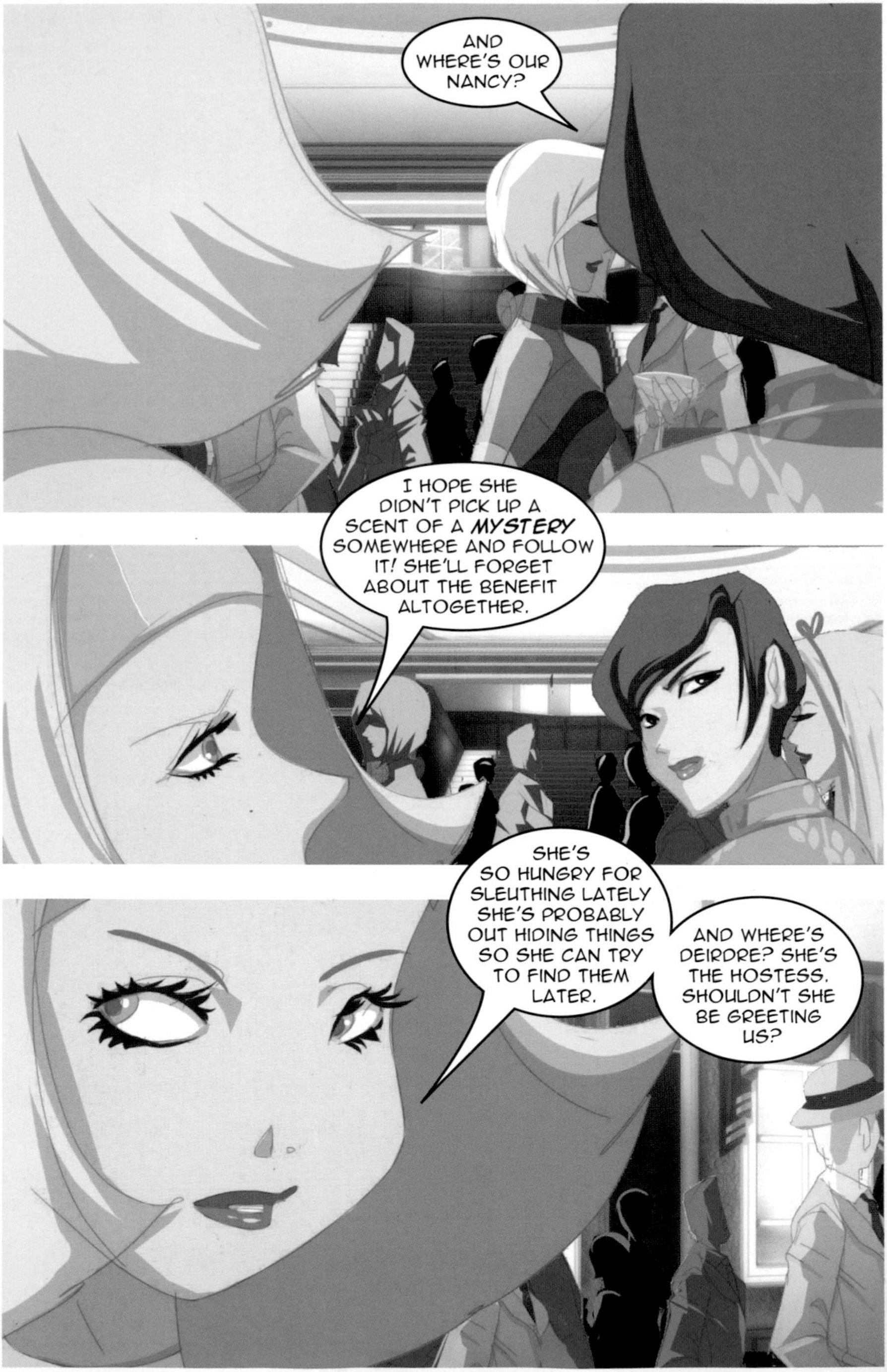
AND WHERE'S OUR NANCY?
I HOPE SHE DIDN'T PICK UP A SCENT OF A *MYSTERY* SOMEWHERE AND FOLLOW IT! SHE'LL FORGET ABOUT THE BENEFIT ALTOGETHER.
SHE'S SO HUNGRY FOR SLEUTHING LATELY SHE'S PROBABLY OUT HIDING THINGS SO SHE CAN TRY TO FIND THEM LATER.
AND WHERE'S DEIRDRE? SHE'S THE HOSTESS. SHOULDN'T SHE BE GREETING US?

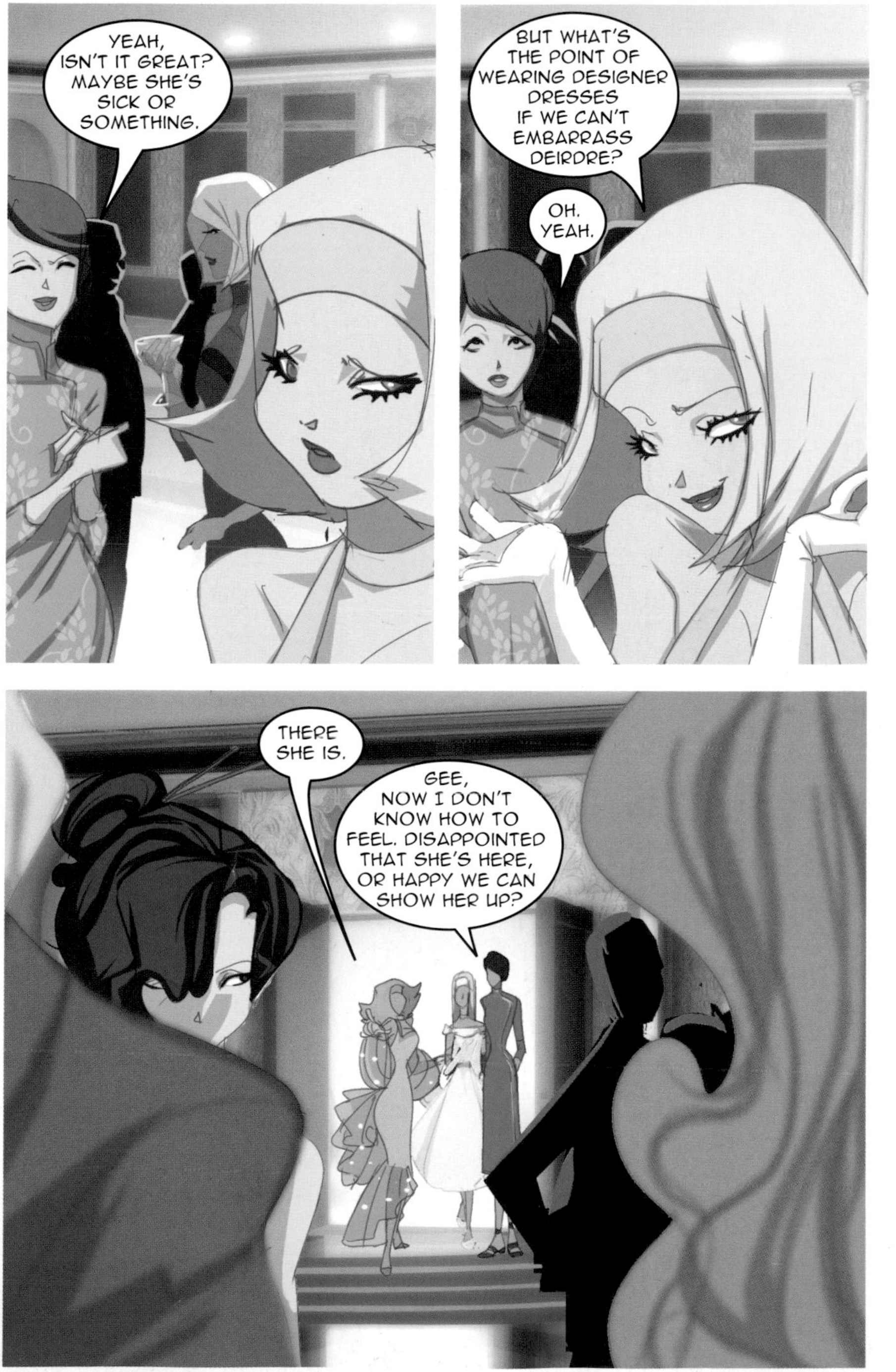
YEAH, ISN'T IT GREAT? MAYBE SHE'S SICK OR SOMETHING.
BUT WHAT'S THE POINT OF WEARING DESIGNER DRESSES IF WE CAN'T EMBARRASS DEIRDRE?
OH. YEAH.
THERE SHE IS.
GEE, NOW I DON'T KNOW HOW TO FEEL. DISAPPOINTED THAT SHE'S HERE, OR HAPPY WE CAN SHOW HER UP?

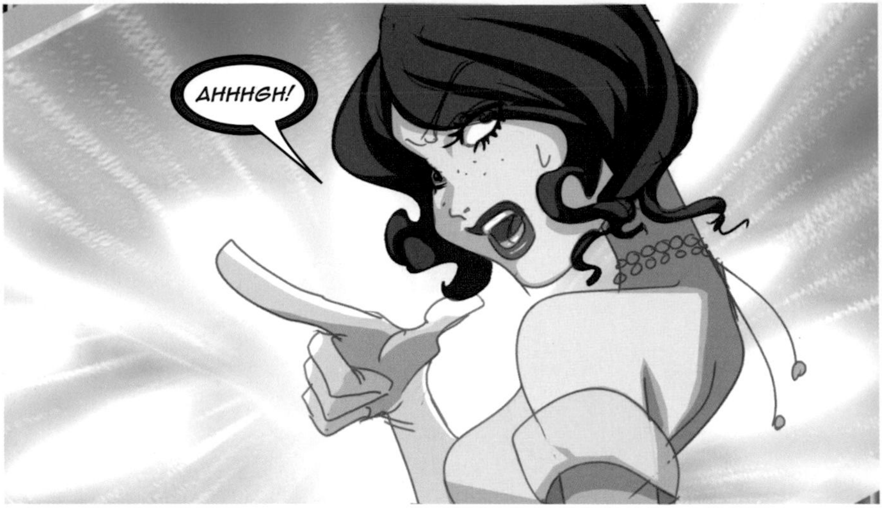
AHHHGH!

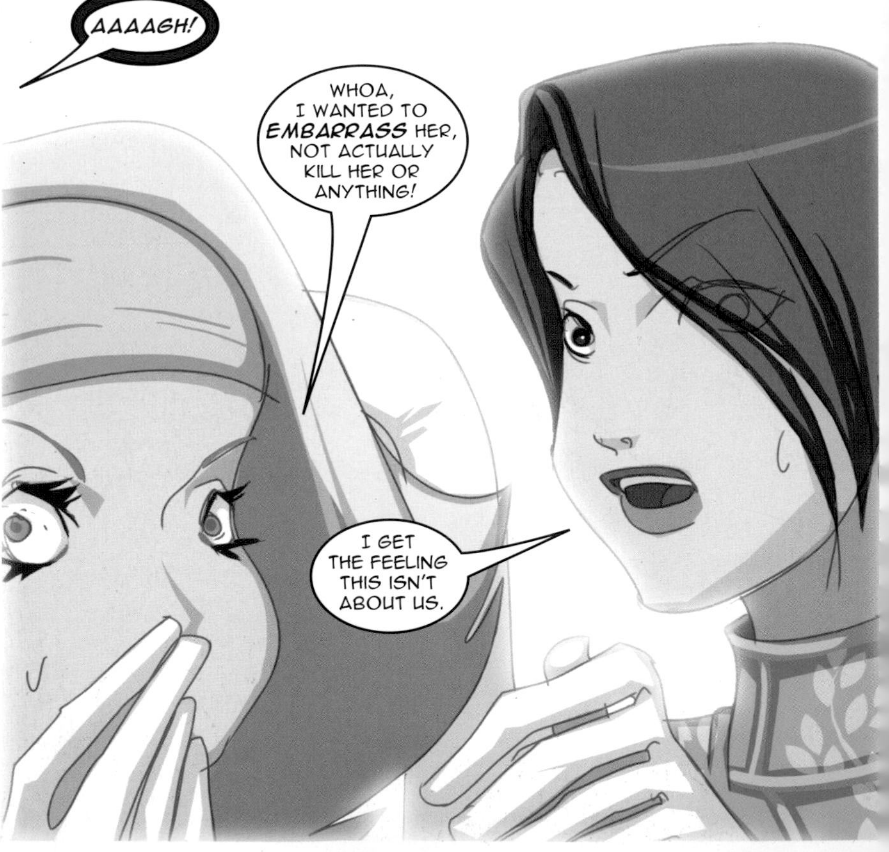
AAAAGH!
WHOA, I WANTED TO EMBARRASS HER, NOT ACTUALLY KILL HER OR ANYTHING!
I GET THE FEELING THIS ISN'T ABOUT US.

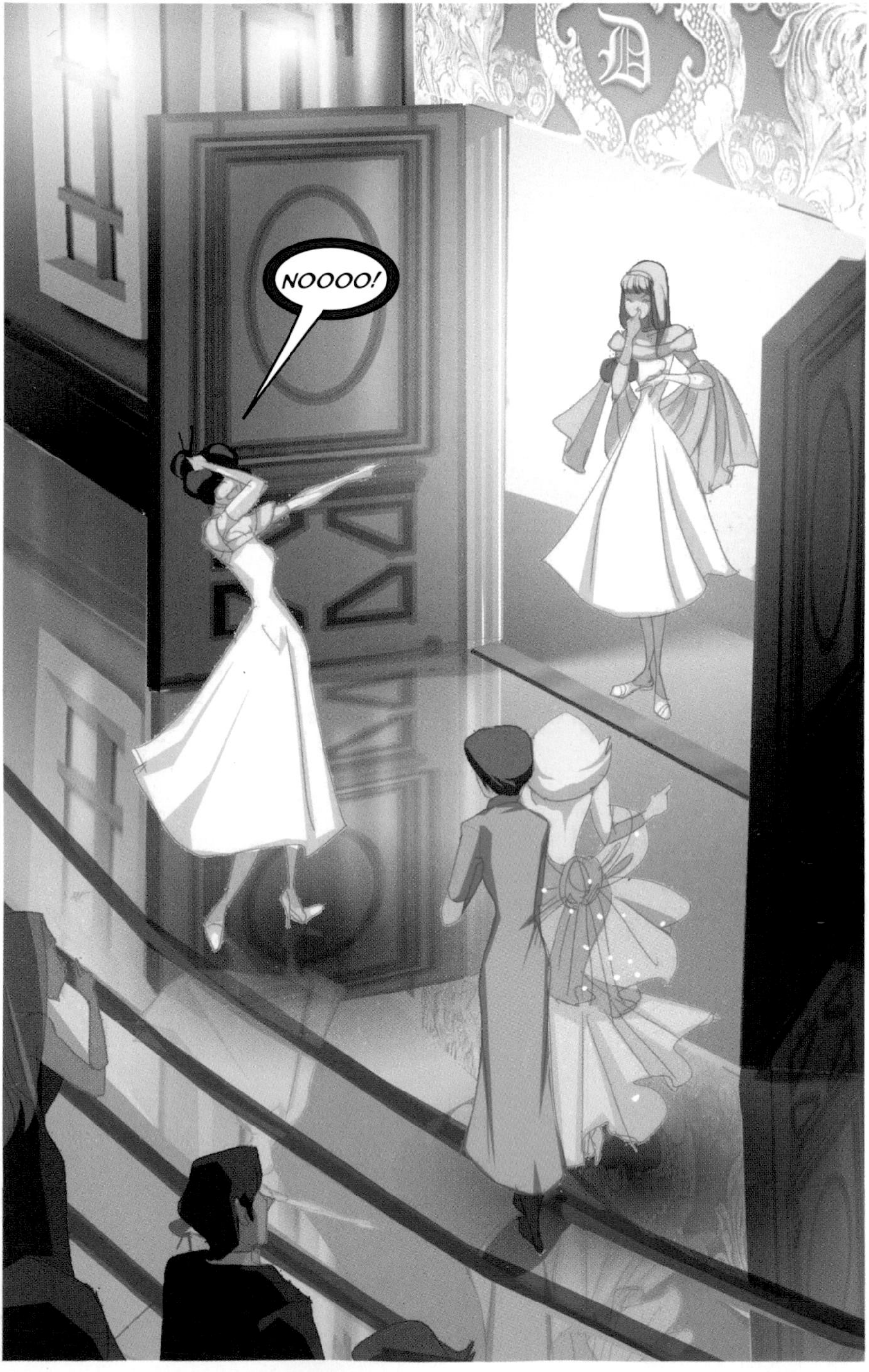
NOOOO!

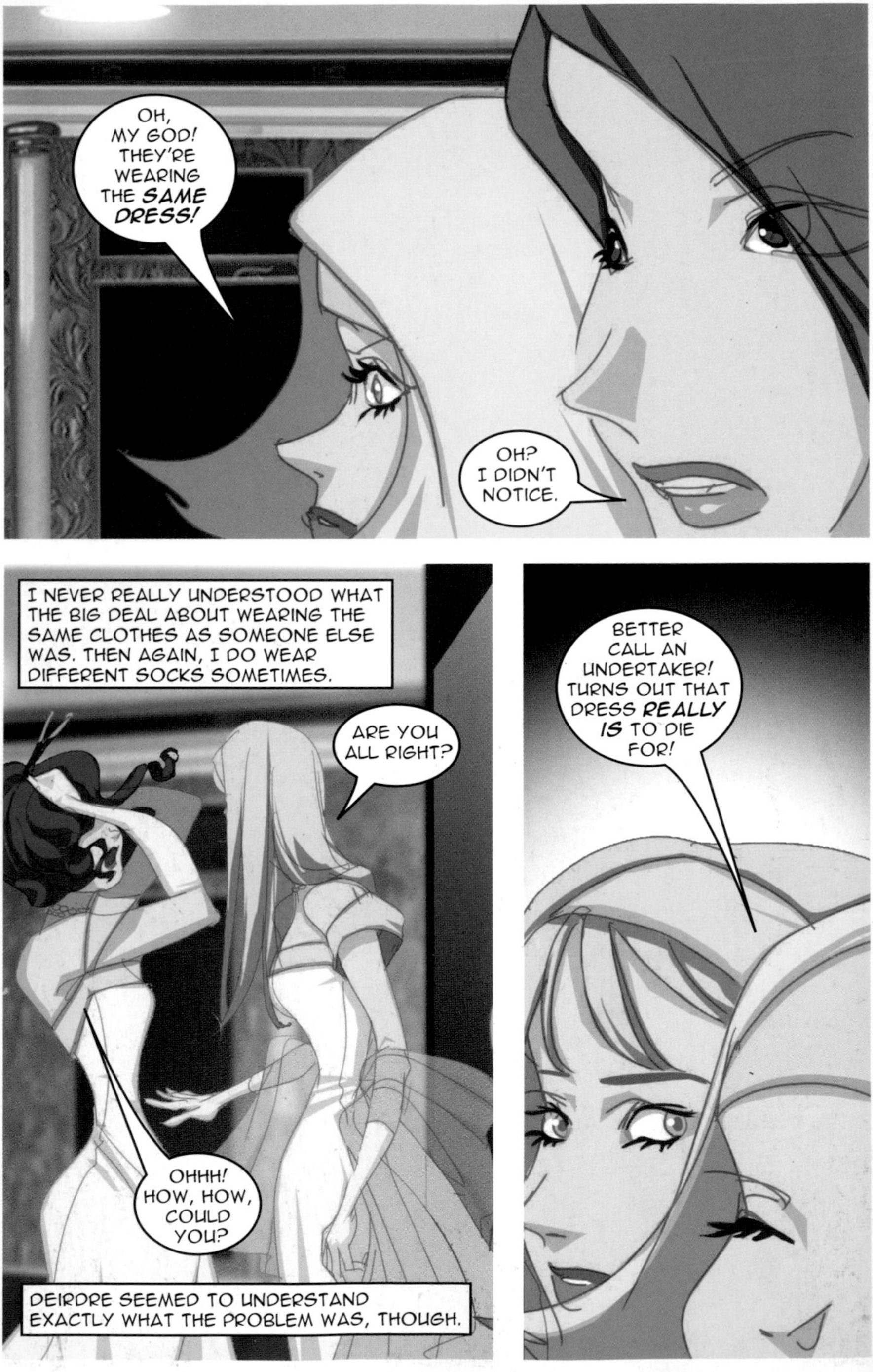
OH, MY GOD! THEY'RE WEARING THE **SAME DRESS!**
OH? I DIDN'T NOTICE.
I NEVER REALLY UNDERSTOOD WHAT THE BIG DEAL ABOUT WEARING THE SAME CLOTHES AS SOMEONE ELSE WAS. THEN AGAIN, I DO WEAR DIFFERENT SOCKS SOMETIMES.
ARE YOU ALL RIGHT?
OHHH! HOW, HOW, COULD YOU?
DEIRDRE SEEMED TO UNDERSTAND EXACTLY WHAT THE PROBLEM WAS, THOUGH.
BETTER CALL AN UNDERTAKER! TURNS OUT THAT DRESS **REALLY IS** TO DIE FOR!

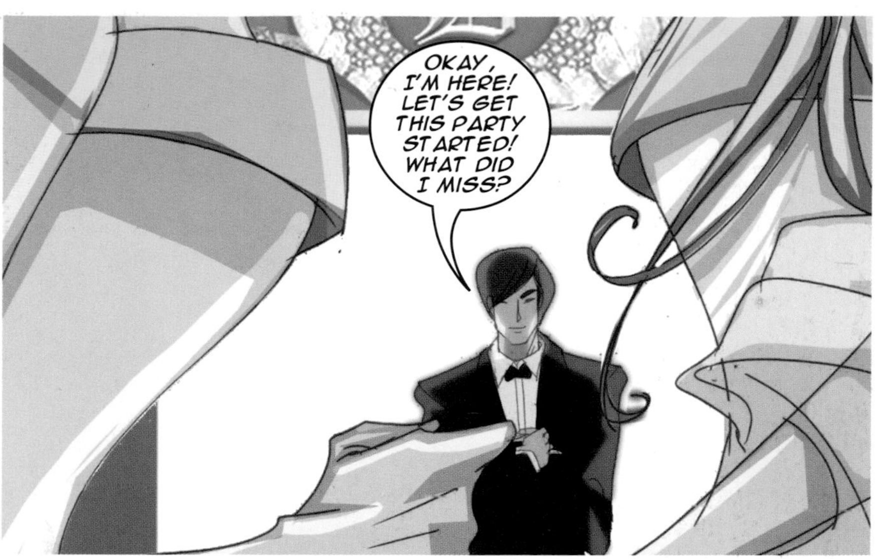
OKAY, I'M HERE! LET'S GET THIS PARTY STARTED! WHAT DID I MISS?

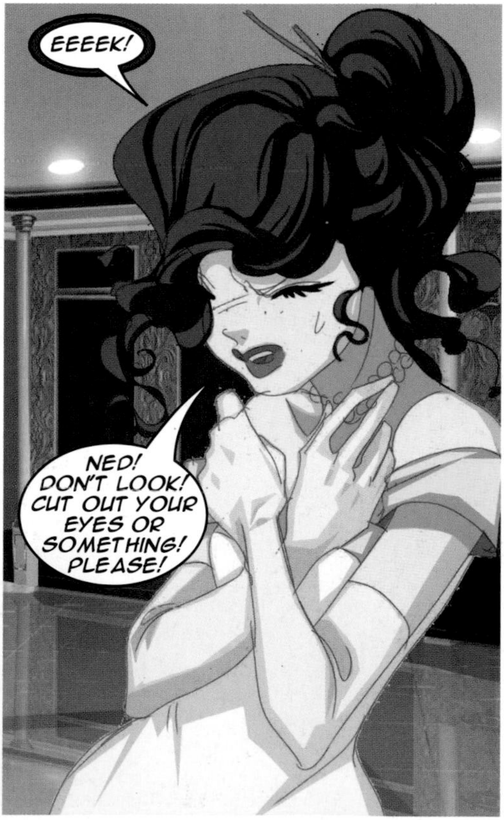
EEEEK!
NED! DON'T LOOK! CUT OUT YOUR EYES OR SOMETHING! PLEASE!

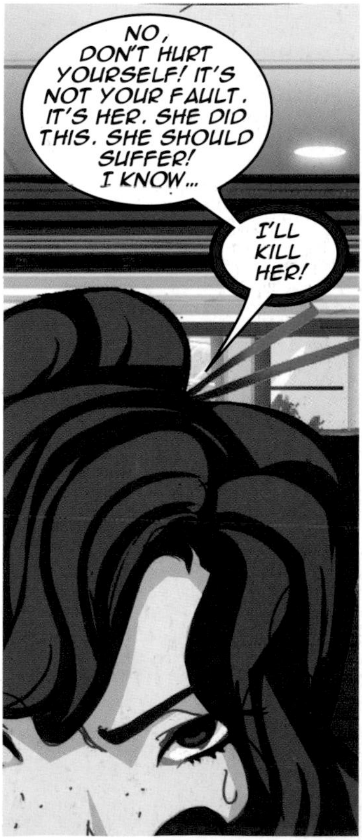
NO, DON'T HURT YOURSELF! IT'S NOT YOUR FAULT. IT'S HER. SHE DID THIS. SHE SHOULD SUFFER! I KNOW...
I'LL KILL HER!

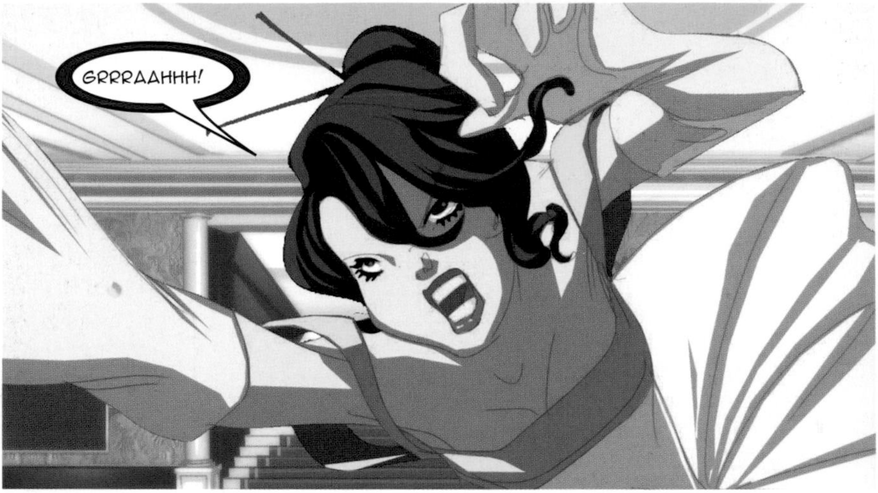
GRRRAAHHH!

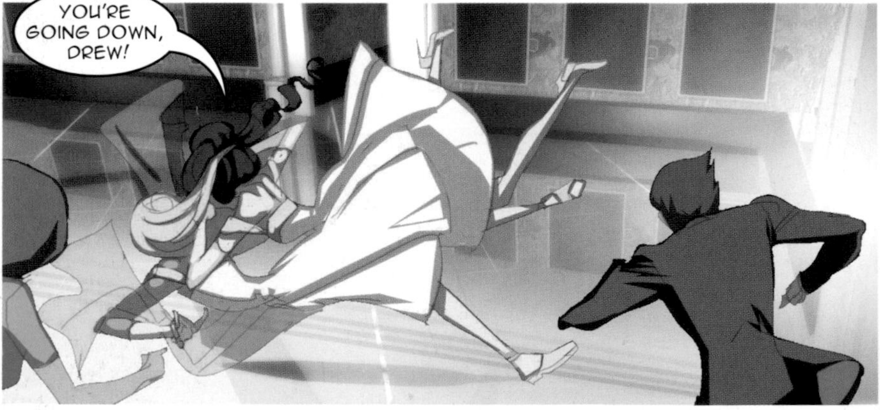
YOU'RE GOING DOWN, DREW!

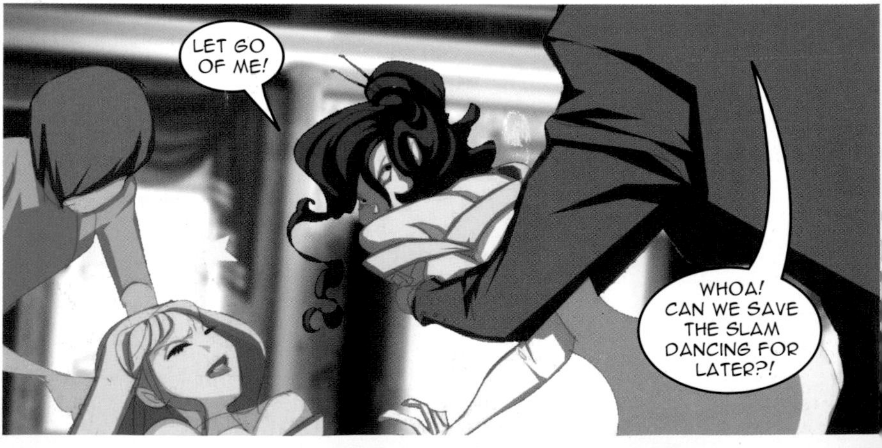
LET GO OF ME!
WHOA! CAN WE SAVE THE SLAM DANCING FOR LATER?!

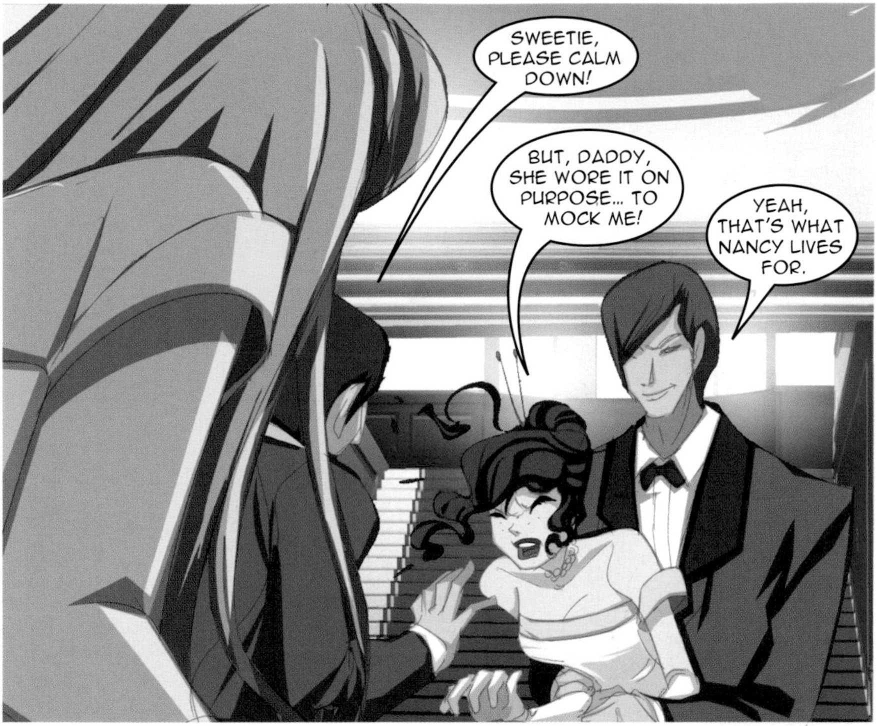
SWEETIE, PLEASE CALM DOWN!
BUT, DADDY, SHE WORE IT ON PURPOSE... TO MOCK ME!
YEAH, THAT'S WHAT NANCY LIVES FOR.

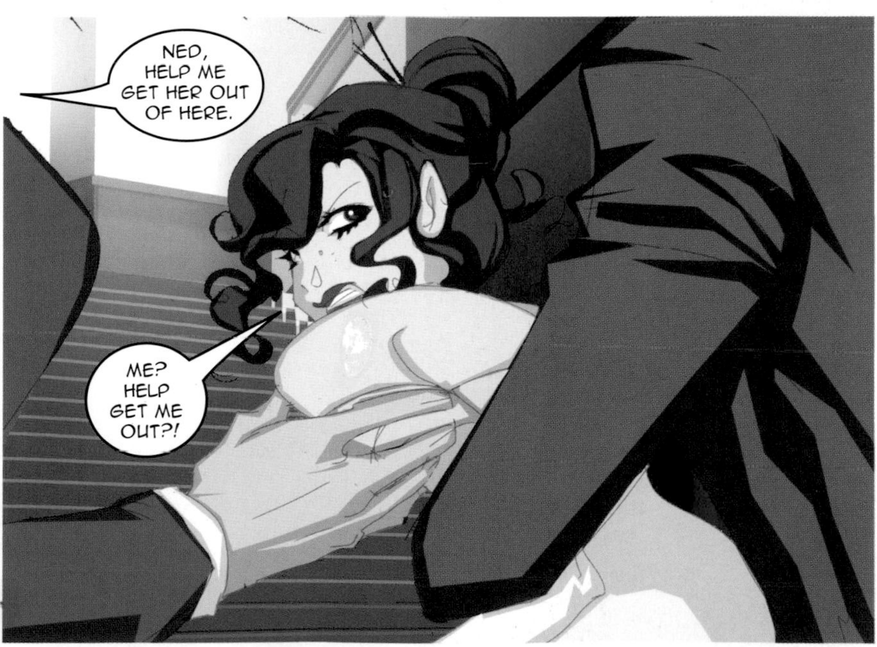
NED, HELP ME GET HER OUT OF HERE.
ME? HELP GET ME OUT?!

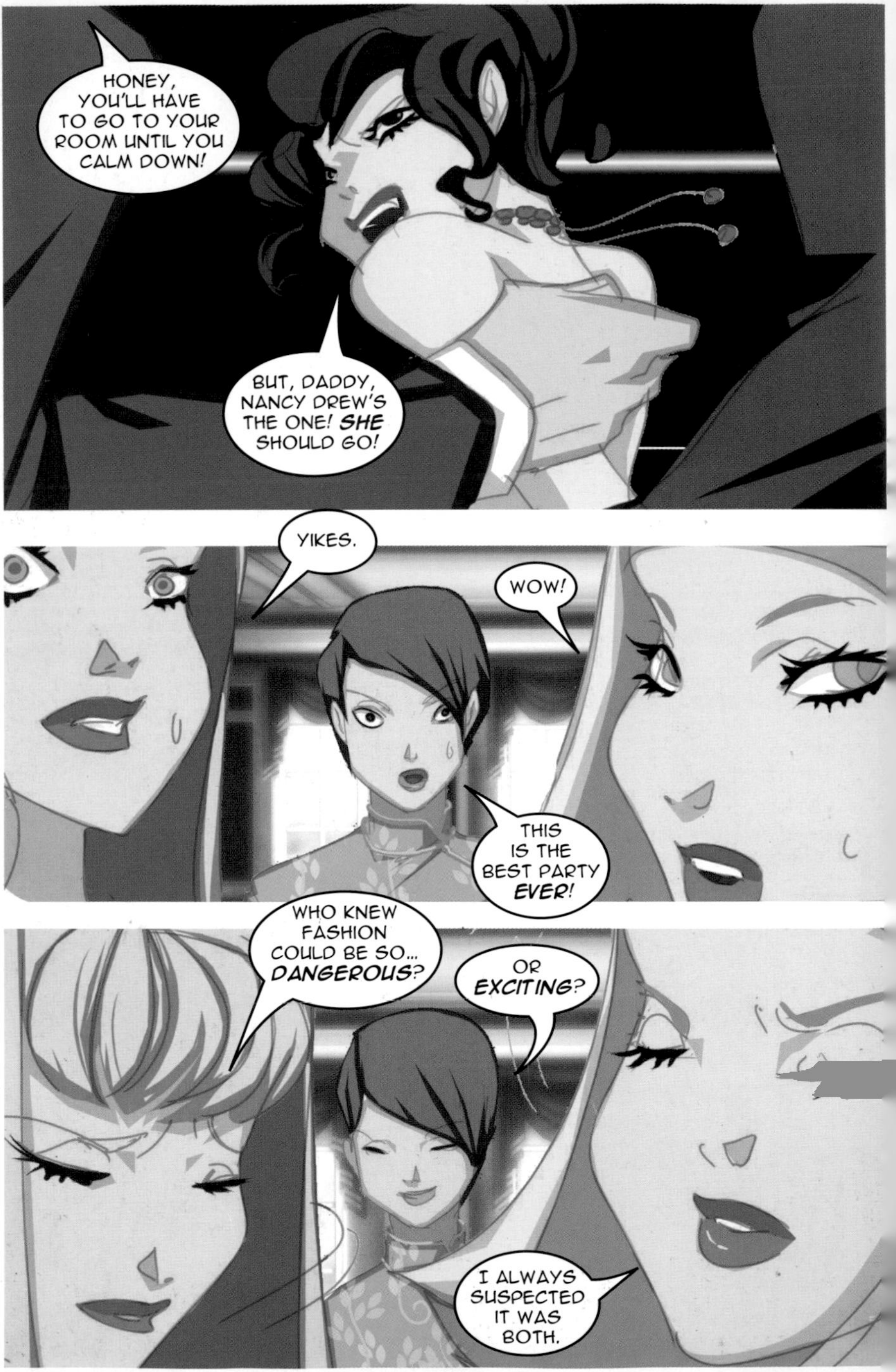
HONEY, YOU'LL HAVE TO GO TO YOUR ROOM UNTIL YOU CALM DOWN!
BUT, DADDY, NANCY DREW'S THE ONE! SHE SHOULD GO!
YIKES.
WOW!
THIS IS THE BEST PARTY EVER!
WHO KNEW FASHION COULD BE SO... DANGEROUS?
OR EXCITING?
I ALWAYS SUSPECTED IT WAS BOTH.

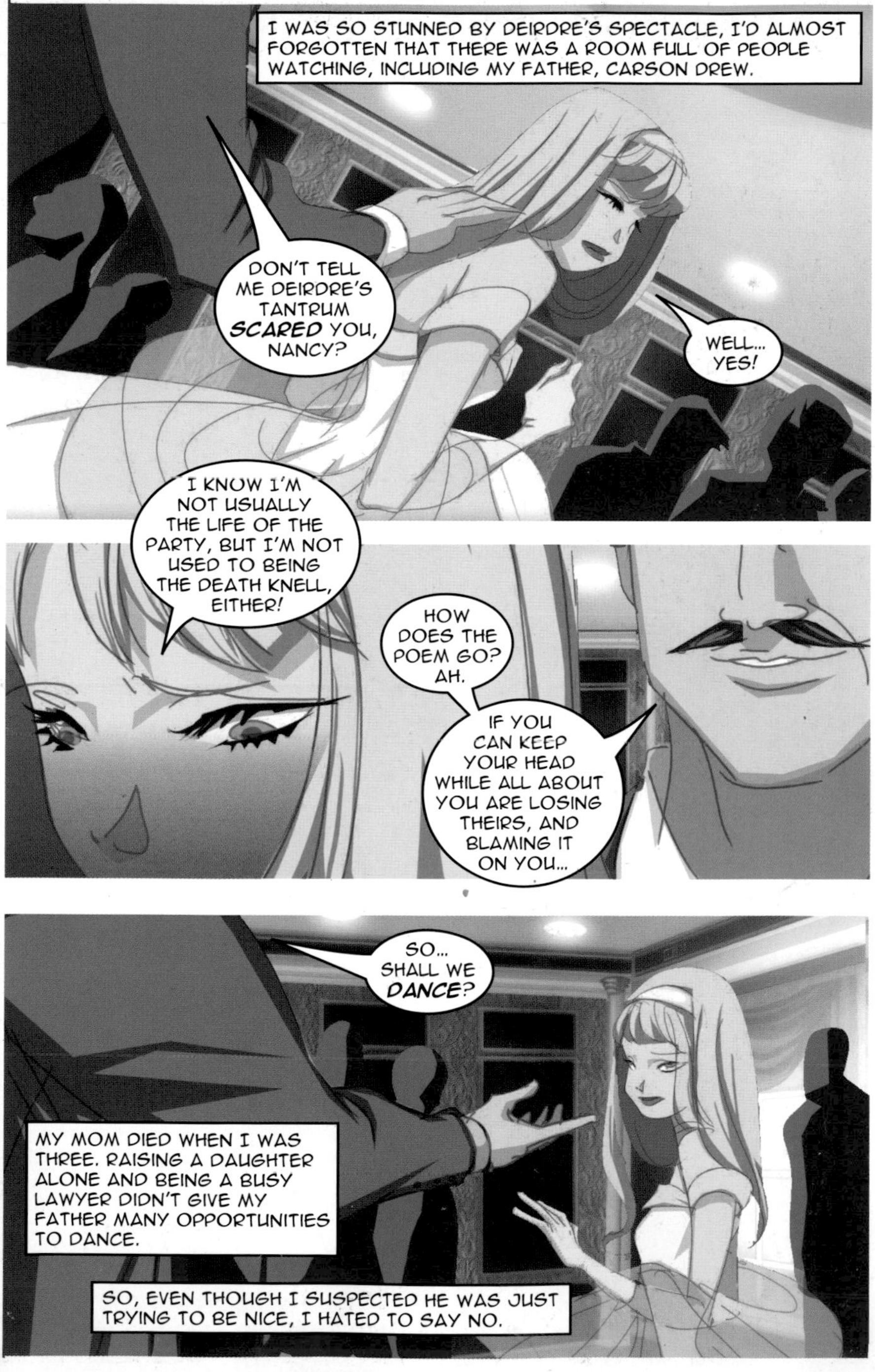
I WAS SO STUNNED BY DEIRDRE'S SPECTACLE, I'D ALMOST FORGOTTEN THAT THERE WAS A ROOM FULL OF PEOPLE WATCHING, INCLUDING MY FATHER, CARSON DREW.
DON'T TELL ME DEIRDRE'S TANTRUM **SCARED** YOU, NANCY?
WELL... YES!
I KNOW I'M NOT USUALLY THE LIFE OF THE PARTY, BUT I'M NOT USED TO BEING THE DEATH KNELL, EITHER!
HOW DOES THE POEM GO? AH.
IF YOU CAN KEEP YOUR HEAD WHILE ALL ABOUT YOU ARE LOSING THEIRS, AND BLAMING IT ON YOU...
SO... SHALL WE **DANCE**?
MY MOM DIED WHEN I WAS THREE. RAISING A DAUGHTER ALONE AND BEING A BUSY LAWYER DIDN'T GIVE MY FATHER MANY OPPORTUNITIES TO DANCE.
SO, EVEN THOUGH I SUSPECTED HE WAS JUST TRYING TO BE NICE, I HATED TO SAY NO.

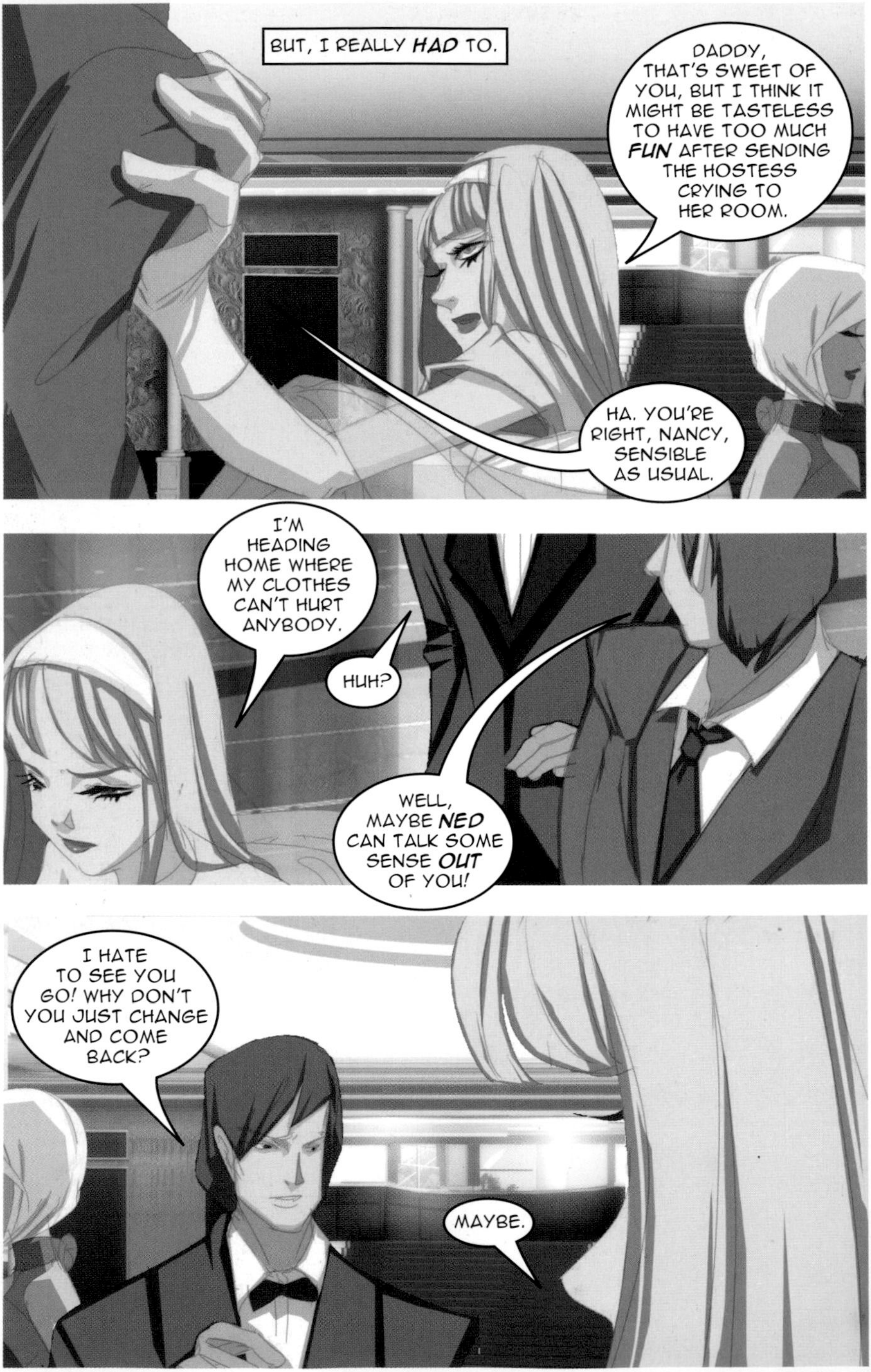
BUT, I REALLY ***HAD*** TO.
DADDY, THAT'S SWEET OF YOU, BUT I THINK IT MIGHT BE TASTELESS TO HAVE TOO MUCH ***FUN*** AFTER SENDING THE HOSTESS CRYING TO HER ROOM.
HA. YOU'RE RIGHT, NANCY, SENSIBLE AS USUAL.
I'M HEADING HOME WHERE MY CLOTHES CAN'T HURT ANYBODY.
HUH?
WELL, MAYBE ***NED*** CAN TALK SOME SENSE ***OUT*** OF YOU!
I HATE TO SEE YOU GO! WHY DON'T YOU JUST CHANGE AND COME BACK?
MAYBE.

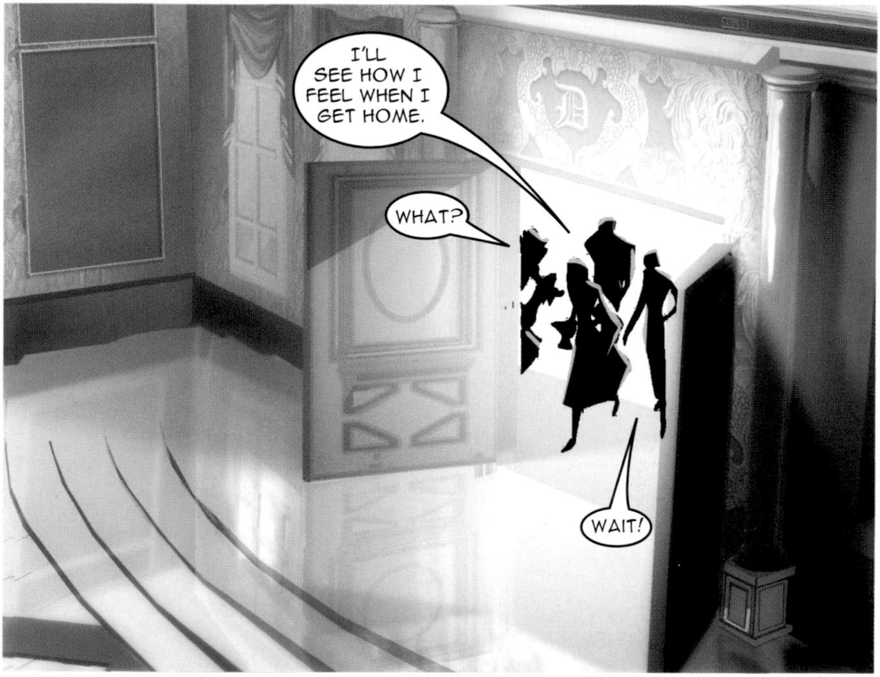
I'LL SEE HOW I FEEL WHEN I GET HOME.
WHAT?
WAIT!

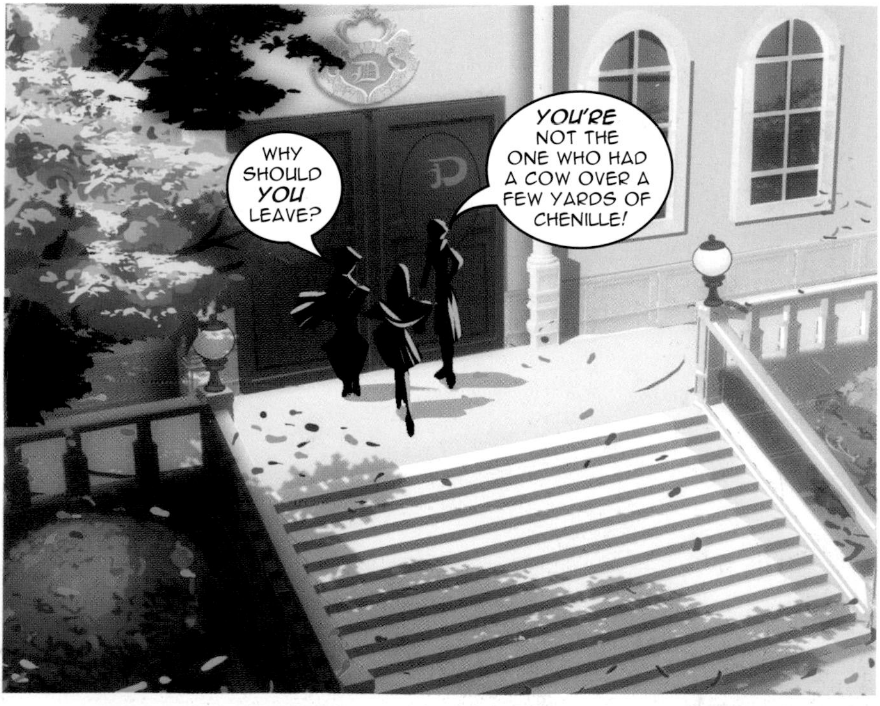
WHY SHOULD *YOU* LEAVE?
YOU'RE NOT THE ONE WHO HAD A COW OVER A FEW YARDS OF CHENILLE!

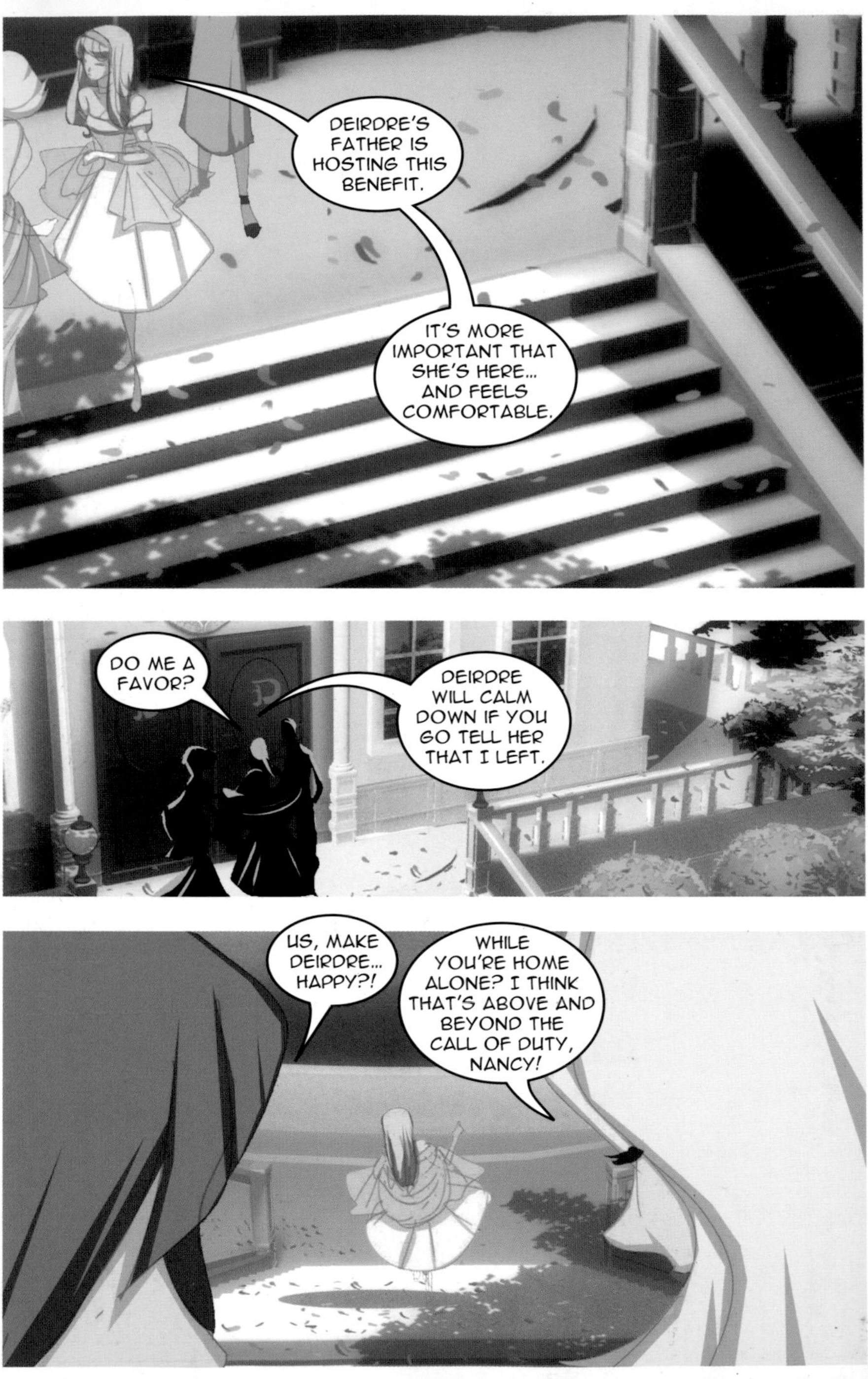
DEIRDRE'S FATHER IS HOSTING THIS BENEFIT.
IT'S MORE IMPORTANT THAT SHE'S HERE... AND FEELS COMFORTABLE.
DO ME A FAVOR?
DEIRDRE WILL CALM DOWN IF YOU GO TELL HER THAT I LEFT.
US, MAKE DEIRDRE... HAPPY?!
WHILE YOU'RE HOME ALONE? I THINK THAT'S ABOVE AND BEYOND THE CALL OF DUTY, NANCY!

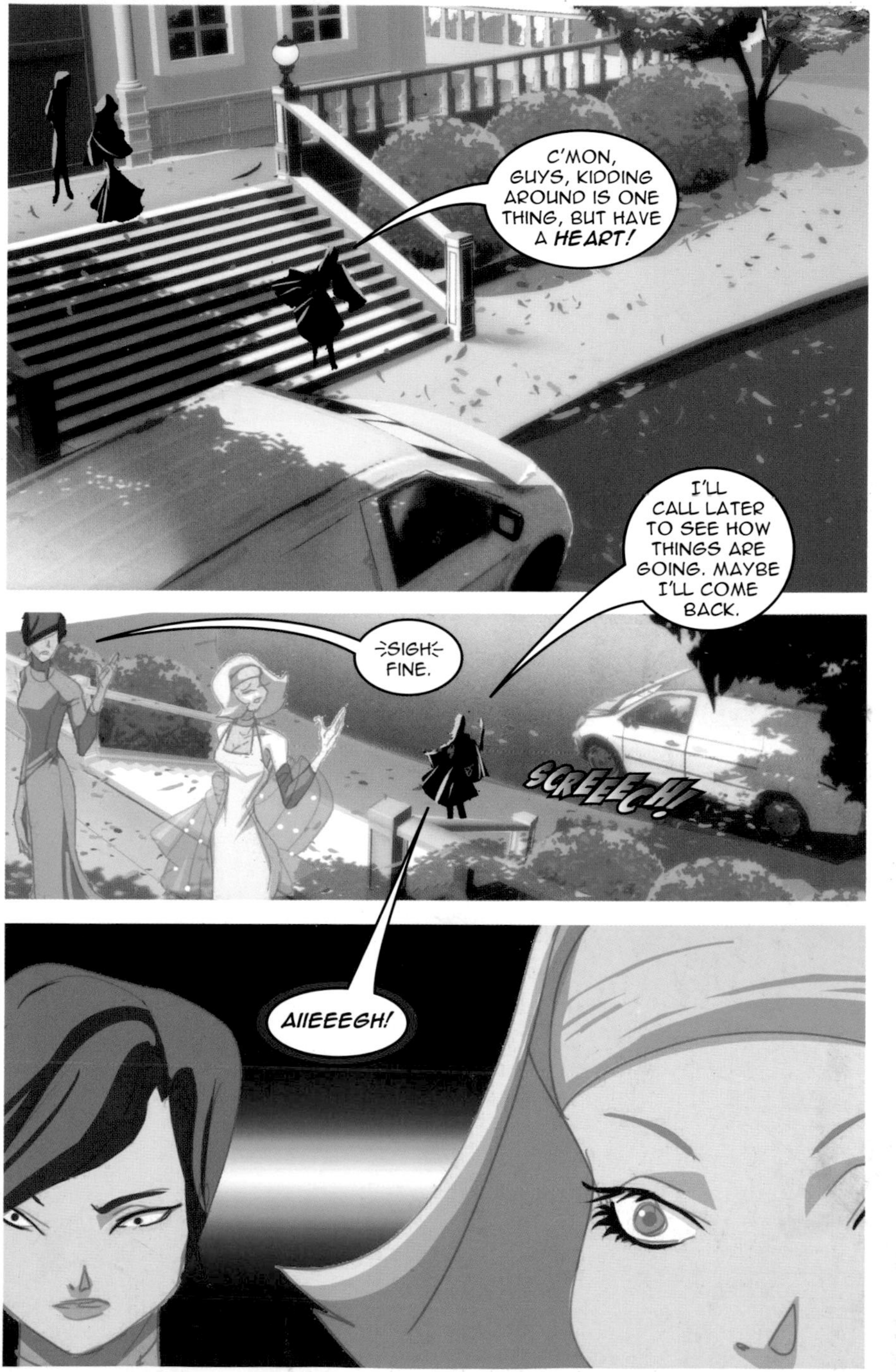
C'MON, GUYS, KIDDING AROUND IS ONE THING, BUT HAVE A HEART!
I'LL CALL LATER TO SEE HOW THINGS ARE GOING. MAYBE I'LL COME BACK.
-SIGH- FINE.
SCREEECH!
AIIEEEGH!

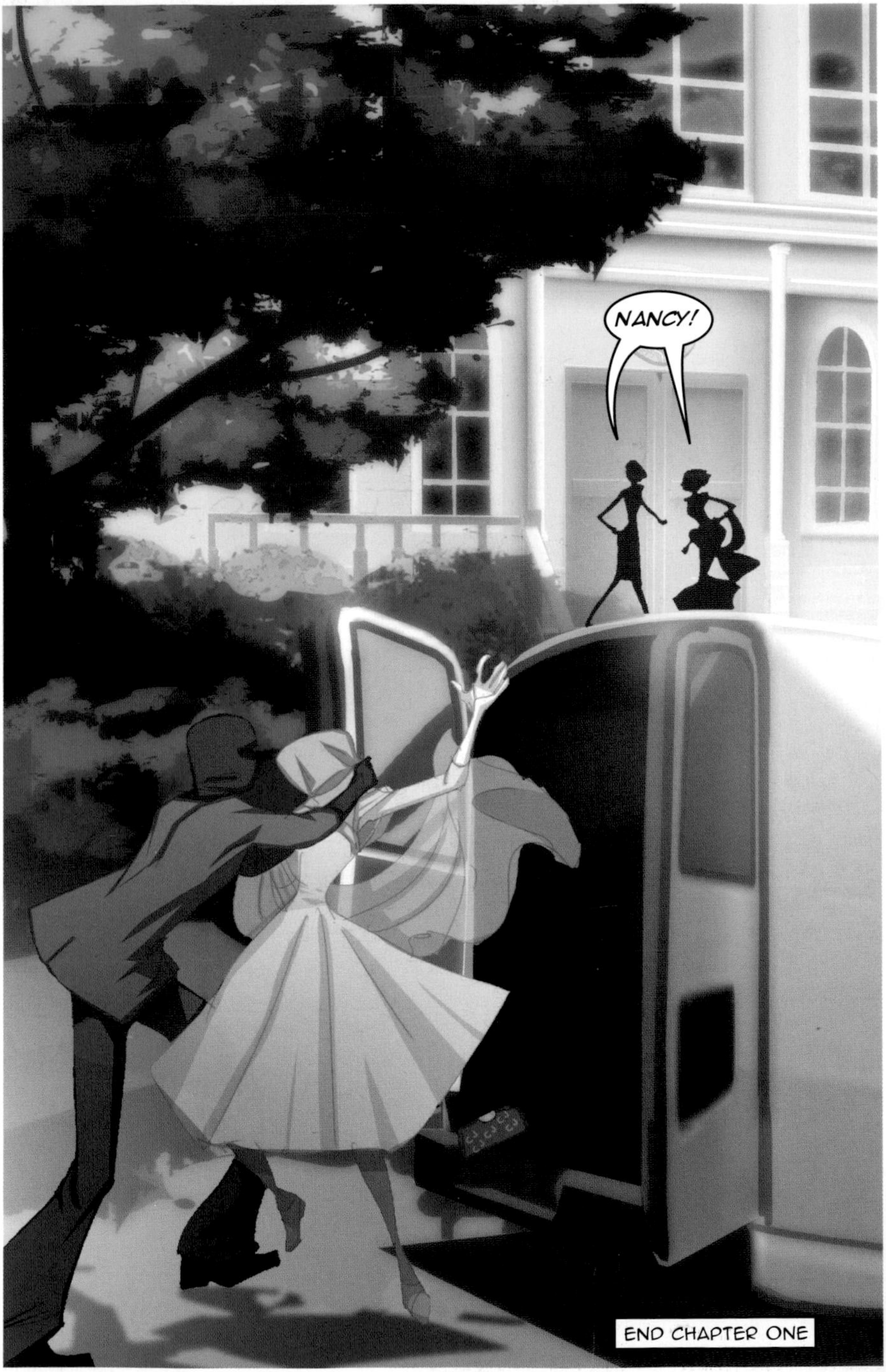
NANCY!
END CHAPTER ONE

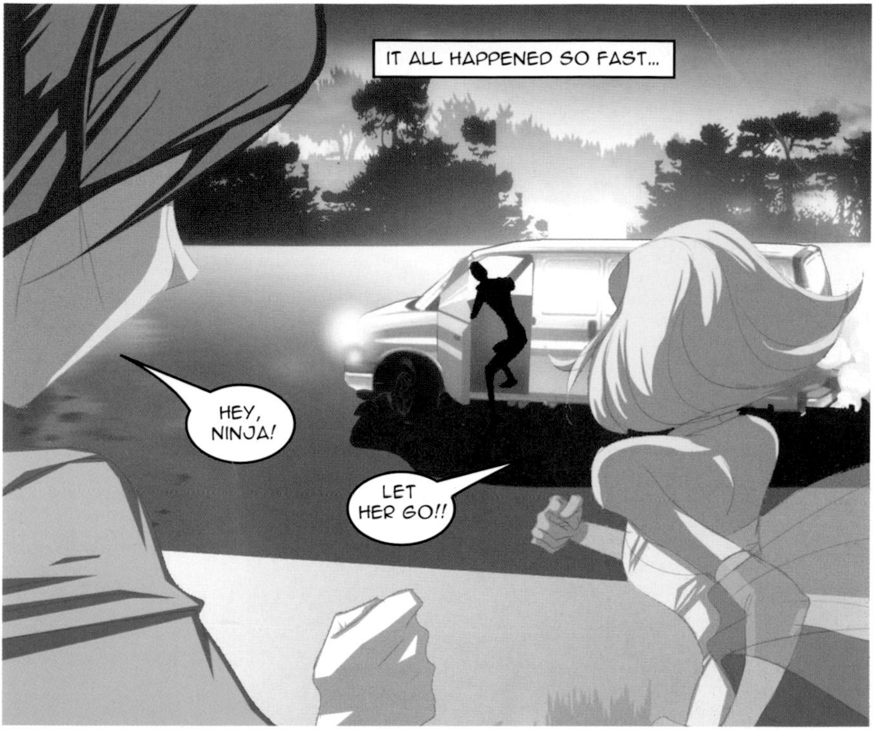
IT ALL HAPPENED SO FAST...
HEY, NINJA!
LET HER GO!!

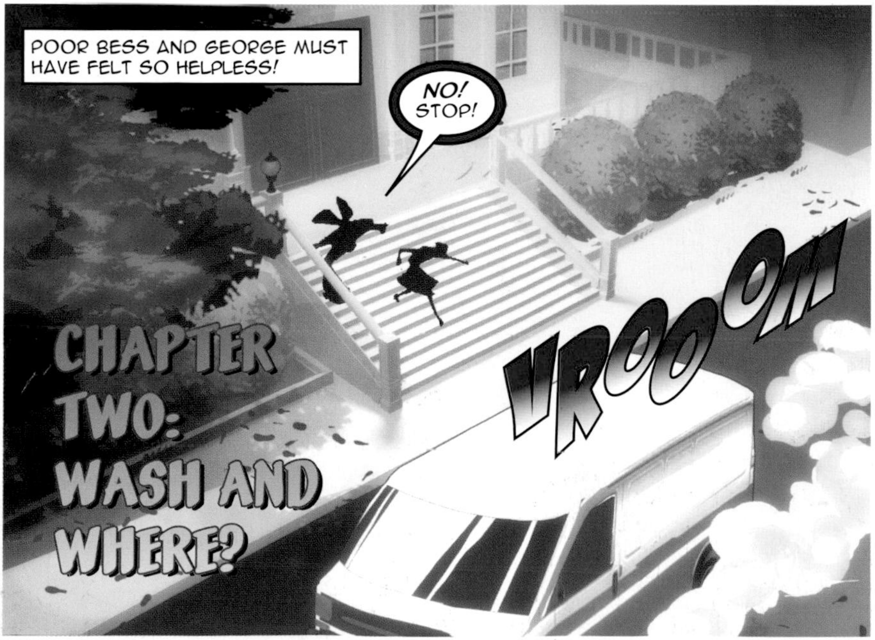
POOR BESS AND GEORGE MUST HAVE FELT SO HELPLESS!
NO! STOP!
CHAPTER TWO: WASH AND WHERE?
VROOOOM

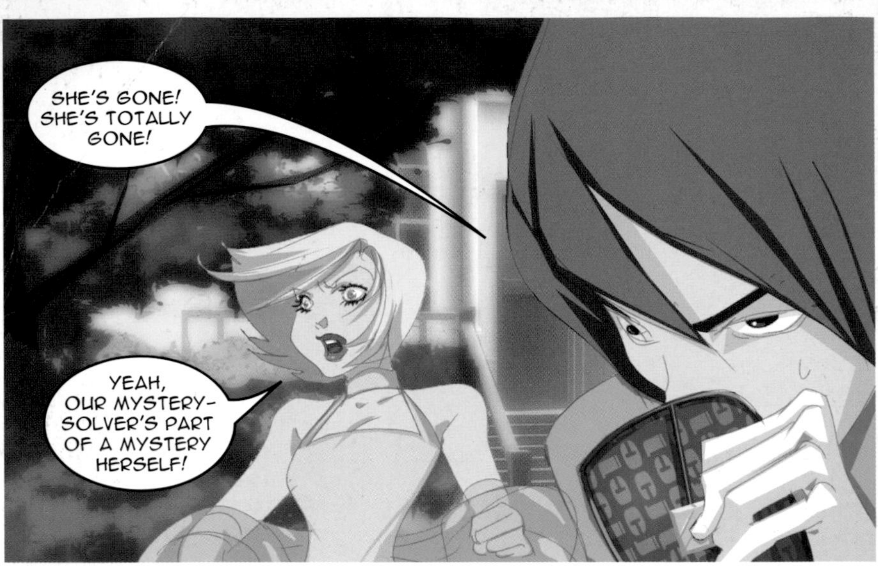
SHE'S GONE! SHE'S TOTALLY GONE!
YEAH, OUR MYSTERY-SOLVER'S PART OF A MYSTERY HERSELF!

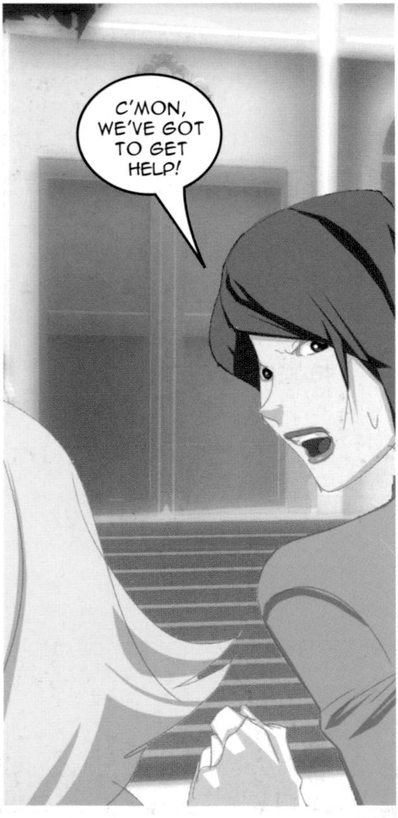
C'MON, WE'VE GOT TO GET HELP!

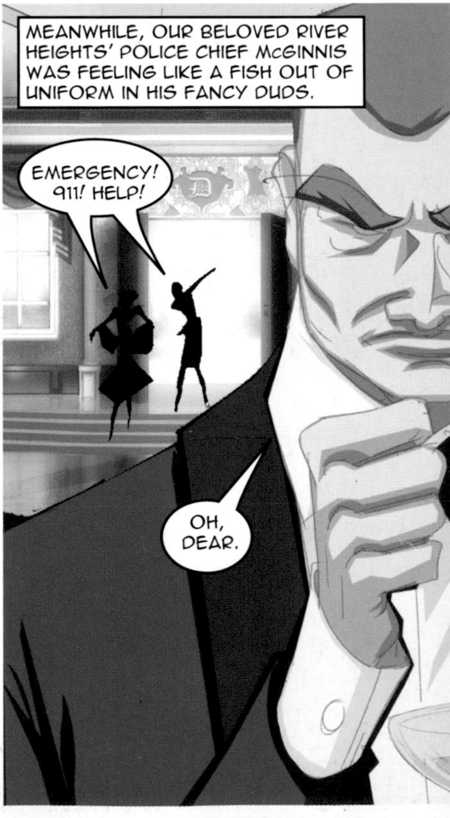
MEANWHILE, OUR BELOVED RIVER HEIGHTS' POLICE CHIEF McGINNIS WAS FEELING LIKE A FISH OUT OF UNIFORM IN HIS FANCY DUDS.
EMERGENCY! 911! HELP!
OH, DEAR.

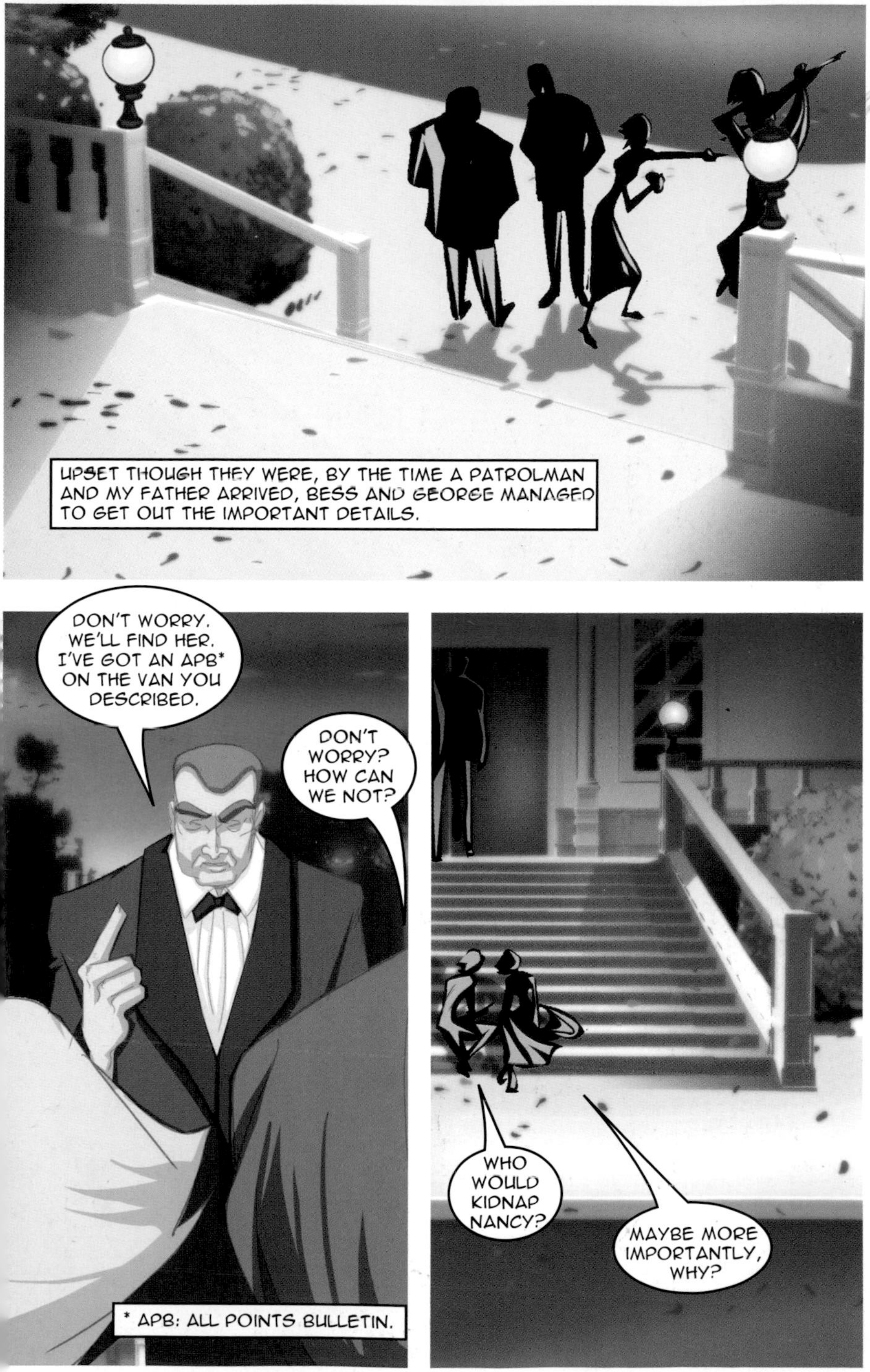
UPSET THOUGH THEY WERE, BY THE TIME A PATROLMAN AND MY FATHER ARRIVED, BESS AND GEORGE MANAGED TO GET OUT THE IMPORTANT DETAILS.
DON'T WORRY. WE'LL FIND HER. I'VE GOT AN APB* ON THE VAN YOU DESCRIBED.
DON'T WORRY? HOW CAN WE NOT?
* APB: ALL POINTS BULLETIN.
WHO WOULD KIDNAP NANCY?
MAYBE MORE IMPORTANTLY, WHY?

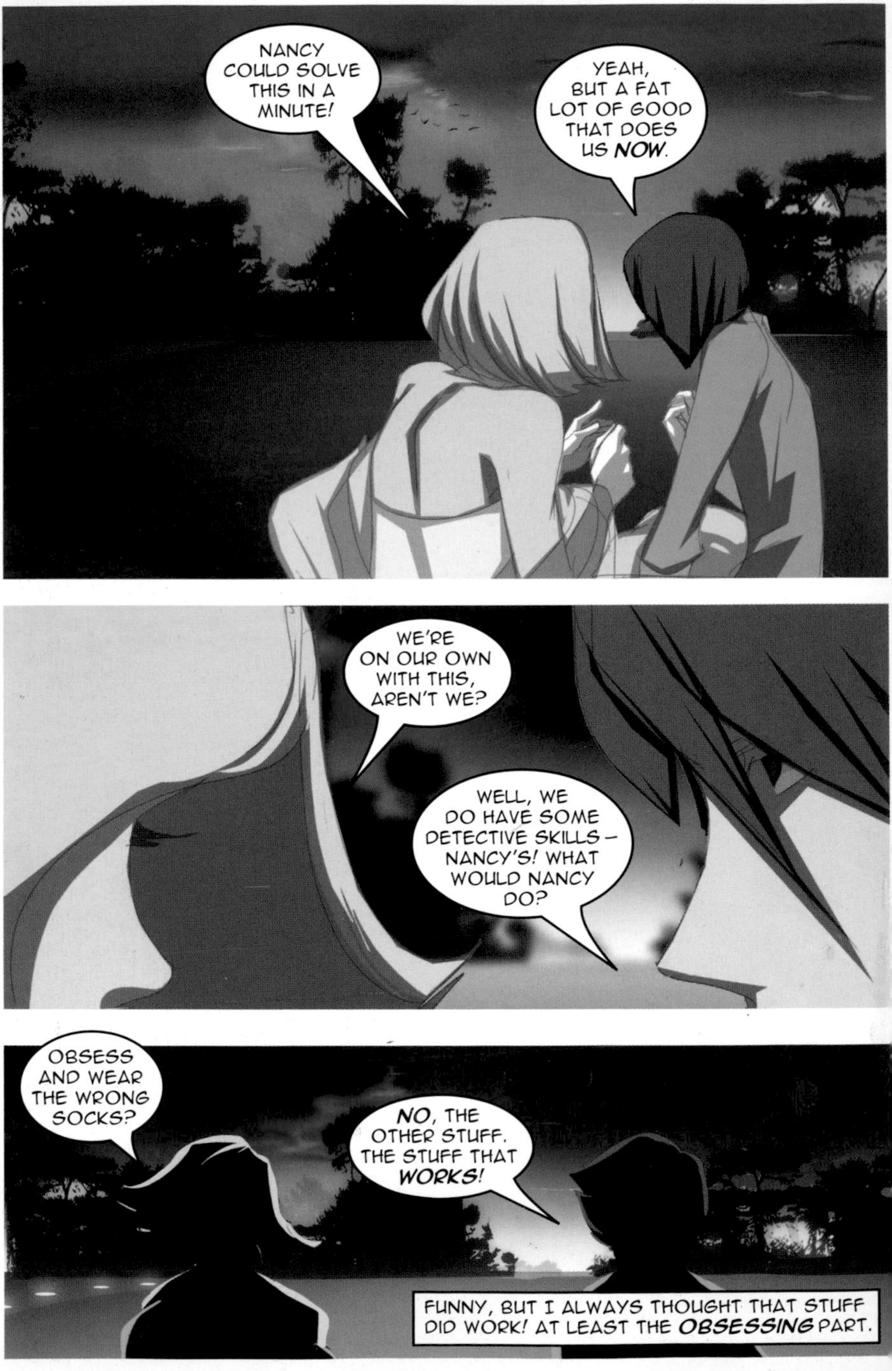
NANCY COULD SOLVE THIS IN A MINUTE!
YEAH, BUT A FAT LOT OF GOOD THAT DOES US **NOW**.
WE'RE ON OUR OWN WITH THIS, AREN'T WE?
WELL, WE DO HAVE SOME DETECTIVE SKILLS – NANCY'S! WHAT WOULD NANCY DO?
OBSESS AND WEAR THE WRONG SOCKS?
NO, THE OTHER STUFF. THE STUFF THAT **WORKS!**
FUNNY, BUT I ALWAYS THOUGHT THAT STUFF DID WORK! AT LEAST THE ***OBSESSING*** PART.

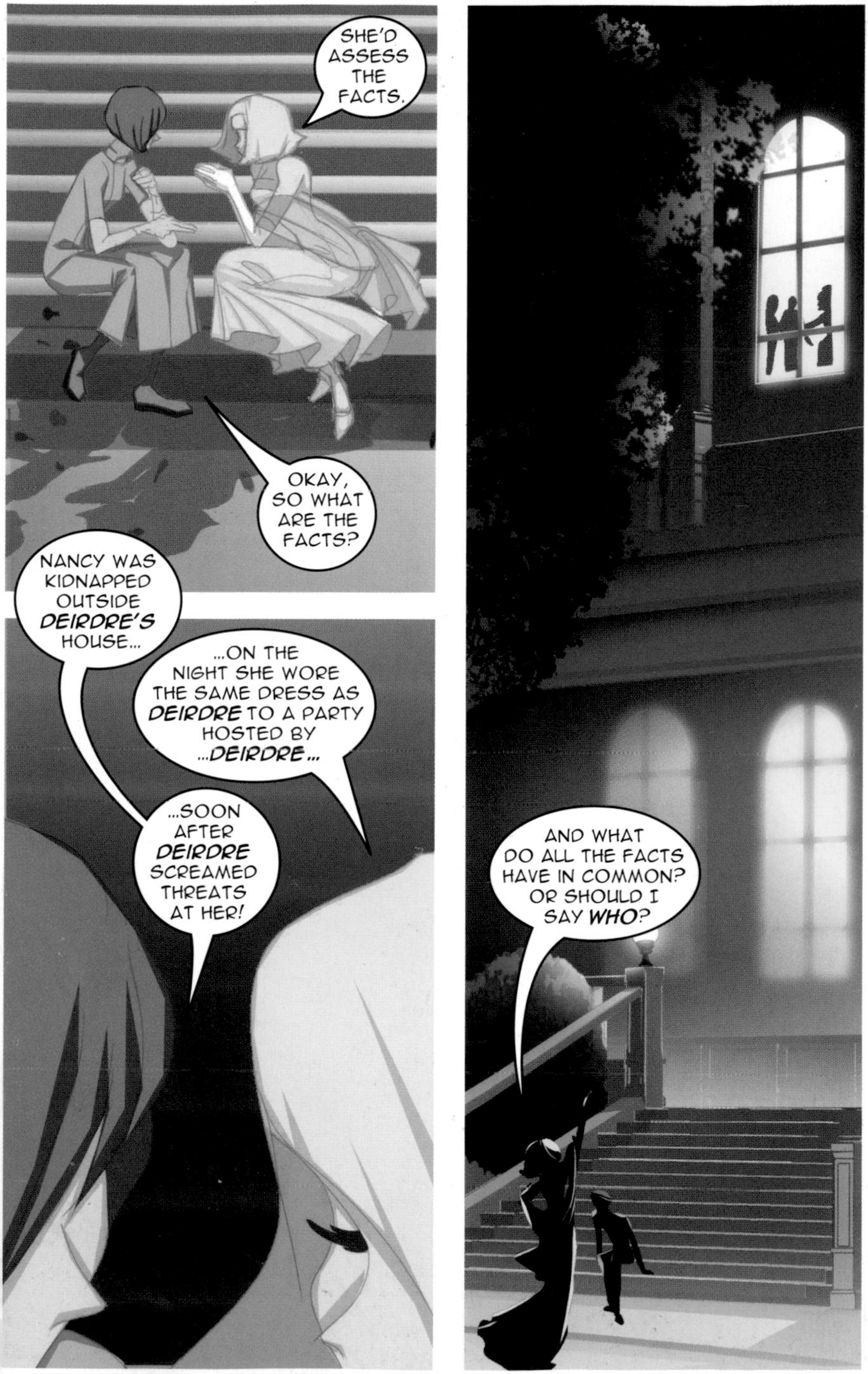
SHE'D ASSESS THE FACTS.
OKAY, SO WHAT ARE THE FACTS?
NANCY WAS KIDNAPPED OUTSIDE DEIRDRE'S HOUSE...
...ON THE NIGHT SHE WORE THE SAME DRESS AS DEIRDRE TO A PARTY HOSTED BY ...DEIRDRE...
...SOON AFTER DEIRDRE SCREAMED THREATS AT HER!
AND WHAT DO ALL THE FACTS HAVE IN COMMON? OR SHOULD I SAY WHO?

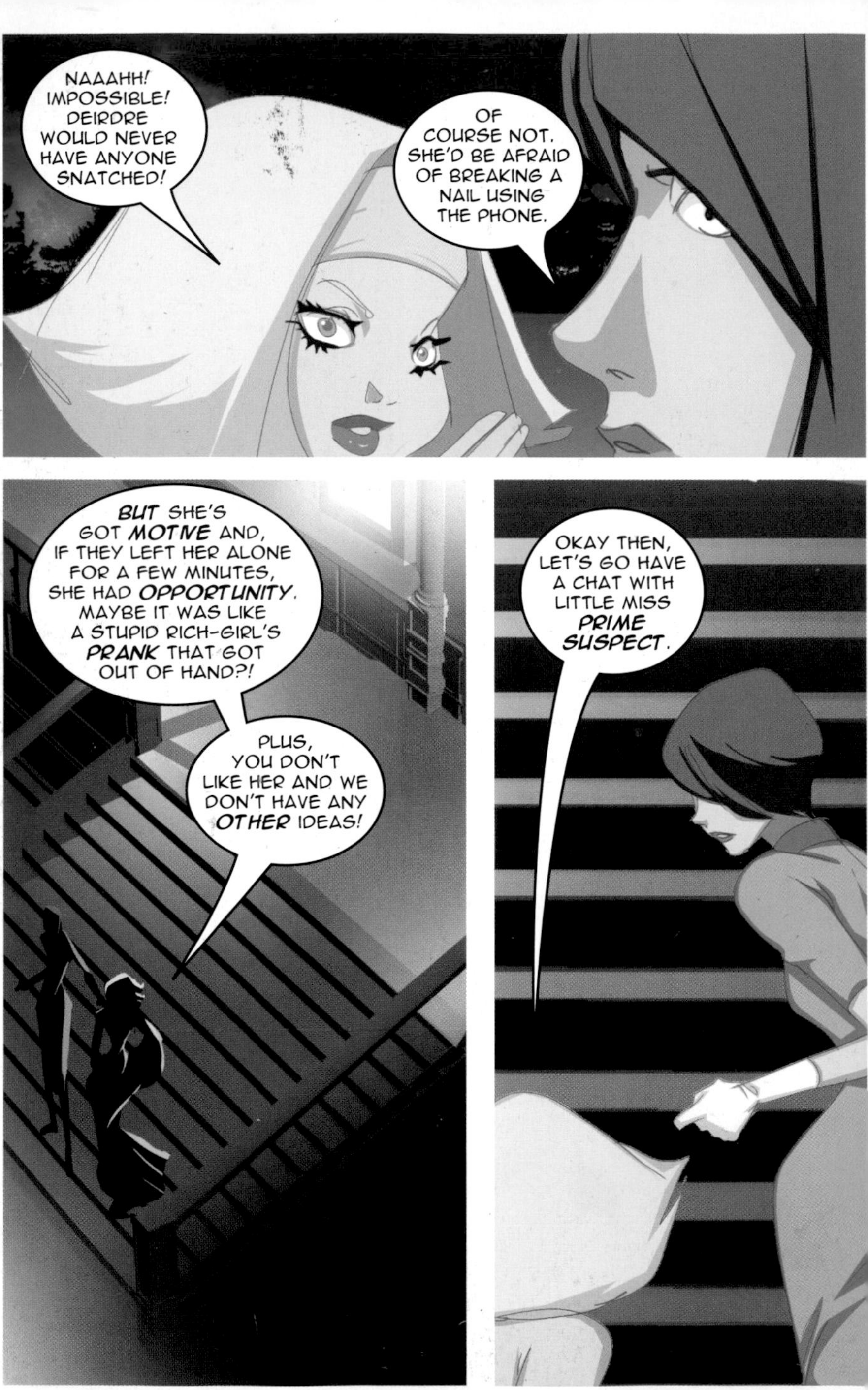
NAAAHH! IMPOSSIBLE! DEIRDRE WOULD NEVER HAVE ANYONE SNATCHED!
OF COURSE NOT. SHE'D BE AFRAID OF BREAKING A NAIL USING THE PHONE.
BUT SHE'S GOT MOTIVE AND, IF THEY LEFT HER ALONE FOR A FEW MINUTES, SHE HAD OPPORTUNITY. MAYBE IT WAS LIKE A STUPID RICH-GIRL'S PRANK THAT GOT OUT OF HAND?!
PLUS, YOU DON'T LIKE HER AND WE DON'T HAVE ANY OTHER IDEAS!
OKAY THEN, LET'S GO HAVE A CHAT WITH LITTLE MISS PRIME SUSPECT.

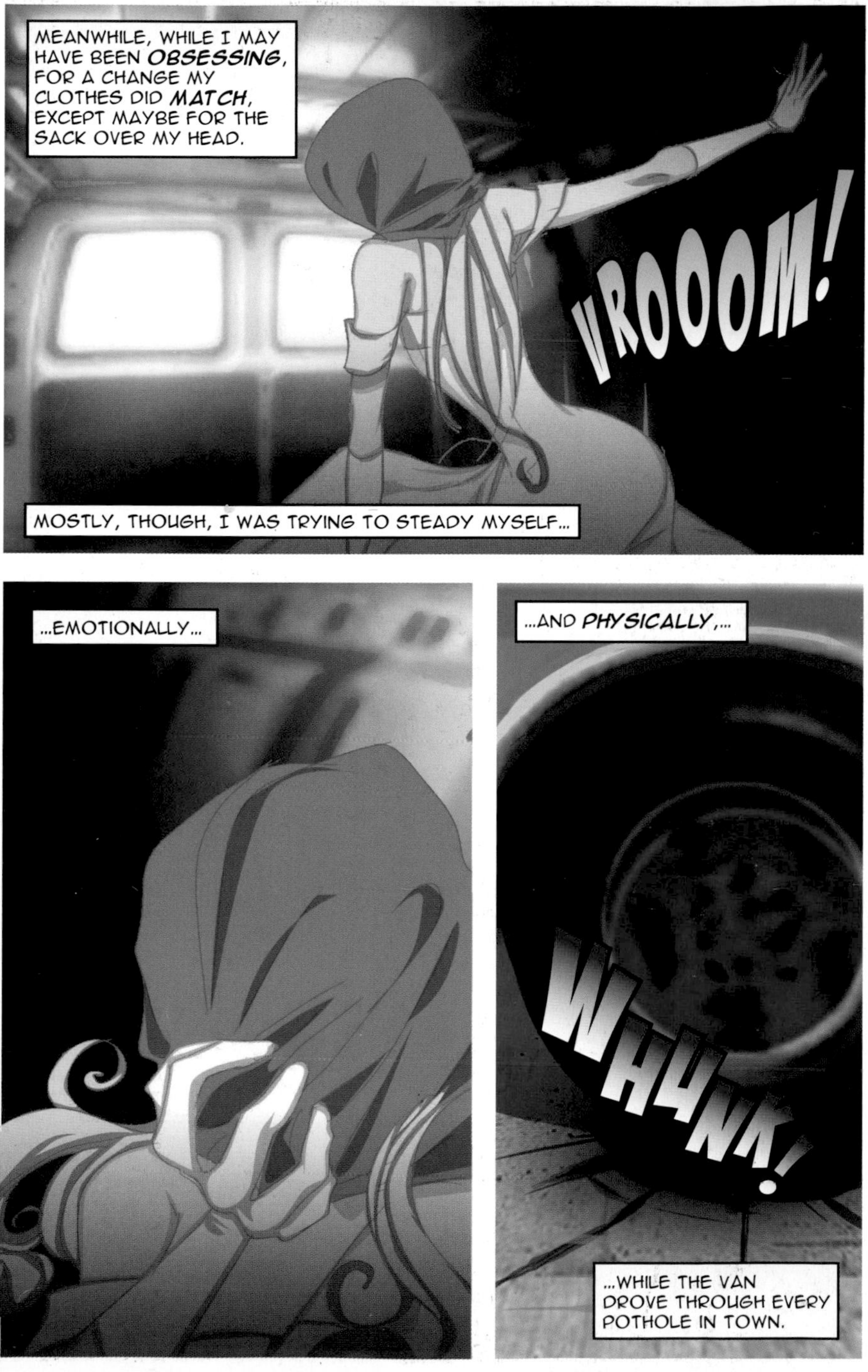
MEANWHILE, WHILE I MAY HAVE BEEN OBSESSING, FOR A CHANGE MY CLOTHES DID MATCH, EXCEPT MAYBE FOR THE SACK OVER MY HEAD.
VROOOM!
MOSTLY, THOUGH, I WAS TRYING TO STEADY MYSELF...
...EMOTIONALLY...
...AND PHYSICALLY,...
WHUNK!
...WHILE THE VAN DROVE THROUGH EVERY POTHOLE IN TOWN.

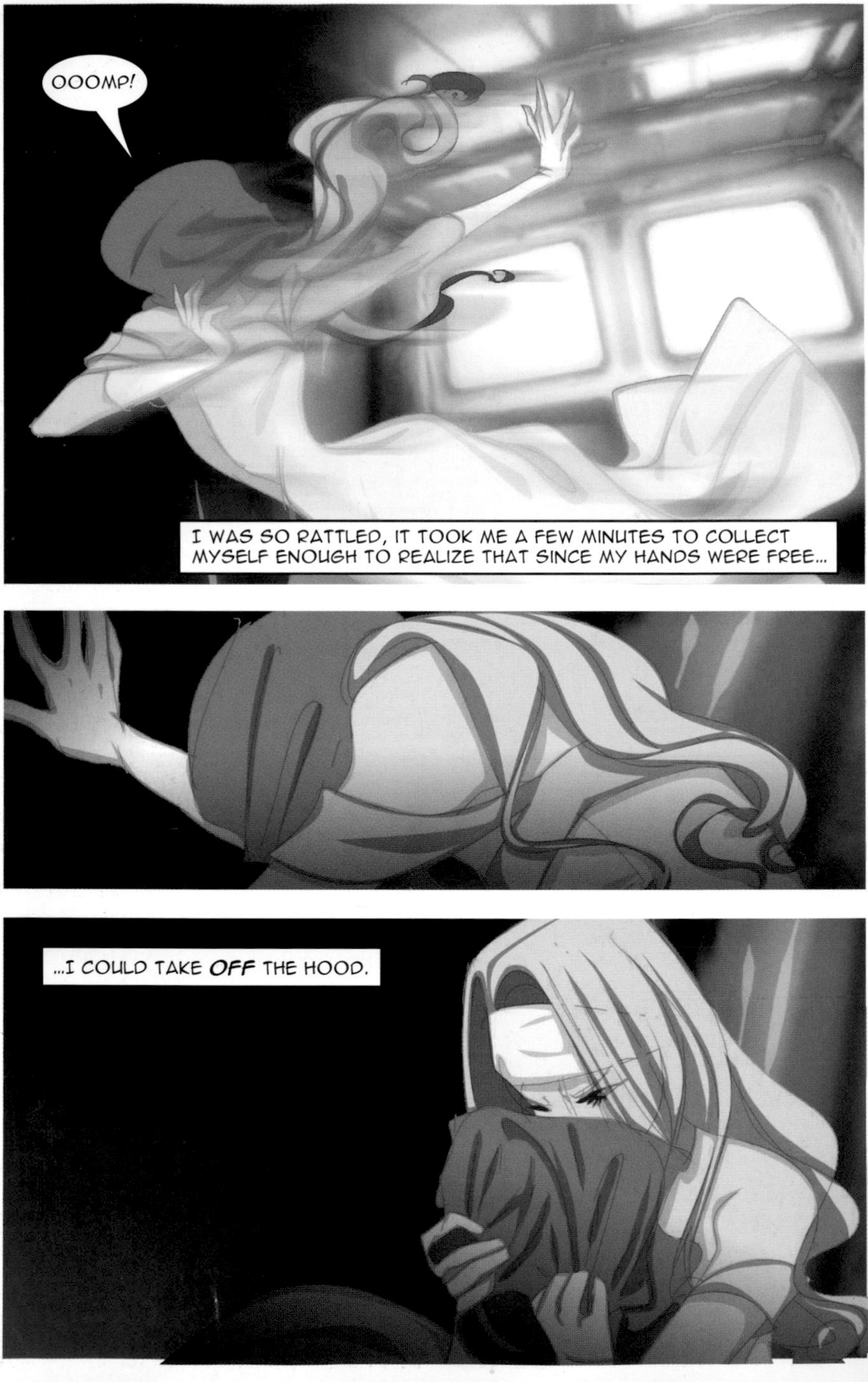
OOOMP!
I WAS SO RATTLED, IT TOOK ME A FEW MINUTES TO COLLECT MYSELF ENOUGH TO REALIZE THAT SINCE MY HANDS WERE FREE...
...I COULD TAKE OFF THE HOOD.

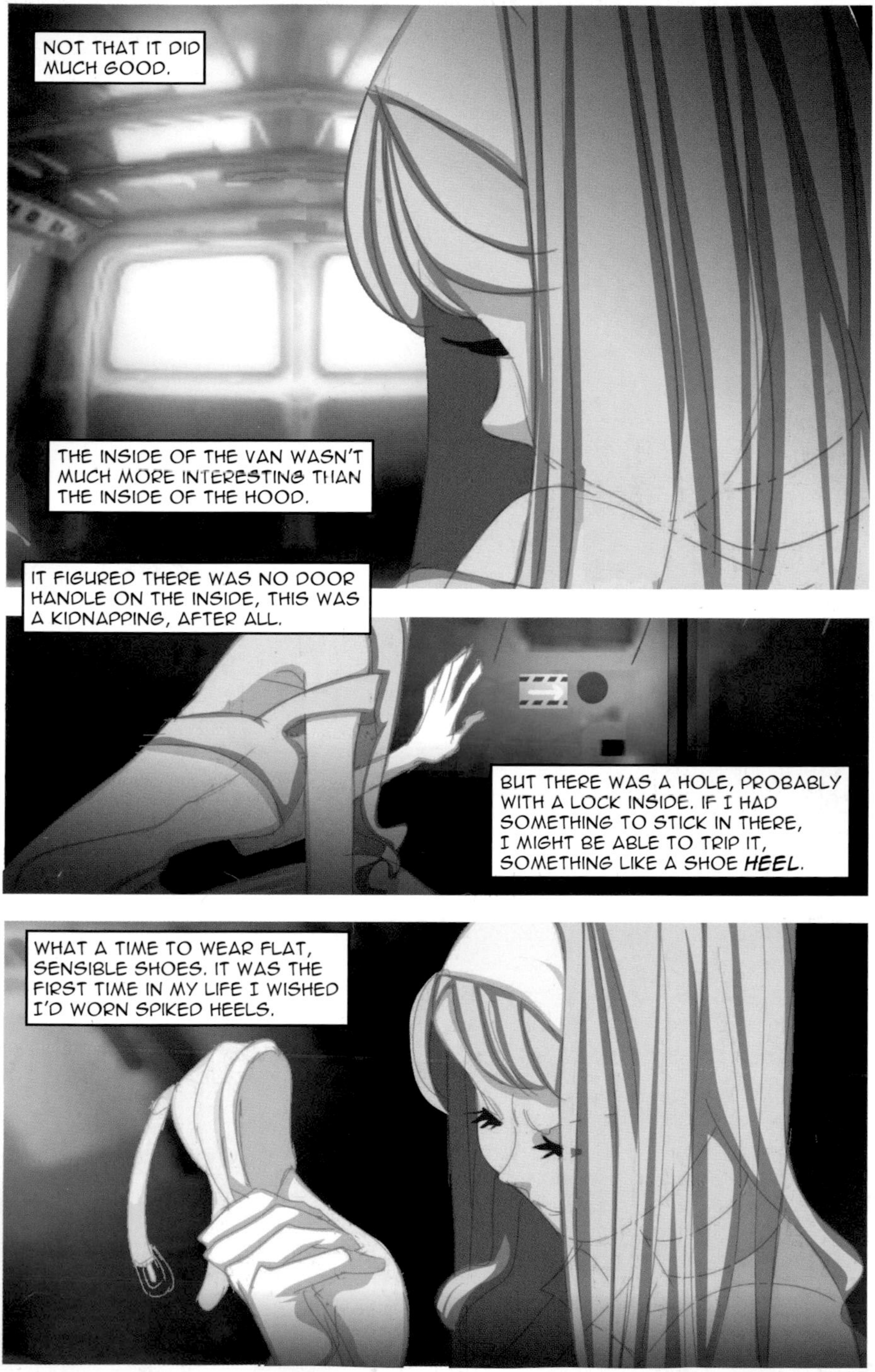
NOT THAT IT DID MUCH GOOD.
THE INSIDE OF THE VAN WASN'T MUCH MORE INTERESTING THAN THE INSIDE OF THE HOOD.
IT FIGURED THERE WAS NO DOOR HANDLE ON THE INSIDE, THIS WAS A KIDNAPPING, AFTER ALL.
BUT THERE WAS A HOLE, PROBABLY WITH A LOCK INSIDE. IF I HAD SOMETHING TO STICK IN THERE, I MIGHT BE ABLE TO TRIP IT, SOMETHING LIKE A SHOE *HEEL*.
WHAT A TIME TO WEAR FLAT, SENSIBLE SHOES. IT WAS THE FIRST TIME IN MY LIFE I WISHED I'D WORN SPIKED HEELS.

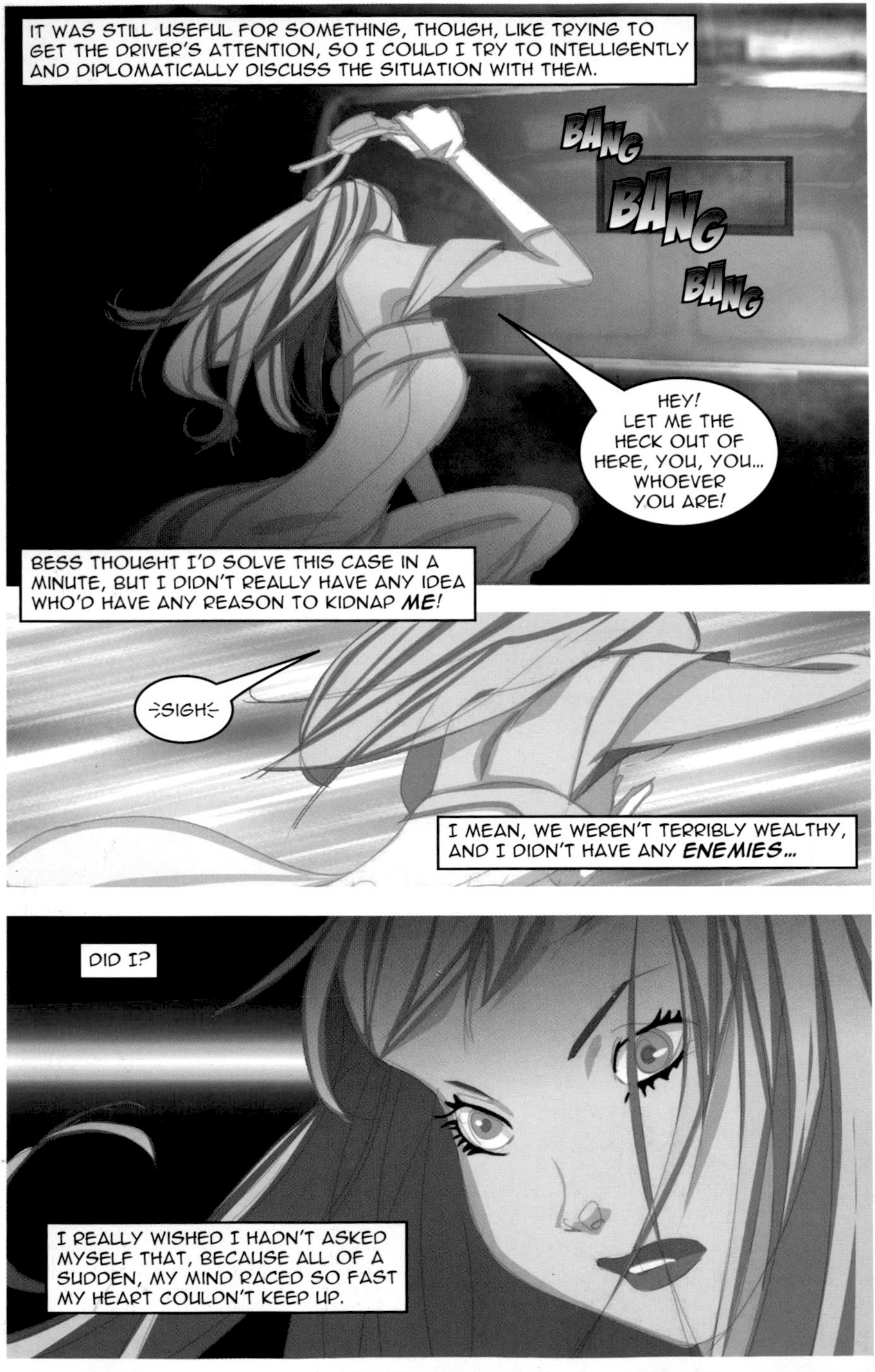
IT WAS STILL USEFUL FOR SOMETHING, THOUGH, LIKE TRYING TO GET THE DRIVER'S ATTENTION, SO I COULD I TRY TO INTELLIGENTLY AND DIPLOMATICALLY DISCUSS THE SITUATION WITH THEM.
BANG
BANG
BANG
HEY! LET ME THE HECK OUT OF HERE, YOU, YOU... WHOEVER YOU ARE!
BESS THOUGHT I'D SOLVE THIS CASE IN A MINUTE, BUT I DIDN'T REALLY HAVE ANY IDEA WHO'D HAVE ANY REASON TO KIDNAP *ME*!
SIGH
I MEAN, WE WEREN'T TERRIBLY WEALTHY, AND I DIDN'T HAVE ANY *ENEMIES...*
DID I?
I REALLY WISHED I HADN'T ASKED MYSELF THAT, BECAUSE ALL OF A SUDDEN, MY MIND RACED SO FAST MY HEART COULDN'T KEEP UP.

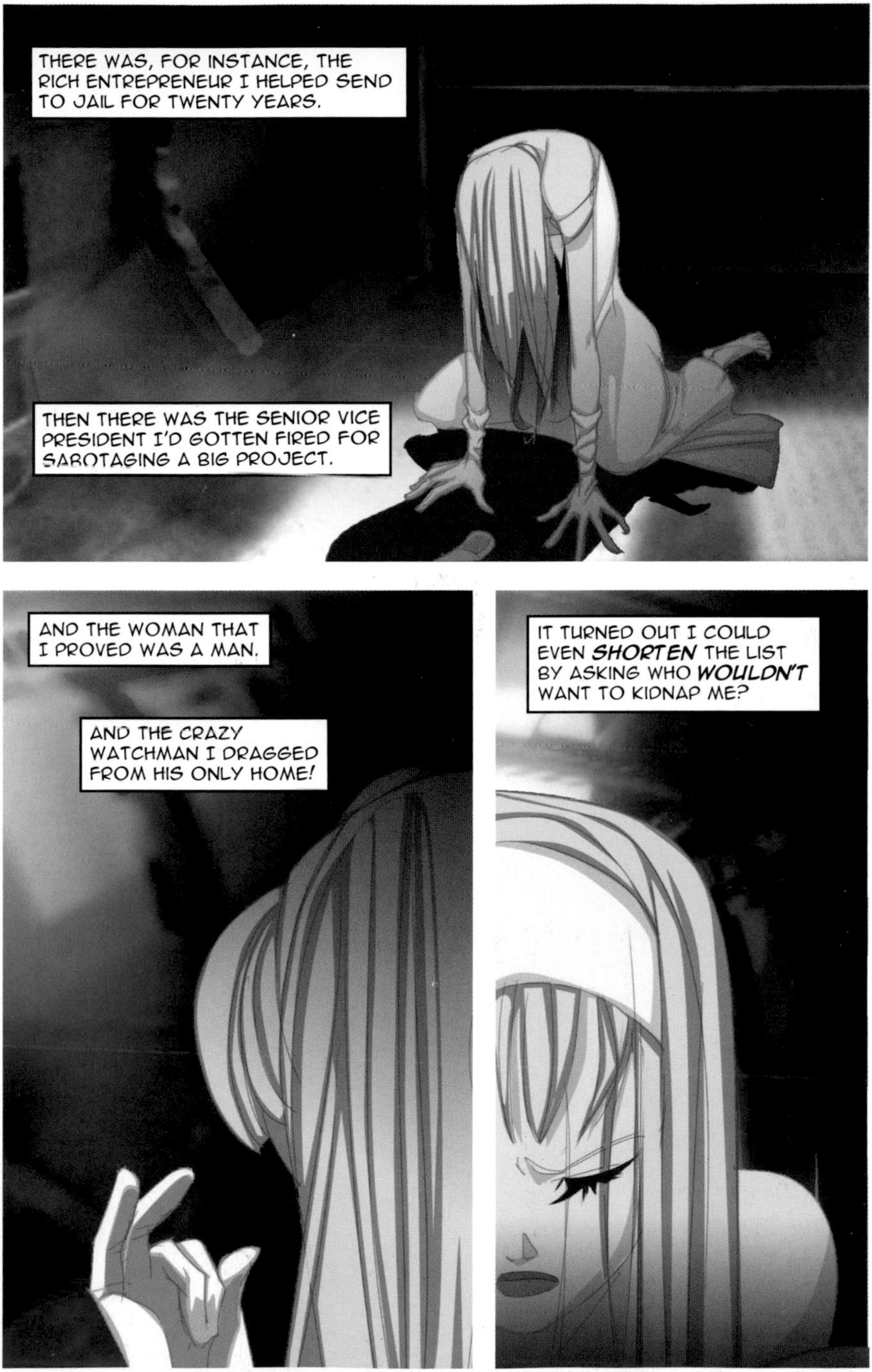
THERE WAS, FOR INSTANCE, THE RICH ENTREPRENEUR I HELPED SEND TO JAIL FOR TWENTY YEARS.
THEN THERE WAS THE SENIOR VICE PRESIDENT I'D GOTTEN FIRED FOR SABOTAGING A BIG PROJECT.
AND THE WOMAN THAT I PROVED WAS A MAN.
AND THE CRAZY WATCHMAN I DRAGGED FROM HIS ONLY HOME!
IT TURNED OUT I COULD EVEN SHORTEN THE LIST BY ASKING WHO WOULDN'T WANT TO KIDNAP ME?

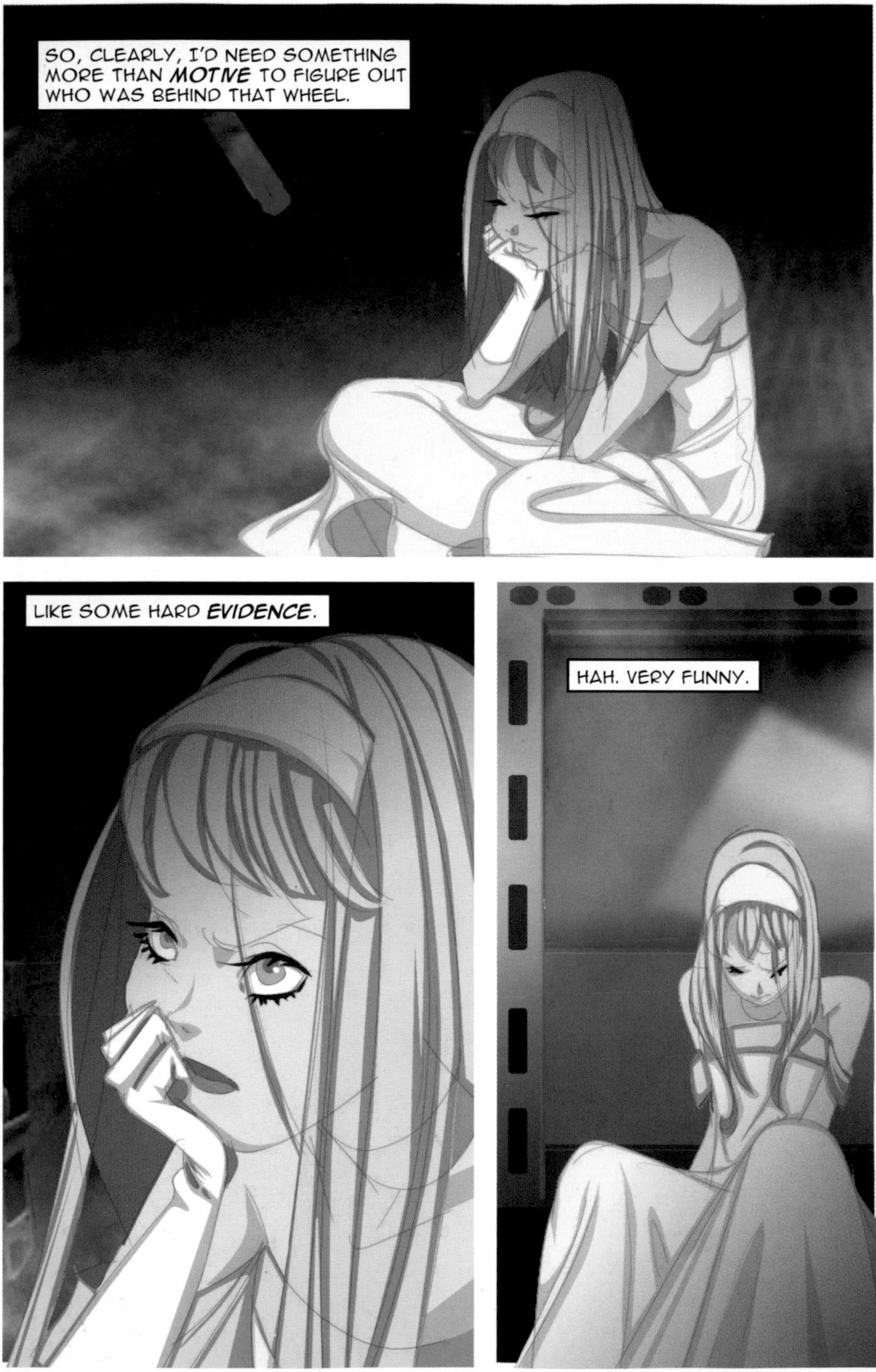
SO, CLEARLY, I'D NEED SOMETHING MORE THAN MOTIVE TO FIGURE OUT WHO WAS BEHIND THAT WHEEL.
LIKE SOME HARD EVIDENCE.
HAH. VERY FUNNY.

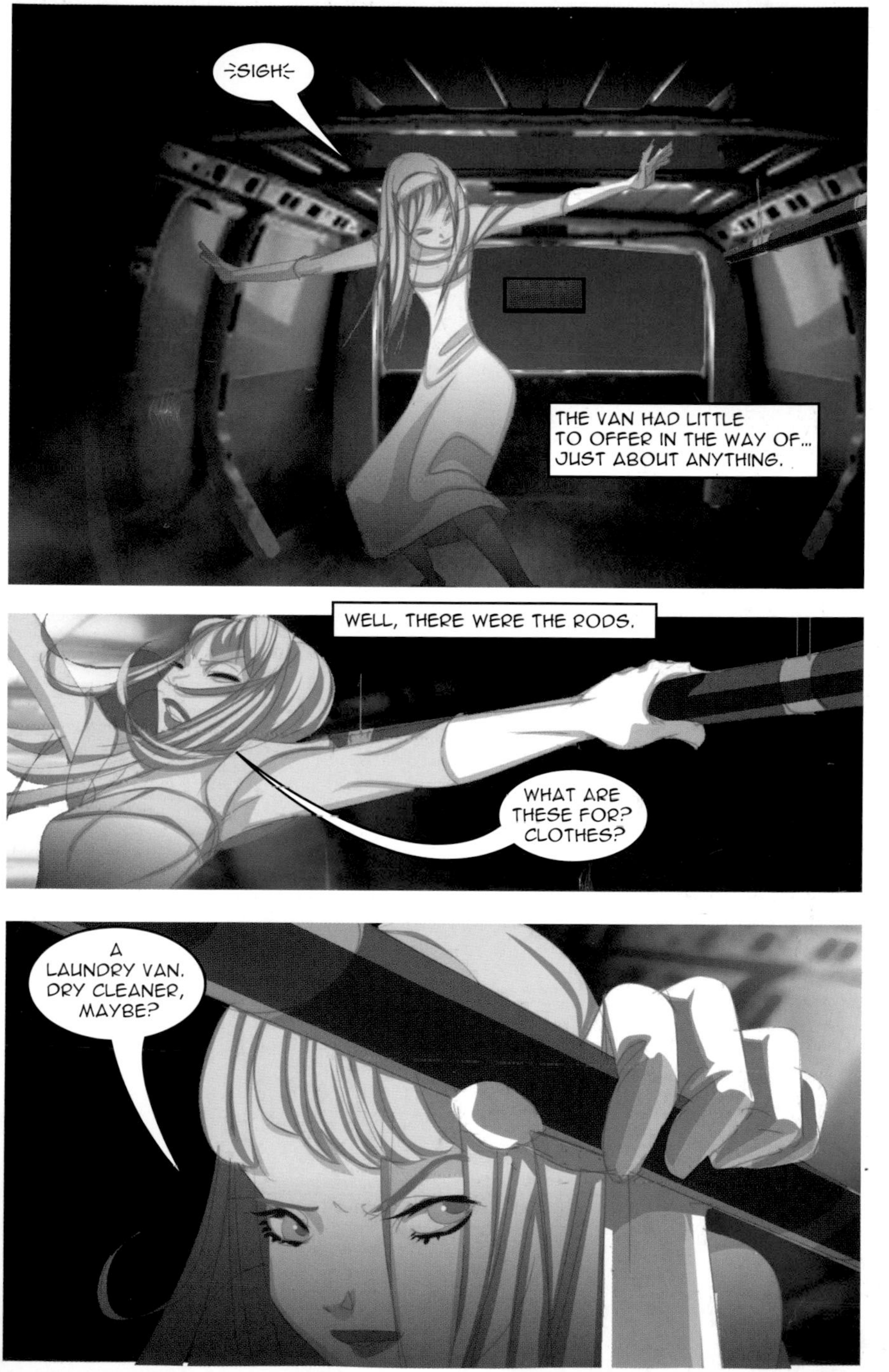

-SIGH-
THE VAN HAD LITTLE TO OFFER IN THE WAY OF... JUST ABOUT ANYTHING.
WELL, THERE WERE THE RODS.
WHAT ARE THESE FOR? CLOTHES?
A LAUNDRY VAN. DRY CLEANER, MAYBE?

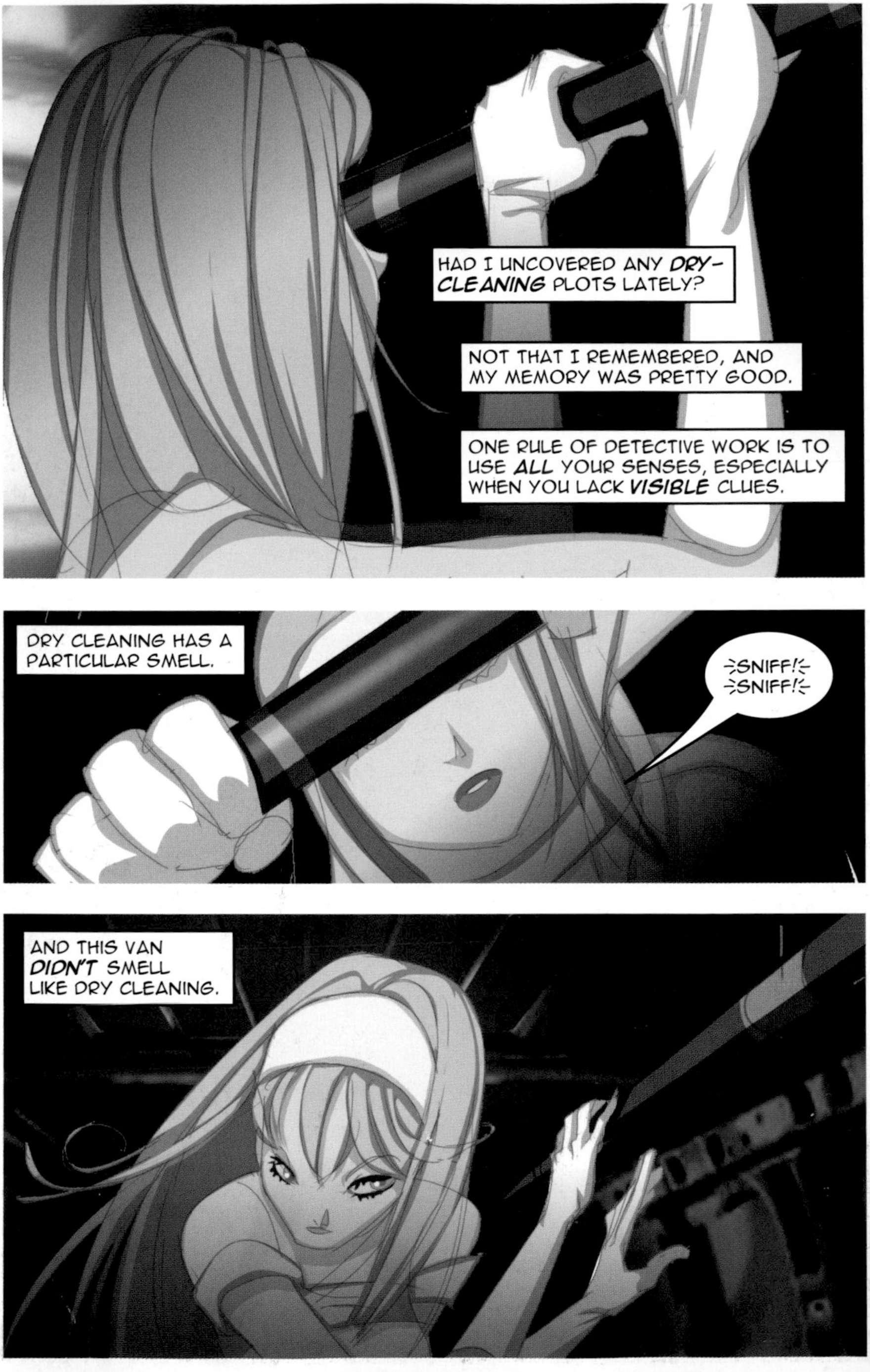
HAD I UNCOVERED ANY DRY-CLEANING PLOTS LATELY?
NOT THAT I REMEMBERED, AND MY MEMORY WAS PRETTY GOOD.
ONE RULE OF DETECTIVE WORK IS TO USE ALL YOUR SENSES, ESPECIALLY WHEN YOU LACK VISIBLE CLUES.
DRY CLEANING HAS A PARTICULAR SMELL.
SNIFF! SNIFF!
AND THIS VAN DIDN'T SMELL LIKE DRY CLEANING.

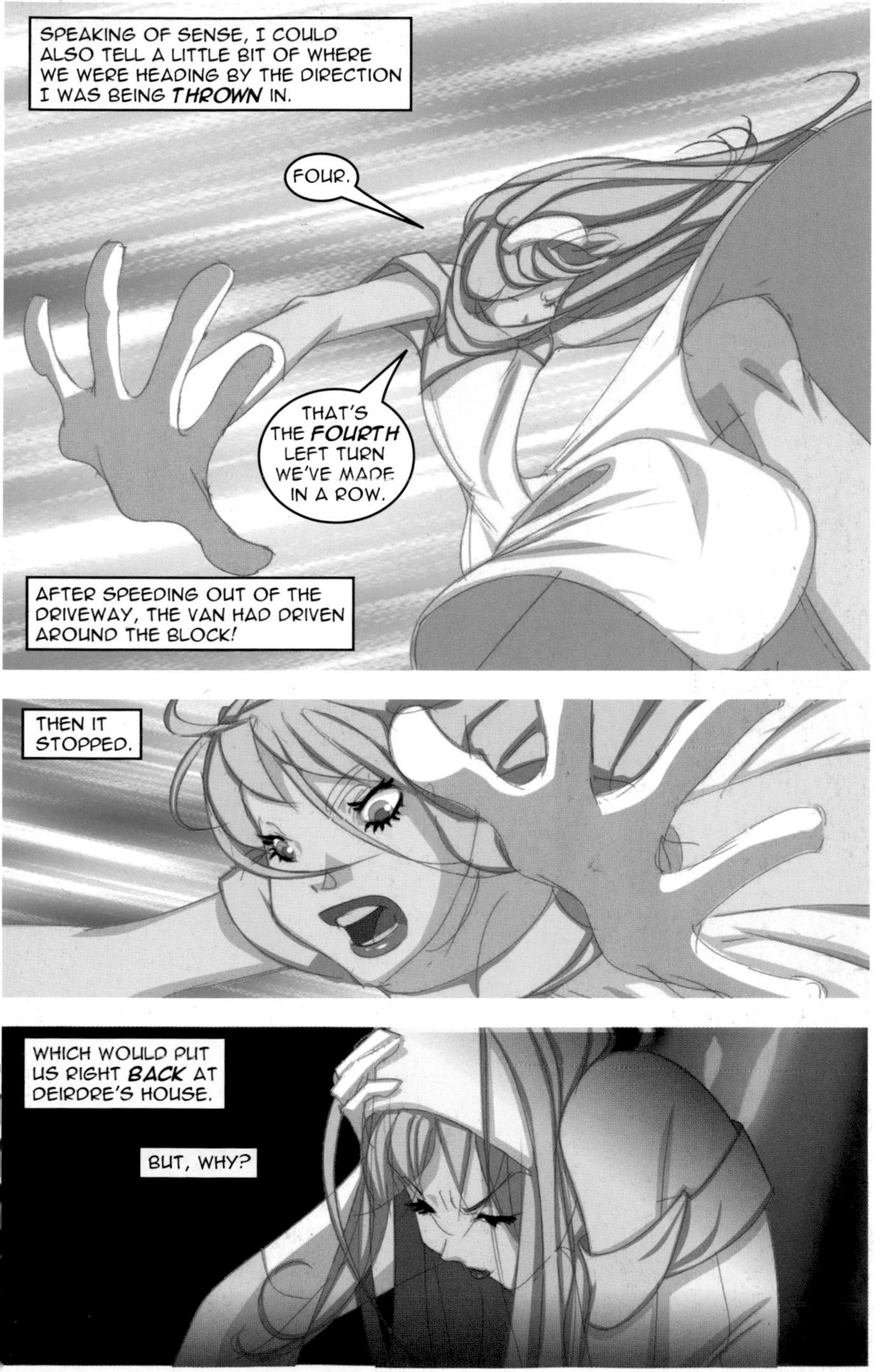
SPEAKING OF SENSE, I COULD ALSO TELL A LITTLE BIT OF WHERE WE WERE HEADING BY THE DIRECTION I WAS BEING *THROWN* IN.
FOUR.
THAT'S THE *FOURTH* LEFT TURN WE'VE MADE IN A ROW.
AFTER SPEEDING OUT OF THE DRIVEWAY, THE VAN HAD DRIVEN AROUND THE BLOCK!
THEN IT STOPPED.
WHICH WOULD PUT US RIGHT *BACK* AT DEIRDRE'S HOUSE.
BUT, WHY?

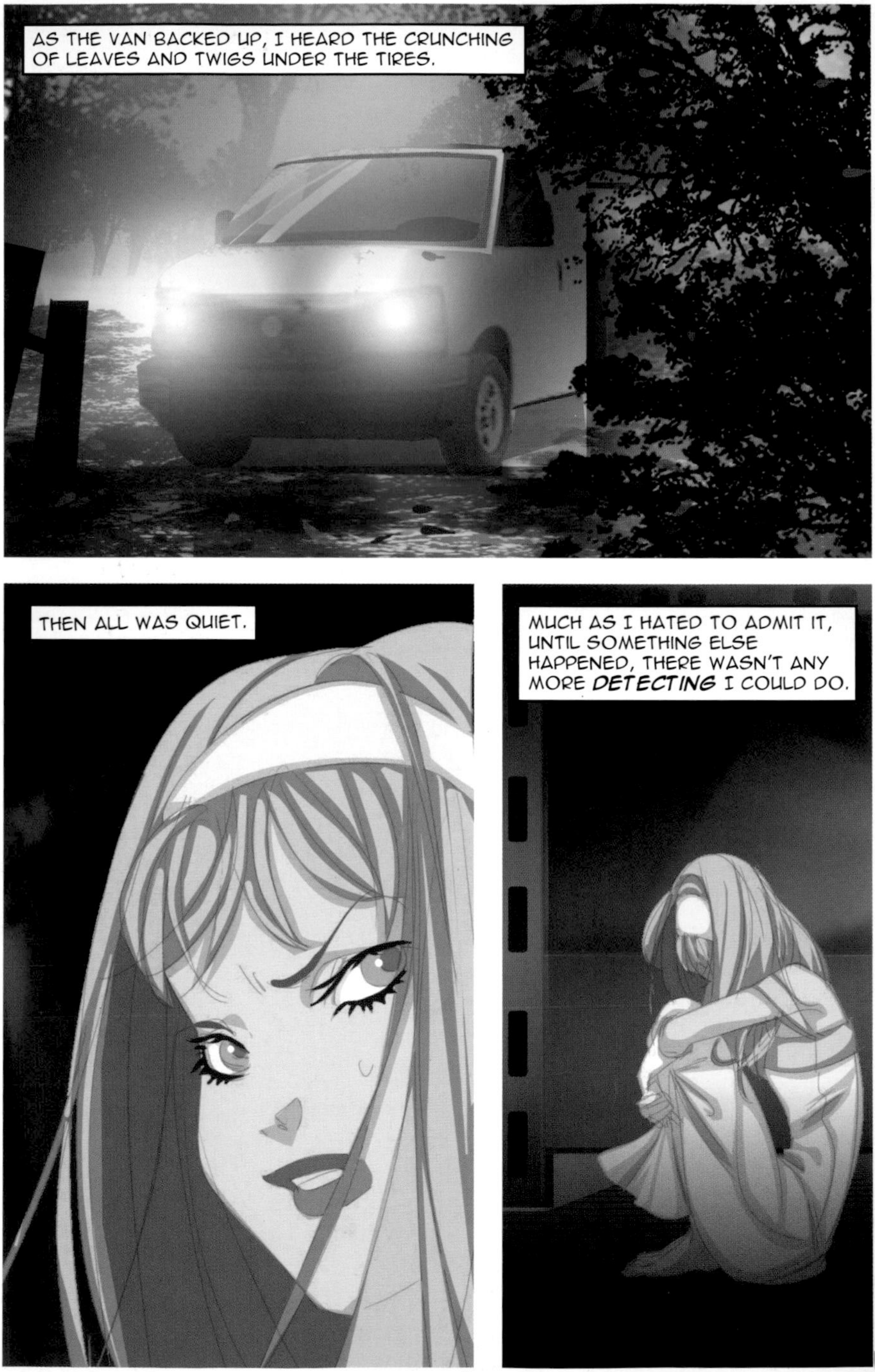
AS THE VAN BACKED UP, I HEARD THE CRUNCHING OF LEAVES AND TWIGS UNDER THE TIRES.
THEN ALL WAS QUIET.
MUCH AS I HATED TO ADMIT IT, UNTIL SOMETHING ELSE HAPPENED, THERE WASN'T ANY MORE *DETECTING* I COULD DO.

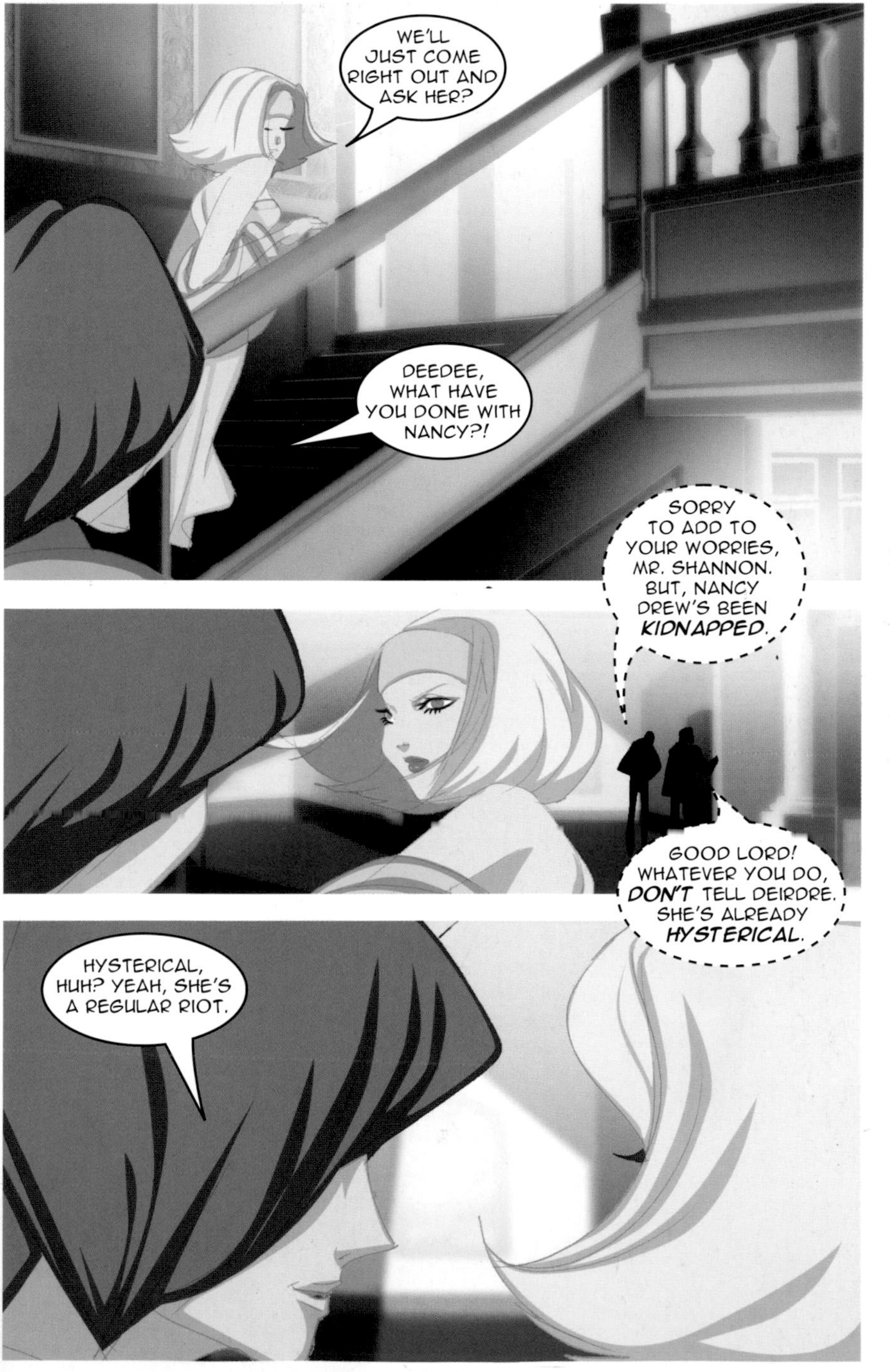

WE'LL JUST COME RIGHT OUT AND ASK HER?
DEEDEE, WHAT HAVE YOU DONE WITH NANCY?!
SORRY TO ADD TO YOUR WORRIES, MR. SHANNON. BUT, NANCY DREW'S BEEN **KIDNAPPED**.
GOOD LORD! WHATEVER YOU DO, **DON'T** TELL DEIRDRE. SHE'S ALREADY **HYSTERICAL**.
HYSTERICAL, HUH? YEAH, SHE'S A REGULAR RIOT.

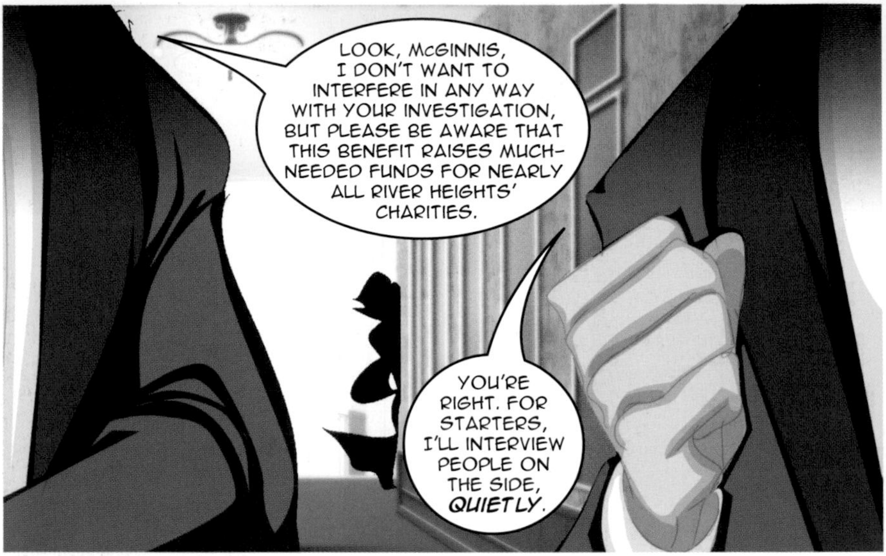
LOOK, McGINNIS, I DON'T WANT TO INTERFERE IN ANY WAY WITH YOUR INVESTIGATION, BUT PLEASE BE AWARE THAT THIS BENEFIT RAISES MUCH-NEEDED FUNDS FOR NEARLY ALL RIVER HEIGHTS' CHARITIES.
YOU'RE RIGHT. FOR STARTERS, I'LL INTERVIEW PEOPLE ON THE SIDE, ***QUIETLY***.

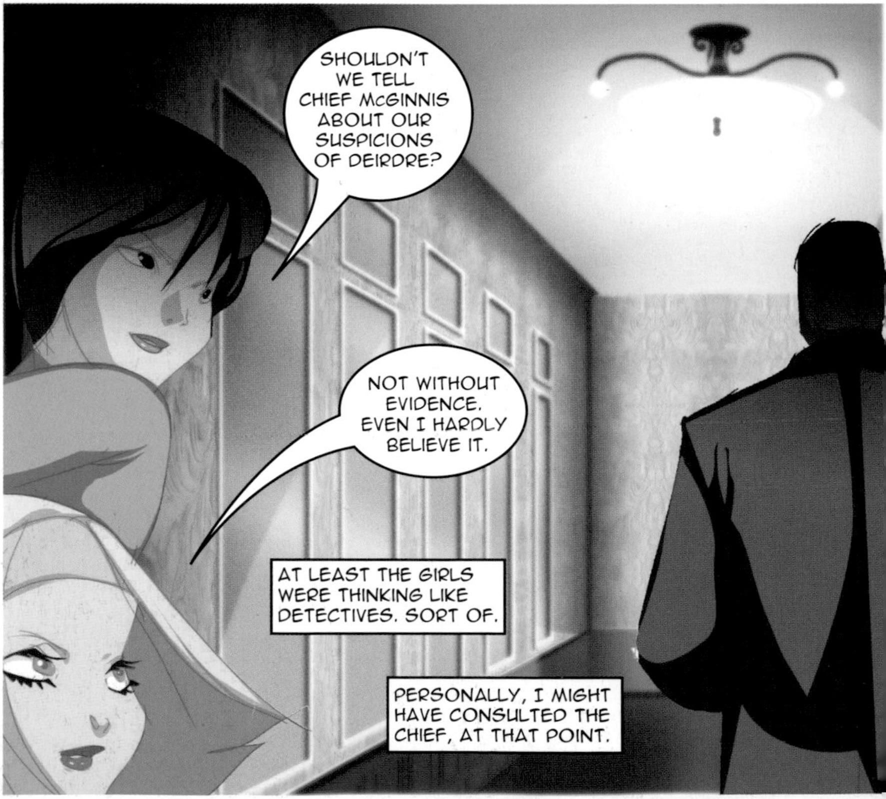
SHOULDN'T WE TELL CHIEF McGINNIS ABOUT OUR SUSPICIONS OF DEIRDRE?
NOT WITHOUT EVIDENCE. EVEN I HARDLY BELIEVE IT.
AT LEAST THE GIRLS WERE THINKING LIKE DETECTIVES. SORT OF.
PERSONALLY, I MIGHT HAVE CONSULTED THE CHIEF, AT THAT POINT.

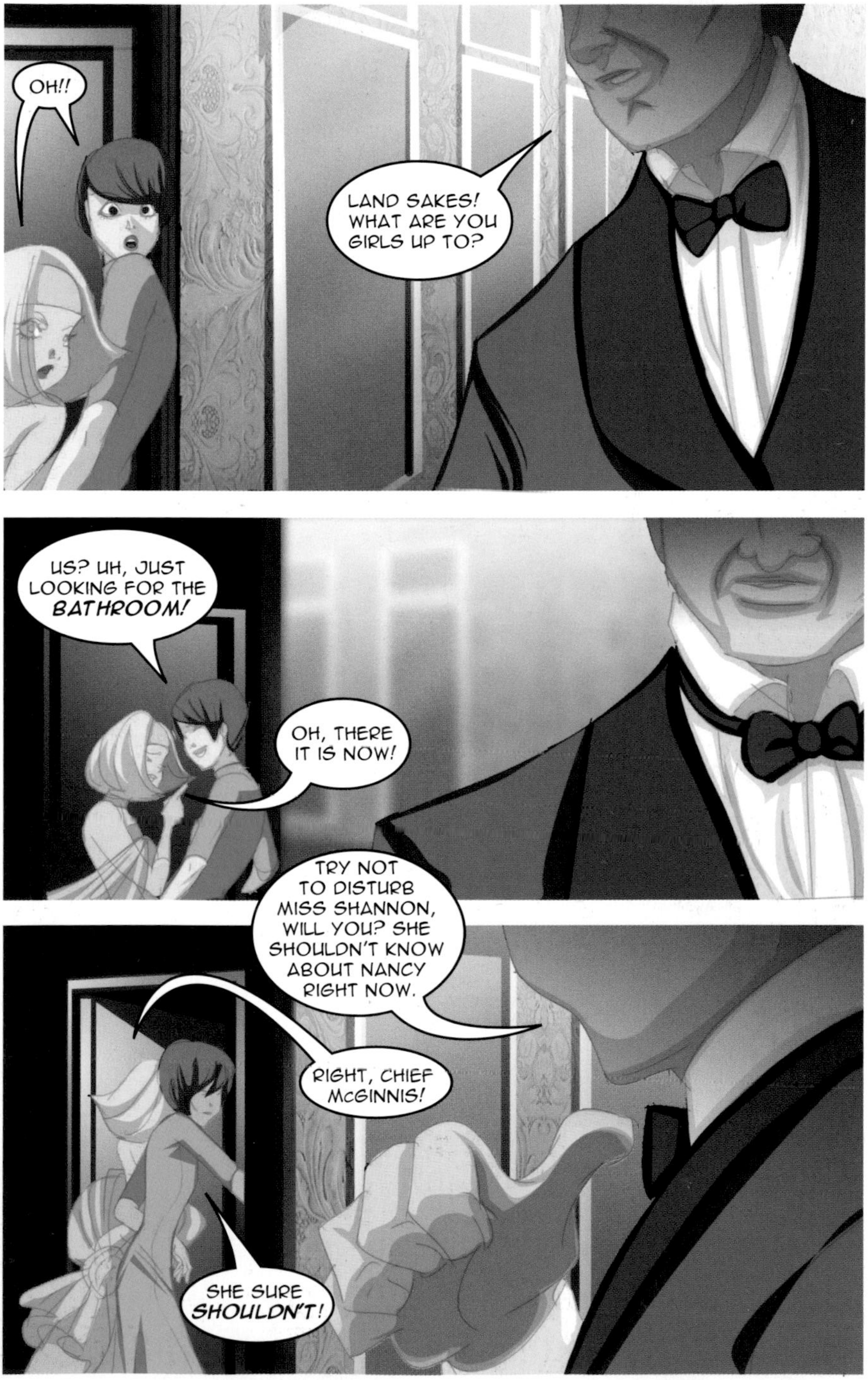
OH!!
LAND SAKES! WHAT ARE YOU GIRLS UP TO?
US? UH, JUST LOOKING FOR THE *BATHROOM!*
OH, THERE IT IS NOW!
TRY NOT TO DISTURB MISS SHANNON, WILL YOU? SHE SHOULDN'T KNOW ABOUT NANCY RIGHT NOW.
RIGHT, CHIEF McGINNIS!
SHE SURE *SHOULDN'T!*

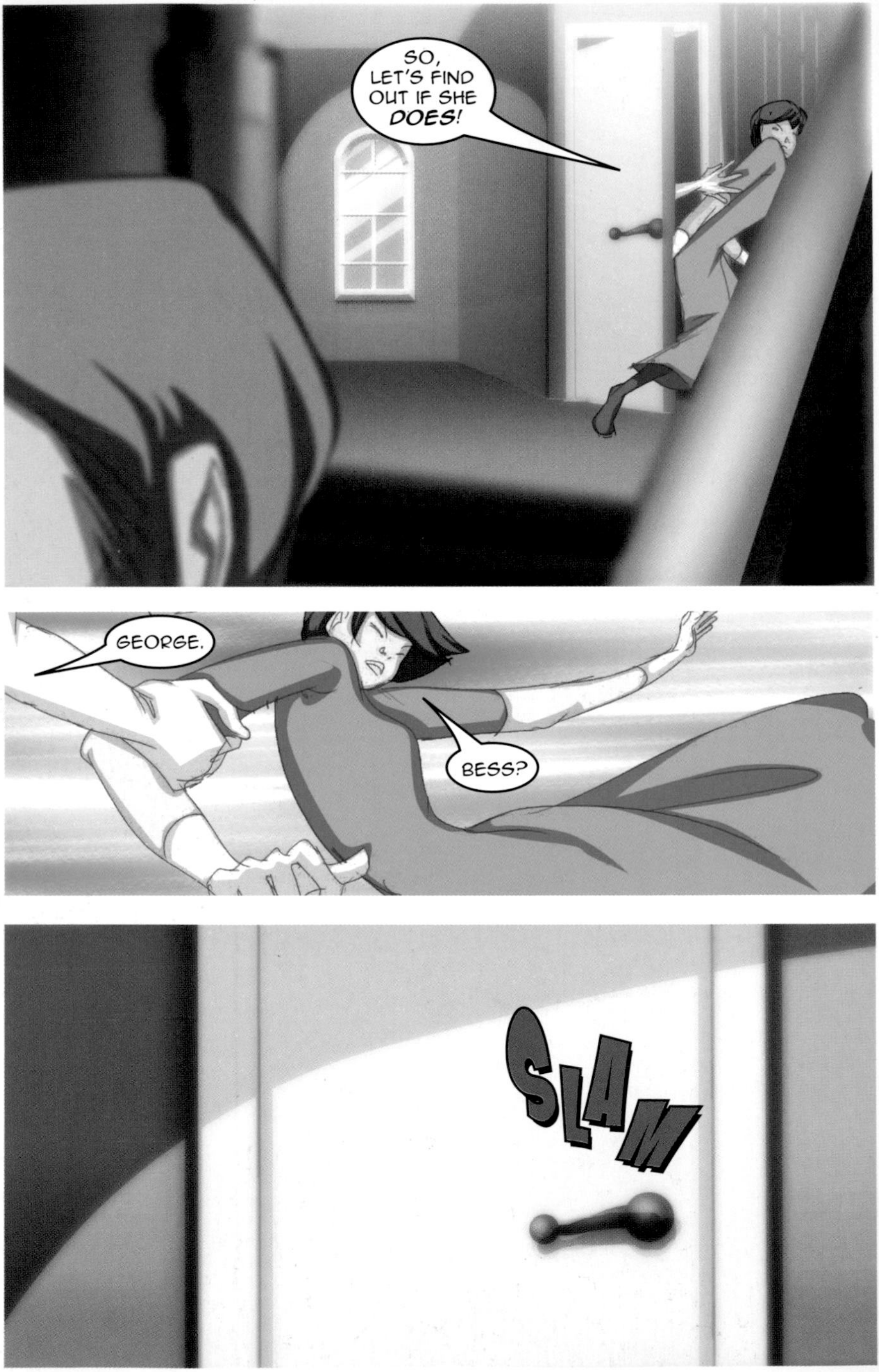
SO, LET'S FIND OUT IF SHE DOES!
GEORGE.
BESS?
SLAM

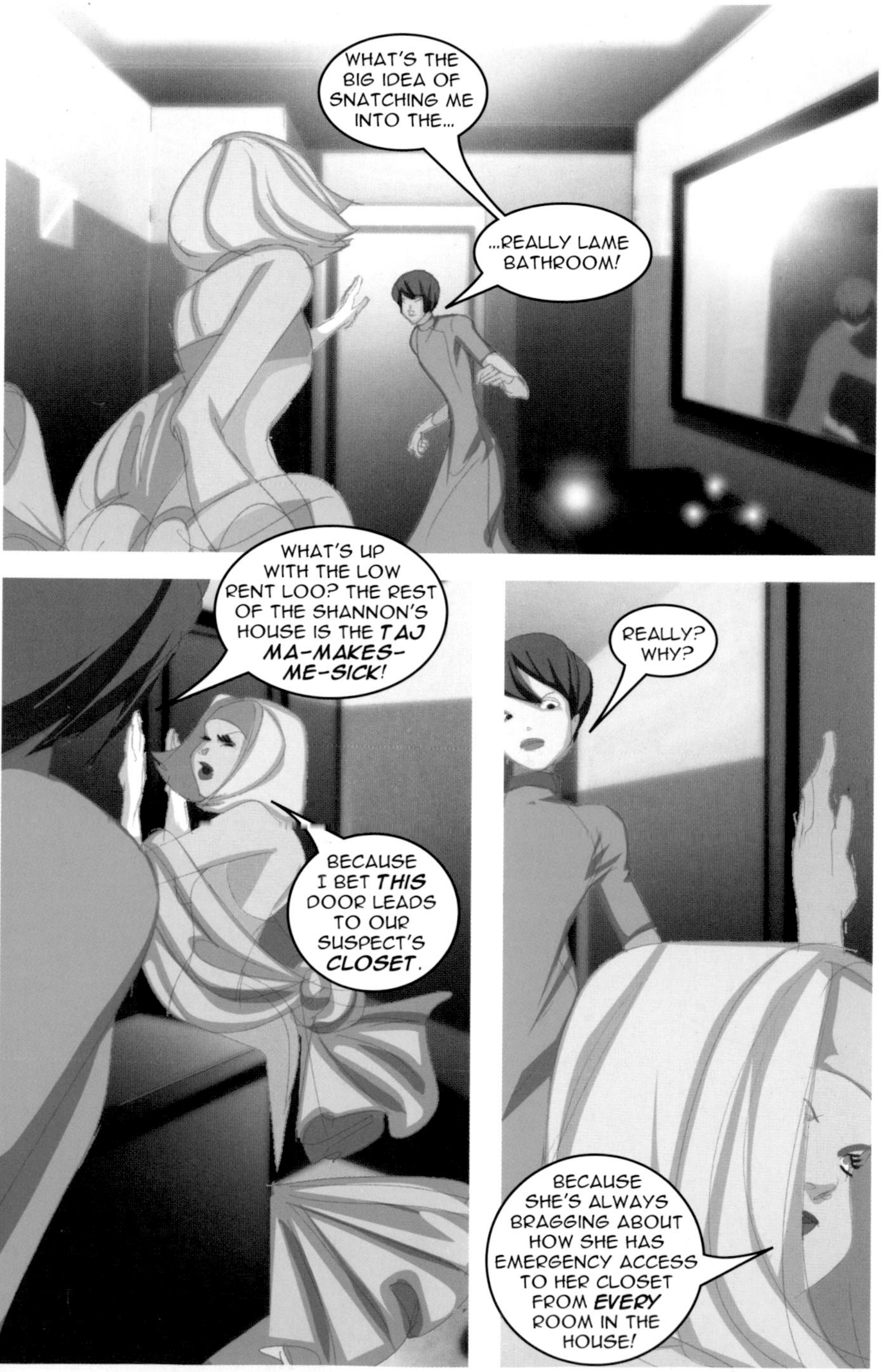
WHAT'S THE BIG IDEA OF SNATCHING ME INTO THE...
...REALLY LAME BATHROOM!
WHAT'S UP WITH THE LOW RENT LOO? THE REST OF THE SHANNON'S HOUSE IS THE ***TAJ MA-MAKES-ME-SICK***!
REALLY? WHY?
BECAUSE I BET ***THIS*** DOOR LEADS TO OUR SUSPECT'S ***CLOSET***.
BECAUSE SHE'S ALWAYS BRAGGING ABOUT HOW SHE HAS EMERGENCY ACCESS TO HER CLOSET FROM ***EVERY*** ROOM IN THE HOUSE!

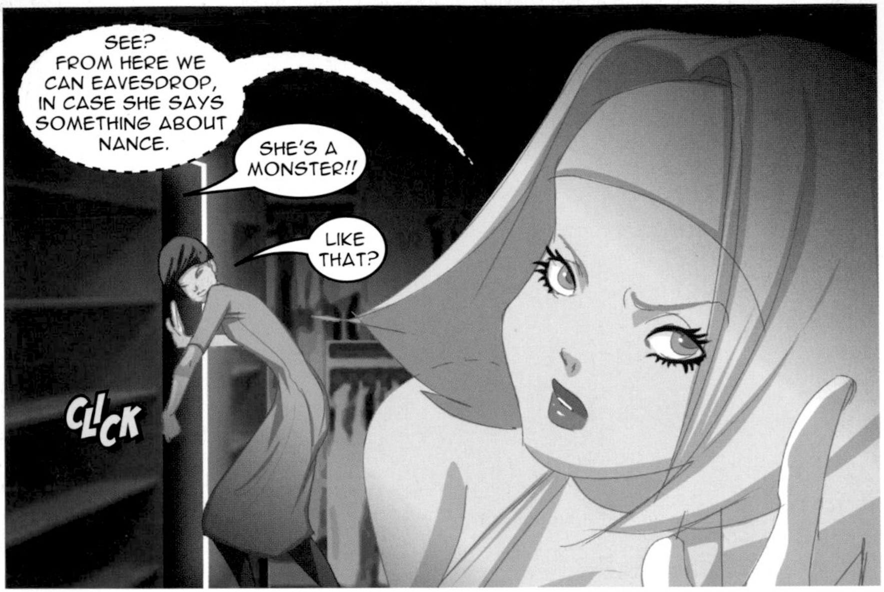
SEE? FROM HERE WE CAN EAVESDROP, IN CASE SHE SAYS SOMETHING ABOUT NANCE.
SHE'S A MONSTER!!
LIKE THAT?
CLICK

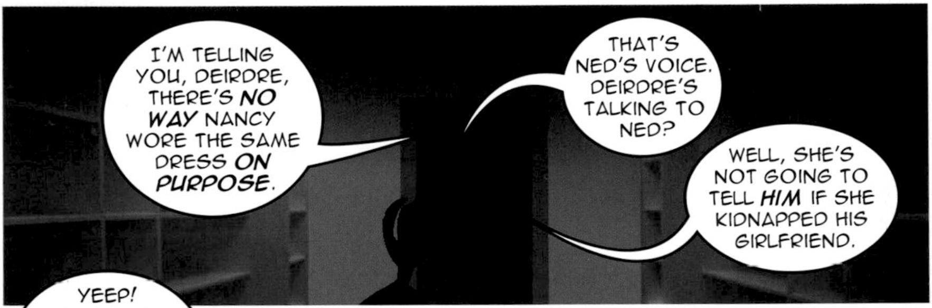
I'M TELLING YOU, DEIRDRE, THERE'S **NO WAY** NANCY WORE THE SAME DRESS **ON PURPOSE**.
THAT'S NED'S VOICE. DEIRDRE'S TALKING TO NED?
WELL, SHE'S NOT GOING TO TELL **HIM** IF SHE KIDNAPPED HIS GIRLFRIEND.

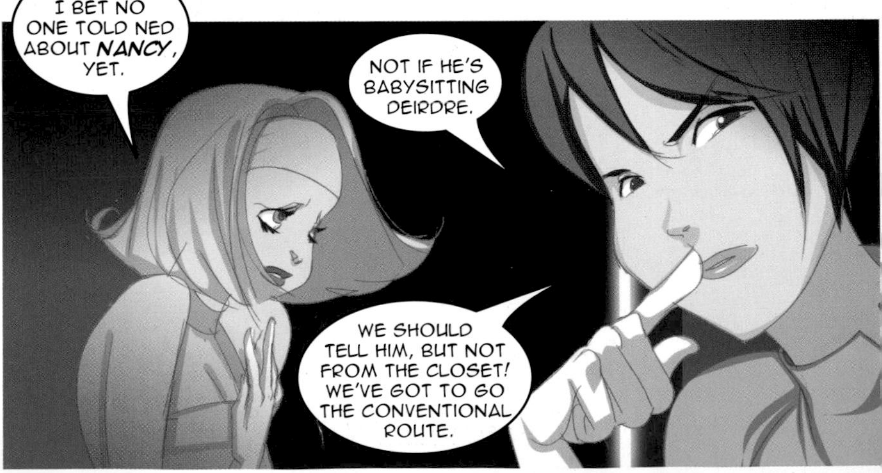
YEEP! I BET NO ONE TOLD NED ABOUT **NANCY**, YET.
NOT IF HE'S BABYSITTING DEIRDRE.
WE SHOULD TELL HIM, BUT NOT FROM THE CLOSET! WE'VE GOT TO GO THE CONVENTIONAL ROUTE.

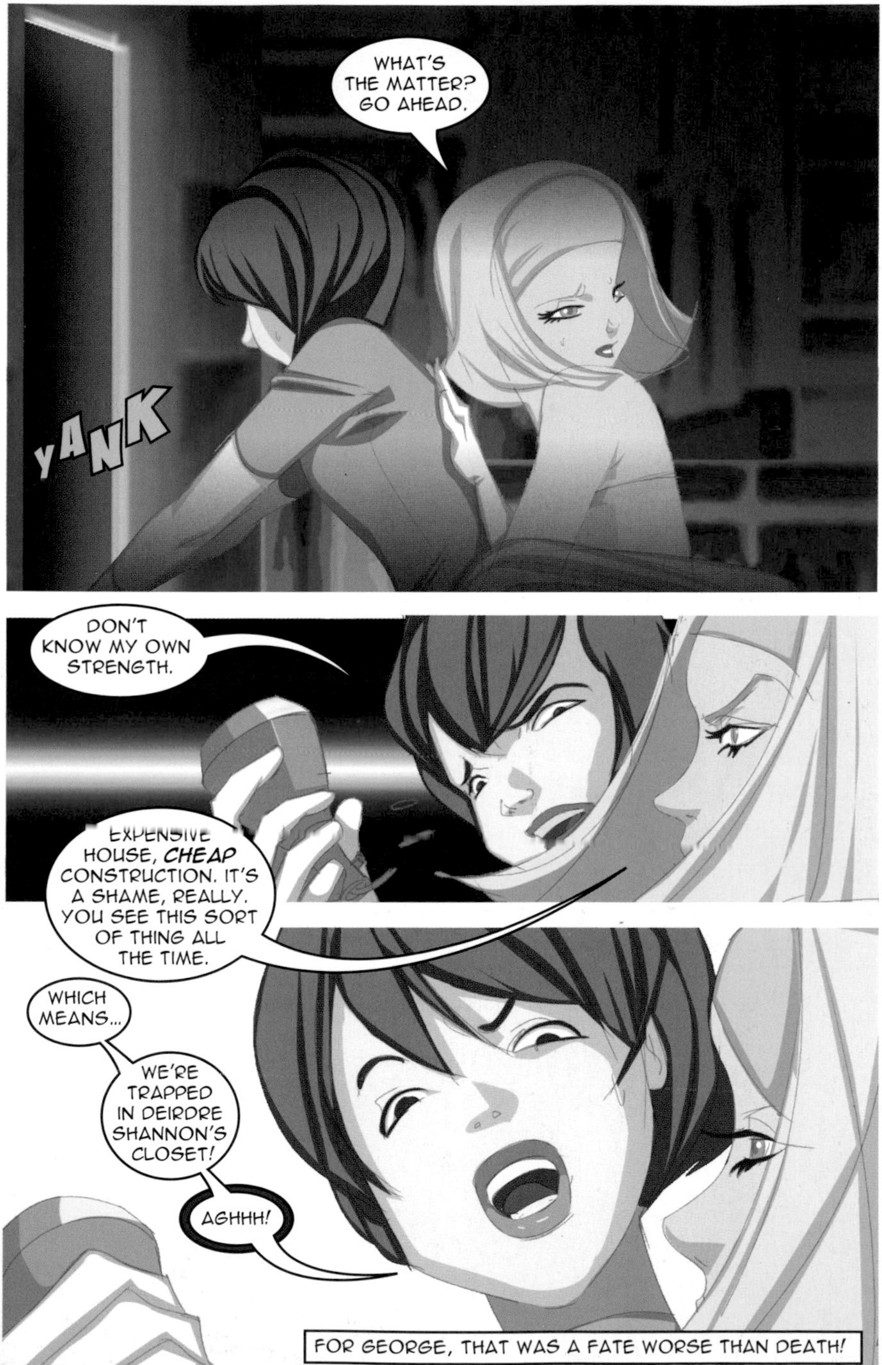
WHAT'S THE MATTER? GO AHEAD.
YANK
DON'T KNOW MY OWN STRENGTH.
EXPENSIVE HOUSE, CHEAP CONSTRUCTION. IT'S A SHAME, REALLY. YOU SEE THIS SORT OF THING ALL THE TIME.
WHICH MEANS...
WE'RE TRAPPED IN DEIRDRE SHANNON'S CLOSET!
AGHHH!
FOR GEORGE, THAT WAS A FATE WORSE THAN DEATH!

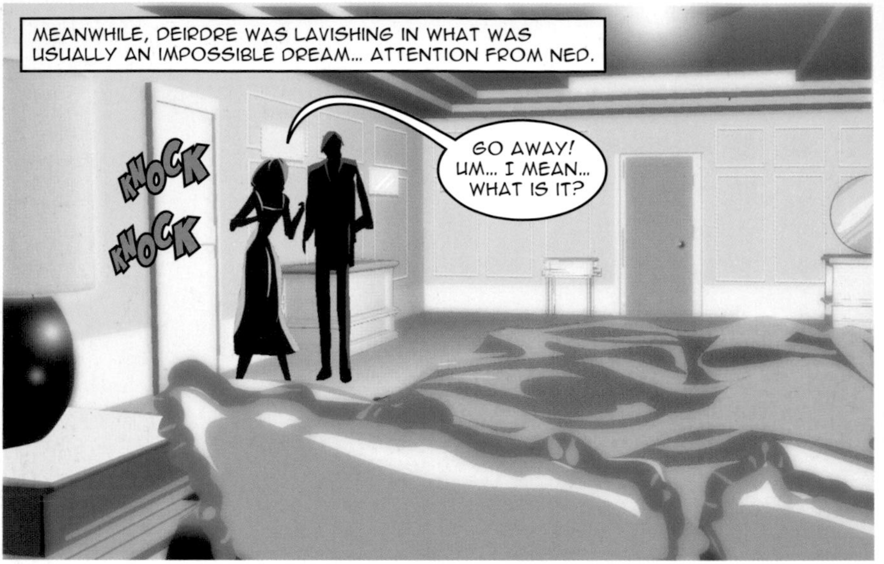
MEANWHILE, DEIRDRE WAS LAVISHING IN WHAT WAS USUALLY AN IMPOSSIBLE DREAM... ATTENTION FROM NED.
KNOCK
KNOCK
GO AWAY! UM... I MEAN... WHAT IS IT?

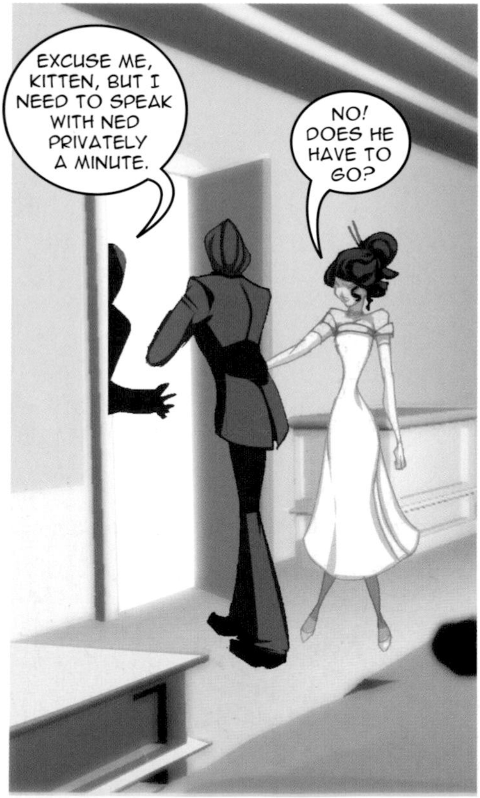
EXCUSE ME, KITTEN, BUT I NEED TO SPEAK WITH NED PRIVATELY A MINUTE.
NO! DOES HE HAVE TO GO?

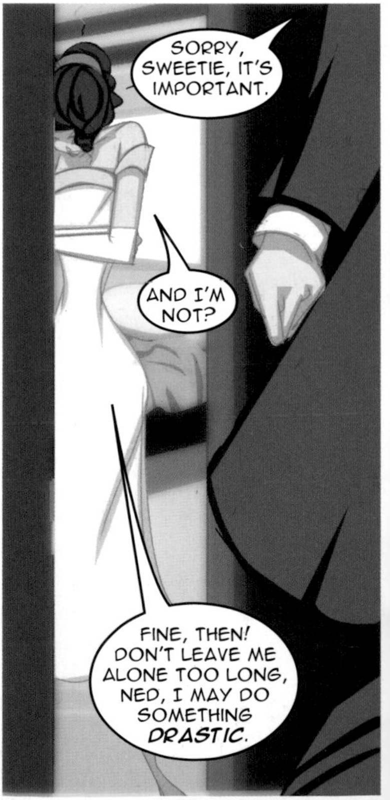
SORRY, SWEETIE, IT'S IMPORTANT.
AND I'M NOT?
FINE, THEN! DON'T LEAVE ME ALONE TOO LONG, NED, I MAY DO SOMETHING *DRASTIC*.

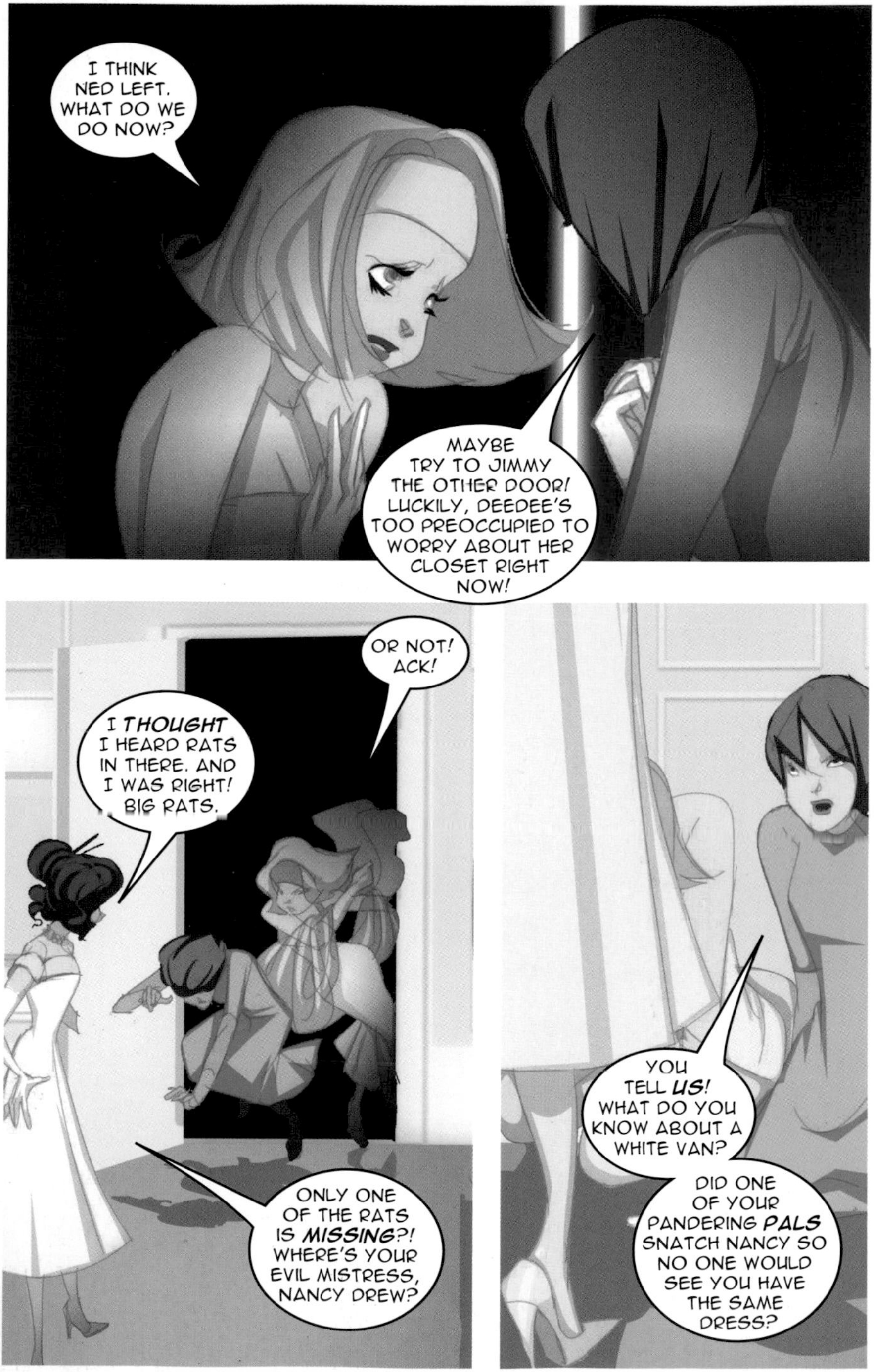
I THINK NED LEFT. WHAT DO WE DO NOW?
MAYBE TRY TO JIMMY THE OTHER DOOR! LUCKILY, DEEDEE'S TOO PREOCCUPIED TO WORRY ABOUT HER CLOSET RIGHT NOW!
OR NOT! ACK!
I *THOUGHT* I HEARD RATS IN THERE. AND I WAS RIGHT! BIG RATS.
ONLY ONE OF THE RATS IS *MISSING*?! WHERE'S YOUR EVIL MISTRESS, NANCY DREW?
YOU TELL *US*! WHAT DO YOU KNOW ABOUT A WHITE VAN?
DID ONE OF YOUR PANDERING *PALS* SNATCH NANCY SO NO ONE WOULD SEE YOU HAVE THE SAME DRESS?

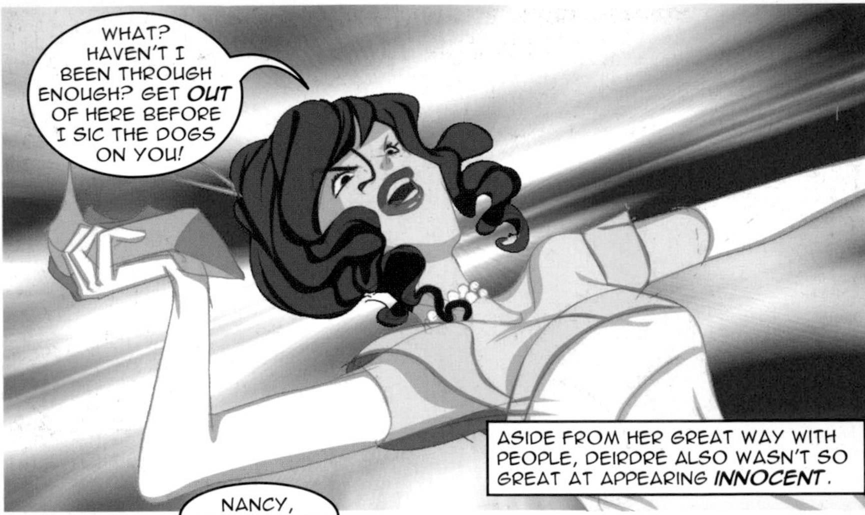
WHAT? HAVEN'T I BEEN THROUGH ENOUGH? GET **OUT** OF HERE BEFORE I SIC THE DOGS ON YOU!
ASIDE FROM HER GREAT WAY WITH PEOPLE, DEIRDRE ALSO WASN'T SO GREAT AT APPEARING **INNOCENT**.

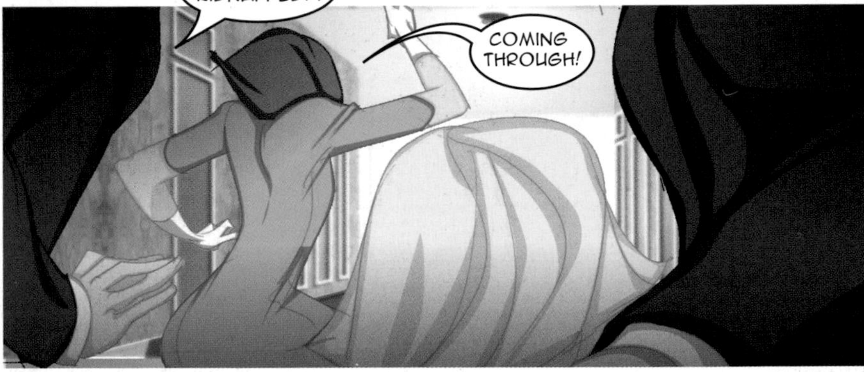
NANCY, KIDNAPPED?!
COMING THROUGH!

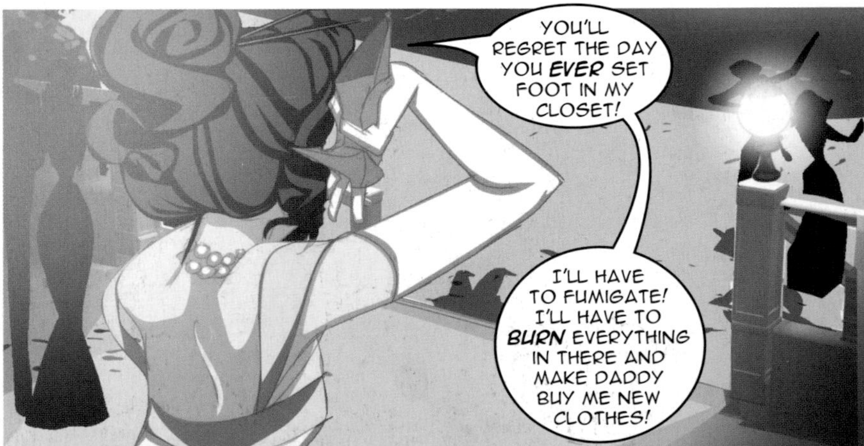
YOU'LL REGRET THE DAY YOU **EVER** SET FOOT IN MY CLOSET!
I'LL HAVE TO FUMIGATE! I'LL HAVE TO **BURN** EVERYTHING IN THERE AND MAKE DADDY BUY ME NEW CLOTHES!

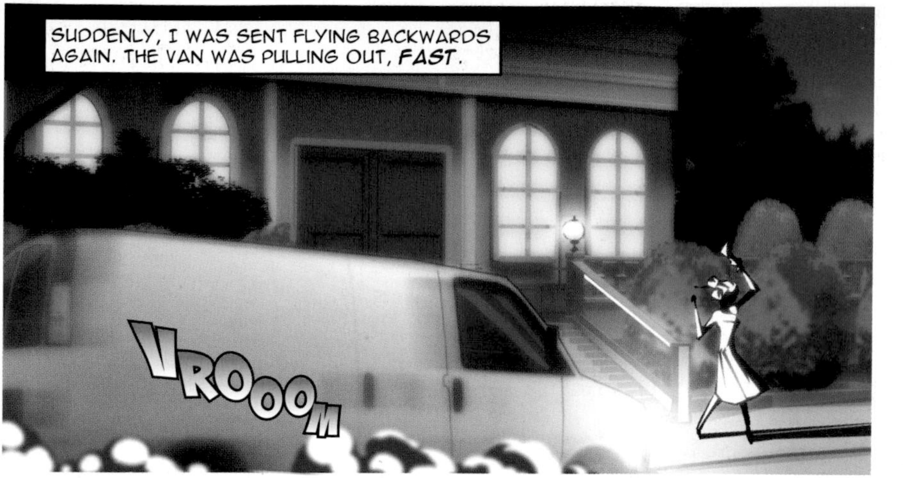
SUDDENLY, I WAS SENT FLYING BACKWARDS AGAIN. THE VAN WAS PULLING OUT, *FAST*.
VROOOM

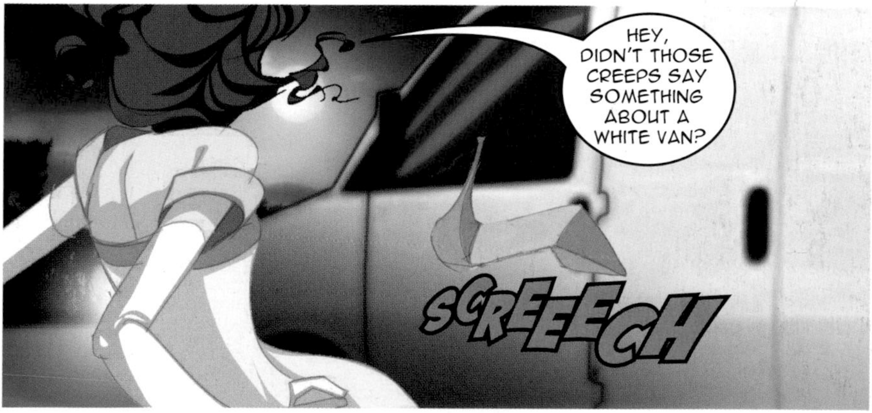
HEY, DIDN'T THOSE CREEPS SAY SOMETHING ABOUT A WHITE VAN?
SCREEECH

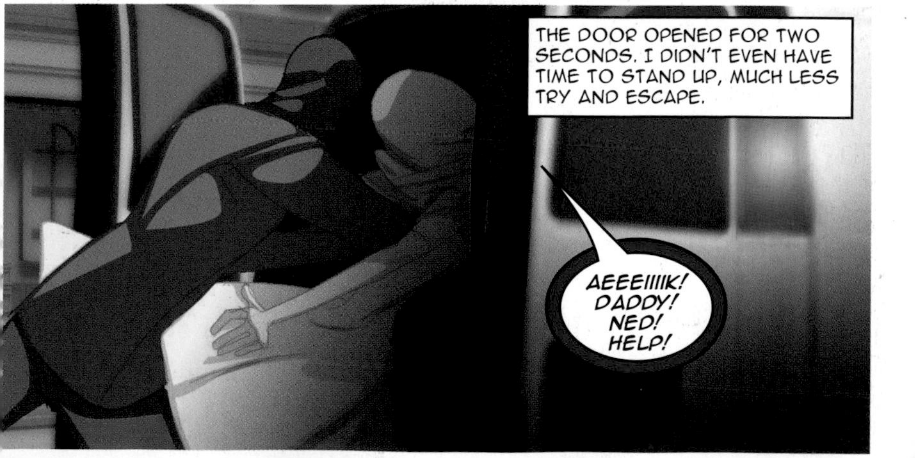
THE DOOR OPENED FOR TWO SECONDS. I DIDN'T EVEN HAVE TIME TO STAND UP, MUCH LESS TRY AND ESCAPE.
AEEEIIIIK! DADDY! NED! HELP!

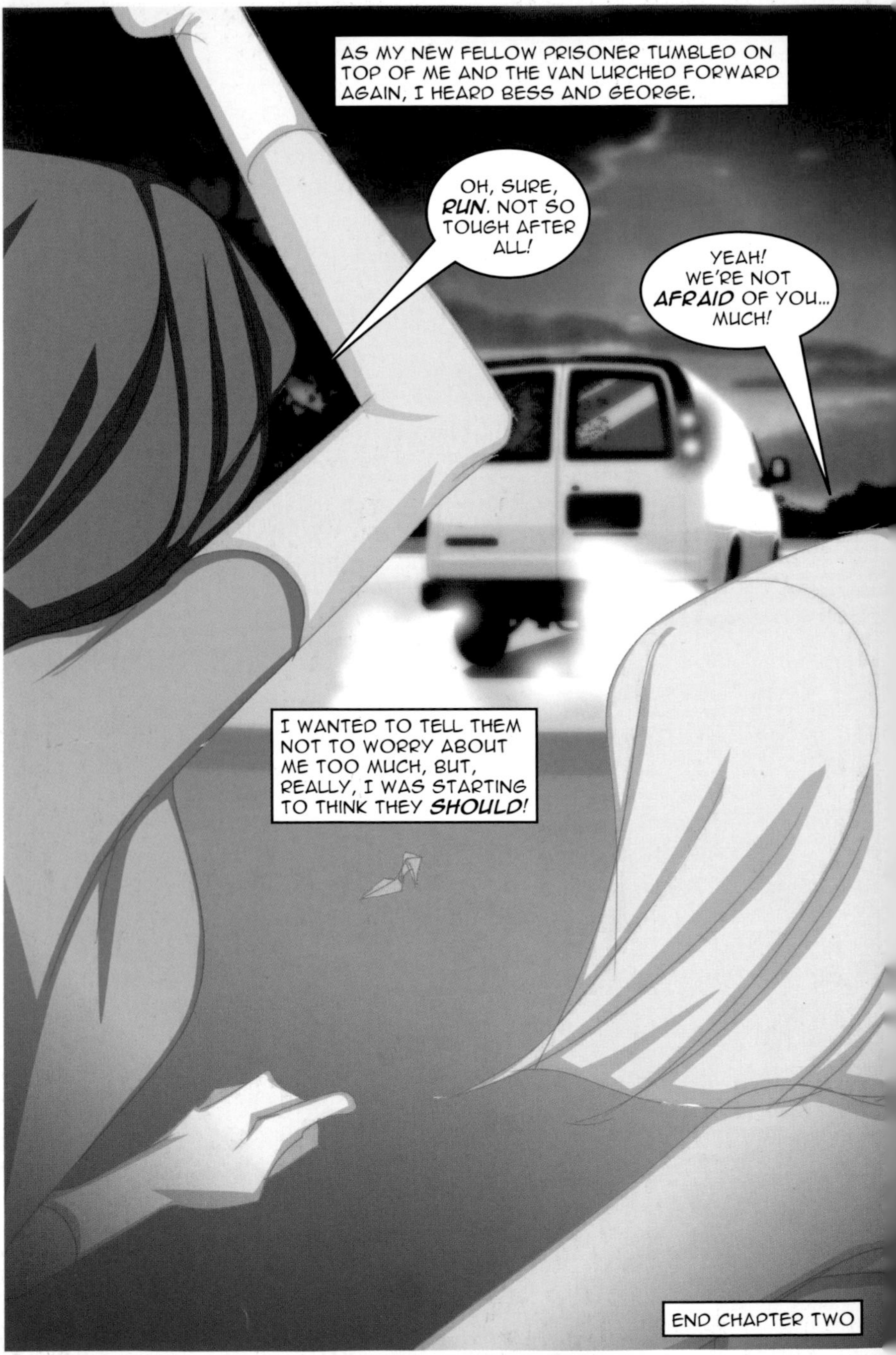
AS MY NEW FELLOW PRISONER TUMBLED ON TOP OF ME AND THE VAN LURCHED FORWARD AGAIN, I HEARD BESS AND GEORGE.
OH, SURE, *RUN*. NOT SO TOUGH AFTER ALL!
YEAH! WE'RE NOT *AFRAID* OF YOU... MUCH!
I WANTED TO TELL THEM NOT TO WORRY ABOUT ME TOO MUCH, BUT, REALLY, I WAS STARTING TO THINK THEY *SHOULD*!
END CHAPTER TWO

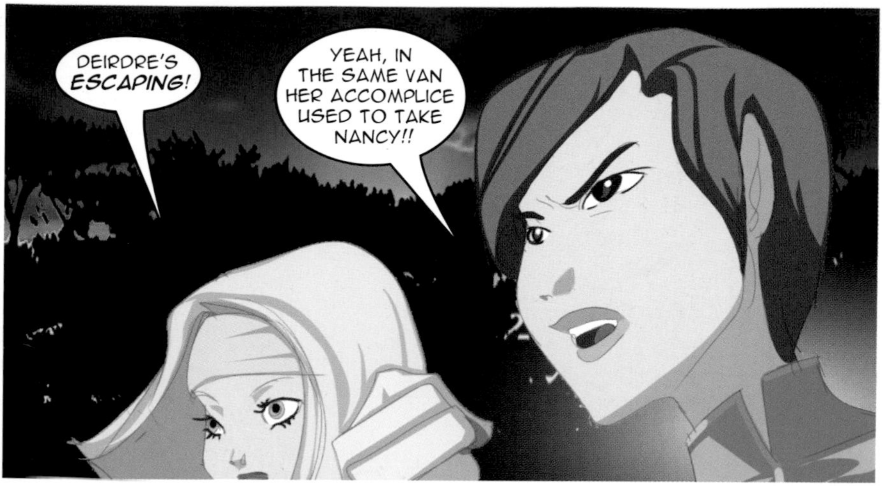
DEIRDRE'S *ESCAPING!*
YEAH, IN THE SAME VAN HER ACCOMPLICE USED TO TAKE NANCY!!
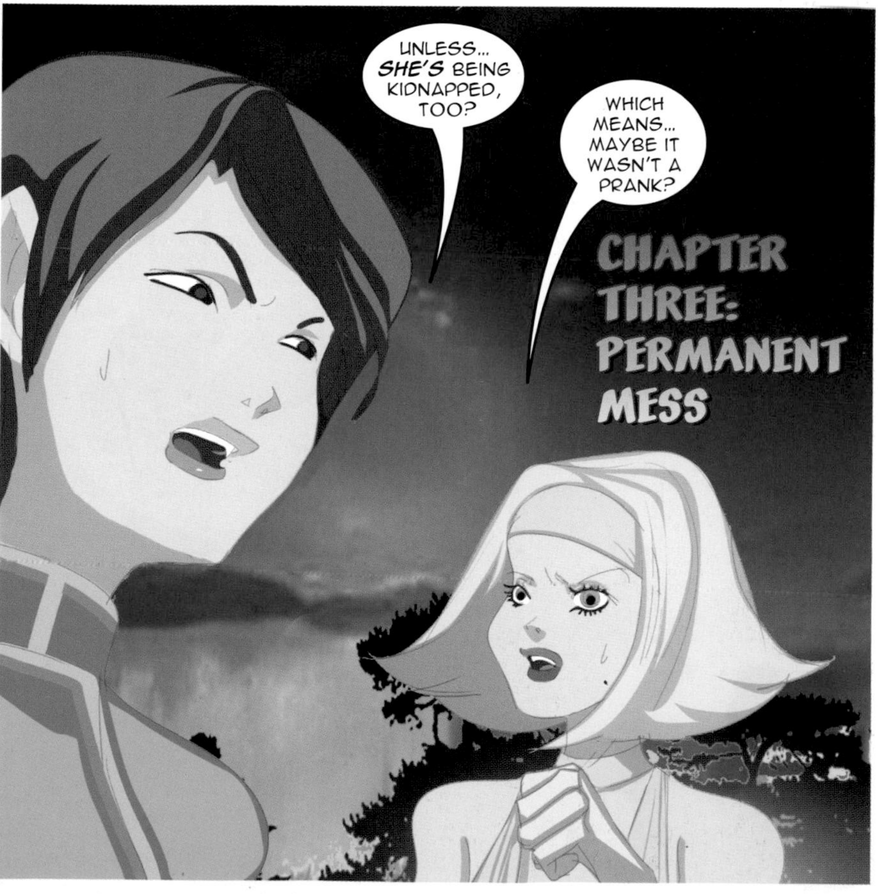
UNLESS... *SHE'S* BEING KIDNAPPED, TOO?
WHICH MEANS... MAYBE IT WASN'T A PRANK?
CHAPTER THREE: PERMANENT MESS

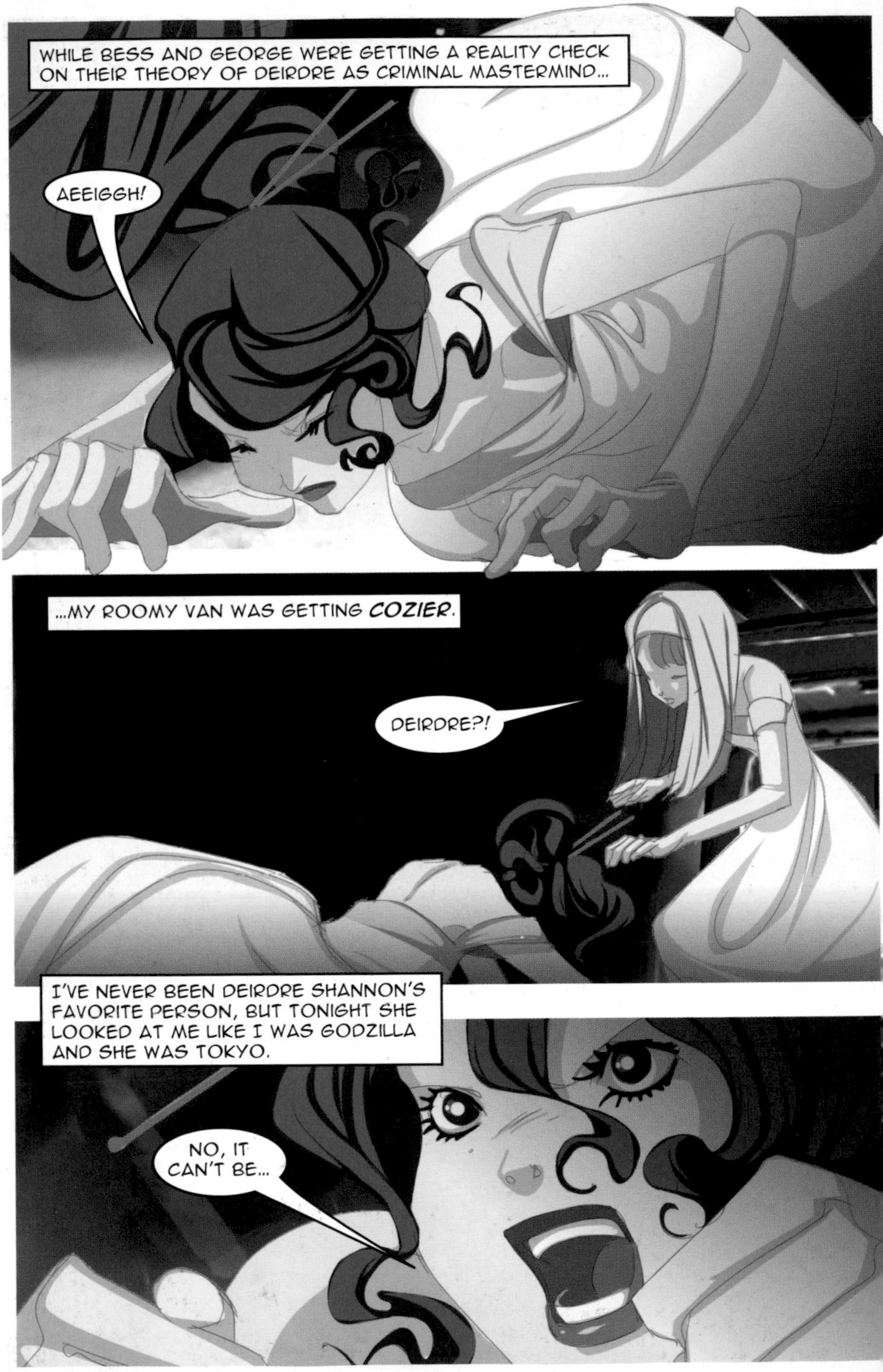
WHILE BESS AND GEORGE WERE GETTING A REALITY CHECK ON THEIR THEORY OF DEIRDRE AS CRIMINAL MASTERMIND...
AEEIGGH!
...MY ROOMY VAN WAS GETTING COZIER.
DEIRDRE?!
I'VE NEVER BEEN DEIRDRE SHANNON'S FAVORITE PERSON, BUT TONIGHT SHE LOOKED AT ME LIKE I WAS GODZILLA AND SHE WAS TOKYO.
NO, IT CAN'T BE...

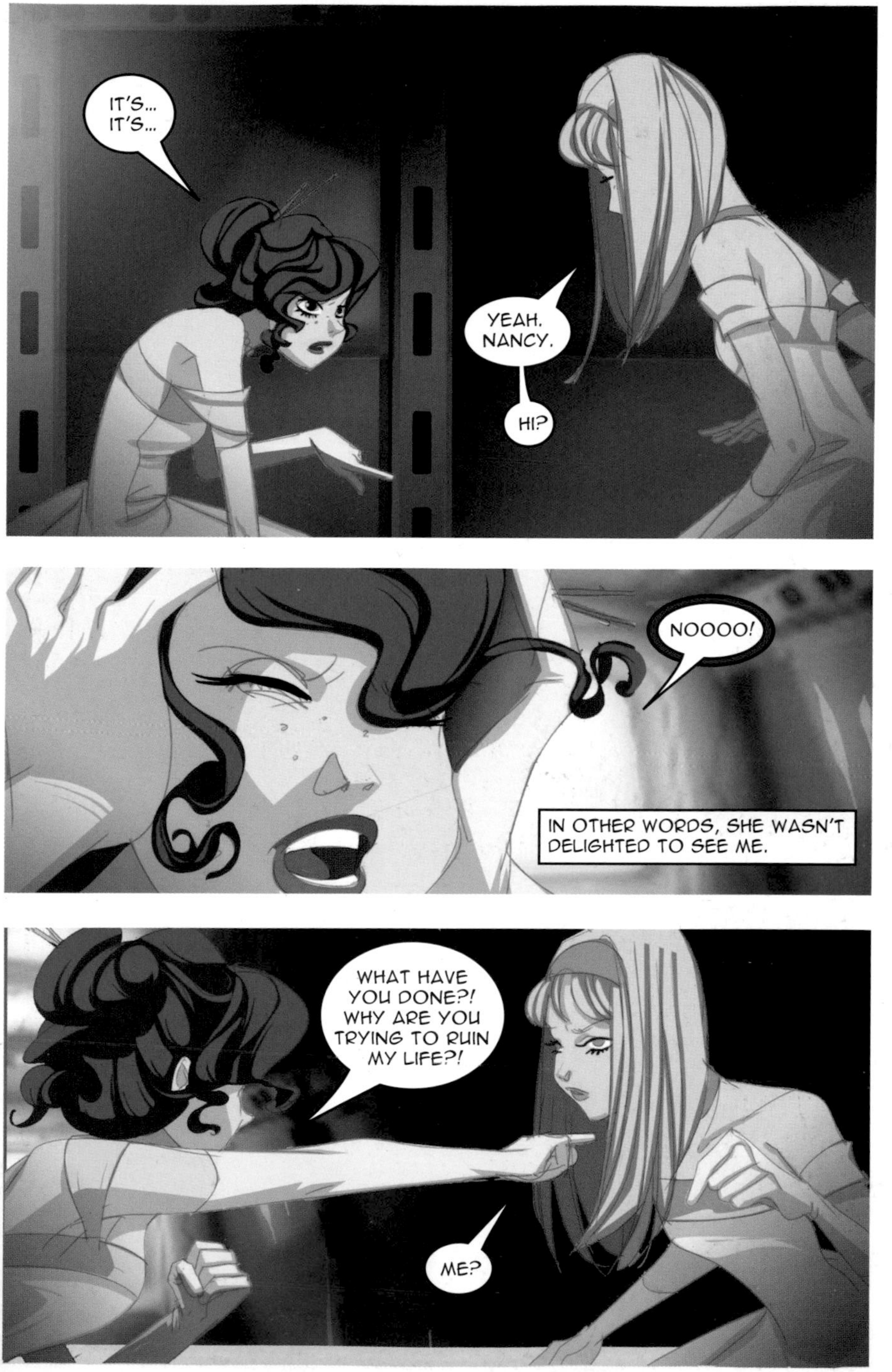
IT'S...
IT'S...
YEAH. NANCY.
HI?
NOOOO!
IN OTHER WORDS, SHE WASN'T DELIGHTED TO SEE ME.
WHAT HAVE YOU DONE?! WHY ARE YOU TRYING TO RUIN MY LIFE?!
ME?

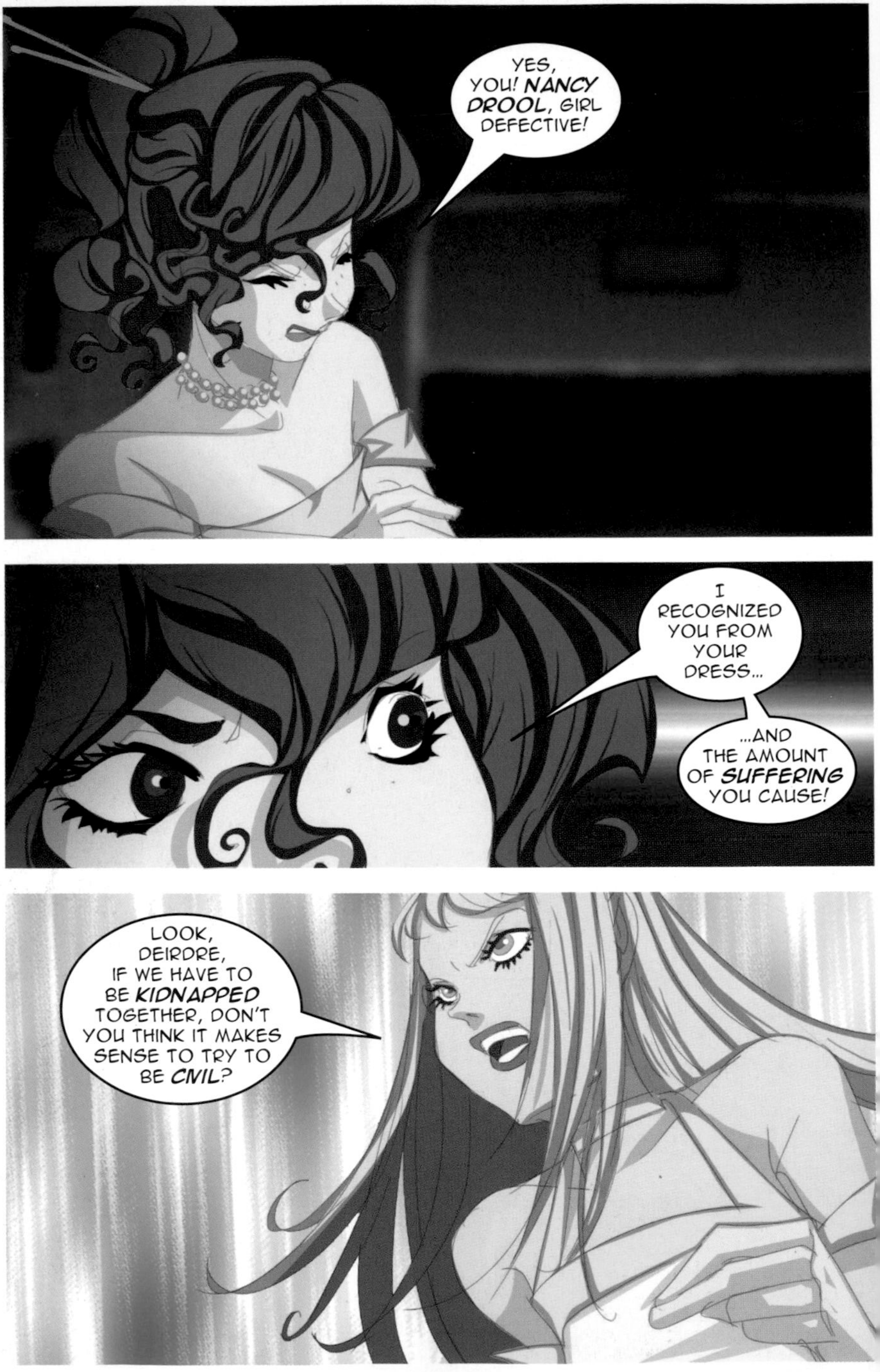
YES, YOU! NANCY DROOL, GIRL DEFECTIVE!
I RECOGNIZED YOU FROM YOUR DRESS...
...AND THE AMOUNT OF SUFFERING YOU CAUSE!
LOOK, DEIRDRE, IF WE HAVE TO BE KIDNAPPED TOGETHER, DON'T YOU THINK IT MAKES SENSE TO TRY TO BE CIVIL?

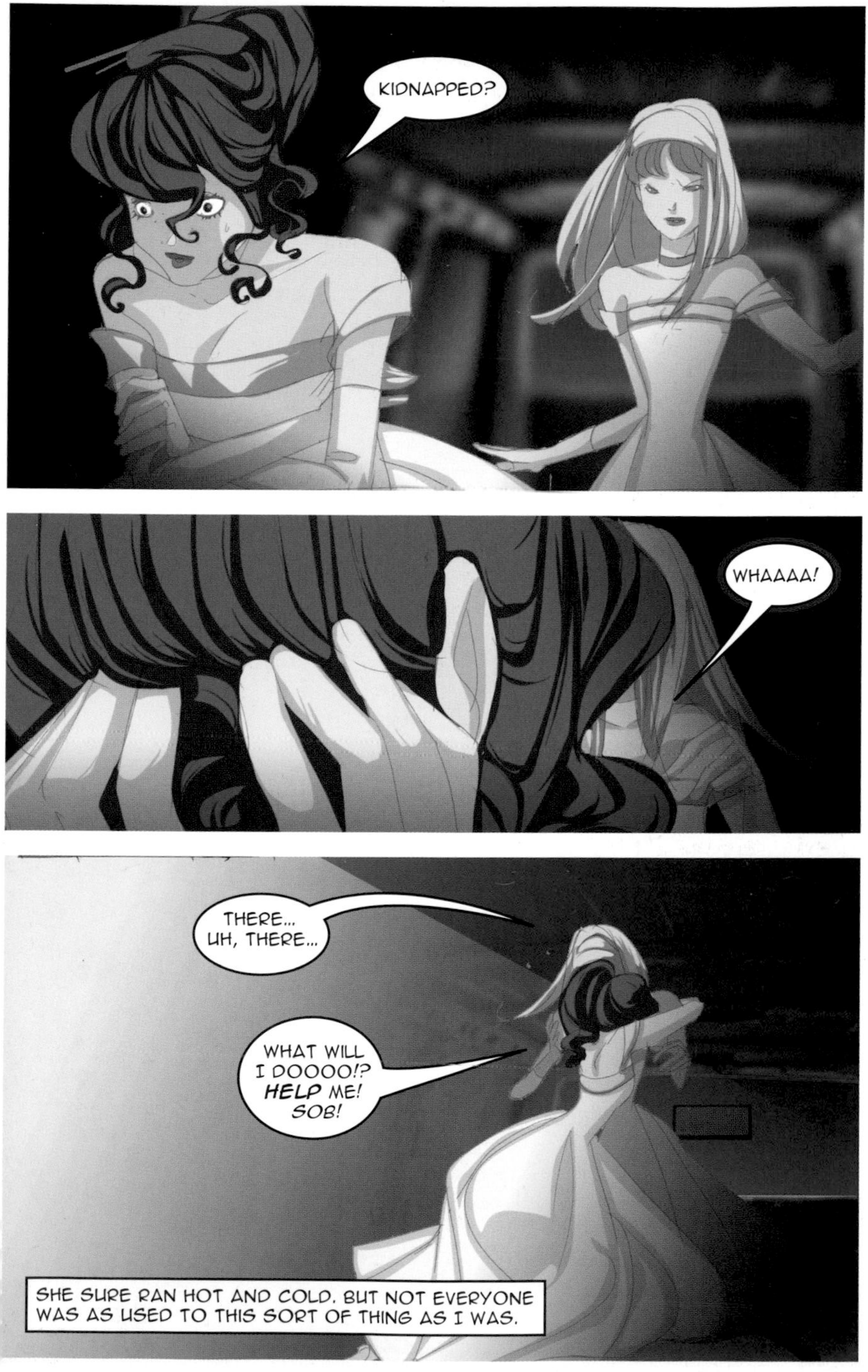
KIDNAPPED?
WHAAAA!
THERE... UH, THERE...
WHAT WILL I DOOOO!? HELP ME! SOB!
SHE SURE RAN HOT AND COLD. BUT NOT EVERYONE WAS AS USED TO THIS SORT OF THING AS I WAS.

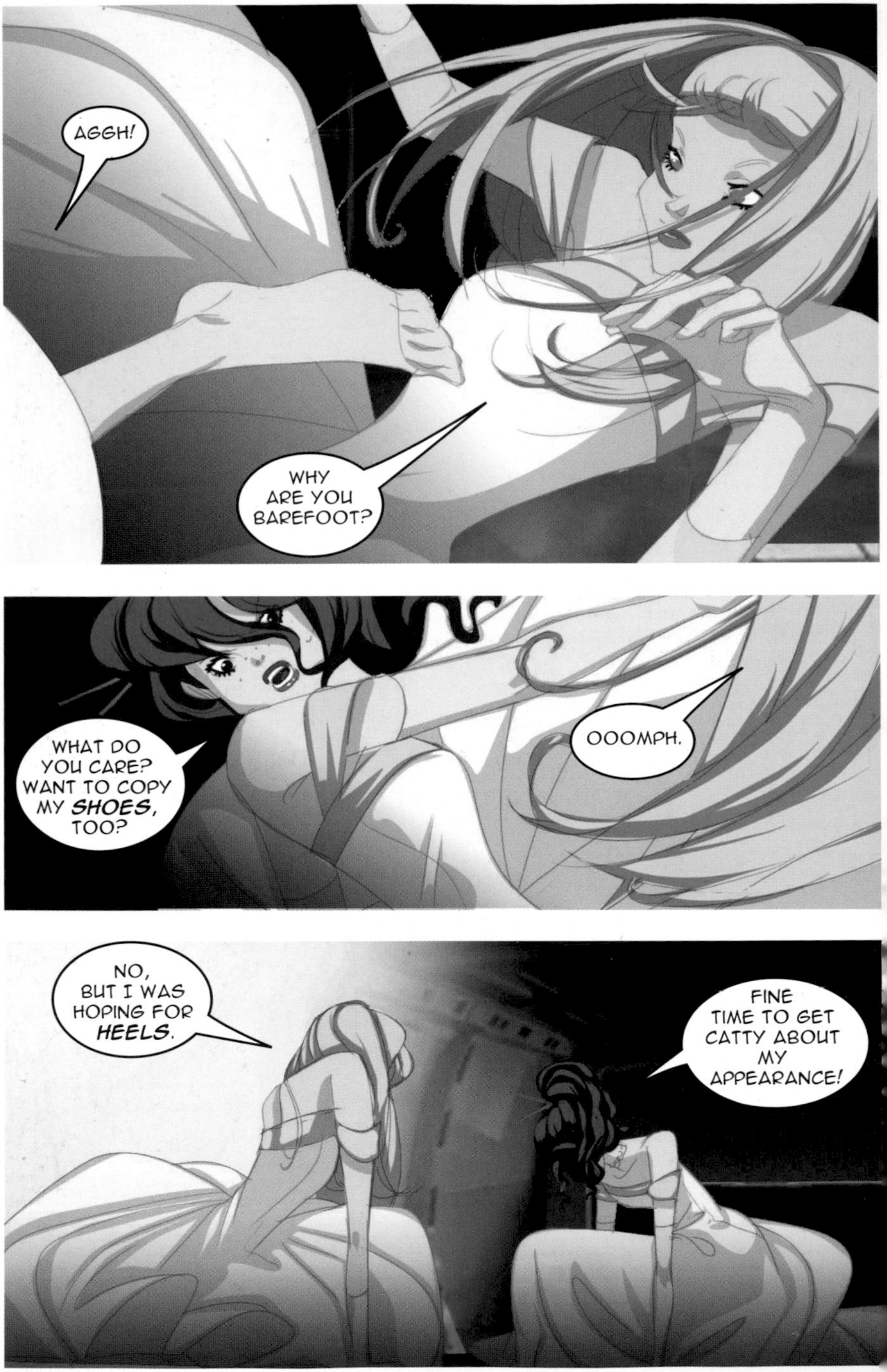
AGGH!
WHY ARE YOU BAREFOOT?
WHAT DO YOU CARE? WANT TO COPY MY SHOES, TOO?
OOOMPH.
NO, BUT I WAS HOPING FOR HEELS.
FINE TIME TO GET CATTY ABOUT MY APPEARANCE!

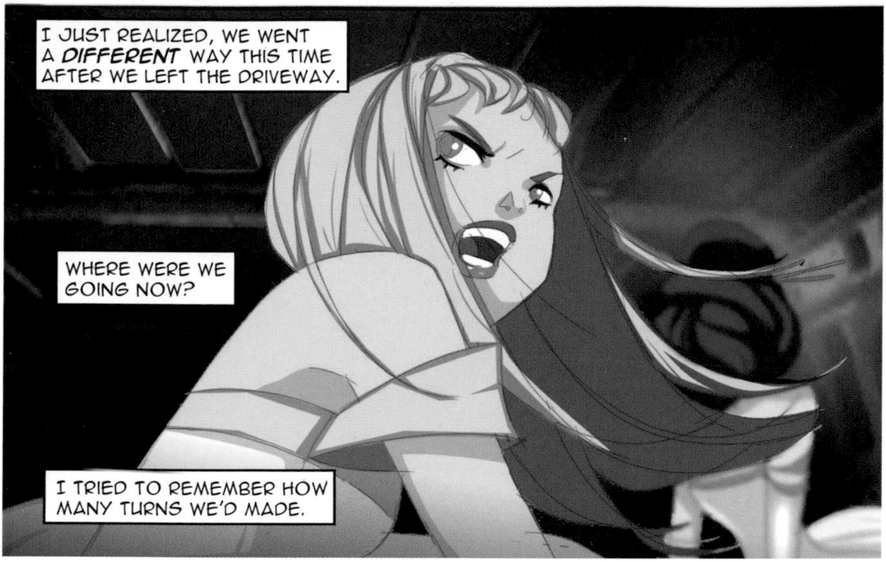
I JUST REALIZED, WE WENT A ***DIFFERENT*** WAY THIS TIME AFTER WE LEFT THE DRIVEWAY.
WHERE WERE WE GOING NOW?
I TRIED TO REMEMBER HOW MANY TURNS WE'D MADE.

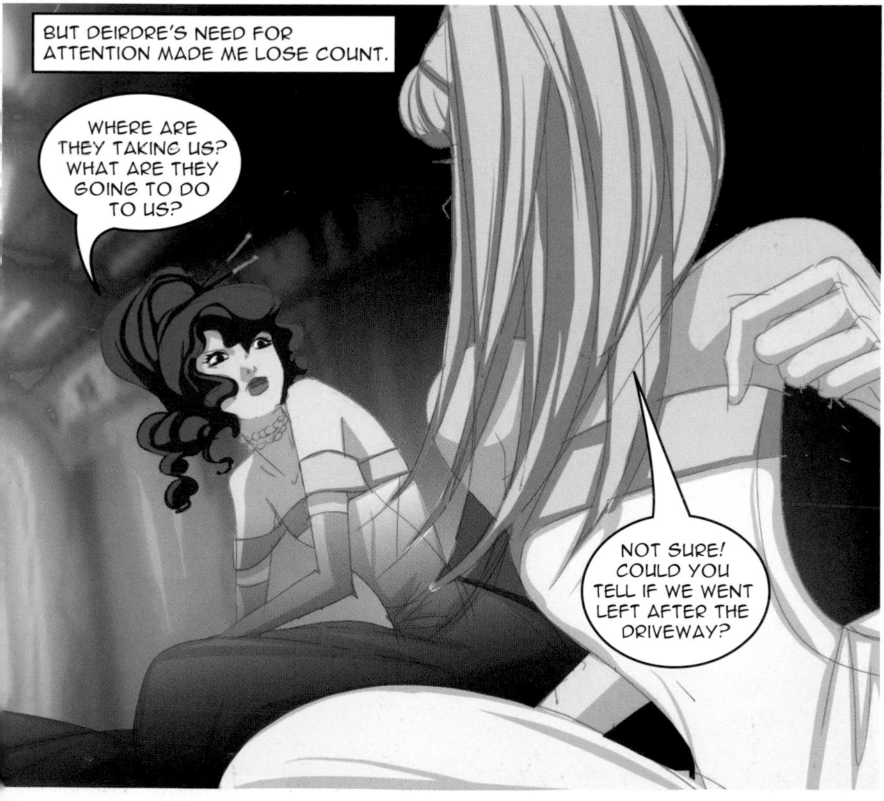
BUT DEIRDRE'S NEED FOR ATTENTION MADE ME LOSE COUNT.
WHERE ARE THEY TAKING US? WHAT ARE THEY GOING TO DO TO US?
NOT SURE! COULD YOU TELL IF WE WENT LEFT AFTER THE DRIVEWAY?

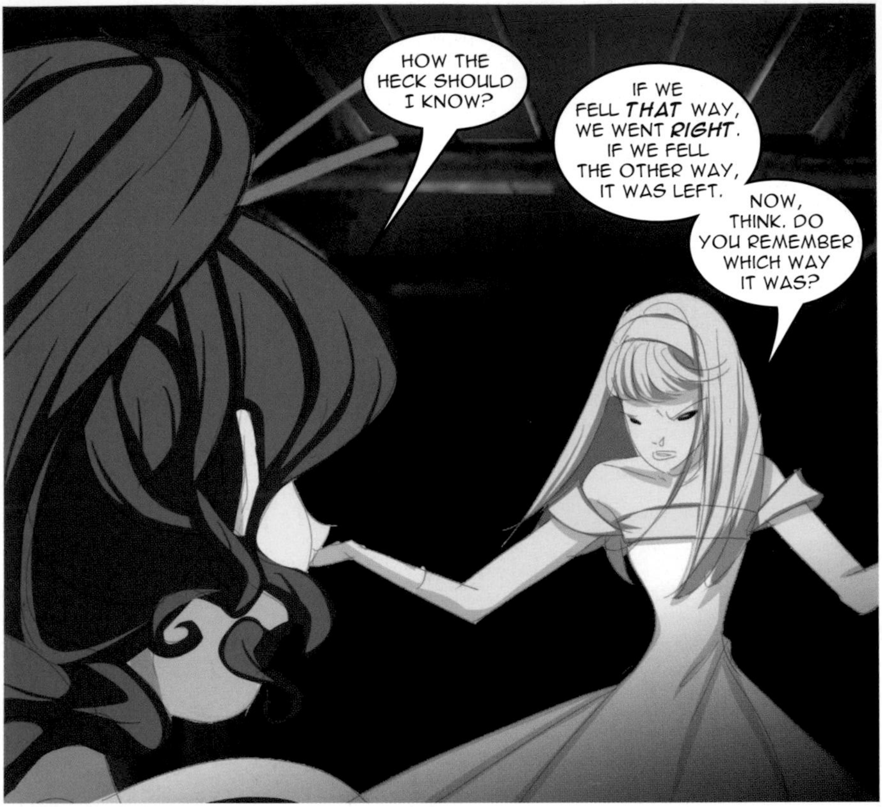
HOW THE HECK SHOULD I KNOW?
IF WE FELL THAT WAY, WE WENT RIGHT. IF WE FELL THE OTHER WAY, IT WAS LEFT.
NOW, THINK. DO YOU REMEMBER WHICH WAY IT WAS?

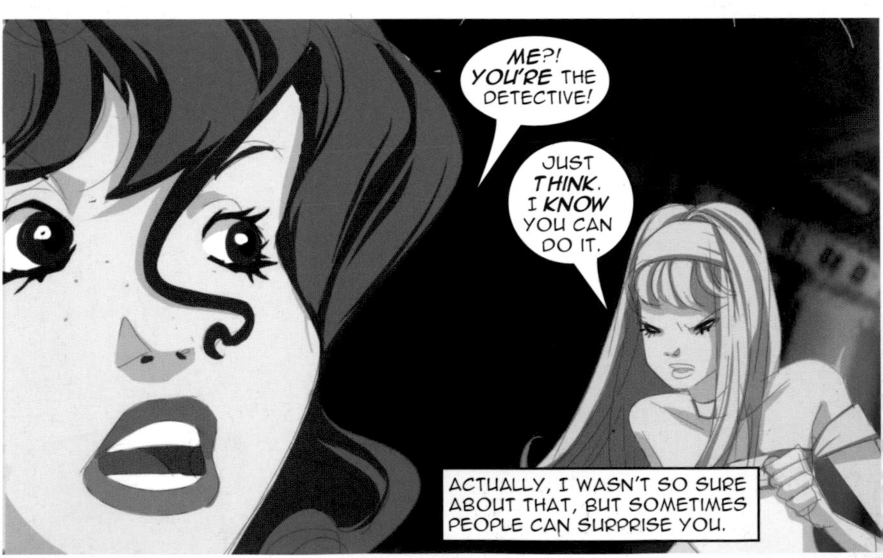
ME?! YOU'RE THE DETECTIVE!
JUST THINK. I KNOW YOU CAN DO IT.
ACTUALLY, I WASN'T SO SURE ABOUT THAT, BUT SOMETIMES PEOPLE CAN SURPRISE YOU.

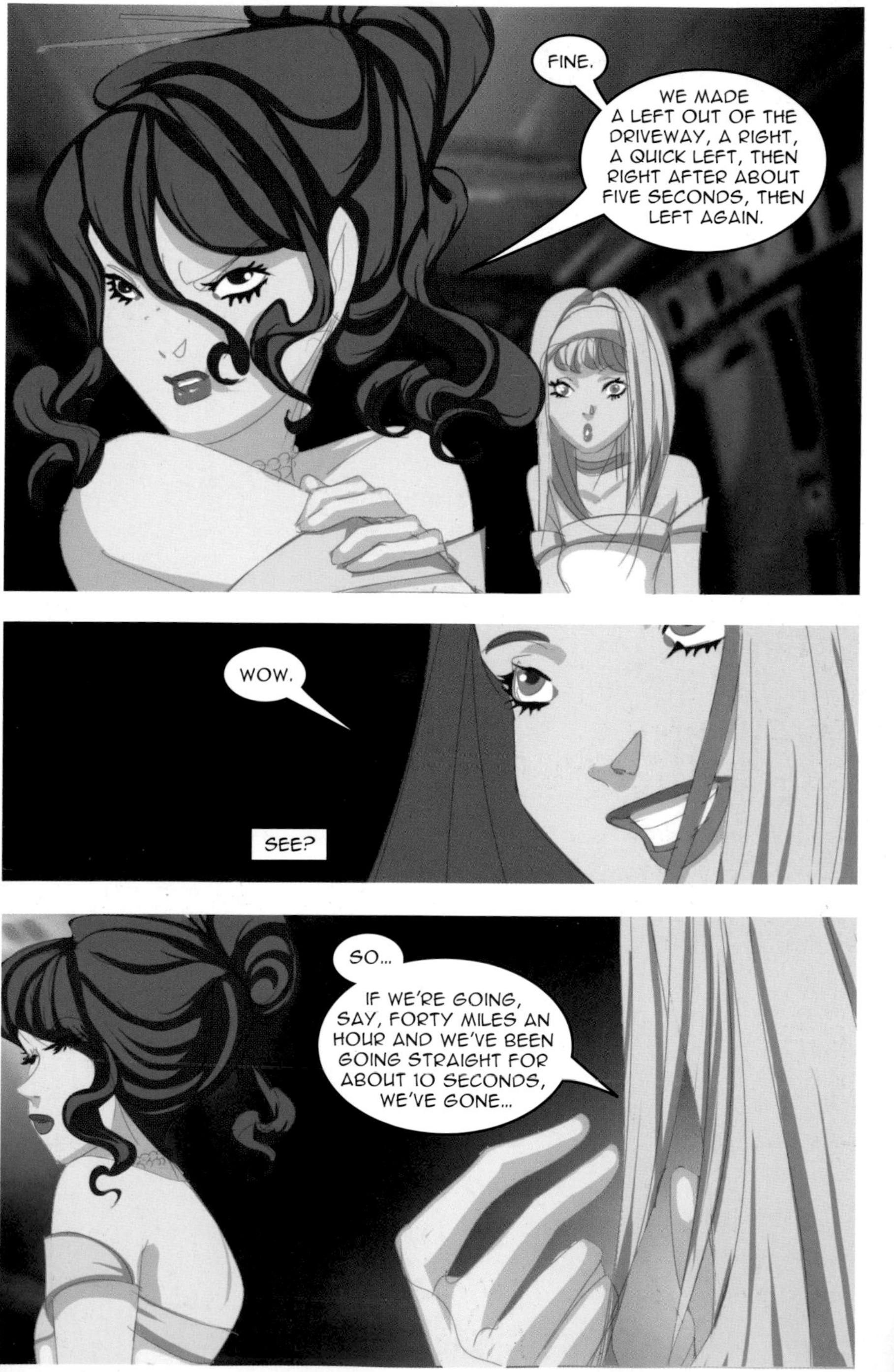
FINE.
WE MADE A LEFT OUT OF THE DRIVEWAY, A RIGHT, A QUICK LEFT, THEN RIGHT AFTER ABOUT FIVE SECONDS, THEN LEFT AGAIN.
WOW.
SEE?
SO...
IF WE'RE GOING, SAY, FORTY MILES AN HOUR AND WE'VE BEEN GOING STRAIGHT FOR ABOUT 10 SECONDS, WE'VE GONE...

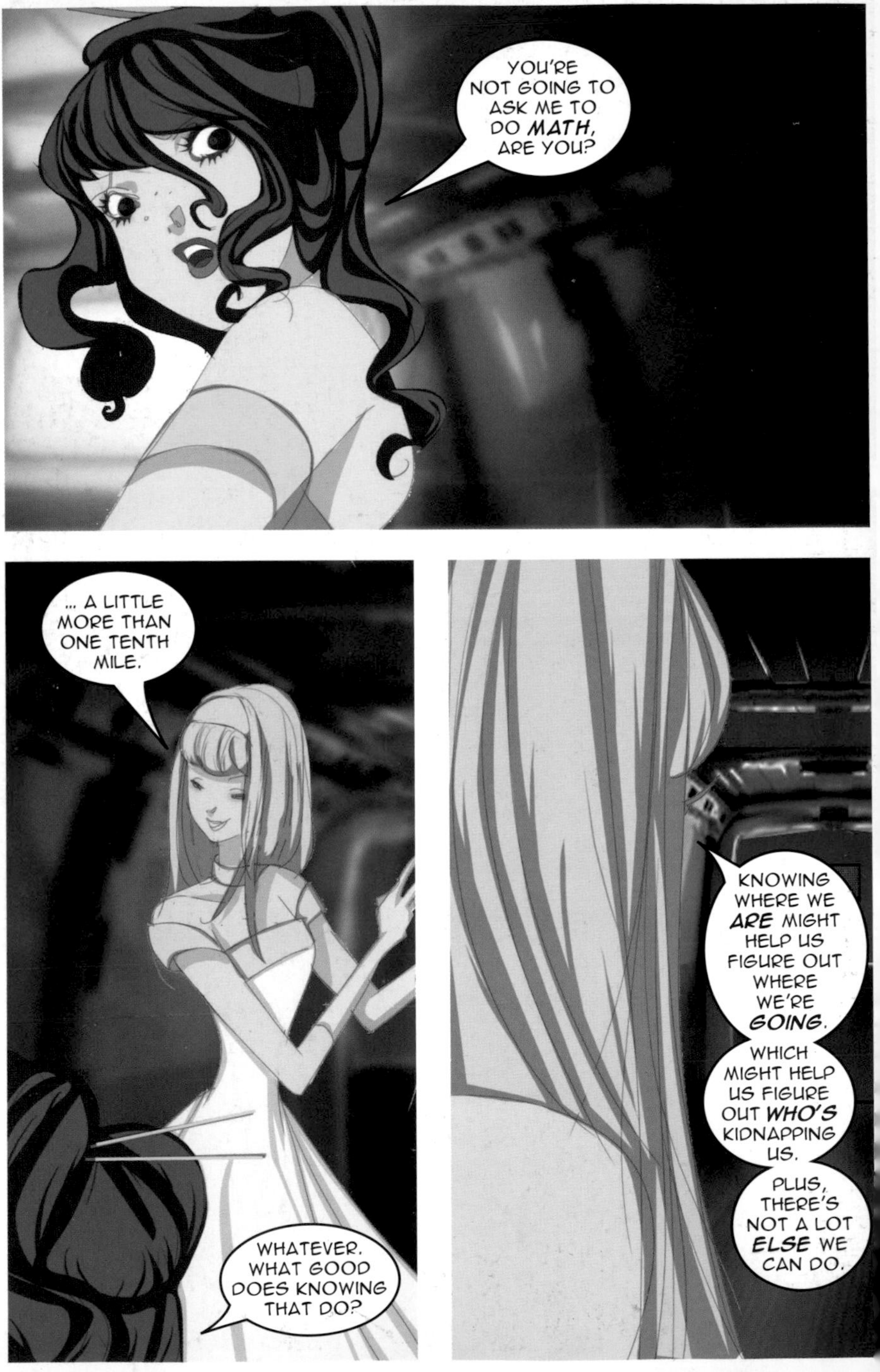
YOU'RE NOT GOING TO ASK ME TO DO MATH, ARE YOU?
... A LITTLE MORE THAN ONE TENTH MILE.
WHATEVER. WHAT GOOD DOES KNOWING THAT DO?
KNOWING WHERE WE ARE MIGHT HELP US FIGURE OUT WHERE WE'RE GOING.
WHICH MIGHT HELP US FIGURE OUT WHO'S KIDNAPPING US.
PLUS, THERE'S NOT A LOT ELSE WE CAN DO.

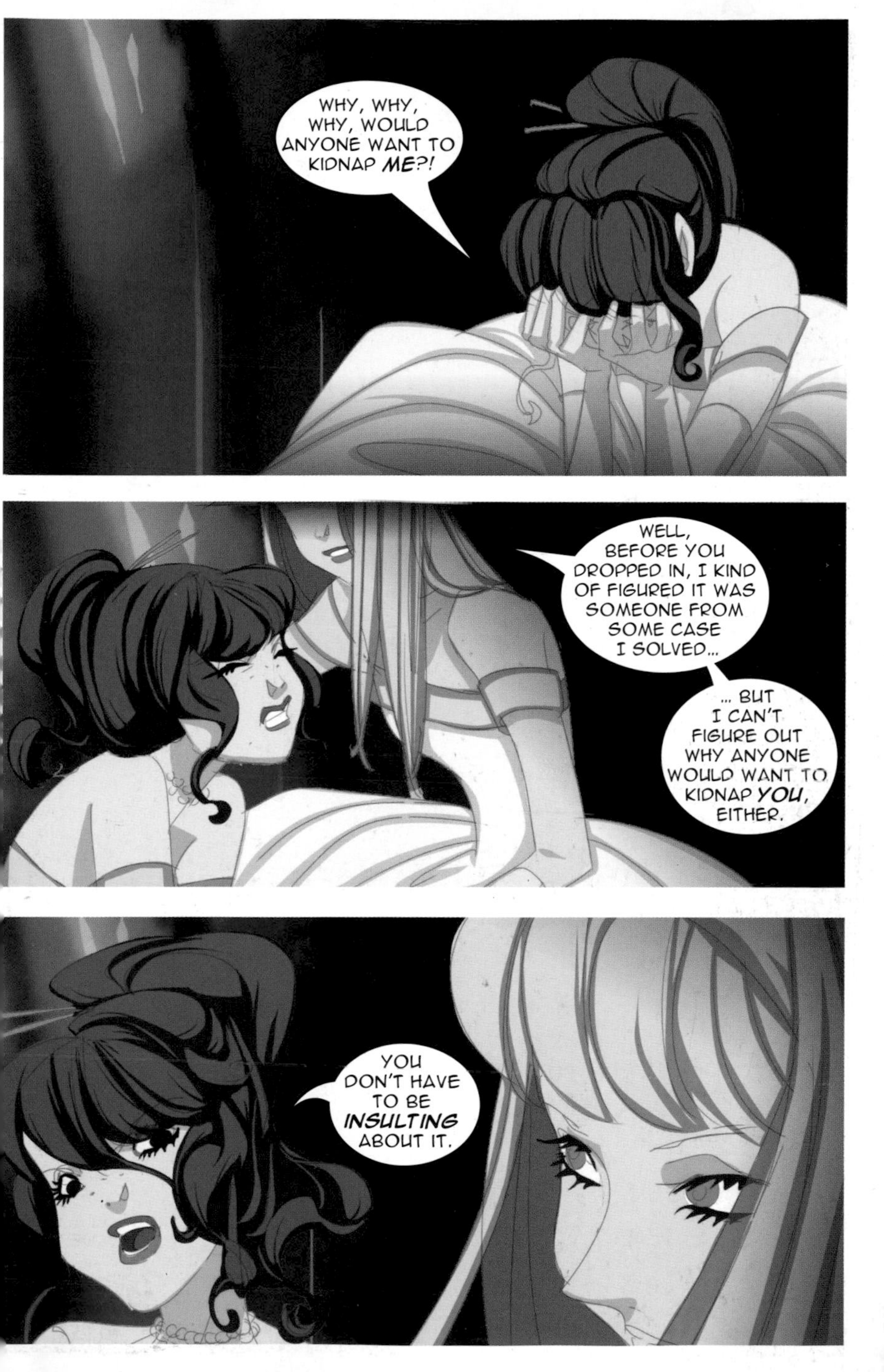
WHY, WHY, WHY, WOULD ANYONE WANT TO KIDNAP *ME*?!
WELL, BEFORE YOU DROPPED IN, I KIND OF FIGURED IT WAS SOMEONE FROM SOME CASE I SOLVED...
... BUT I CAN'T FIGURE OUT WHY ANYONE WOULD WANT TO KIDNAP *YOU*, EITHER.
YOU DON'T HAVE TO BE *INSULTING* ABOUT IT.

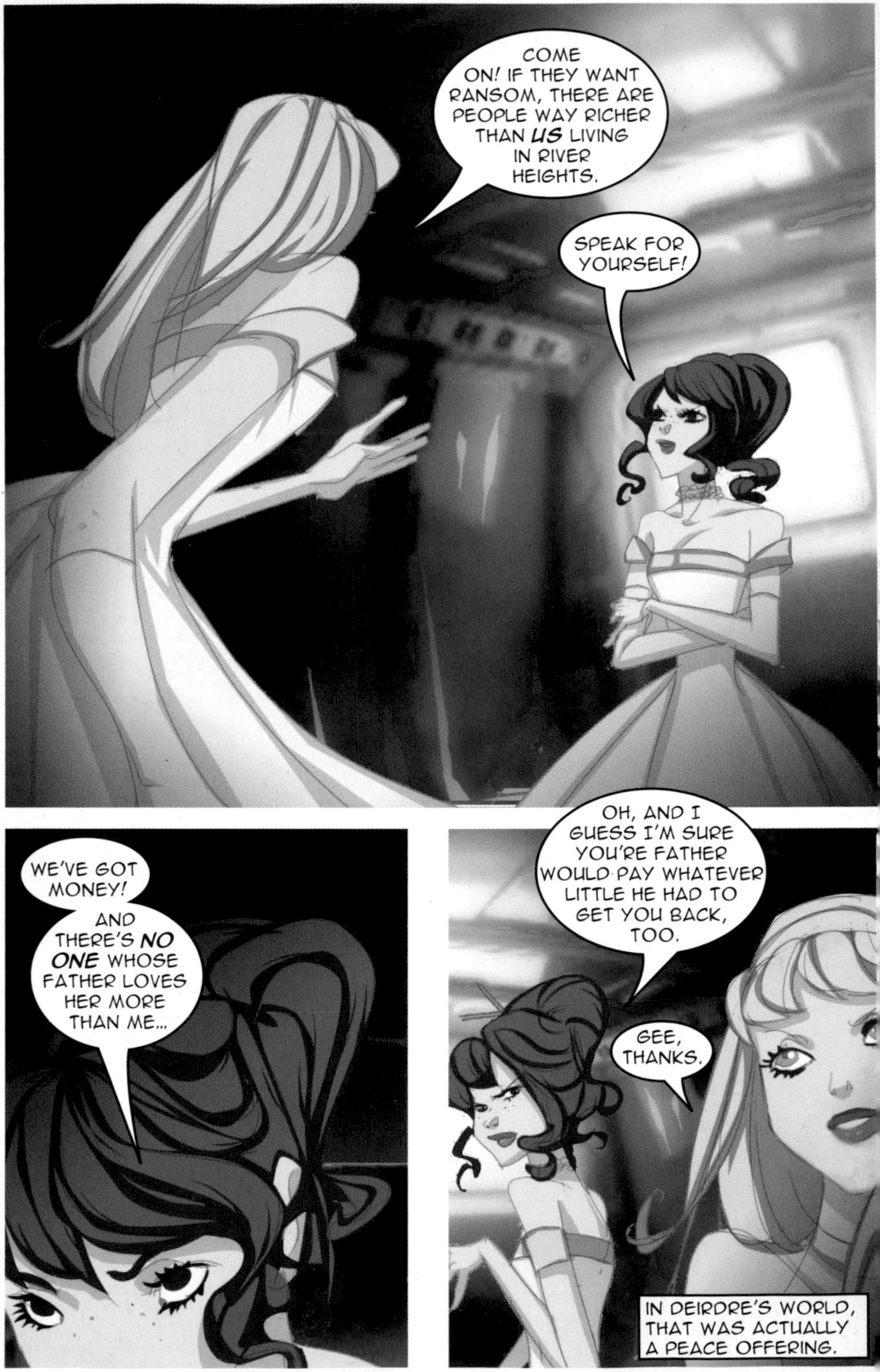
COME ON! IF THEY WANT RANSOM, THERE ARE PEOPLE WAY RICHER THAN *US* LIVING IN RIVER HEIGHTS.
SPEAK FOR YOURSELF!
WE'VE GOT MONEY!
AND THERE'S **NO ONE** WHOSE FATHER LOVES HER MORE THAN ME...
OH, AND I GUESS I'M SURE YOU'RE FATHER WOULD PAY WHATEVER LITTLE HE HAD TO GET YOU BACK, TOO.
GEE, THANKS.
IN DEIRDRE'S WORLD, THAT WAS ACTUALLY A PEACE OFFERING.

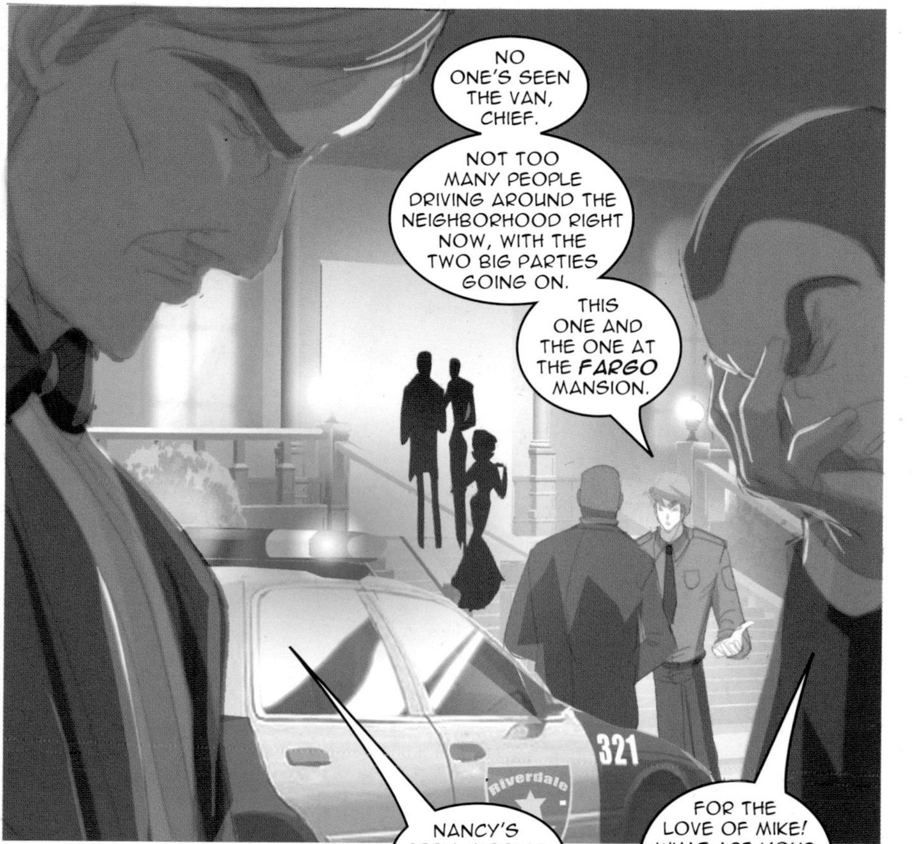
NO ONE'S SEEN THE VAN, CHIEF.
NOT TOO MANY PEOPLE DRIVING AROUND THE NEIGHBORHOOD RIGHT NOW, WITH THE TWO BIG PARTIES GOING ON.
THIS ONE AND THE ONE AT THE FARGO MANSION.
321
Riverdale
NANCY'S BEEN MISSING ALMOST AN HOUR!
FOR THE LOVE OF MIKE! WHAT ARE YOUR PEOPLE DOING TO FIND OUR DAUGHTERS?!
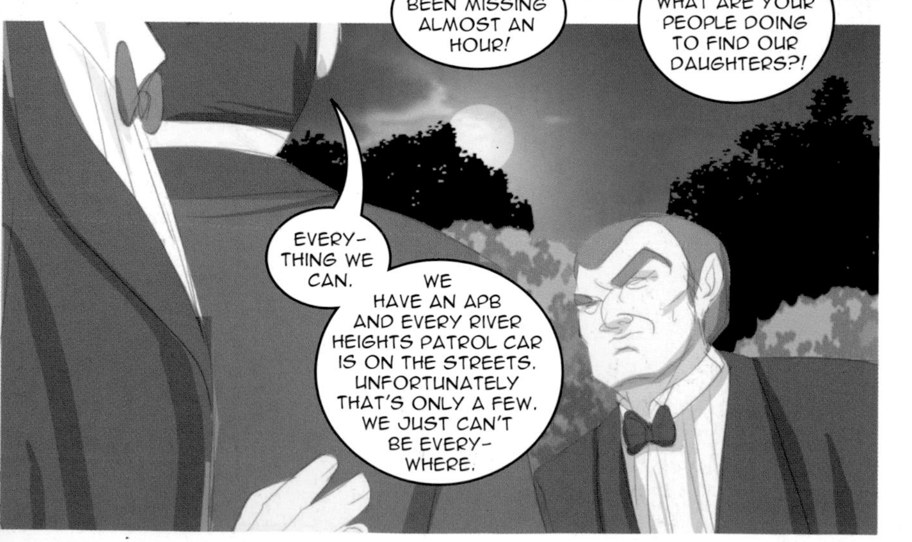
EVERY-THING WE CAN.
WE HAVE AN APB AND EVERY RIVER HEIGHTS PATROL CAR IS ON THE STREETS. UNFORTUNATELY THAT'S ONLY A FEW. WE JUST CAN'T BE EVERY-WHERE.

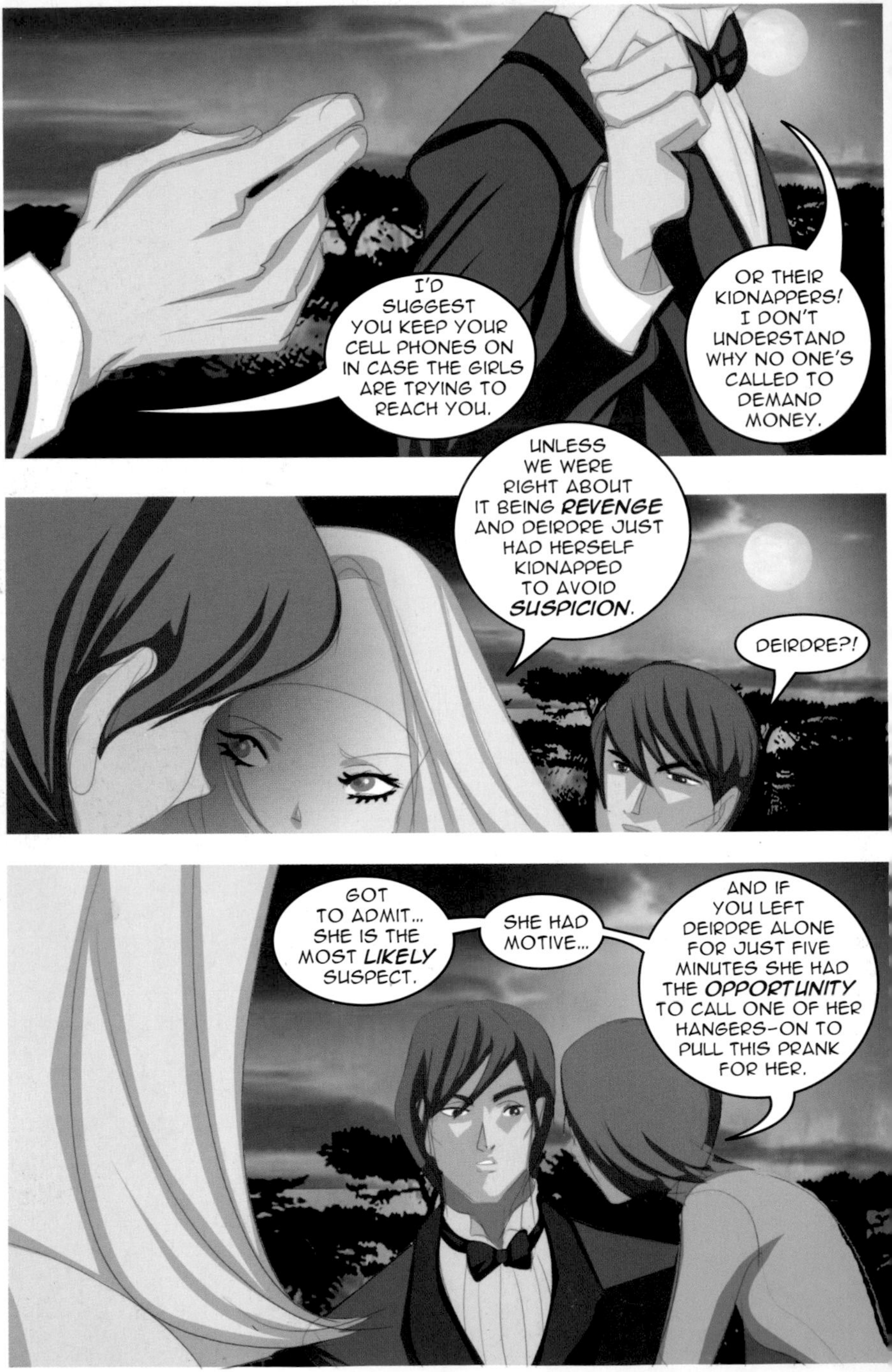
I'D SUGGEST YOU KEEP YOUR CELL PHONES ON IN CASE THE GIRLS ARE TRYING TO REACH YOU.
OR THEIR KIDNAPPERS! I DON'T UNDERSTAND WHY NO ONE'S CALLED TO DEMAND MONEY.
UNLESS WE WERE RIGHT ABOUT IT BEING REVENGE AND DEIRDRE JUST HAD HERSELF KIDNAPPED TO AVOID SUSPICION.
DEIRDRE?!
GOT TO ADMIT... SHE IS THE MOST LIKELY SUSPECT.
SHE HAD MOTIVE...
AND IF YOU LEFT DEIRDRE ALONE FOR JUST FIVE MINUTES SHE HAD THE OPPORTUNITY TO CALL ONE OF HER HANGERS-ON TO PULL THIS PRANK FOR HER.

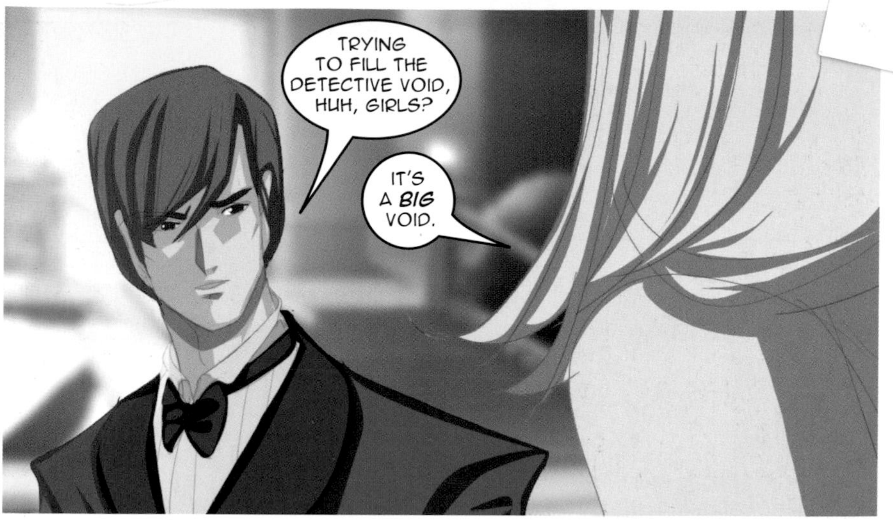
TRYING TO FILL THE DETECTIVE VOID, HUH, GIRLS?
IT'S A **BIG** VOID.
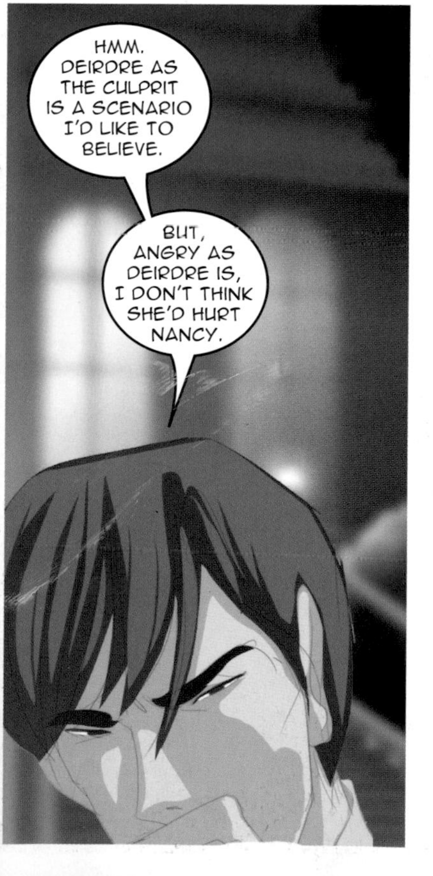
HMM. DEIRDRE AS THE CULPRIT IS A SCENARIO I'D LIKE TO BELIEVE.
BUT, ANGRY AS DEIRDRE IS, I DON'T THINK SHE'D HURT NANCY.
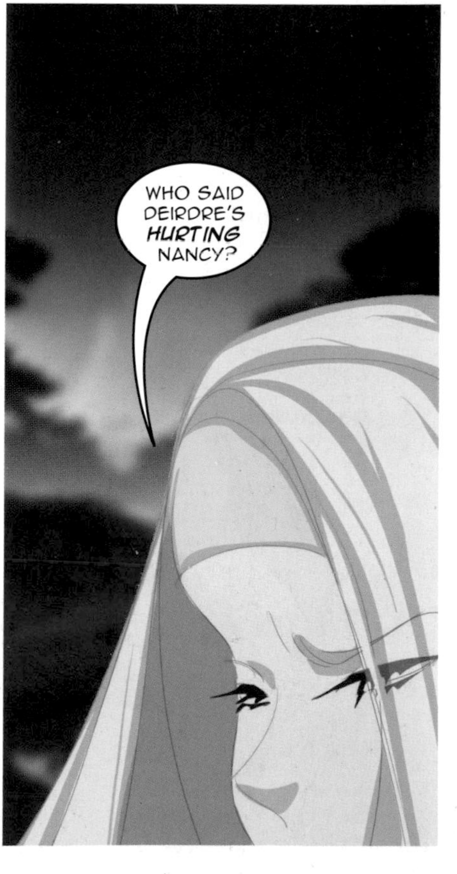
WHO SAID DEIRDRE'S ***HURTING*** NANCY?

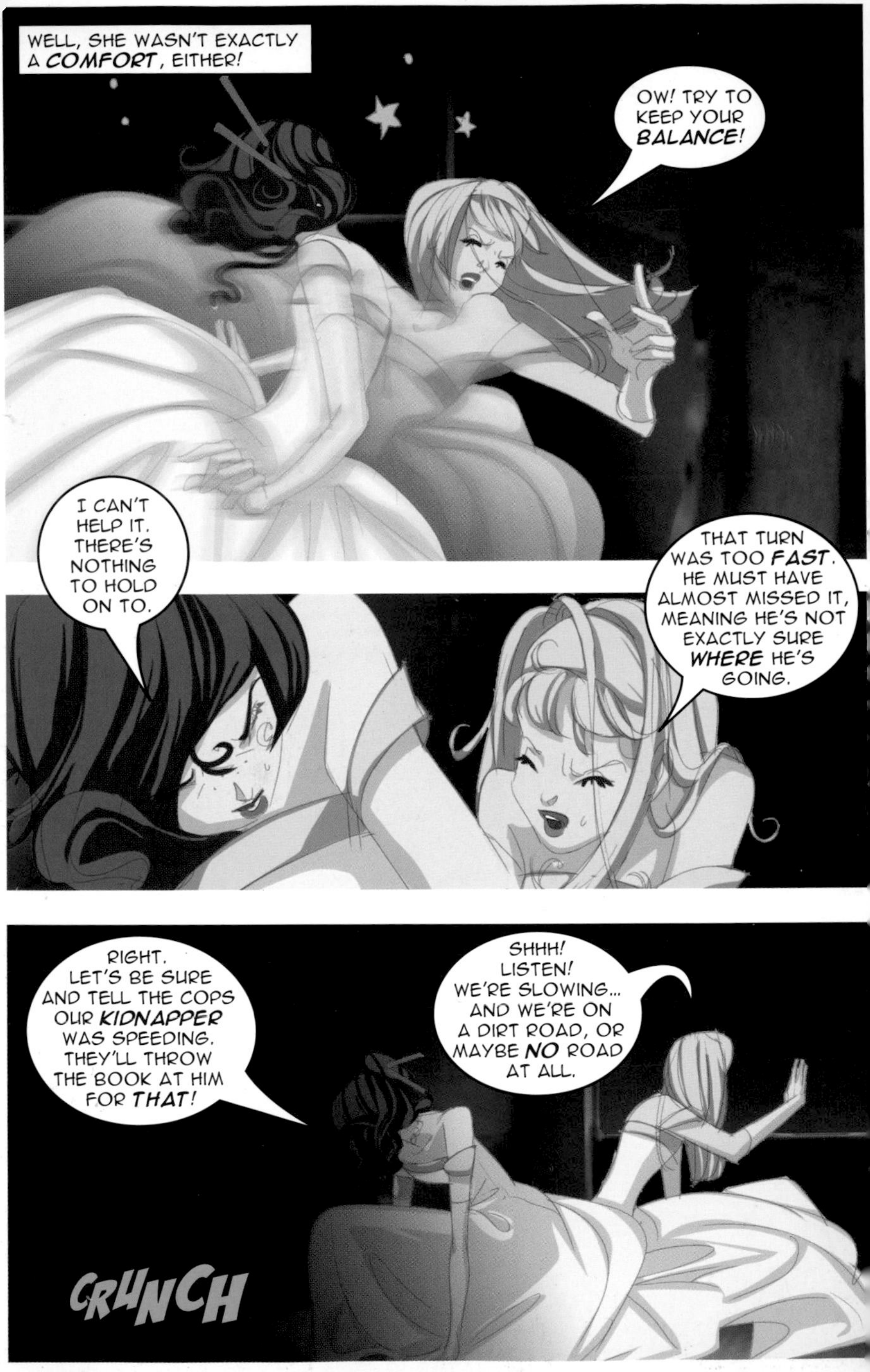
WELL, SHE WASN'T EXACTLY A COMFORT, EITHER!
OW! TRY TO KEEP YOUR BALANCE!
I CAN'T HELP IT. THERE'S NOTHING TO HOLD ON TO.
THAT TURN WAS TOO FAST. HE MUST HAVE ALMOST MISSED IT, MEANING HE'S NOT EXACTLY SURE WHERE HE'S GOING.
RIGHT. LET'S BE SURE AND TELL THE COPS OUR KIDNAPPER WAS SPEEDING. THEY'LL THROW THE BOOK AT HIM FOR THAT!
SHHH! LISTEN! WE'RE SLOWING... AND WE'RE ON A DIRT ROAD, OR MAYBE NO ROAD AT ALL.
CRUNCH

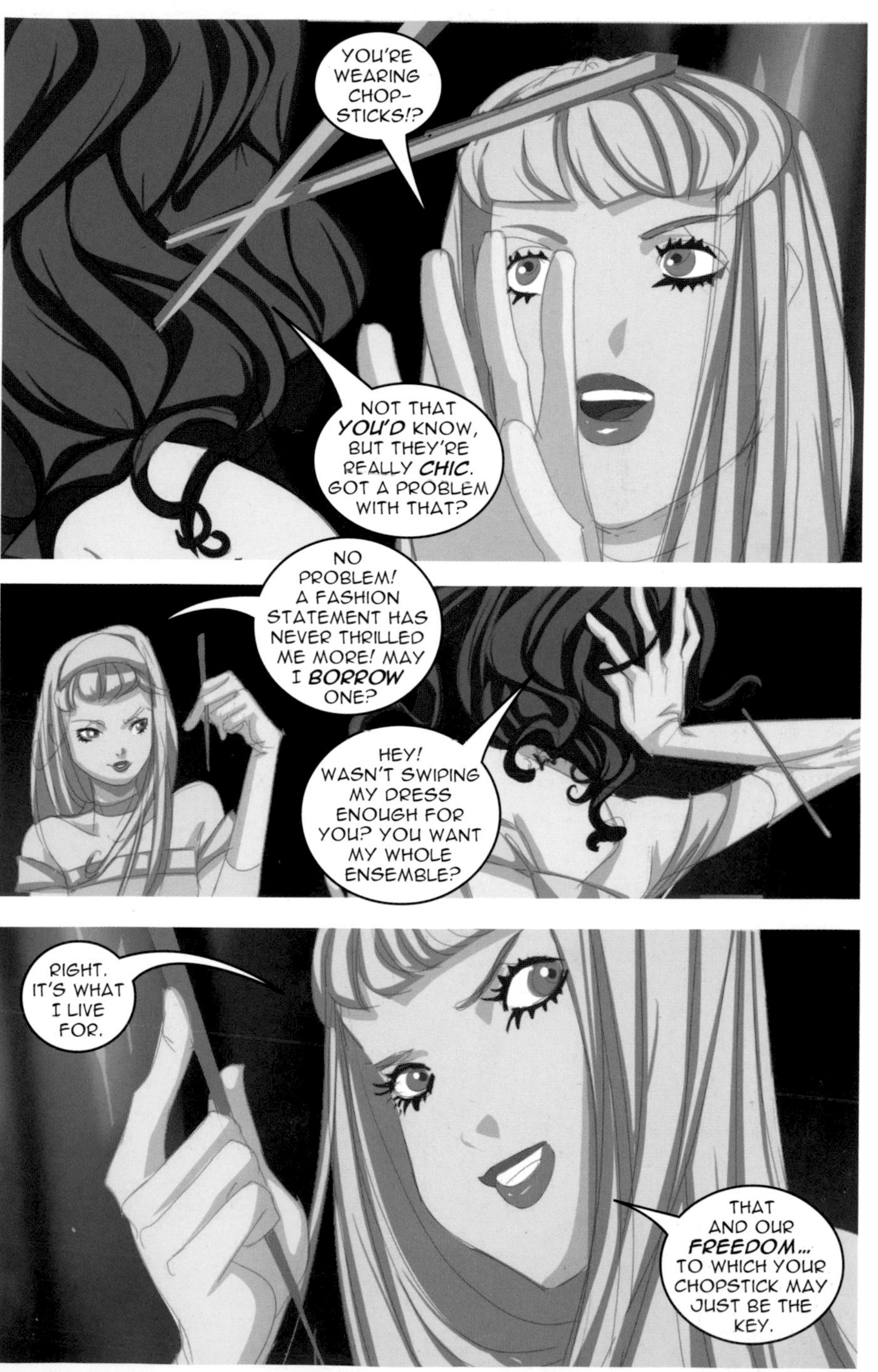
YOU'RE WEARING CHOP-STICKS!?
NOT THAT YOU'D KNOW, BUT THEY'RE REALLY CHIC. GOT A PROBLEM WITH THAT?
NO PROBLEM! A FASHION STATEMENT HAS NEVER THRILLED ME MORE! MAY I BORROW ONE?
HEY! WASN'T SWIPING MY DRESS ENOUGH FOR YOU? YOU WANT MY WHOLE ENSEMBLE?
RIGHT. IT'S WHAT I LIVE FOR.
THAT AND OUR FREEDOM... TO WHICH YOUR CHOPSTICK MAY JUST BE THE KEY.

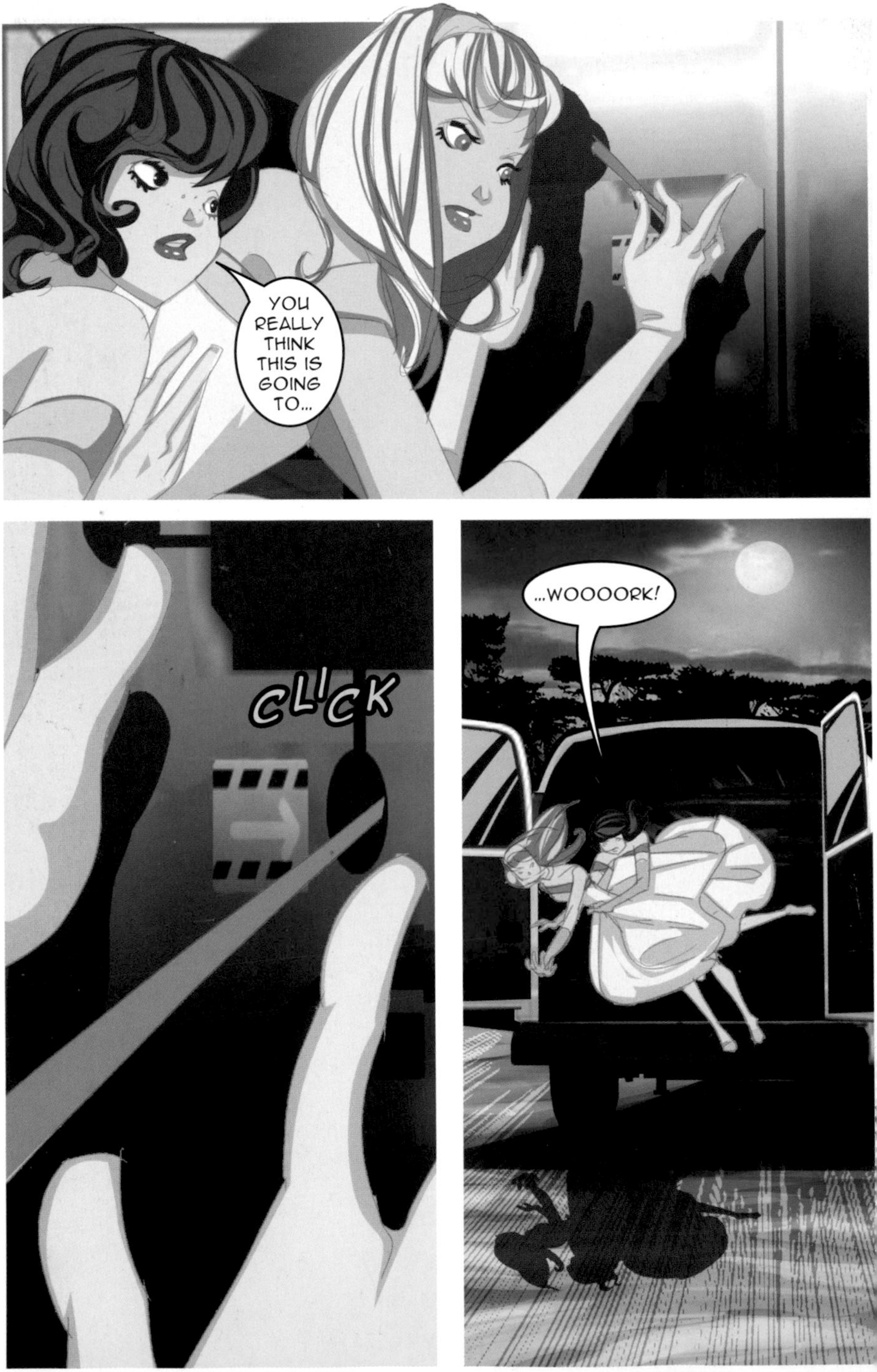
YOU REALLY THINK THIS IS GOING TO...
CLICK
...WOOOORK!

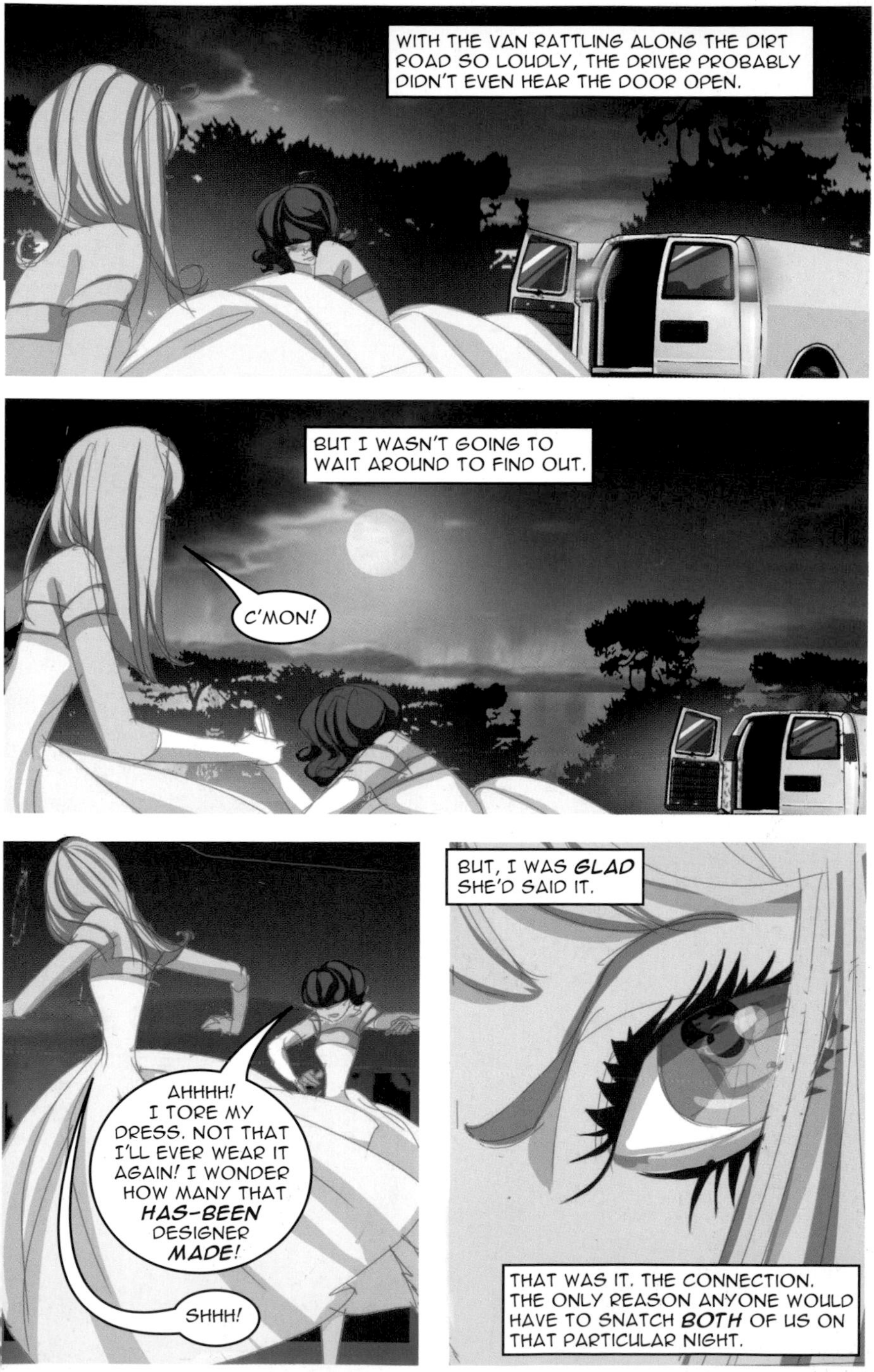

WITH THE VAN RATTLING ALONG THE DIRT ROAD SO LOUDLY, THE DRIVER PROBABLY DIDN'T EVEN HEAR THE DOOR OPEN.
BUT I WASN'T GOING TO WAIT AROUND TO FIND OUT.
C'MON!
AHHHH! I TORE MY DRESS. NOT THAT I'LL EVER WEAR IT AGAIN! I WONDER HOW MANY THAT HAS-BEEN DESIGNER MADE!
SHHH!
BUT, I WAS GLAD SHE'D SAID IT.
THAT WAS IT. THE CONNECTION. THE ONLY REASON ANYONE WOULD HAVE TO SNATCH BOTH OF US ON THAT PARTICULAR NIGHT.

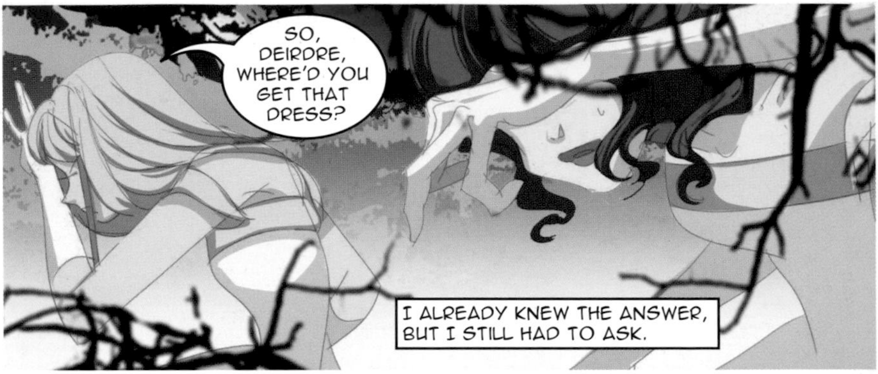
SO, DEIRDRE, WHERE'D YOU GET THAT DRESS?
I ALREADY KNEW THE ANSWER, BUT I STILL HAD TO ASK.

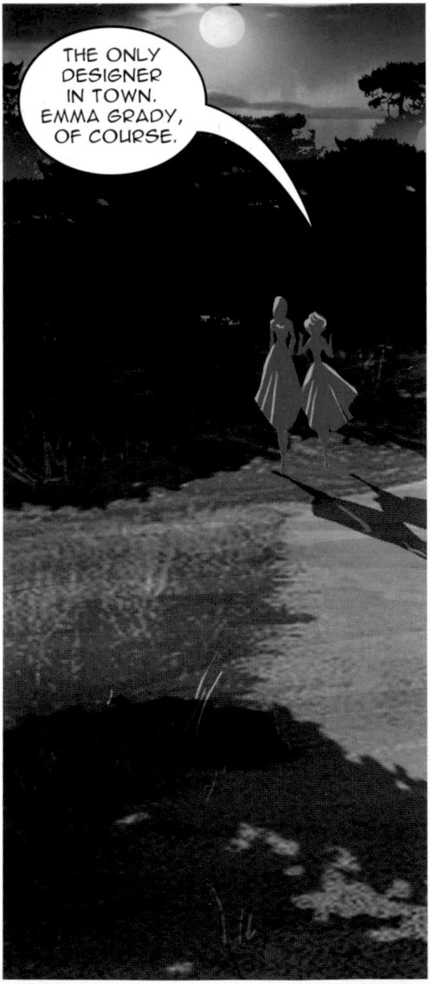
THE ONLY DESIGNER IN TOWN. EMMA GRADY, OF COURSE.

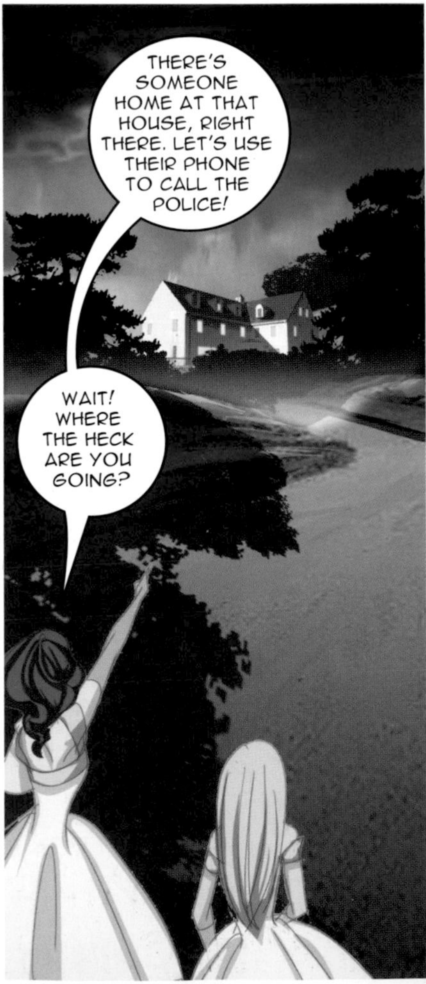
THERE'S SOMEONE HOME AT THAT HOUSE, RIGHT THERE. LET'S USE THEIR PHONE TO CALL THE POLICE!
WAIT! WHERE THE HECK ARE YOU GOING?

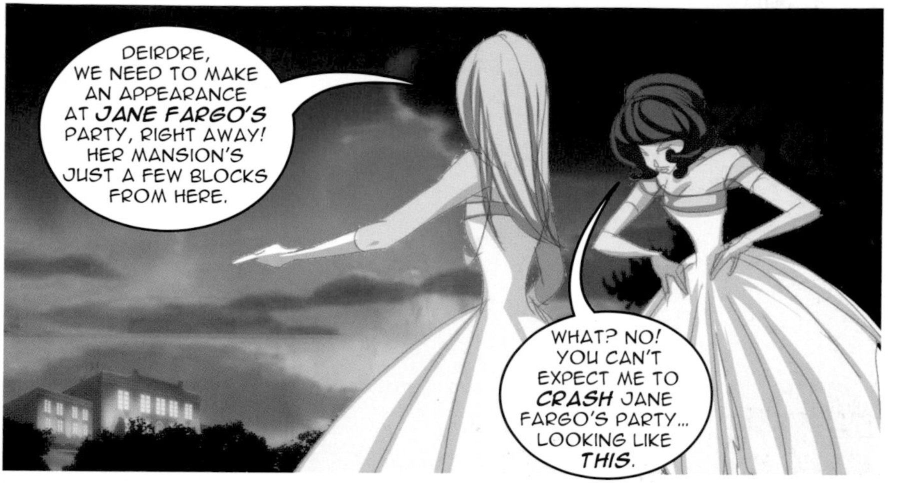
DEIRDRE, WE NEED TO MAKE AN APPEARANCE AT JANE FARGO'S PARTY, RIGHT AWAY! HER MANSION'S JUST A FEW BLOCKS FROM HERE.
WHAT? NO! YOU CAN'T EXPECT ME TO CRASH JANE FARGO'S PARTY... LOOKING LIKE THIS.

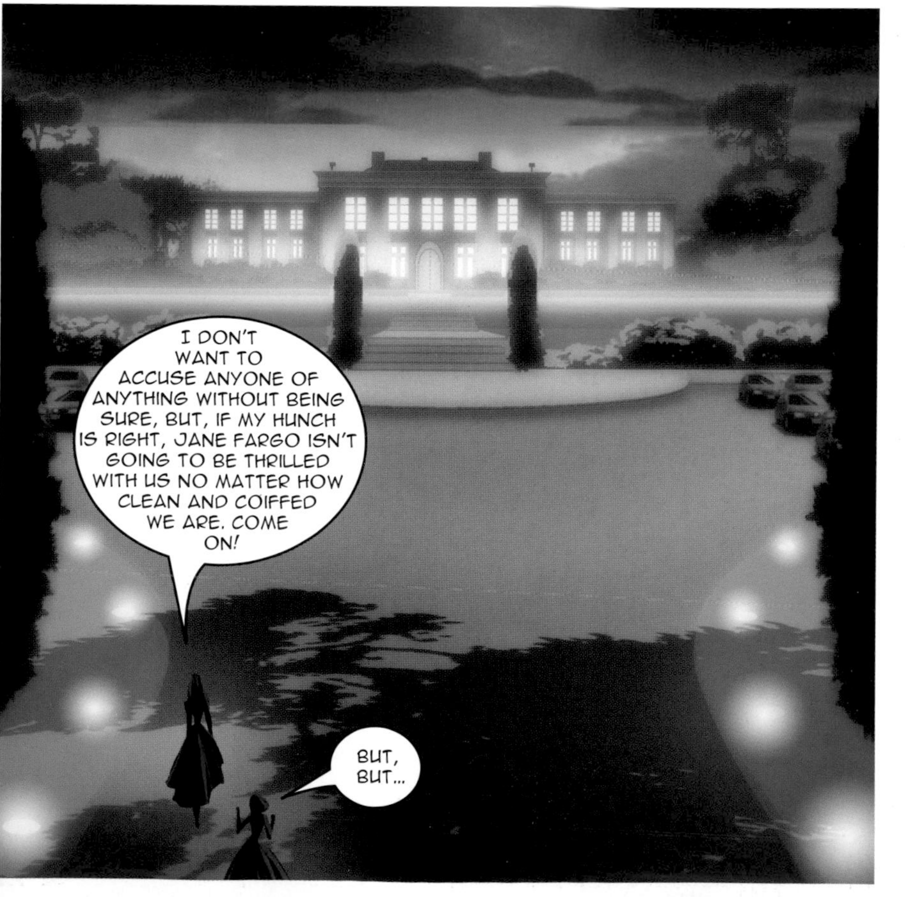
I DON'T WANT TO ACCUSE ANYONE OF ANYTHING WITHOUT BEING SURE, BUT, IF MY HUNCH IS RIGHT, JANE FARGO ISN'T GOING TO BE THRILLED WITH US NO MATTER HOW CLEAN AND COIFFED WE ARE. COME ON!
BUT, BUT...

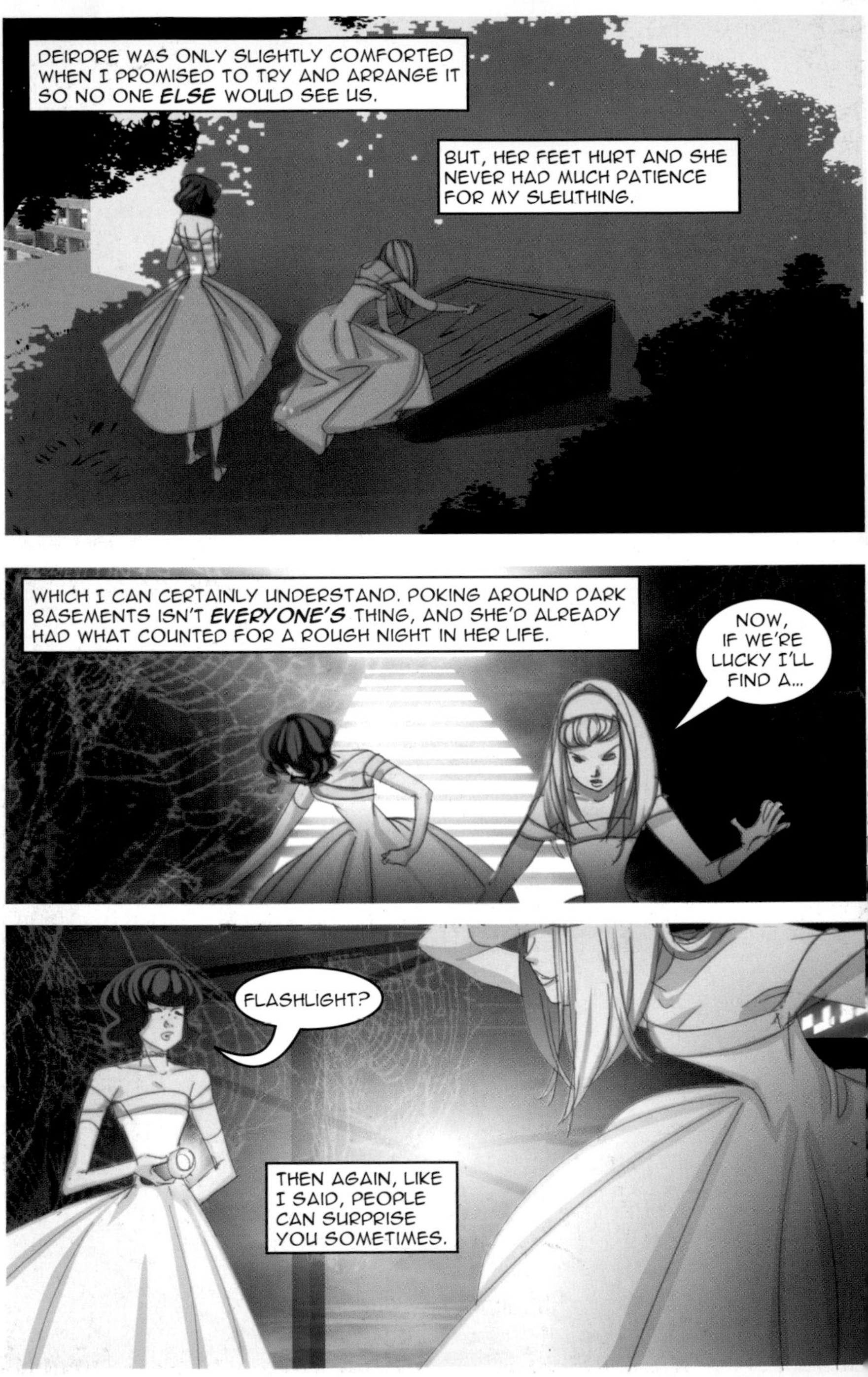

DEIRDRE WAS ONLY SLIGHTLY COMFORTED WHEN I PROMISED TO TRY AND ARRANGE IT SO NO ONE *ELSE* WOULD SEE US.
BUT, HER FEET HURT AND SHE NEVER HAD MUCH PATIENCE FOR MY SLEUTHING.
WHICH I CAN CERTAINLY UNDERSTAND. POKING AROUND DARK BASEMENTS ISN'T *EVERYONE'S* THING, AND SHE'D ALREADY HAD WHAT COUNTED FOR A ROUGH NIGHT IN HER LIFE.
NOW, IF WE'RE LUCKY I'LL FIND A...
FLASHLIGHT?
THEN AGAIN, LIKE I SAID, PEOPLE CAN SURPRISE YOU SOMETIMES.

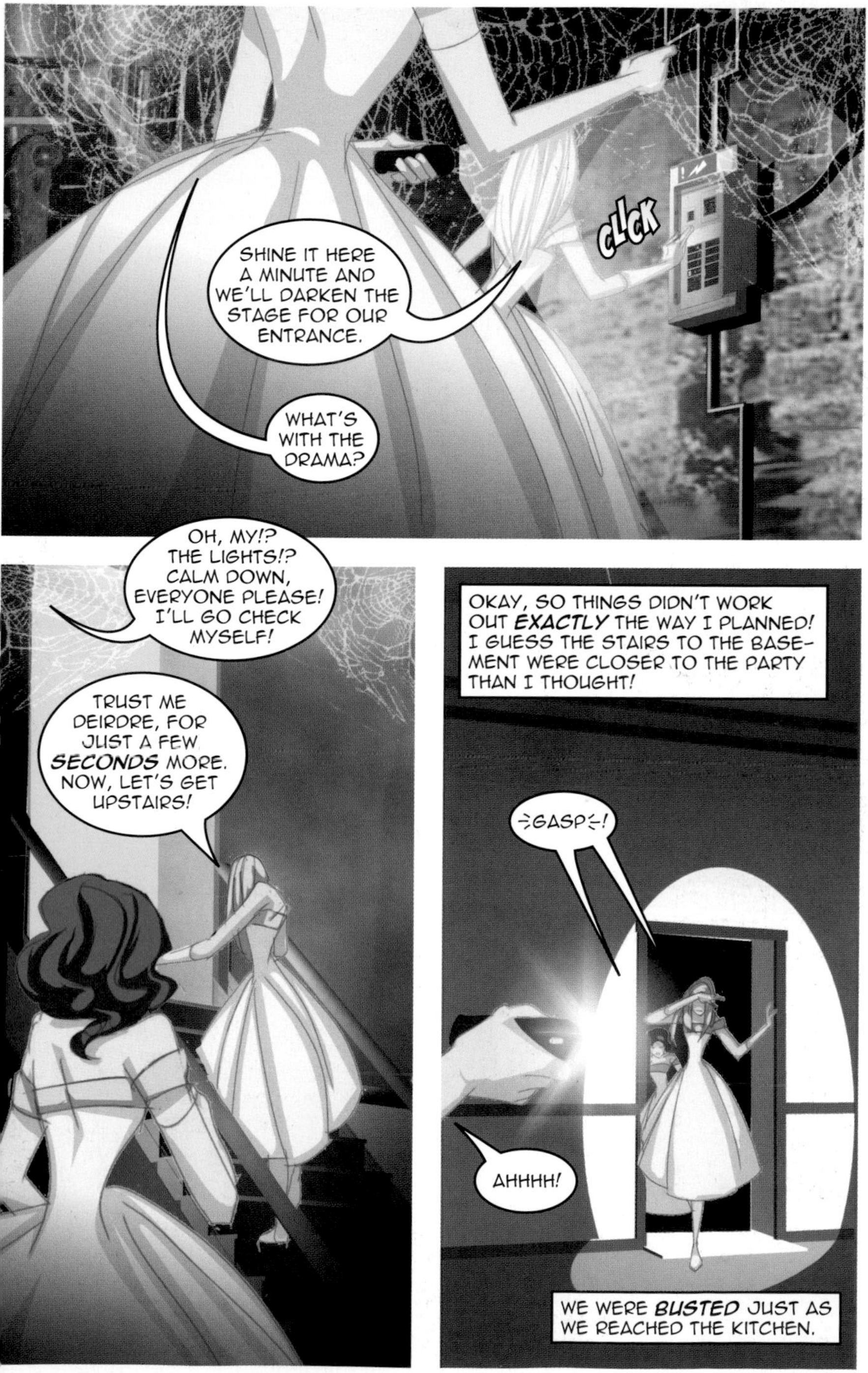
SHINE IT HERE A MINUTE AND WE'LL DARKEN THE STAGE FOR OUR ENTRANCE.
WHAT'S WITH THE DRAMA?
CLICK
OH, MY!? THE LIGHTS!? CALM DOWN, EVERYONE PLEASE! I'LL GO CHECK MYSELF!
TRUST ME DEIRDRE, FOR JUST A FEW **SECONDS** MORE. NOW, LET'S GET UPSTAIRS!
OKAY, SO THINGS DIDN'T WORK OUT **EXACTLY** THE WAY I PLANNED! I GUESS THE STAIRS TO THE BASE-MENT WERE CLOSER TO THE PARTY THAN I THOUGHT!
GASP!
AHHHH!
WE WERE **BUSTED** JUST AS WE REACHED THE KITCHEN.

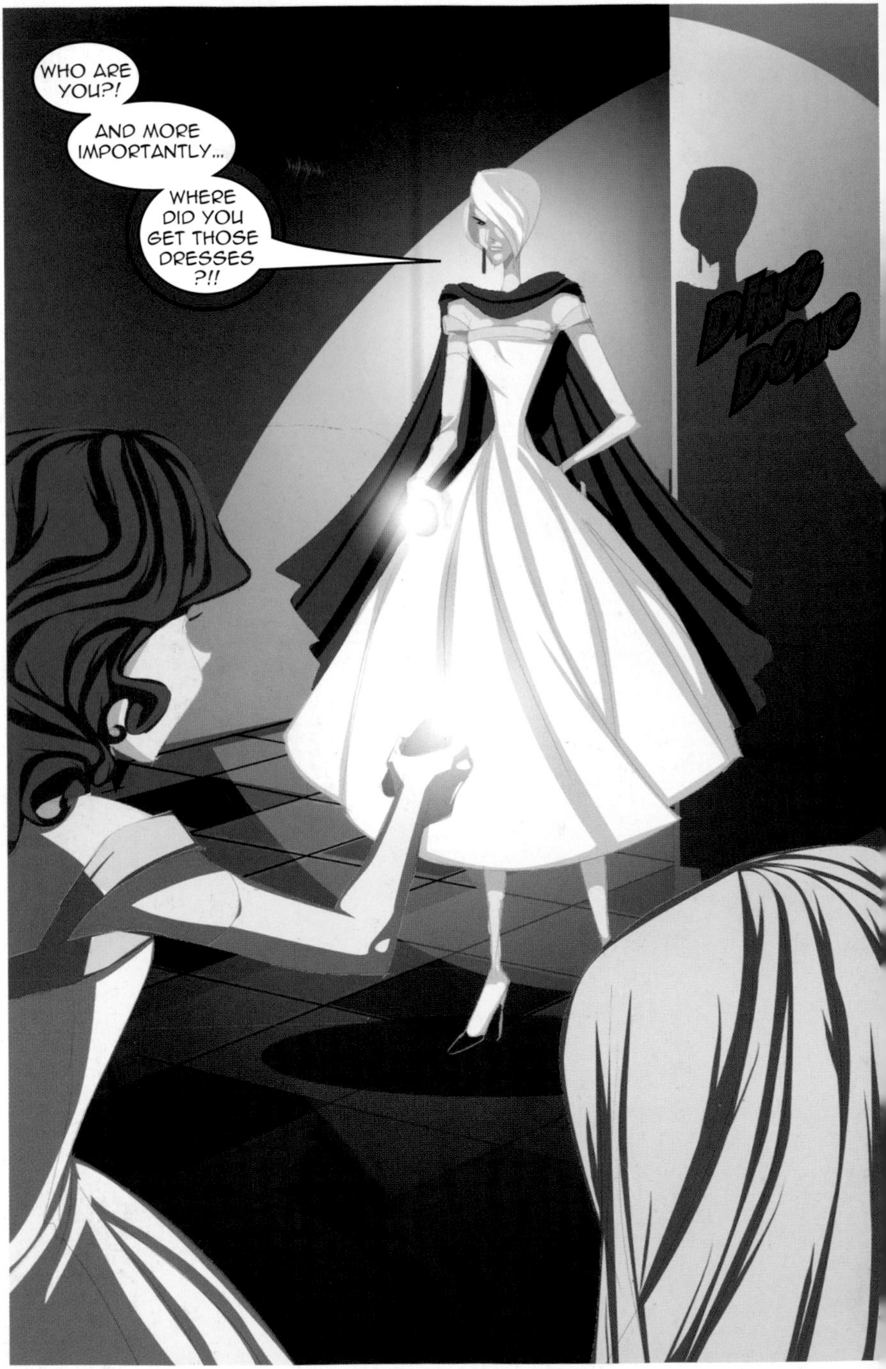
WHO ARE YOU?!
AND MORE IMPORTANTLY...
WHERE DID YOU GET THOSE DRESSES ?!!
DING DONG

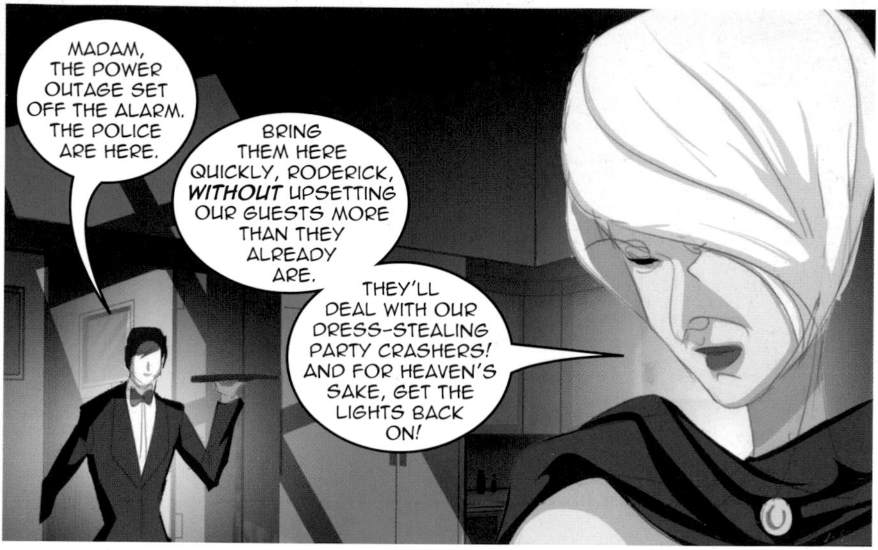
MADAM, THE POWER OUTAGE SET OFF THE ALARM. THE POLICE ARE HERE.
BRING THEM HERE QUICKLY, RODERICK, WITHOUT UPSETTING OUR GUESTS MORE THAN THEY ALREADY ARE.
THEY'LL DEAL WITH OUR DRESS-STEALING PARTY CRASHERS! AND FOR HEAVEN'S SAKE, GET THE LIGHTS BACK ON!

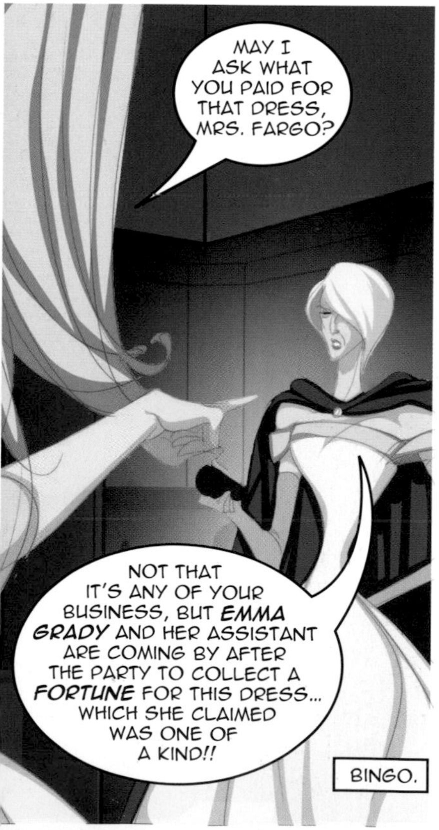
MAY I ASK WHAT YOU PAID FOR THAT DRESS, MRS. FARGO?
NOT THAT IT'S ANY OF YOUR BUSINESS, BUT EMMA GRADY AND HER ASSISTANT ARE COMING BY AFTER THE PARTY TO COLLECT A FORTUNE FOR THIS DRESS... WHICH SHE CLAIMED WAS ONE OF A KIND!!
BINGO.

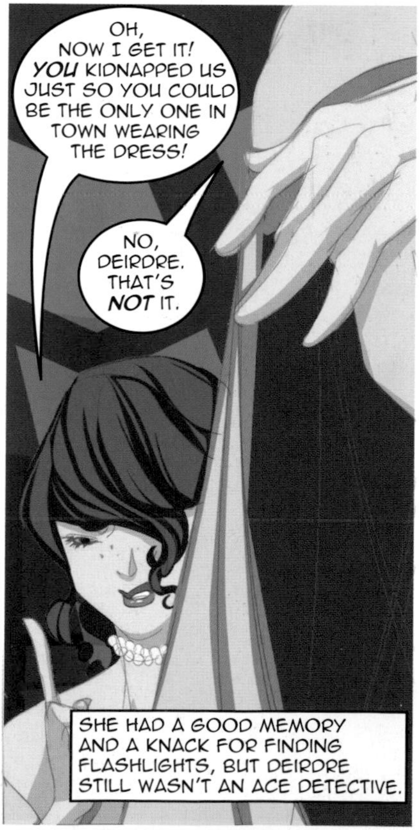
OH, NOW I GET IT! YOU KIDNAPPED US JUST SO YOU COULD BE THE ONLY ONE IN TOWN WEARING THE DRESS!
NO, DEIRDRE. THAT'S NOT IT.
SHE HAD A GOOD MEMORY AND A KNACK FOR FINDING FLASHLIGHTS, BUT DEIRDRE STILL WASN'T AN ACE DETECTIVE.

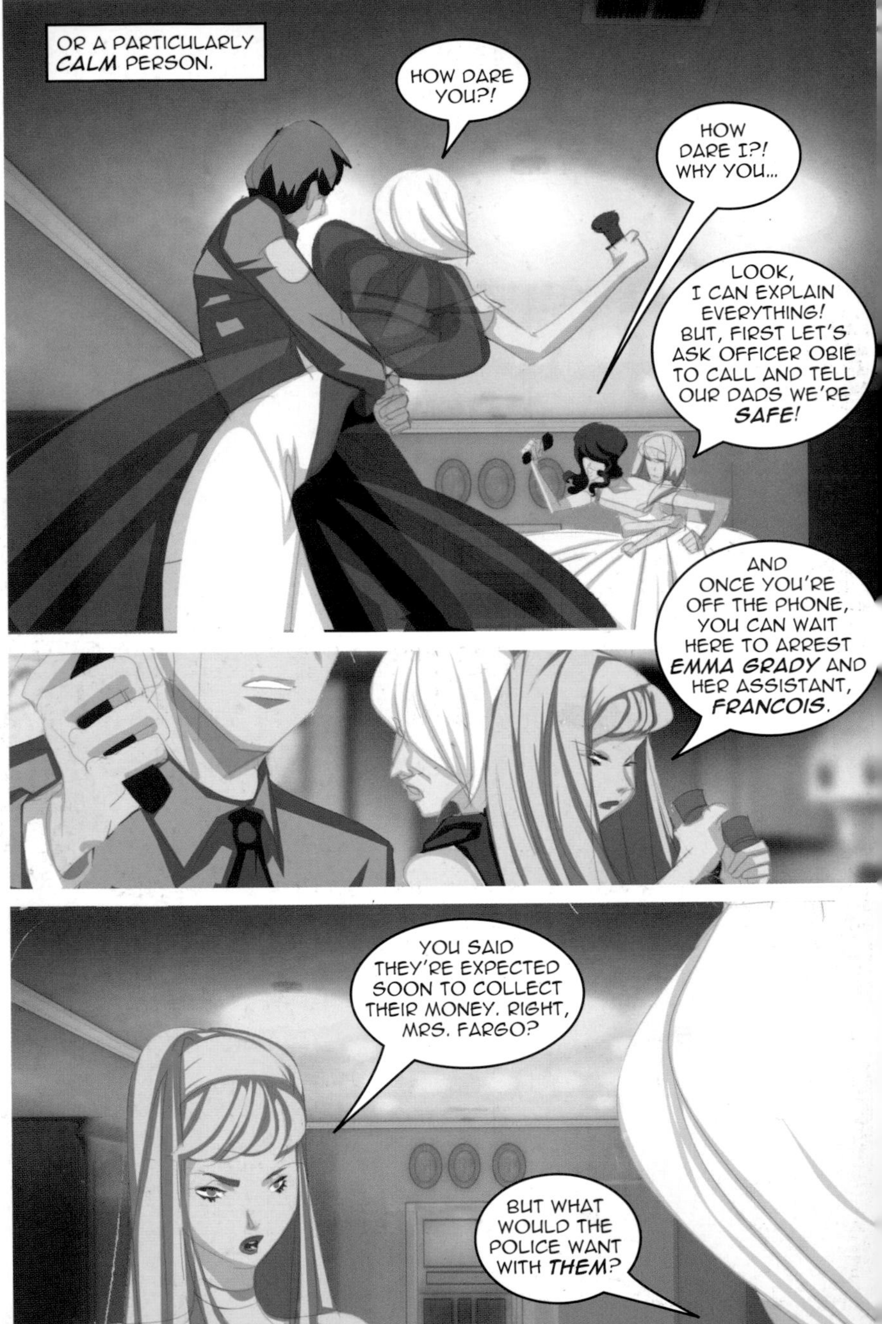
OR A PARTICULARLY CALM PERSON.
HOW DARE YOU?!
HOW DARE I?! WHY YOU...
LOOK, I CAN EXPLAIN EVERYTHING! BUT, FIRST LET'S ASK OFFICER OBIE TO CALL AND TELL OUR DADS WE'RE SAFE!
AND ONCE YOU'RE OFF THE PHONE, YOU CAN WAIT HERE TO ARREST EMMA GRADY AND HER ASSISTANT, FRANCOIS.
YOU SAID THEY'RE EXPECTED SOON TO COLLECT THEIR MONEY. RIGHT, MRS. FARGO?
BUT WHAT WOULD THE POLICE WANT WITH THEM?

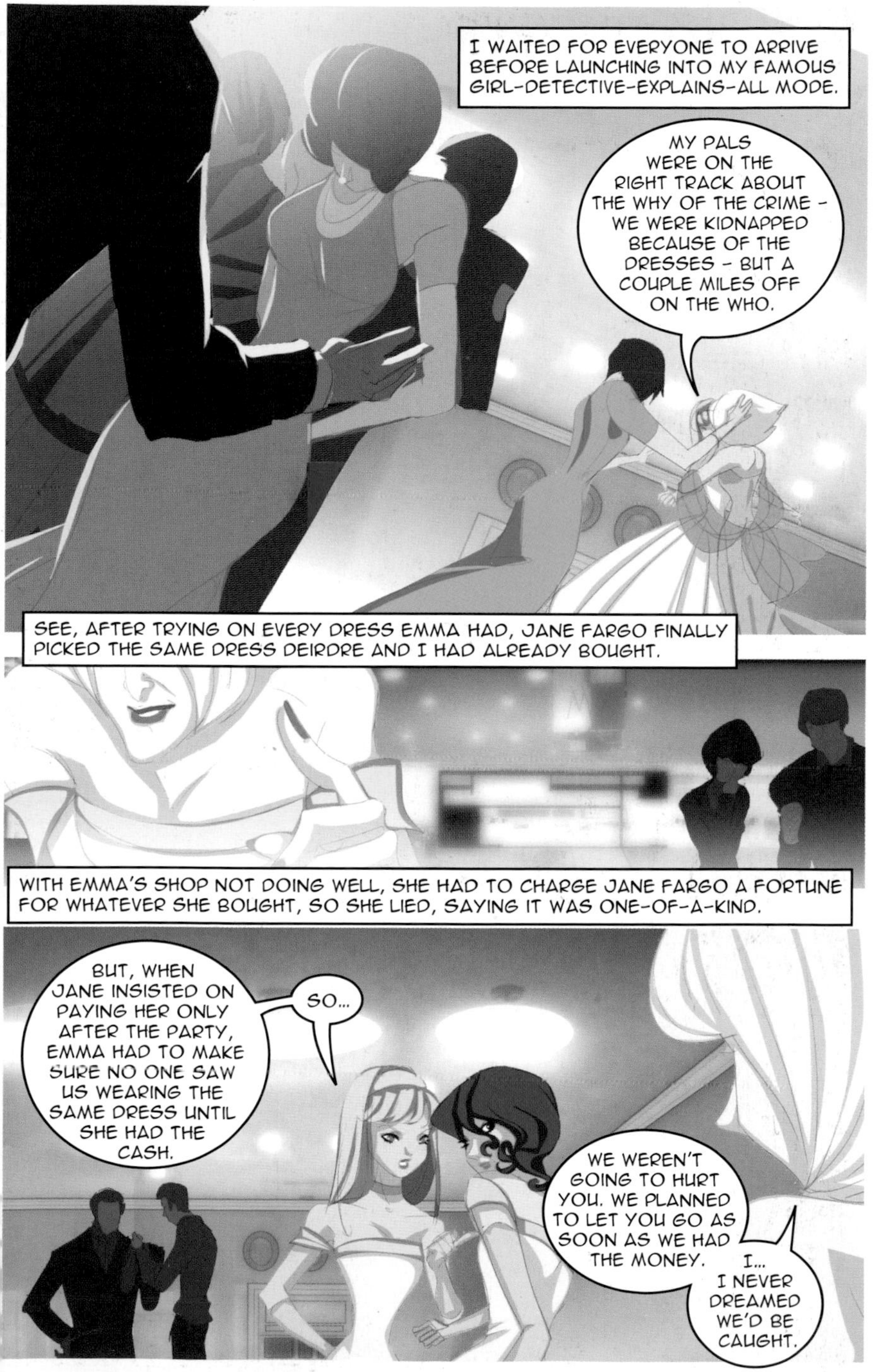
I WAITED FOR EVERYONE TO ARRIVE BEFORE LAUNCHING INTO MY FAMOUS GIRL-DETECTIVE-EXPLAINS-ALL MODE.
MY PALS WERE ON THE RIGHT TRACK ABOUT THE WHY OF THE CRIME - WE WERE KIDNAPPED BECAUSE OF THE DRESSES - BUT A COUPLE MILES OFF ON THE WHO.
SEE, AFTER TRYING ON EVERY DRESS EMMA HAD, JANE FARGO FINALLY PICKED THE SAME DRESS DEIRDRE AND I HAD ALREADY BOUGHT.
WITH EMMA'S SHOP NOT DOING WELL, SHE HAD TO CHARGE JANE FARGO A FORTUNE FOR WHATEVER SHE BOUGHT, SO SHE LIED, SAYING IT WAS ONE-OF-A-KIND.
SO...
BUT, WHEN JANE INSISTED ON PAYING HER ONLY AFTER THE PARTY, EMMA HAD TO MAKE SURE NO ONE SAW US WEARING THE SAME DRESS UNTIL SHE HAD THE CASH.
WE WEREN'T GOING TO HURT YOU. WE PLANNED TO LET YOU GO AS SOON AS WE HAD THE MONEY.
I... I NEVER DREAMED WE'D BE CAUGHT.

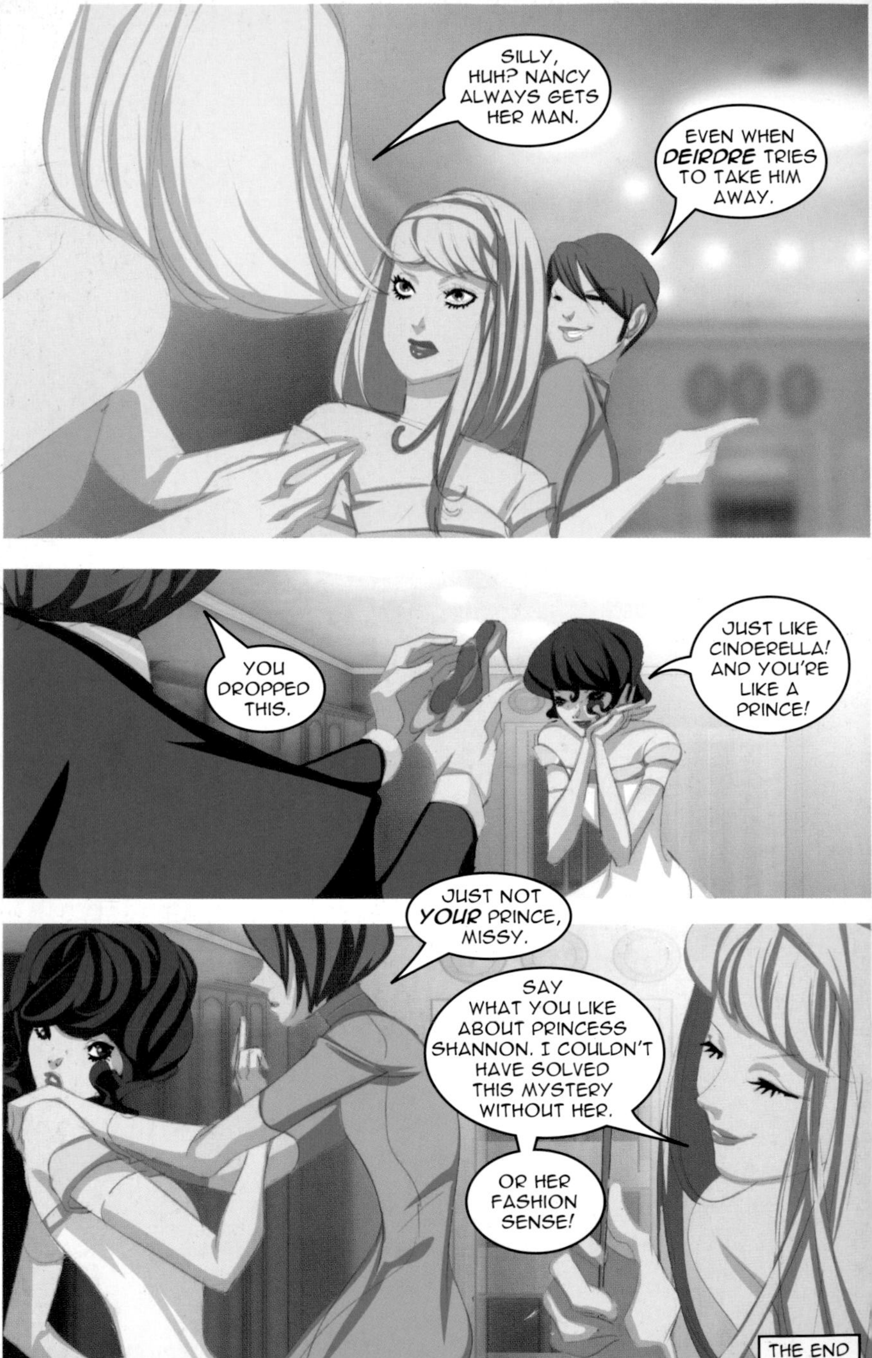
SILLY, HUH? NANCY ALWAYS GETS HER MAN.
EVEN WHEN DEIRDRE TRIES TO TAKE HIM AWAY.
YOU DROPPED THIS.
JUST LIKE CINDERELLA! AND YOU'RE LIKE A PRINCE!
JUST NOT YOUR PRINCE, MISSY.
SAY WHAT YOU LIKE ABOUT PRINCESS SHANNON. I COULDN'T HAVE SOLVED THIS MYSTERY WITHOUT HER.
OR HER FASHION SENSE!
THE END

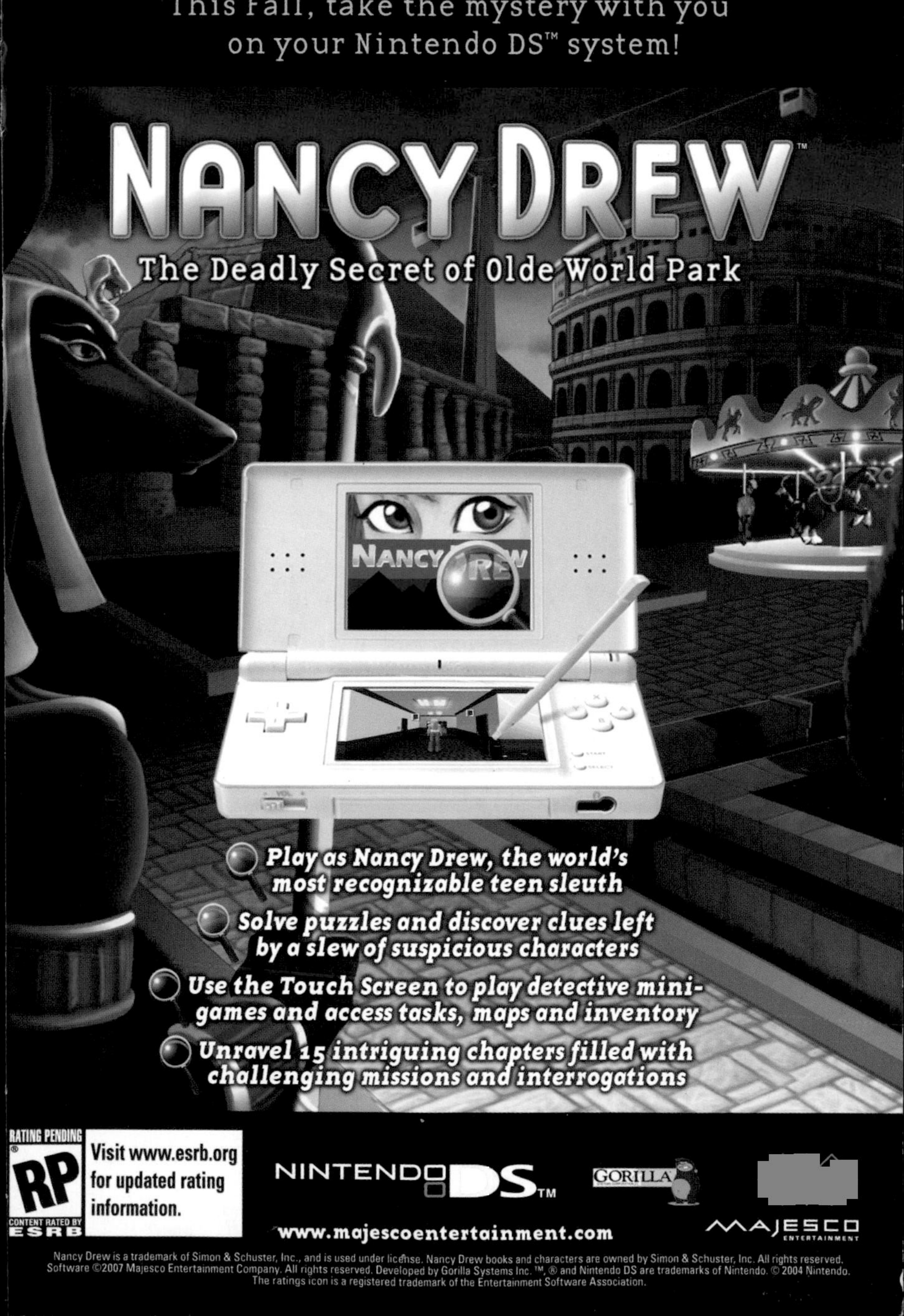
This Fall, take the mystery with you
on your Nintendo DS™ system!
NANCY DREW™
The Deadly Secret of Olde World Park
NANCY DREW
Play as Nancy Drew, the world's most recognizable teen sleuth
Solve puzzles and discover clues left by a slew of suspicious characters
Use the Touch Screen to play detective mini-games and access tasks, maps and inventory
Unravel 15 intriguing chapters filled with challenging missions and interrogations
RATING PENDING
RP
CONTENT RATED BY ESRB
Visit www.esrb.org for updated rating information.
NINTENDO DS™
GORILLA
www.majescoentertainment.com
MAJESCO ENTERTAINMENT
Nancy Drew is a trademark of Simon & Schuster, Inc., and is used under license. Nancy Drew books and characters are owned by Simon & Schuster, Inc. All rights reserved. Software ©2007 Majesco Entertainment Company. All rights reserved. Developed by Gorilla Systems Inc. ™, ® and Nintendo DS are trademarks of Nintendo. © 2004 Nintendo.
The ratings icon is a registered trademark of the Entertainment Software Association.

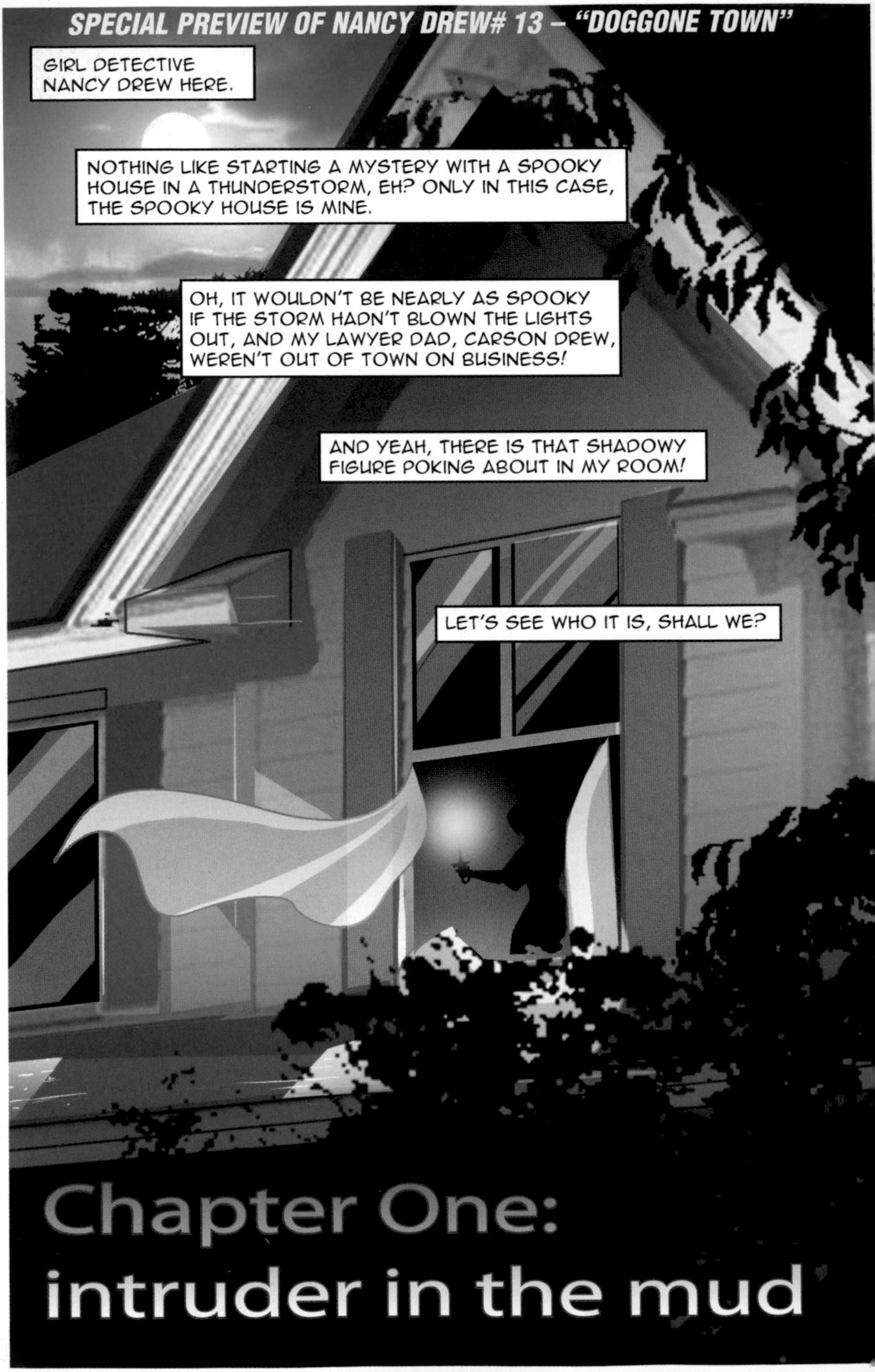
SPECIAL PREVIEW OF NANCY DREW# 13 – "DOGGONE TOWN"
GIRL DETECTIVE NANCY DREW HERE.
NOTHING LIKE STARTING A MYSTERY WITH A SPOOKY HOUSE IN A THUNDERSTORM, EH? ONLY IN THIS CASE, THE SPOOKY HOUSE IS MINE.
OH, IT WOULDN'T BE NEARLY AS SPOOKY IF THE STORM HADN'T BLOWN THE LIGHTS OUT, AND MY LAWYER DAD, CARSON DREW, WEREN'T OUT OF TOWN ON BUSINESS!
AND YEAH, THERE IS THAT SHADOWY FIGURE POKING ABOUT IN MY ROOM!
LET'S SEE WHO IT IS, SHALL WE?
Chapter One:
intruder in the mud

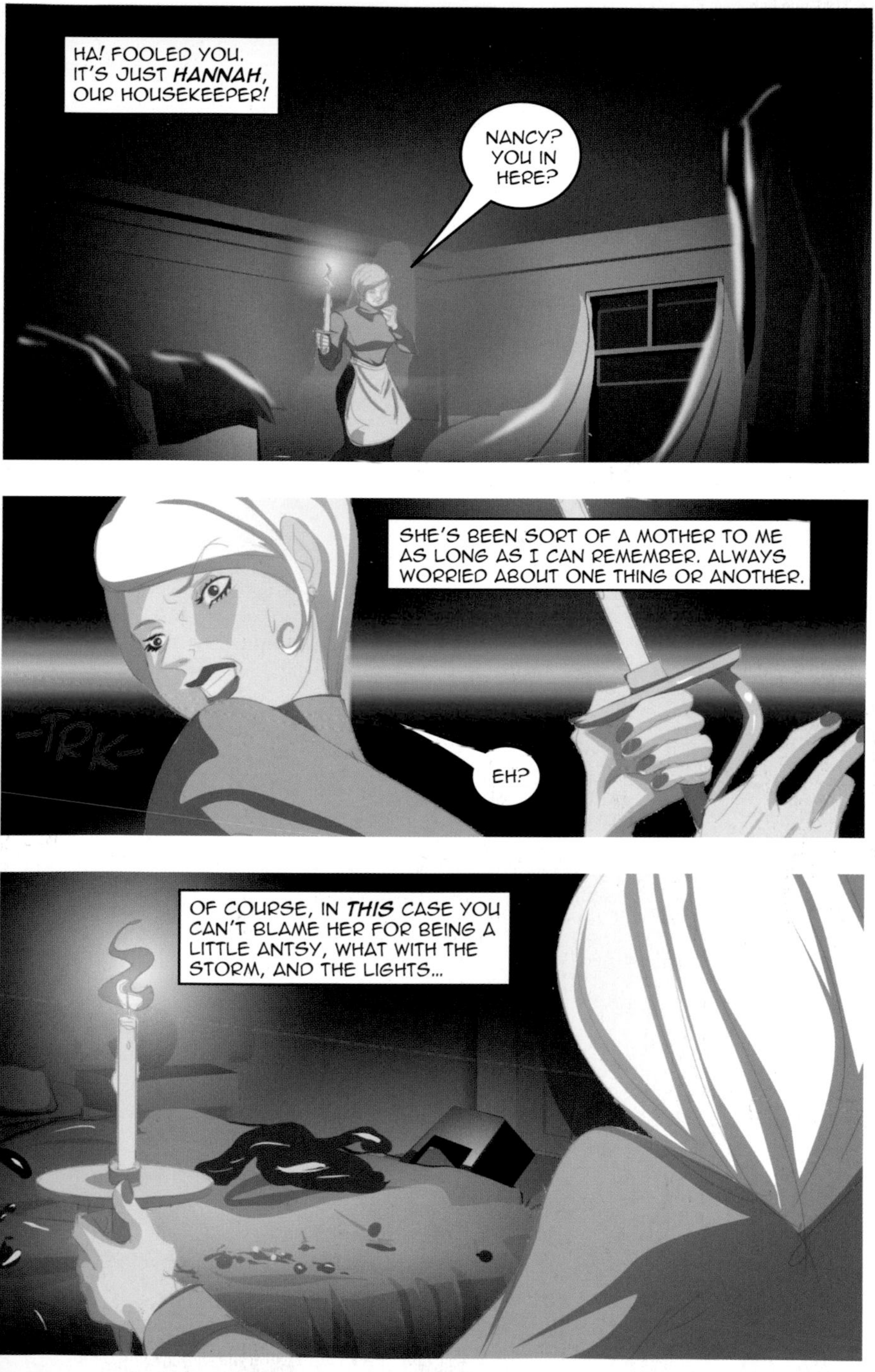
HA! FOOLED YOU. IT'S JUST HANNAH, OUR HOUSEKEEPER!
NANCY? YOU IN HERE?
SHE'S BEEN SORT OF A MOTHER TO ME AS LONG AS I CAN REMEMBER. ALWAYS WORRIED ABOUT ONE THING OR ANOTHER.
-TRK-
EH?
OF COURSE, IN THIS CASE YOU CAN'T BLAME HER FOR BEING A LITTLE ANTSY, WHAT WITH THE STORM, AND THE LIGHTS...

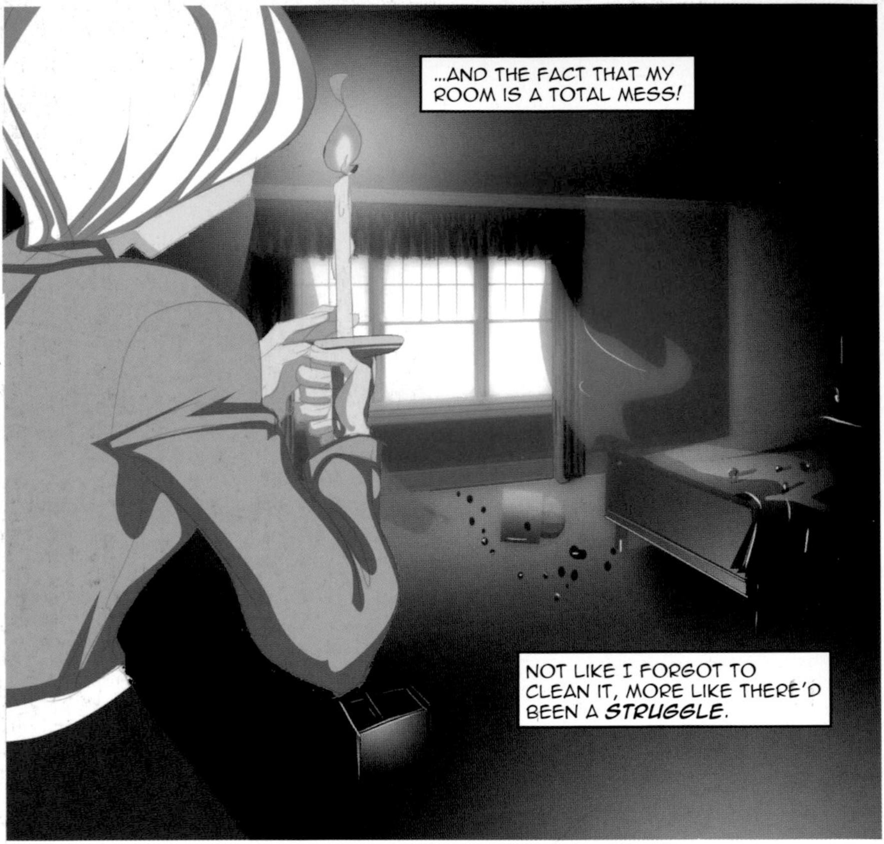
...AND THE FACT THAT MY ROOM IS A TOTAL MESS!
NOT LIKE I FORGOT TO CLEAN IT, MORE LIKE THERE'D BEEN A STRUGGLE.

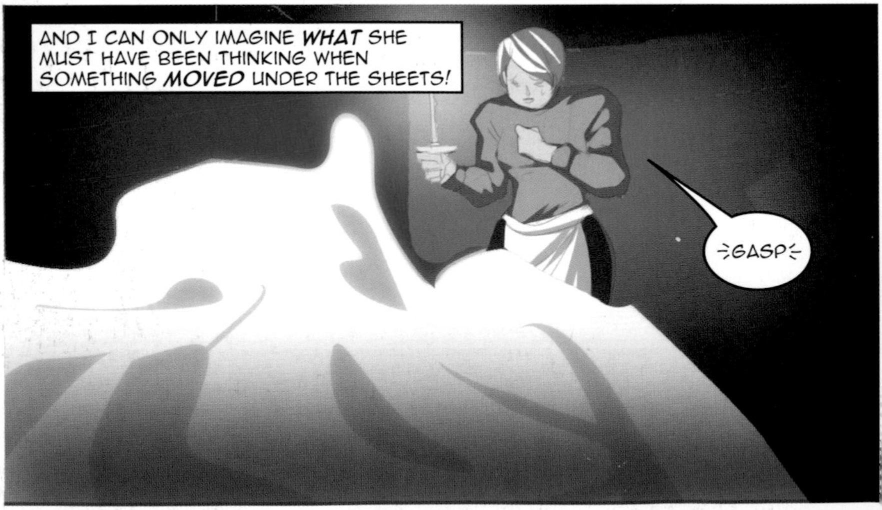
AND I CAN ONLY IMAGINE WHAT SHE MUST HAVE BEEN THINKING WHEN SOMETHING MOVED UNDER THE SHEETS!
GASP

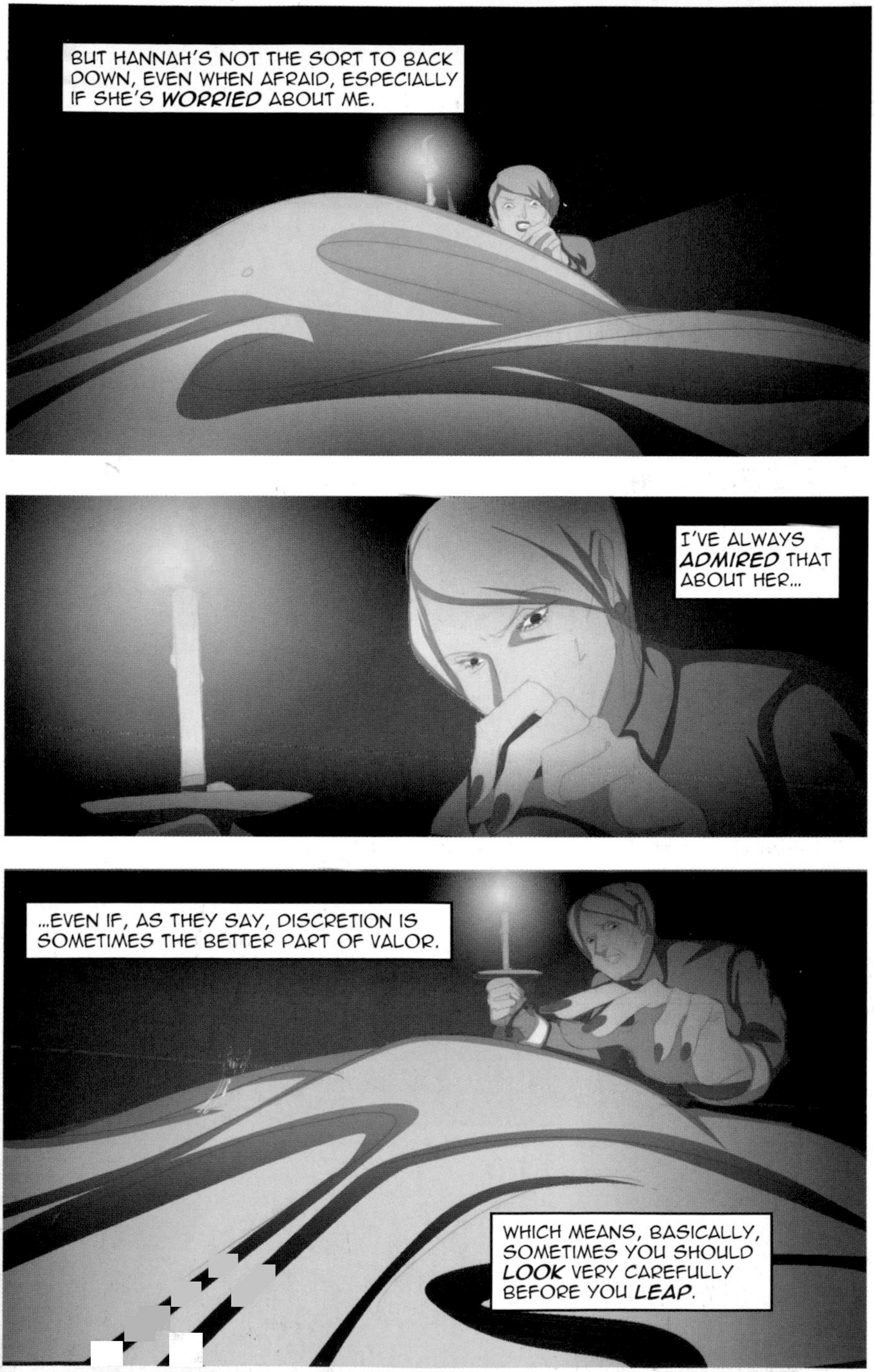
BUT HANNAH'S NOT THE SORT TO BACK DOWN, EVEN WHEN AFRAID, ESPECIALLY IF SHE'S WORRIED ABOUT ME.
I'VE ALWAYS ADMIRED THAT ABOUT HER...
...EVEN IF, AS THEY SAY, DISCRETION IS SOMETIMES THE BETTER PART OF VALOR.
WHICH MEANS, BASICALLY, SOMETIMES YOU SHOULD LOOK VERY CAREFULLY BEFORE YOU LEAP.

DON'T MISS NANCY DREW GRAPHIC NOVEL # 13 – "DOGGONE TOWN"

Go Undercover in Paris
as Nancy Drew® in
Danger by Design

You, as Nancy Drew, are in
Paris to work undercover
for a prestigious fashion
designer. Minette is all the
rage in the fashion world,
but strange threats and
unwelcome guests are
causing her to unravel.
It's up to you to stitch the
clues together and unmask
the mystery in this PC
adventure game.

dare to play™

FOR MYSTERY FANS 10 to Adult

Nancy Drew PC Adventure Game #14
Order online at www.HerInteractive.com
Also in stores!

Compatible with WINDOWS® 98/2000/Me/XP/Vista

Created by

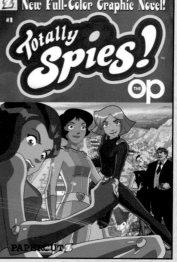

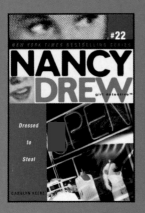

WATCH OUT FOR PAPERCUTZ™

If this is your very first Papercutz graphic novel, then allow me, Jim Salicrup, your humble and lovable Editor-in-Chief, to welcome you to the Papercutz Backpages where we check out what's happening in the ever-expanding Papercutz Universe! If you're a long-time Papercutz fan, then welcome back, friend!

Things really have been popping at Papercutz! In the last few editions of the Backpages we've announced new titles such as TALES FROM THE CRYPT, CLASSICS ILLUSTRATED, and CLASSICS ILLUSTRATED DELUXE. Well, guess what? The tradition continues, and we're announcing yet another addition to our line-up of blockbuster titles. So, what is our latest and greatest title? We'll give you just one hint -- the stars of the next Papercutz graphic novel series just happen to be the biggest, most exciting line of constructible action figures ever created! That's right -- BIONICLE is coming! Check out the power-packed preview pages ahead!

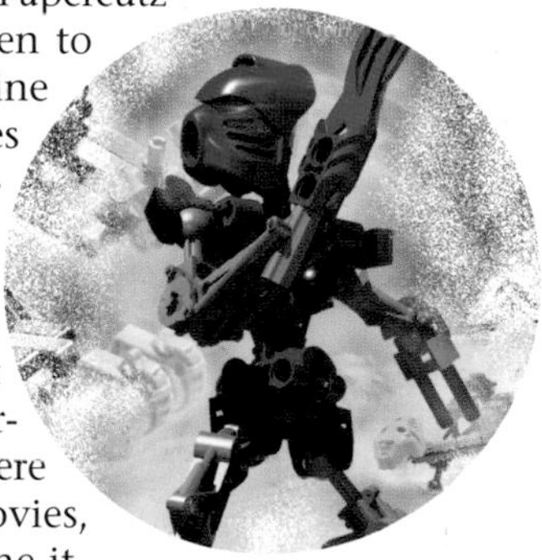

Before I run out of room, let me say that we're always interested in what you think! Are there characters, TV shows, movies, books, videogames, you-name-it, that you'd like to see Papercutz turn into graphic novels? Don't be shy, let's us know! You can contact me at salicrup@papercutz.com or Jim Salicrup, PAPERCUTZ, 40 Exchange Place, Ste. 1308, New York, NY 10005 and let us know how we're doing. After all, we want you to be as excited about Papercutz as we are!

Thanks,

Jim

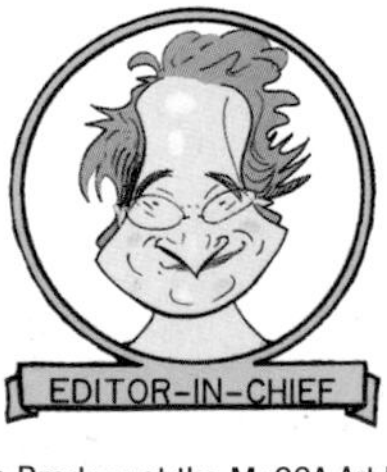
EDITOR-IN-CHIEF

Caricature drawn by Steve Brodner at the MoCCA Art Fest.

TWO DOZEN TEEN DETECTIVE GRAPHIC NOVELS NOW IN PRINT!

NEW STORY! FULL-COLOR GRAPHIC NOVEL
NANCY DREW
girl detective
#12
DRESS REVERSAL
BASED ON THE SERIES BY CAROLYN KEENE
PETRUCHA & KINNEY
MURASE & GUZMAN
PAPERCUT

You know, while it's exciting to be adding so many new titles, we don't want anyone to think we've forgotten any of our previous Papercutz publications! For example, can you believe there are now two dozen all-new, full-color graphic novels starring America's favorite teen sleuths?! In fact, let's check out what's happening in the 12th volumes of both NANCY DREW and HARDY BOYS...

Writers Stefan Petrucha and Sarah Kinney and artists Sho Murase and Carlos Jose Guzman present Nancy's latest case, "Dress Reversal." After showing up at River Height's social event of the year, in the identical dress as the party's hostess, Deirdre Shannon, things get worse for Nancy when she's suddenly kidnapped! That leaves Bess, George, and Ned to solve the mystery of the missing Girl Detective.

Meanwhile, writer Scot Lobdell, and artist Paulo Henrique Marcondes have sent Frank and Joe Hardy way out West to the "Dude Ranch O' Death!" (You'd think people would think twice before going there, right?) When kids turn up missing at a "tough love" camp for troubled teens, A.T.A.C. sends the Undercover Brothers in to investigate. What they find will surprise you!

Behold. . .

BIONICLE®

At the start of the new millennium,

a new line of toys from Lego made their dramatic debut. Originally released in six color-coded canisters, each containing a constructible, fully-poseable, articulated character, BIONICLE was an instant hit!

The BIONICLE figures were incredibly intriguing. With their exotic names hinting at a complex history, fans were curious to discover more about these captivating characters. Even now, over six years later, there are still many unanswered questions surrounding every facet of the ever-expanding BIONICLE universe.

A comicbook, written by leading BIONICLE expert and author of most of the BIONICLE novels Greg Farshtey, was created by DC Comics and given away to members of the BIONICLE fan club. The action-packed comics revealed much about these mysterious biomechanical (part biological, part mechanical) beings and the world they inhabited. A world filled with many races, most prominent being the Matoran. A world once protected millennia ago by a Great Spirit known as Mata Nui, who has fallen asleep. A world that has begun to decay as its inhabitants must defend themselves from the evil forces of Makuta.

These early comics are incredibly hard-to-find, and many new BIONICLE fans have never seen these all-important early chapters in this epic science fantasy. But soon, those comics will be collected as the first two volumes in the Papercutz series of BIONICLE graphic novels.

In the following pages, enjoy a special preview of BIONICLE graphic novel #1...

TOMMY!
ARE YOU STILL PLAYING WITH THOSE HORRIBLE DOLLS?
YOU'RE GONNA BE LATE FOR WORK!
THEY AREN'T DOLLS, MOM!
THEY'RE FULLY-POSEABLE, MICRO-ARTICULATED ACTION FIGURES!
AND I WASN'T EVEN LOOKING AT 'EM!

In TALES FROM THE CRYPT graphic novel #1 "Ghouls Gone Wild!" Tommy expresses what most action figure fans think.

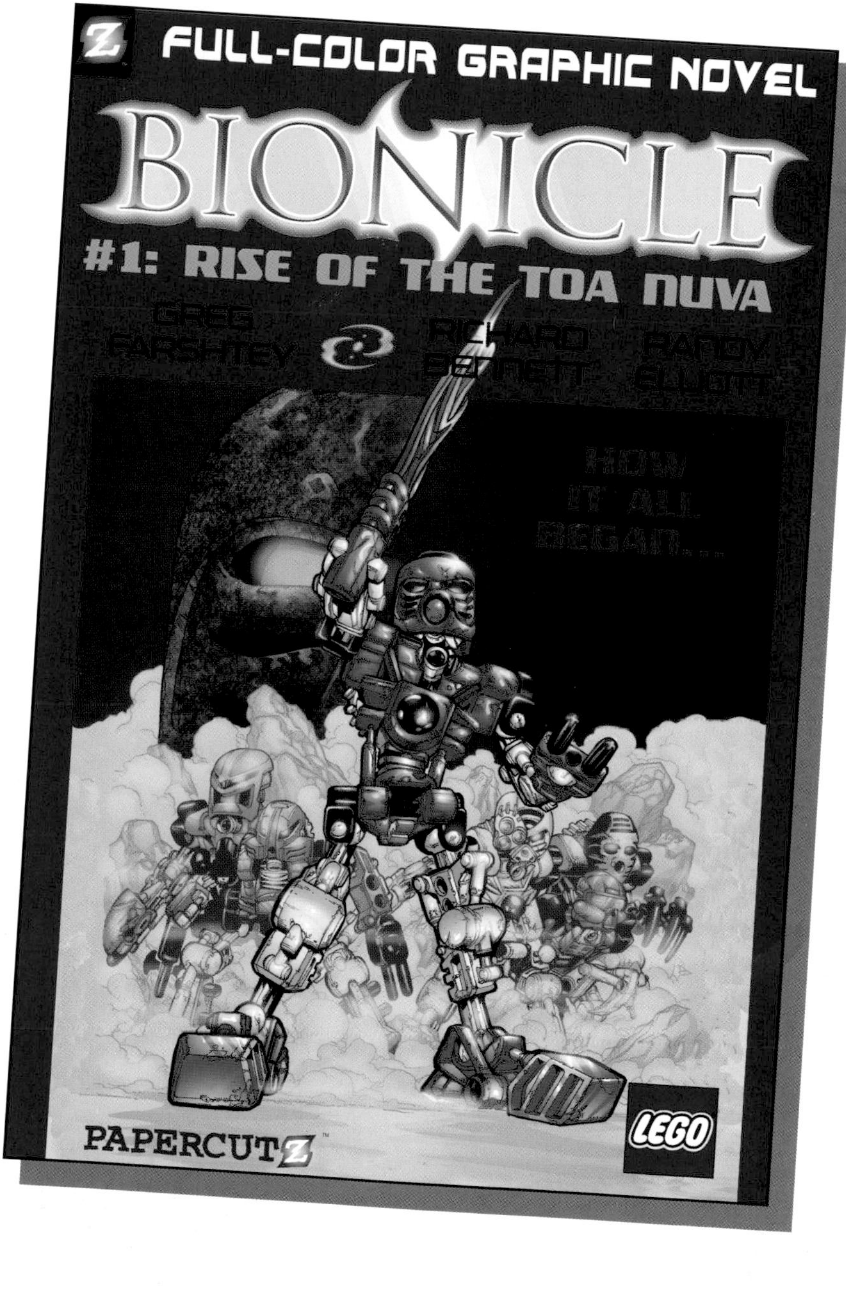
FULL-COLOR GRAPHIC NOVEL
BIONICLE
#1: RISE OF THE TOA NUVA
GREG FARSHTEY
RICHARD BENNETT
RANDY ELLIOTT
HOW IT ALL BEGAN...
PAPERCUTZ
LEGO

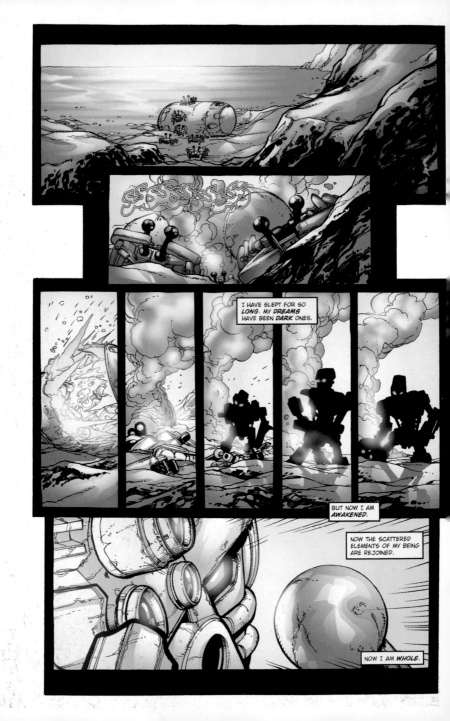

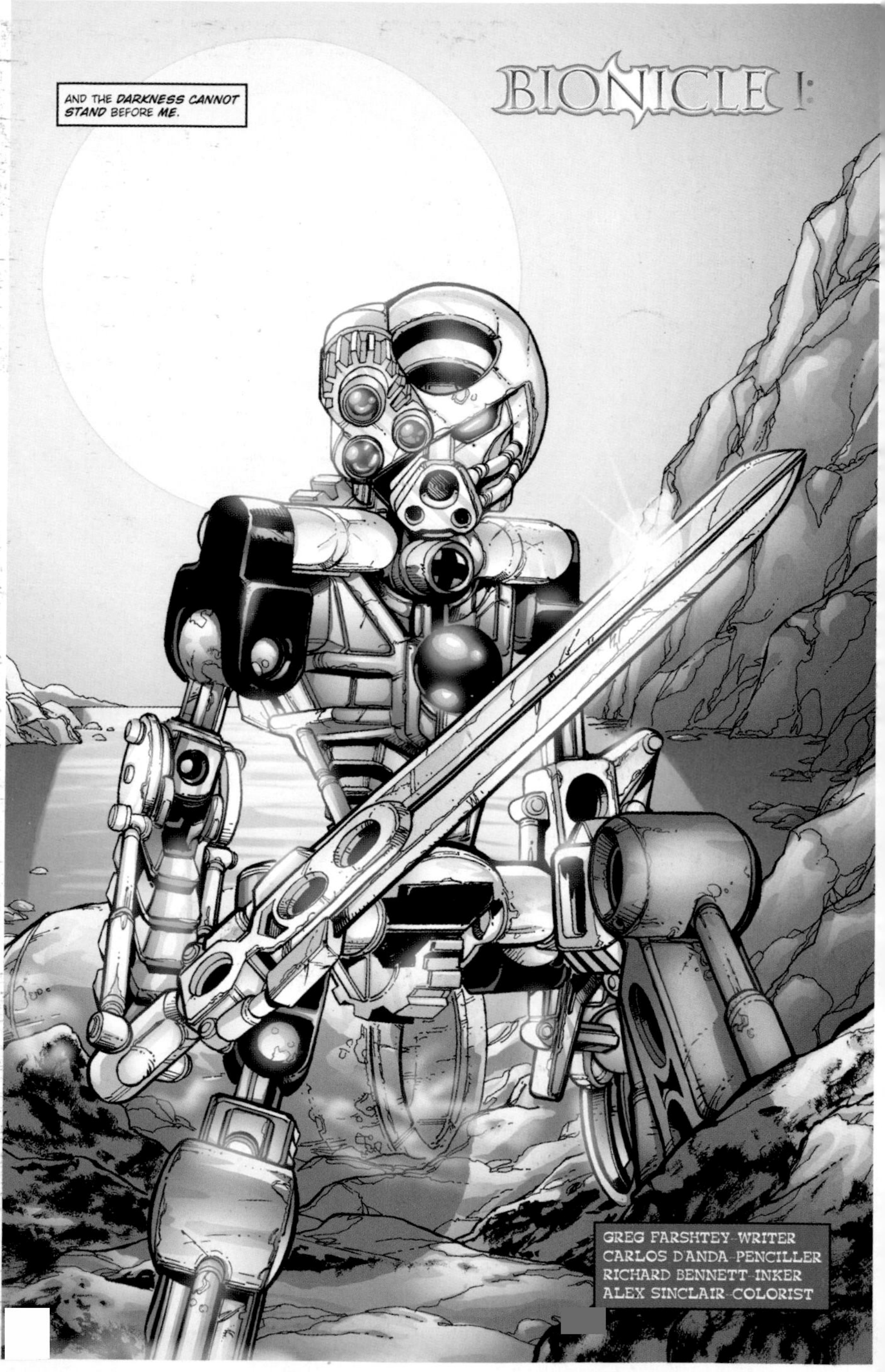
AND THE *DARKNESS CANNOT STAND* BEFORE *ME*.
BIONICLE I:
GREG FARSHTEY–WRITER
CARLOS D'ANDA–PENCILLER
RICHARD BENNETT–INKER
ALEX SINCLAIR–COLORIST

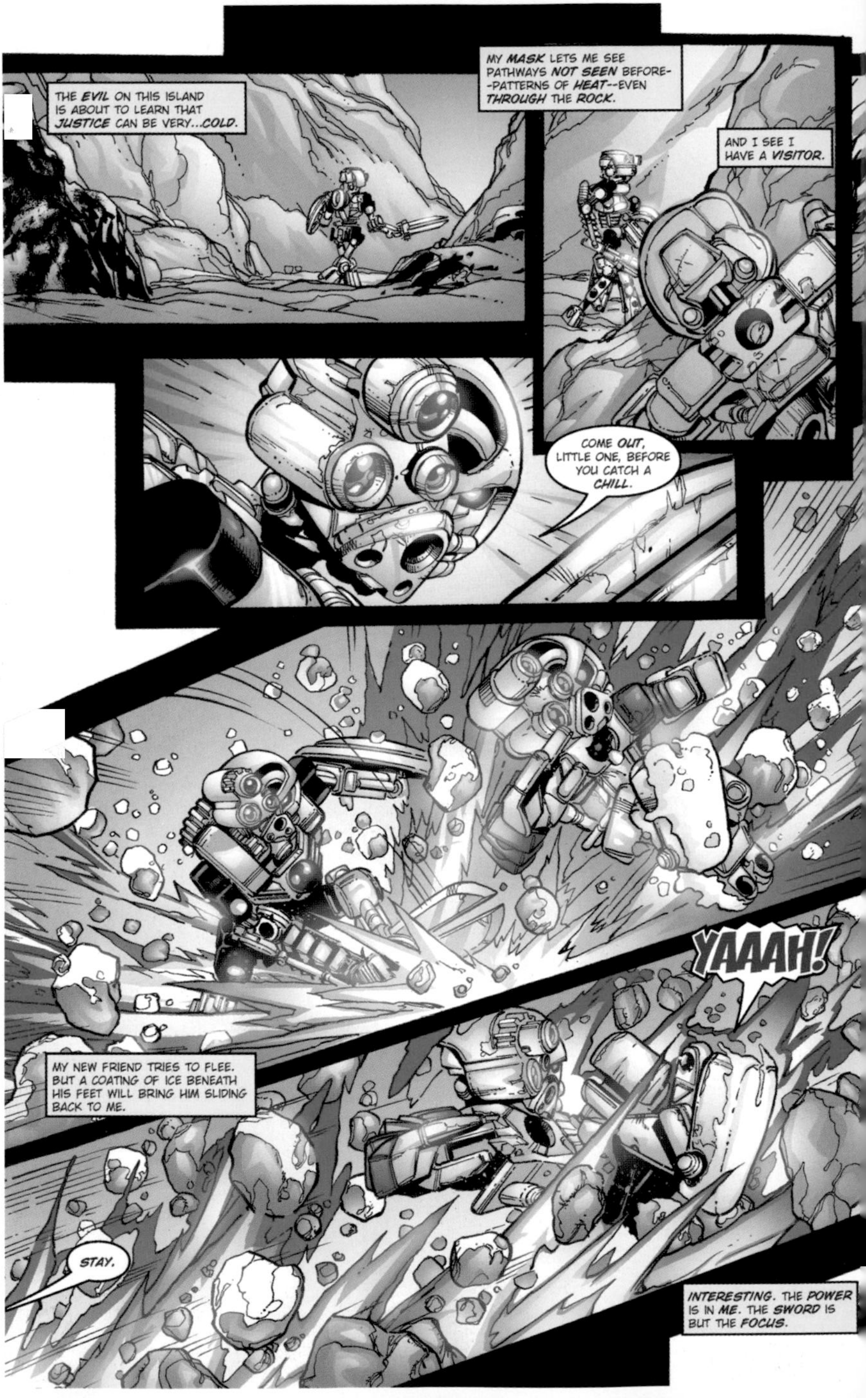
THE EVIL ON THIS ISLAND IS ABOUT TO LEARN THAT JUSTICE CAN BE VERY...COLD.
MY MASK LETS ME SEE PATHWAYS NOT SEEN BEFORE--PATTERNS OF HEAT--EVEN THROUGH THE ROCK.
AND I SEE I HAVE A VISITOR.
COME OUT, LITTLE ONE, BEFORE YOU CATCH A CHILL.
YAAAH!
MY NEW FRIEND TRIES TO FLEE. BUT A COATING OF ICE BENEATH HIS FEET WILL BRING HIM SLIDING BACK TO ME.
STAY.
INTERESTING. THE POWER IS IN ME. THE SWORD IS BUT THE FOCUS.

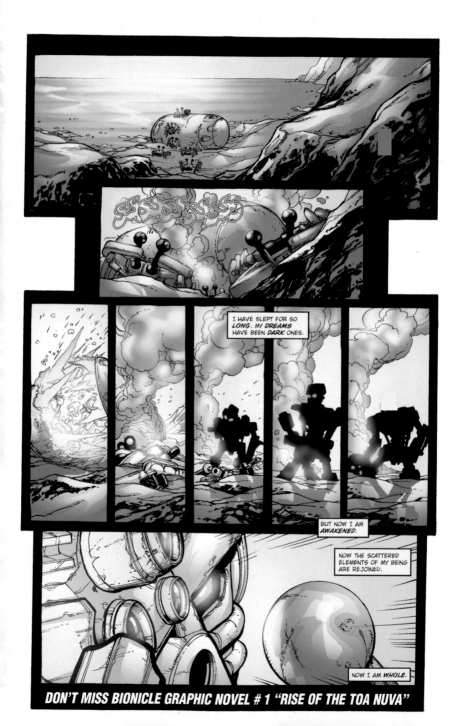

I HAVE SLEPT FOR SO *LONG*. MY *DREAMS* HAVE BEEN *DARK* ONES.

BUT NOW I AM *AWAKENED*.

NOW THE SCATTERED ELEMENTS OF MY BEING ARE REJOINED.

NOW I AM *WHOLE*.

DON'T MISS BIONICLE GRAPHIC NOVEL # 1 "RISE OF THE TOA NUVA"

A SPECIAL EXCLUSIVE

NANCY

DREW

girl detective

BONUS FEATURE!

A long time ago, young Jim Salicrup, and even younger Stefan Petrucha, would talk about writing and drawing comics. They even worked on writing and drawing their own comics. Not that long ago, Jim got to edit a series X-Files comics written by Stefan. Even more recently, Jim asked his childhood friend to write the all-new Papercutz graphic novel series, NANCY DREW, and he agreed. And very recently, Stefan's wife Sarah Kinney, who's a writer as well, started helping him write NANCY DREW.

Last year, Mrs. Schreiber's third grade class had a very special project -- create a Nancy Drew comic. What's even more amazing is that Margo Kinney-Petrucha, daughter of Stefan and Sarah, was a member of that class. While all the students did wonderful work, we just had to show you Margot's terrific tale of everyone's favorite Girl Detective. So without further ado, check out this awesome artistic debut!

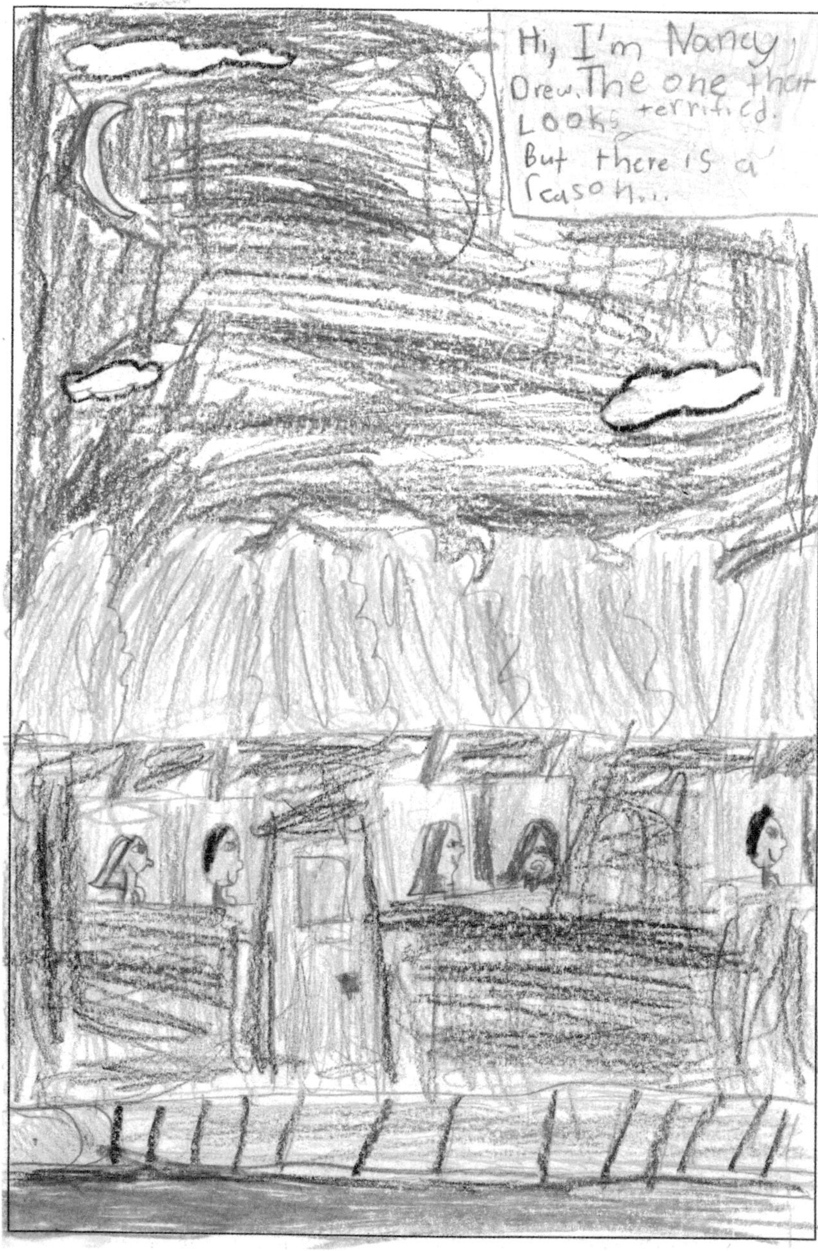
Hi, I'm Nancy, Drew. The one that Looks terrified. But there is a reason...

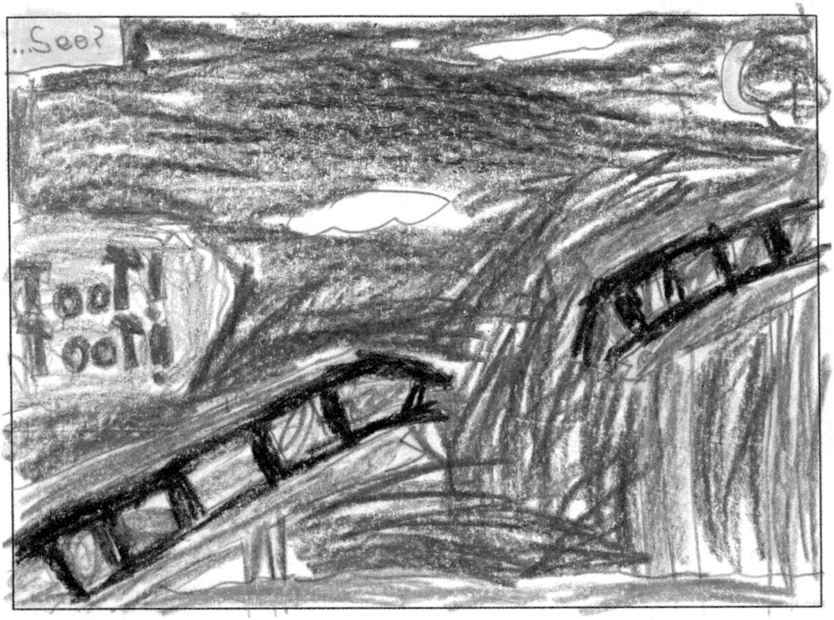
...See?
Toot! Toot!

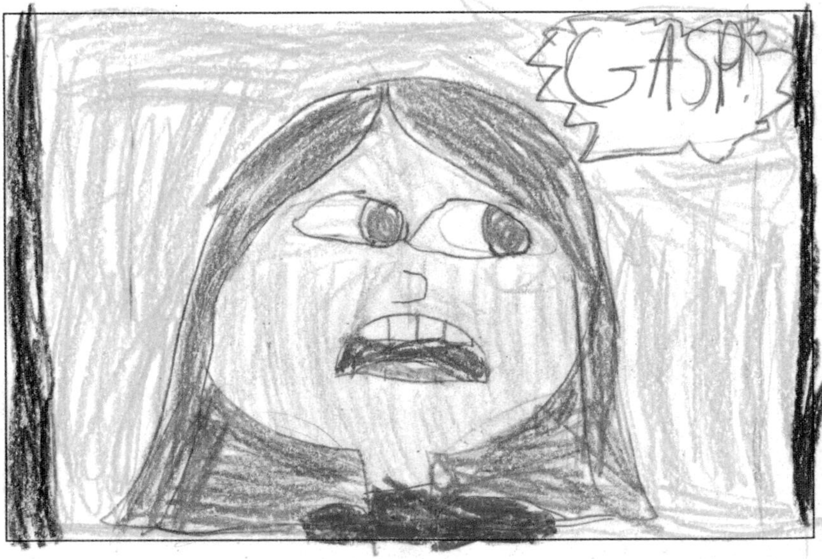
GASP!

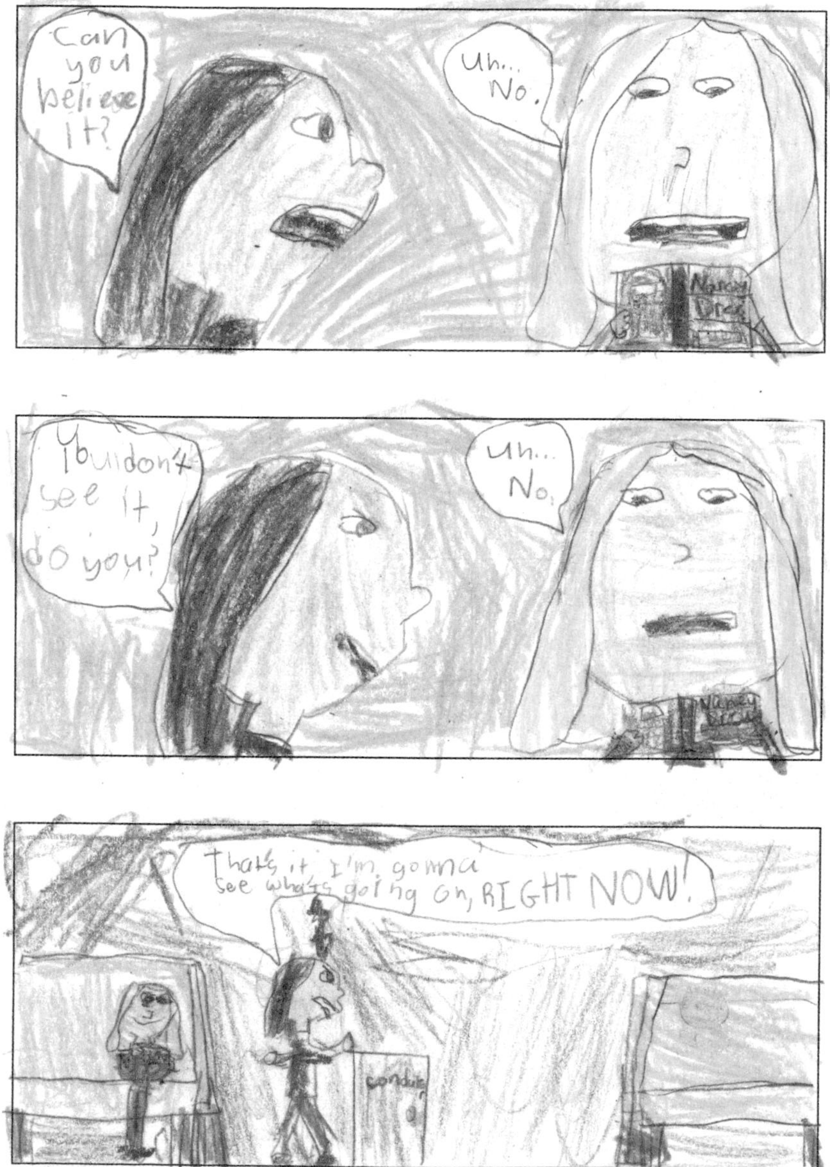
Can you believe it?
Uh... No.
You don't see it, do you?
Uh... No.
That's it I'm gonna see what's going on, RIGHT NOW!

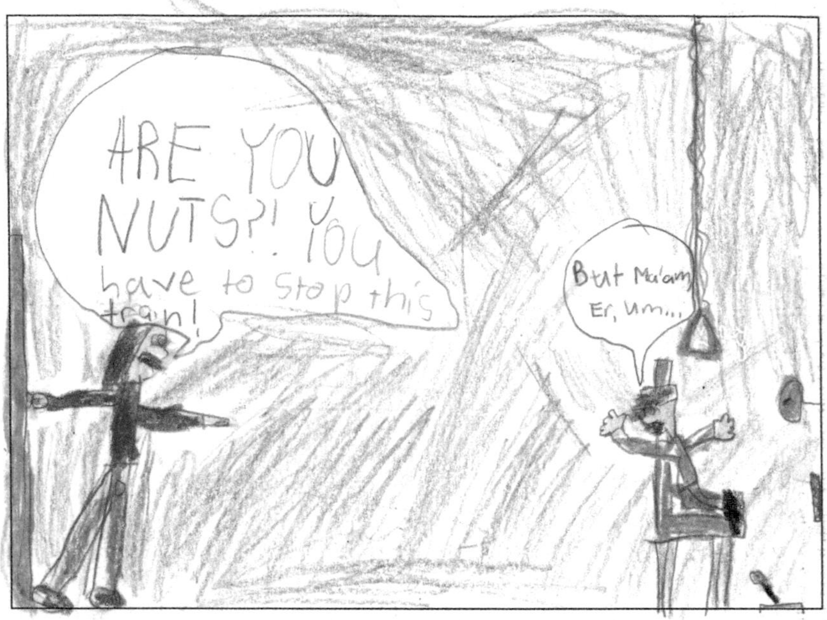
ARE YOU NUTS?! YOU have to Stop this train!
But Ma'am Er, um...

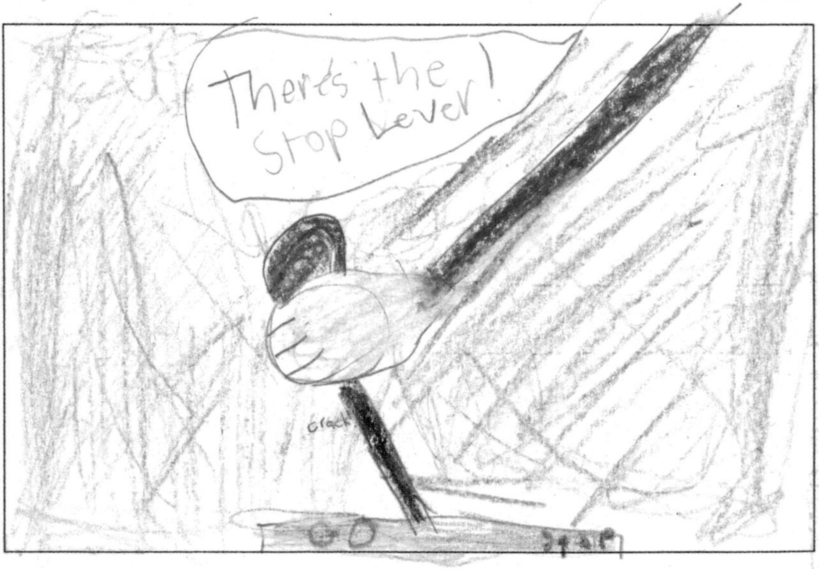
There's the Stop lever!
crack
Stop

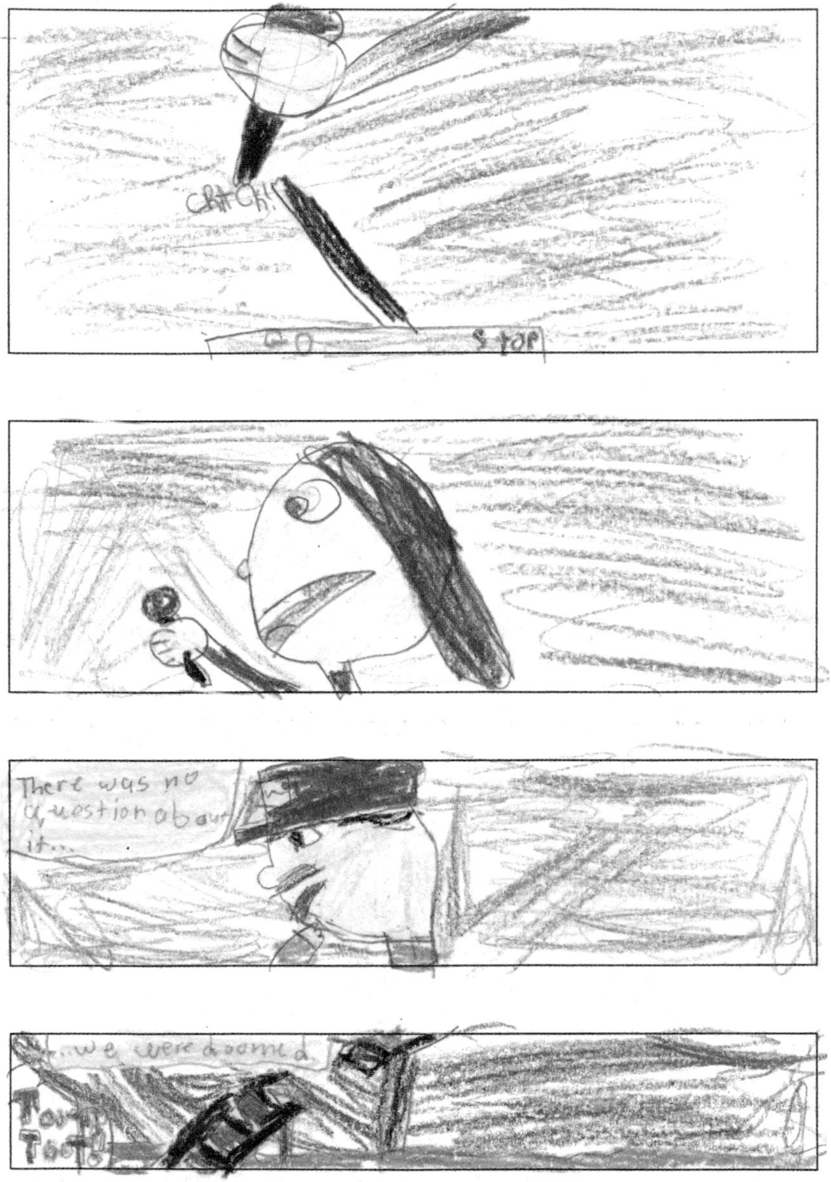
CRATCH!
GO
STOP
There was no question about it...
...we were doomed
Toot! Toot!

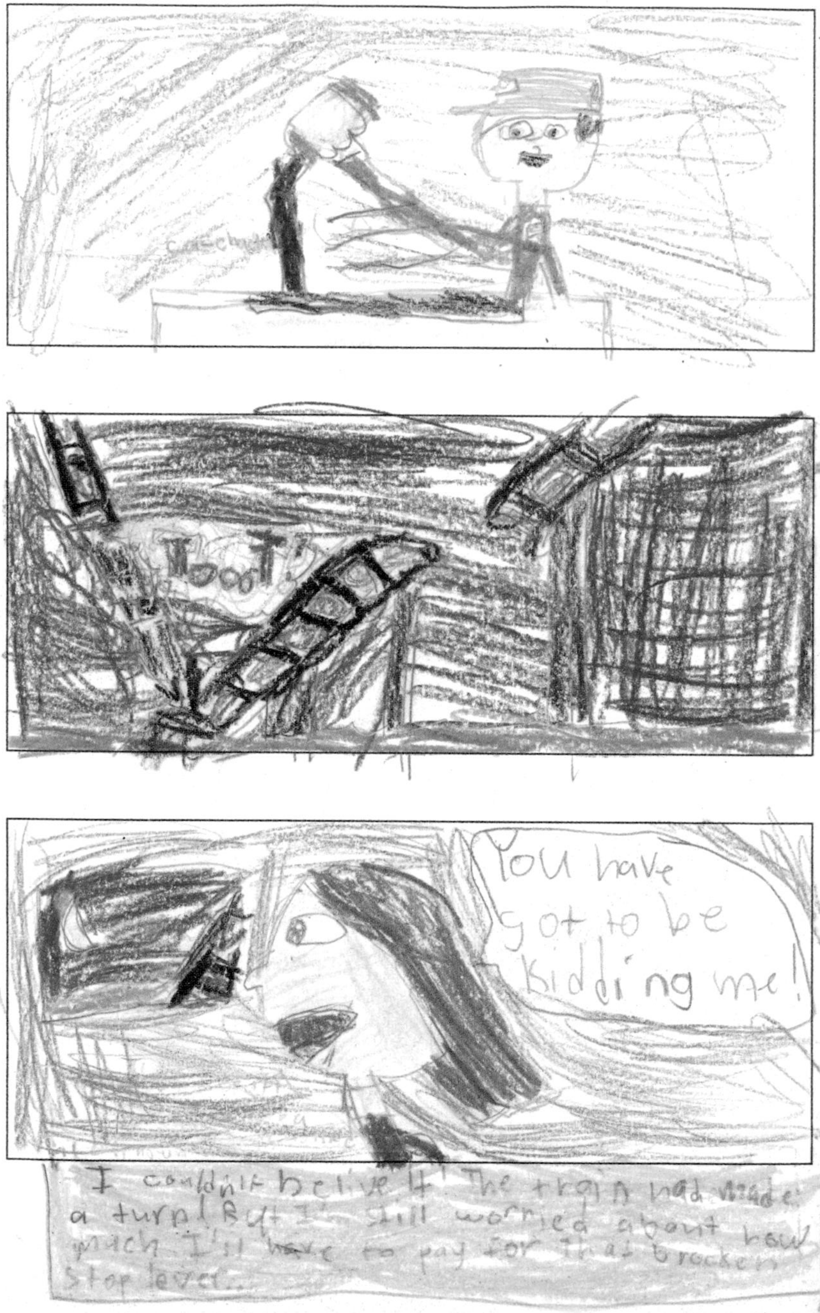
Tooot!
You have got to be kidding me!
I couldn't belive it! The train had made a turn! But I'm still worried about how much I'll have to pay for that brocken stop lever.